The Mysteries of Madness

A Serial Club Adventure

B.D. Carlson

Edited by C.K. Carlson

Published with the assistance of Apathy Productions LLC

https://apathyproductions.com/

Contents

Chapter 1

The lightning strike flashed what should have been blinding light into the night-vision goggles of the cross-department tactical team. Luckily, the team's new goggles came with the latest autogating technology, so the lightning only caused the display to 'bloom out' and flash greenish white for a moment. While not painful or damaging to the eyes, this caused the team to pause each time the lightning struck, allowing them to regain their bearings before continuing to the target.

The slog through the woods was deliberately slow going. It's best that way, thought the team leader, in case of any surprises, they would be poised and ready for action. He was responsible for a significant effort, with independent funding, and led a cross-county, multi-department task force. A dozen tactical officers were on the ground, communicating and converging on the potential crime scene. All were equipped with AR-15s, and some were loaded with expanding bullets to cause the maximum damage on impact. The night before, as a few of the more rambunctious officers were celebrating with some drinks, they decided it would be fun to try out some dumdum bullets a recruit had been making in his basement. They loaded their guns in secret before piling out of the heavy, machine-gun-mounted, armored troop vehicle typically seen in active combat zones.

The team was supported from above by a police helicopter and a military-grade drone controlled by an operator in the troop carrier. Both were equipped with infrared (IR) and night vision. At this point, drones were only used for surveillance by the police, but the operator was excited that soon they would be mounting a high-capacity machine gun on them. Finally, he would be able to see some real action.

As tough as these men were, and with as much backup as they had, every sound in the forest and every breath of wind that blew through the trees seemed to terrify the relatively inexperienced team. Most of the tactical team were recruits, with only a few street-hardened veterans. This can create an environment of high tension and excitement, bolstered by inexperience and naivete. The slightest noise or movement could cause a young team member to pull a little too hard on his trigger and start a bloodbath.

The sound of a squirrel dashing through the woods almost caused young recruit Smith to unload his clip. Just in time, he pulled it back, and the little critter hid behind a tree, waiting for the danger to pass. Glad I didn't waste a dumdum on him, Smith reflected.

It was good that the team had IR in addition to night vision, as the drone had spotted three distinct heat signatures several hundred yards north of the team's position. The drone operator sent the coordinates of the signatures to the team, and they automatically came up on their GPS display. The team leader signaled to his team with a hand signal, and they shifted slightly to their right to intercept the targets.

As the point man approached the IR targets, he came to a clearing in the woods lit by a spectral glow that seemed otherworldly. An orangish hue mixed with smoke and fog filled the small clearing. As the officer focused his eyes, he saw that the light was coming from a near-extinguished trail of embers on the ground. Upon further inspection, it was clear the trail of embers was part of a larger design that he could not quite make out.

Just as he thought that, an image was transmitted to the team from the drone operator: an HD shot of the clearing, showing a five-point star on the ground —a pentagram made out of firewood and brush that had been set on fire.

The team members' fear upon seeing this 'sigil' was palpable. The pentagram was an ancient sign of magical power used in the darkest corners of witchcraft and black magic to bend the world to the conjurer's will. None of the lightly educated officers knew what it meant, only that it instilled ancient fear and dread. There was danger here, and it was dark and terrible. They needed to be ready for anything.

As the team surrounded the clearing, it became apparent that there was more going on than just a homemade pentagram being burnt. In the center of the clearing, on what looked like a crude altar made from a cut log, the team saw the remains of a dead chicken, its head cut off, and blood covering the log and ground. Next to the chicken, stuck into the log, was the bloody hatchet that had ceremoniously removed its head. Gomez, the second point officer, almost wretched in his helmet, pulling it back at the last second. What type of foul magic was at play here, he thought to himself, praying to God the Father and the Holy Spirit.

The Team Leader was not as emotionally affected. There was great danger to him and his team here. Whoever committed this atrocity must be close, as the IR signatures from the burning pentagram and the people were mixed, making pinpointing their location difficult. It would be the green recruit, Smith, who would be the first to stumble upon the perpetrators, hiding in a bush just outside the clearing. As he shouted for them to get out from under the cover and communicated their position to the team and aerial units, spotlights and officers converged on the location, guns drawn and ready to engage.

Out of the bushes came three young skinny girls, shaking and covered in dirt and mud. They couldn't have been more than fifteen years old. Their eyes were wide with terror and fear, having about ten assault rifles pointed at their heads, and officers yelling at them, with helicopter spotlights and drone lights illuminating them from above.

As soon as all the girls were entirely out of the bush, a lightning flash caused the team's night-vision goggles to bloom for a few seconds, and at that very moment, a small squirrel, frightened by the commotion, also bolted out of the bush, heading to another tree. The two events were too much for recruit Smith, who saw the squirrel move and then bloom out, and thought the girls were trying to escape. He immediately opened up in full auto, then did the entire team, as well as the sniper from the helicopter, in a blinding flash of light...

At the worst possible moment, Hudson heard a familiar bellowing from the depths below, ruining his near-total immersion in the TV show he was watching.

"HUDSON!"

Are you fucking kidding me? Hudson said under his breath. Always, at the very best part, he interrupts me. It never fails.

"WHAT?" Hudson wasn't having it today.

'GET DOWN HERE, NOW!!!"

"WHY? I'M IN THE MIDDLE OF SOMETHING."

"I'M NOT GOING TO ASK AGAIN!"

Uh oh, thought Hudson. He must be pissed. That is his ultimate threat. What was the point in fighting it, Hudson wondered. Just submit and get on with your day. Was Hudson growing up? He hoped not. He slowly went downstairs, surrendering to his reality.

Chapter 2

Hudson's father was standing at the bottom of the stairs, frustrated as always. What was up with this kid, he wondered to himself? At least he could communicate with his older brother, Brody, and get him to respond, but Hudson was just so…insolent. He didn't seem to respect or even recognize any authority structure. It made every interaction with him an endless power struggle, in which he tried to get Hudson to follow some basic rules and oversight, while Hudson fought him every step of the way. Sometimes, his father wasn't sure if Hudson was trying to get under his skin or if he was just fundamentally… different.

"Why do you have to make this so hard on me every single time, Hudson? You know I am trying to get to work." His father looked at Hudson for recognition, but he didn't seem to get it.

"I'm sorry, Dad." Hudson just wanted to get this over as fast as possible. Regret and compliance were usually the key. But he didn't put enough effort into his delivery, and his father wasn't buying it.

Hudson's father didn't have the time to reprimand Hudson. "Hudson, I am getting put on a special assignment at work, and it's going to mean some extra money for us, but it also means I will have to work some longer hours."

Hudson was secretly relieved. He loved his father, but to Hudson, it felt like he was forever busting his chops and getting on his case. There was nothing he wanted more than alone time so he could do his own thing. No one seemed to get that about him. They were always trying to corral him and direct him.

"Don't worry about me, Dad, I can take care of myself. I'm fifteen now." Hudson felt confident in his statement. His father, not so much.

"Yeah, I'm sure you are a very competent young man; no one doubts that. But you need supervision, and with me working longer hours, I thought it might be time to start up a similar arrangement to what we had last year."

"Hang on one sec, Dad. You know I have my podcast now with Cai and Sage? We do those three days a week. It's not like I am sitting around here alone for hours or anything."

"I know you're a big internet star now, but that doesn't mean you still don't need supervision. Like last time, Brody will watch you and the home, and a few kids with parents who need to work late will be here after school. Obviously, Sage and Cai will be here as usual, but we need to accommodate at least one more child."

Oh great, here it comes, thought Hudson. He raised his eyebrow. "Like who, Dad?"

His father hesitated momentarily, and Hudson could tell his dad was a little embarrassed. "It's the son of the family who owns my company. He is about your age, and I think you two will get along."

At that very moment, the doorbell rang, and Hudson's blood ran cold. He hoped there would be some lag time before he got this new person dumped on his lap, but his dad loved surprising him. Hudson hated surprises.

"Oh, good, he's here now. I can introduce you before I go to work."

"Super." Hudson was barely hiding his irritation.

Chapter 3

When the door opened, Hudson expected to see an adult with his new after-school mate, but it was just a solitary kid standing there. On the street at the end of their walkway, Hudson could see what looked like a very expensive car, like a Bentley or something, just beginning to drive away. Huh, Hudson thought, I'm guessing we won't meet his parents today. I wonder why? Did they even drop him off, or did they have 'the help' do it?

Outside, standing alone, was a tall, skinny boy. Ugh, thought Hudson, he's even skinnier than me.

"Why hello, um, you must be, Wick?" Hudson's father was as surprised as Hudson not to see one of the young boy's parents or a guardian accompanying him. And this kid didn't look very healthy; he was pale and sickly looking. I hope he doesn't have anything Hudson can catch; Hudson's father thought a bit concerned.

The young man flipped his jet-black hair from his eyes a bit. "Um, yeah. That's me. Nice meeting you." He had a languid way about his speech. Like, he didn't care about being there all that much.

"Nice meeting you, Wick. This is my son, Hudson. He's about your age."

"Hey," Hudson said, not extending his hand to shake. He looked the new kid up and down and noticed he was dressed weirdly; he was wearing all black. And it's not like he was in a black T-shirt like most kids; he was in black pants and a black button-down shirt, like a 20-something hipster from the 90s. Hudson wasn't sure he liked this guy at all. Did he think he was cool or something? Who was he trying to impress?

Hudson's father was shooting Hudson a look. Maybe he wasn't being social and welcoming enough. "So, Wick. Where do you go to school?" said his father, interrupting the awkward pause.

Wick hesitated, but he figured, what the hell, they already know I'm a rich brat. "I go to Old Springs Academy, up on the hill near our family home."

Hudson's father knew the place; he spent many hours there supervising lawn and maintenance crews for Wick's family, which owns most of Old Springs' more respected foundations and institutions. Old Springs Academy was a stately stone-and-brick school dating back to post-Revolutionary times, with expansive grounds and a dozen fields for its state-champion lacrosse and field hockey teams.

Seeing that Hudson would not take up the slack conversationally, his father continued. "Wick, it's very nice meeting you. I'd love to show you around a bit, but I do need to get to work. Hudson, can you show Wick around and introduce him to Brody?"

Before Hudson could object or ask his father what they should do for the next three hours, his father walked out the door, jumped into his truck, and was off. Hudson was dumbfounded. Thanks, Dad!

Wick didn't seem too offended by the whole situation. He was used to being the odd man out, an unwanted presence to most people. He looked down at the ground, nonplussed by Hudson's father's unceremonious exit. Hudson figured he would play this like he did when the two girls got dumped on his lap last year. If he was honest with himself, that worked out pretty well. He had two new friends and a podcast out of it; maybe this wouldn't be so bad.

"Do you want to have a bowl of cereal or something and watch a show?"

Wick barely looked at him. "I'm not hungry. But whatever, you have some."

What a weirdo, thought Hudson. What kind of kid doesn't like cereal?

"Sure, um, follow me."

Hudson uncomfortably led Wick into the kitchen, where he made himself a bowl of cereal and grabbed his favorite bowl and spoon.

"Do you want anything else, like a granola bar or something?"

"Nah, I'm good."

Hudson just shrugged, put his food on the table, and went to get his tablet to put on the kitchen table so they could watch a show. But when he got back, Wick was already holding his large phone and watching his own show, apparently engrossed. Hudson just shrugged again, put the tablet down for himself, and then they sat, spending the next few hours in silence, both watching their individual shows, together in proximity yet totally separate.

Chapter 4

Overall, Hudson didn't like school. It's not that he didn't like to learn things; he did, but they moved at a glacial pace in school, and the information was so weak and biased that he didn't fully trust what he was being told. Regardless, due to other kids' bullying, he had to focus on protecting himself. Education and learning were the farthest thing from the mind of a child forced to survive any of our public institutions.

While Hudson was young, he was well-read, even for a typical American adult. He started reading fiction like 'The Lord of the Rings' and 'The Chronicles of Narnia', books his mom had introduced him to before she passed away when he was twelve. But since he had begun their series of investigations into the disappearance of children by serial killers a year prior, Hudson had expanded his reading queue far beyond fiction for young adults. He was reading books on history, religion, science, myth, and nature. He loved nature and animals. Animals seemed so pure and so authentic to him. People, not so much. People often put on a front and a false face for others to see and believe in. Animals were real. If they liked you, you knew it. If they didn't, you knew that too.

Today, it was history class, and Hudson loved history overall. However, the history he learned in public school differed significantly from the accurate history he encountered in some of his more adult books. For instance, he was reading the book 'A People's History of the United States' by Howard Zinn, which gave an exhaustive, evidence-based retelling of US history from the perspective of the millions of poor and working-class people who lived through it, not the elitist professors and historians telling a nice propaganda story while working for wealthy handlers.

The lesson today was about the Middle Ages, also known as the Dark Ages, when people were a little more honest about things. The teacher read from the prescribed lesson plan, not modifying a single word or providing any additional information or insights. Her endless, drone-like speech put at least a third of the class to sleep within five minutes. She would repeatedly raise her voice slightly to wake people up, then resume her drone. On and on.

"That was when the collapse of the Western Roman Empire, and the embrace of Christianity by the Roman Emperor Charlamange, led to the end of what is known as the classical period. Population decline, the collapse of centralized authority, tribal invasions, and mass migrations of tribes, which had begun in late classical times, continued into the Early Middle Ages.

"The Middle Ages began around 476 A.D., after a significant loss of power throughout Europe by the ancient Roman Empire. The Middle Ages lasted from the 5th to the late 15th centuries, eventually giving way to the Renaissance and the Age of Discovery. The medieval period is subdivided into the Early, High, and Late Middle Ages…"

Hudson was numb to the information's statistic-based, analysis-free delivery. It didn't seem to him that this was intended to educate anyone, only to test how well people could regurgitate a bunch of numbers. There was no attempt to explain how or why any of this happens.

The teacher continued, completely unfazed that most of the class was zoning out, "An essential group during the Middle Ages was a military religious order called the Knights Templar. The Knights Templar, a Catholic order, primarily protected Christian pilgrims on their long and dangerous journey to the Holy Land. Their headquarters were located on the current Temple Mount and existed for nearly two centuries during the Middle Ages. The Templar Knights were among the most skilled fighting units of the Crusades…"

At that point, though he would have personally found this information very interesting, Hudson himself dozed off. It's almost as if the teacher's mannerisms and lack of passion for her craft impeded his desire and ability to learn. If only Hudson had been born into more fortuitous circumstances, like Wick Beale, he might have found his experience at school to be quite different.

Chapter 5

Across town and up the hill, Wick felt completely different about school than Hudson did. And it's not because Wick was popular; he wasn't. He sat in the corner, hoping not to get picked on, just like Hudson did. But Wick was bright, like Hudson, and he naturally desired information and education, just as Hudson did. In that way, they were very similar.

What Wick appreciated about his school was the quality of the teachers and the diversity and maturity of the curriculum. It was the equivalent of an undergraduate college; his parents frequently told him, and he didn't doubt it was true. Being rich had its benefits, Wick thought to himself, as he quickly refocused on what was turning into a fascinating history of the Middle Ages, particularly the Knights Templar.

Professor Marlow continued his thirty-minute-long monologue, all done from memory with no notes or book. All the kids were transfixed by his story, which was now culminating in what he called a more accurate historical account of Templar history. He spoke in an eloquent tone, like a very refined person, and when he taught you something, you knew it for good. To the kids, he seemed like an old man, but he probably wasn't more than forty-five. Unlike the public-school teacher, he spoke with genuine interest and passion about the subject.

"This is the period following the collapse of the Roman Empire, when Roman Catholic Christianity dominated Europe and imposed a horrific religious Inquisition on all people, forcing them to convert to and worship their form of Christianity under threat of torture and death. People, or more accurately peasants, weren't even allowed to read books then, under threat of torture." The professor looked around for signs of revulsion in their little eyes and saw enough to still have faith in humanity.

"You could only know what a Catholic priest told you the Bible or other books were about." All the kids looked at each other in horror. One of them blurted out, "But what if the priest was a liar!" Then, he realized he had spoken out of turn and lowered his head. Professor Marlow ignored the outburst, agreeing with the sentiment, if not the etiquette.

"It wasn't enough for the Roman Catholic Church to dominate people's minds in Europe; they wanted to force others around the world to believe what they believed. So, under the guise of protecting pilgrims on their trip to the Holy Land, the Catholic Church partnered with a group known as the Knights Templar, a non-Christian, I repeat, a non-Christian order of pagan warrior monks, and launched what is commonly known as the Crusades.

"It is little known today, but the Templars were the first international bankers. They are the ones who built our modern global banking system. Their wealth was primarily created based on a system called usury, which is charging obscenely high interest rates on loans intended to make debt slaves out of people. If you charge people high enough interest rates, they will never be able to pay back their loans. They are forever indebted to you.

"In this case, the debtors were Christian pilgrims traveling to Jerusalem and the Holy Land, as undertaking a pilgrimage was both costly and very dangerous. The great irony here is that early Christians at the time were morally opposed to any form of interest or usury, and it was the Templars who normalized it for them by exploiting them. This becomes the foundation of modern capitalism.

"The Templars were prominent movers and shakers in Christian finance. Not widely known is that almost 90% of their members weren't even knights who fought in the Crusades. How do you like that? It was the order's non-combatant members who managed the extensive economic infrastructure of their financial empire.

"Aside from the wealth of the members, which they must relinquish when joining the Order, the other way Templars acquired their fortune was by looting the Holy Land for treasures and relics. Protecting pilgrims was a convenient cover story, but the real motive was their desire to pillage and plunder the remnants of the Eastern Roman Empire for Biblical artifacts…and to slaughter heretics, of course. I mean, that is the real goal of the crusades, the elimination of all forms of opposition, also known as heretics, to the Roman Catholic Church.

"In 1162, the Papal Bull *Omne Datum Optimum* became the foundational document of the Templars' power. In this, the Pope gave them an obscene amount of power and control. The Templars did not have to pay a kickback to the church, then called a tithe. And they could collect protection money from regular people. Oh, and nobody who entered the Templar Order could ever leave it. You were a member for life, upon threat of death. Sounds a bit like a modern mafia organization running a protection racket, no?" The kids all nodded, seeing the obvious connection once it was explained to them.

"After a few hundred years, the Templars were getting way too powerful, and both the King of France and the Pope wanted to see them reined in. They were the wealthiest order in the world, richer than many Kings of major countries at the time. The Templars owned churches, chapels, farms, villages, and mills. They owned rights to pasturage, fishing, and wood.

"With all this money and power, the Templars were getting arrogant. They were pushing Christians around, because guess what, they weren't Christian. It is a significant myth and propagandized narrative that the Knights Templar were established to protect pilgrims on their way to Jerusalem and the Holy Land. This is a cover story. They were established primarily as a branch of the ancient Mystery Schools. But that will be a discussion for another day.

"It was at dawn on Friday, the 13th, October 1307, that King Philip IV of France had hundreds of French Templars arrested simultaneously. Among the crimes the Templars were accused of were acts during admissions ceremonies in which recruits were forced to spit on the cross, deny the existence of Christ, and engage in homosexual practices. The Templars were accused of idolatry and were charged with worshipping either a figure known as Baphomet, a winged hermaphroditic demonic deity, or a mummified severed head they recovered at their original headquarters on the Temple Mount. These guys believed they could make that head speak, and it would tell the future. That is not a joke.

"The secret French orders said that all Templars were to be seized, tortured, and interrogated. Confessions were to be obtained from them, and all their goods were to be seized. Now, here comes the interesting part, which you will not read about in most history books. The original sealed letters were sent out a whole month, thirty days, before October 13th, on September 12th. These letters went all over France. All someone had to do was open one of them, and all the plans would have been exposed. Well, it seems someone did. And the Templars were given a heads-up so they could get a head start on being on the run. This is where the legend of Friday the 13th being an unlucky day comes from.

"But the Templars had even more help than a thirty-day heads-up that they were about to be arrested in France. When the Pope wrote to the King of England on November 22, 1307, he requested that the King arrest all Templars in England and seize their lands and property. But, like in France, there was not a one-month gap, but a three-month gap until the English King enforced the Pope's orders. This gave the Templars in England ample time to move underground, with the help and support of elements of the English aristocracy. In the end, before either the king of France or England took action, the Templars had transferred their wealth, treasure, and holdings out of France and into England, Scotland, Portugal, and other overseas havens.

"In the end, the only thing that the King of France got from the Templars was their real estate properties, which were extensive. None of their gold, their wealth, their jewels, their treasures, and none of the relics that had been stolen from Jerusalem were ever found. Hmm, I wonder where they went?" The kids were all furrowing their brows, thinking about all the adventures they could have while looking for Templar treasure!

"One thing I want you to think about is where these Templars went after they were criminalized? They had one of the largest navies in the world. Where did it go? Well, at some point in the late Middle Ages, thousands of pirate ships appeared around the world flying the Skull and Bones flag, which, if you are well-informed like me, you would know was how Templars used to bury their dead. Most Templar gravestones show the crossed thighbones and the skull known as the Skull and Bones — the same Skull and Bones always seen on the flag of the pirates, The Jolly Roger!"

The professor then displayed a large Skull and Bones symbol on his projector for the class. Everyone couldn't wait to hear about the pirates. How could anyone not like school, thought Wick?

At that moment, Wick realized he had to go to the bathroom very badly. But there was no way he was going to miss one minute of this. He would hold it.

Chapter 6

The Serial Club had become a very popular internet-based true-crime podcast over the past year, following the resolution of the Doctor Dedorius serial killer case, which was, at the time, a national news story. Based on downloads and listeners, they had one of the largest true-crime podcasts specifically covering serial killers globally. One of the things that made their podcast stand out from others on the market is Hudson's and his team's behavioral profiling abilities.

Hudson, along with his best friends Sage and Cai, would take turns explaining the motivations and development of the disturbed individual they were investigating, each based on their area of interest. Hudson was the thinker, the analyst. He would help connect the dots and explain the larger picture that may often get lost amid a wave of emotion. Cai, being African American and coming from a more economically challenging environment, had developed street smarts through hard-learned lessons, which gave her an unvarnished understanding of true human motivation and behavior.

Sage was much different than her two friends, who both had a chip on their shoulder and something to prove. She was an indigenous young woman who had a more loving, if not exactly extravagant, upbringing, so she did not have the same level of distrust and skepticism towards people that Hudson and Cai had. While Sage may have been more empathetic than her companions, she was shrewd and no dummy. She could look at a situation and understand the human element, as well as how it connected to other interpersonal elements that Hudson and Cai could not comprehend. Between the three of them, they were the perfect investigative team: intelligence, intuition, and compassion.

Their latest series had been a historical one. The Serial Club had been reviewing some of the most interesting serial killer cases throughout history, then conducting behavioral analyses of a select few to show what creates and motivates serial killers. Based on their extensive research, one of the most common elements all male serial killers seem to have is a deep-seated anger and hatred towards their mothers. This is the crucial missing element that all those other true-crime shows seem to ignore. This was not something the Serial Club would shy away from.

Hudson continued his narration, "For men to have so much anger towards women to commit such horrible atrocities towards them, they must have been seething with rage for years based on resentment towards their mother. This deep resentment is so intolerable to the young man who is feeling it that he displaces that anger onto other women as a surrogate for his mother.

"So, the mother-hating serial killer is out doing all the horrible things to women that he wants to do to his mother, but can't. He is so deep in denial that he doesn't even know that his anger towards his mother is what drives him. He just knows that he is angry and hates women.

"Time and time again, from serial killers like Ed Kemper, the Co-Ed Killer, to Ed Gein, the Butcher of Plainfield, these malformed and maldeveloped men can never reconcile their conflicting love and hatred for the abusive women who bore them."

Everyone in the room kept quiet while Hudson was recording. Sage and Cai had already done their parts, and it was then up to Hudson to finish the project, assemble it with his video and audio editors, and add an overlay that displayed all the Serial Club's social media accounts and contact details, allowing people to send information about new cases to them. The audio-only version would have similar details, but with short URLs so people could write them down.

The only one who was not involved in the podcast was their new after-school partner, Wick Beale. A few weeks earlier, Wick had been dumped on Hudson's doorstep, and since then, he just sat in the corner, not really engaging with anyone, looking down or on his phone most of the time. Sometimes he napped; he would often fall asleep sitting in his folding chair in the corner of the room. The Serial Club would look over, and Wick would be nodding off again. Weird, they all thought. What young kid falls asleep like an old man during the day?

While Hudson's skills at producing video and audio have been evident since their first investigations into missing children, his videos still had a child-like, primitive quality that was very endearing. But not apparently to Wick, who, for the first time, spoke up from the corner as Hudson was doing the editing process.

"Those overlays suck." Wick barely looked up from his phone as he uttered this insult.

Huson and the team were floored. Not just that Wick was being a jerk, but that he said anything at all. He was like a ghost sitting in the corner that they barely considered.

Hudson hated being criticized. He was too delicate and sensitive. He took everything as a personal insult. He immediately shot back, "Like how?"

Wick looked up slowly and sleepily, flipping his black hair from his eyes. "It's just choppy, and your timing is off. I'm not sure about some of the font choices, given this is a podcast about serial killers." He looked back down at his phone.

Hudson was in shock. Cay and Sage never challenged him like that; they always delivered their input more politically. But the more Hudson thought about what Wick was saying, the more he agreed. "Ok, maybe you have a point, but do you think you could do better?"

"Sure, happy to." Wick then took a MicroSD card out of his bag and threw it to Hudson. "Just put the main file and supporting ones on there. I have the professional versions of the software you are using, and I'll be able to access higher-quality fonts and effects. Give me like two or three days, and I'll send the finished files over." Wick looked back down at his phone, like it was nothing.

Hudson, Cai, and Sage were speechless, again. Who was this guy? He not only backed up his tough talk but also said he would help them produce their podcast. They would have to see if he actually delivered.

Chapter 7

The next time they got together, just a few days later, Wick had the episode done and ready to upload. He threw the SD card to Hudson with a lazy motion after sitting in his usual seat.

"Here you go, sport." Hudson grabbed the card out of the air effortlessly and put it in his laptop, ignoring Wick's put-down.

Hudson played the full episode for everyone in the room, including Sage and Cai. Wick seemed to be barely paying attention, as was his way. During the opening credits, the room fell totally silent, and all three of The Serial Club were blown away by how slick the video Wick put together was. It was like they were watching a professionally-produced show on broadcast or cable TV, not some internet show put on by a few kids. And Wick was right that he had access to higher-quality fonts, transitions, music, and still images than Hudson did with his free-to-try software. Everything had a top-tier, high-resolution quality that only money and talent can buy.

And that was what was dawning on each Club member as they watched the 30-minute video. This wasn't just about Wick having access to better quality software than Hudson; he had real talent as a producer. The opening music was ominous, like it should be for a podcast on serial killers. The title sequence of The Serial Club came out at you, and you felt it when it hit. The font Wick used was modern yet retro.

"Wick, I like that font and title treatment a lot. I want to use that as our new Serial Club logo if that is OK with you," Sage loved working with art and creatives. She was hoping she and Wick could be friends and work together on this. But Wick barely acknowledged her. She thought she heard a 'whatever', but she wasn't sure. It was going to take some real effort to penetrate this mystery boy, thought Sage.

As the podcast continued, everything about it felt more polished, complete, and professionally produced. It occurred to Hudson as they watched that this would mean they could start charging more for sponsorship positions. Not that he cared about that stuff, but he did need to keep the engine rolling here, and that meant revenue.

This also occurred to Cai at the same time. "Wow, guys, this looks so good now, we may be able to make a few bucks from it." Wick, again, if he heard, didn't acknowledge her. Cai wondered if this guy thought he was too good for the rest of us, but decided it was too early to judge. He may have a bad attitude. And who could blame him for that, Cai thought? She decided to give him a break, for now. Besides, this podcast was great. Maybe they could find a spot in the Club for this kid?

By the end of the 30-minute video, all three members of The Serial Club knew they wanted Wick to produce all their podcasts. However, they didn't know if he would be willing to do that, so they turned pensively to ask Wick if he would continue to do what he had done on this one with future episodes. When they did, Hudson, Cai, and Sage were yet again shocked that Wick was sound asleep, still sitting upright in his chair. His head was down, and now that it was silent, they could hear soft sounds coming from him. First, it was like shallow breathing, but then it became more like breathless mumbling. After a few seconds, it dawned on the group that Wick was talking in his sleep. And as they listened, they could make out some words.

"...I am the Star Child...follower of Thoth, Keeper of the Mysteries...master of knowledge..."

Hudson looked at Cai and Sage and mouthed the words, "What the fuck!"

Wick continued after a pause, "...I am the son of Isis...of the serpent and the horns...I am the wicker king...the bender..."

Sage was starting to feel uncomfortable. Whatever Wick was saying was not healthy or normal. This did not sound like a typical dream. What was going on in this kid's mind?

Just then, almost like he knew he was being watched, Wick woke up. He saw that three people were staring at him, and realized he must have dozed off.

"Sorry, I must have been sleeping." All three of them were looking at him in shock.

"Wick, are you OK?" Sage was looking at him, genuinely concerned. Wick looked at Hudson and Cai, and they both looked worried, too. Oh, great, what was he doing?

"I'm fine." His feeble acknowledgment didn't seem to assuage these people. Wick didn't know it yet, but he was dealing with three people who had genuine emotions and cared about what was going on with him. This was not something Wick was used to dealing with. Usually, people just left him alone.

"Look, man, you were just saying some messed-up stuff about Thoth and Star Children and whatnot." Cai wasn't one to mince words. "Was that an act or for real?"

She could tell that Wick didn't know what she was talking about. He looked genuinely confused and unaware of anything she was saying.

"I'm sure it was just a dream." Wick didn't seem too concerned about it.

Hudson, Sage, and Cai looked at each other, unsure what to do or say. So, they all just let it drop, for now.

Chapter 8

During their next after-school session, Wick was nowhere to be found. His absence and bizarre behavior in the last meeting had disturbed everyone. So far, they hadn't talked about Wick too much in general. It was clear he didn't want to be there, and he barely interacted with the Serial Club. If he didn't want to interact with them, the team figured, no problem, and they let him be. However, after yesterday, they began to think that a hands-off approach might not be the best idea.

"I'm worried about Wick, you guys." Sage was the first to address the topic, not surprisingly, since she served as the team's compassionate conscience. Both Hudson and Cai were nodding in agreement. "I get that he is not the nicest person, and he has not been the greatest to us, but I think there may be something more serious going on with him."

"And how much he sleeps is strange, isn't it?" Cai was reflecting. "Like he just falls asleep sitting in a chair, like he is eighty years old. In the middle of the day! The kid must be fifteen."

Hudson was in complete agreement. "And then to not only talk in his sleep, but to say such weird things. What in the actual fuck was that?"

"I have never heard of anything he was talking about; it was all Greek to me," Sage replied. Cai was nodding her head in agreement.

The team sat in silence for a few moments, each considering what they had heard and witnessed.

"I feel like we should look into it and try to help him," Sage said, looking at her friends intently. "Who knows what is going on with him in his private life?"

Cai wasn't so sure. "I hear you, Sage, and I want to help. But what if he doesn't want our involvement? Is it right for us to force ourselves on him against his wishes?"

Hudson could see the logic of that argument. "I see what Cai is talking about. If it were me, and I wanted to be private, and others were stepping into my life, I wouldn't appreciate it."

"But what if he is being abused or something, Hudson?" Sage was looking at him with compassion. "And he is too messed up and scared to say anything. Shouldn't we at least offer him our hand so he doesn't drown in the water? Don't we owe any living being that simple level of consideration?"

Both Cai and Hudson were silent for a few seconds. Sage was making a good point. To stay out of someone's business was one thing, but to refuse to offer assistance to a suffering person was another. The Serial Club had built its reputation and identity on doing the right thing, whether other adults or the authorities thought so or not.

"You don't need a weatherman to know which way the wind blows," Cai repeated her mom's favorite lyric from Bob Dylan. Common sense decency is just that, she reminded herself. You don't need to be a genius or have a degree to do the right thing by others. "Ok, I'm in. As long as we back off if he really does not want us around, or don't find anything too disturbing."

Hudson was nodding in agreement as well. "Yeah, let's start with some basic recon and try to create a profile of this kid and his family situation. I can conduct my online research;

maybe you two can put a tracker on his car next time he comes over to see if we can find out where he goes and what he is up to. Make sense?"

Sage was visibly pleased and relieved. This could turn out to be nothing, but at least she felt like they took it seriously and didn't let this kid suffer in silence.

Chapter 9

Hudson's online research had yielded some pretty significant results on the Beale family. Today, with so much information available digitally online, if you knew what you were doing, you could dig up quite a bit.

Hudson had set up their meeting room, also known as his bedroom, so that he could present his findings on Wick's family to the group. He had not put any of the materials out yet because he was unsure whether Wick would attend today's meeting. Wick had not shown up since his rantings while sleeping a few days earlier, and Hudson was not sure if he would be back at all. There was no communication with Wick or his family, so Hudson had no way of knowing what was going on. He was excited, though, to hear Cai and Sage's report on the car tracker they put on Wick's family car.

Just then, Hudson heard the door open below and two sets of feet coming up. They didn't need to knock; if they were on time, Hudson was OK with them just coming in. But if anyone tried to change Hudson's schedule without him knowing, watch out!

"Well, how did it go? Did you find anything good?" Cai knew Hudson had been working hard.

Hudson had found quite a bit. But he wanted to know about the car tracking operation first. "Oh, I have found out some good stuff. But what about you guys? How did the tracking op go?"

Sage was shaking her head. "We know where Wick's house is; that is easy to find online. But it is gated as expected, so we waited until we saw the family driver going out and doing some errands, and then Cai was able to slip a tracker under his back bumper while he was getting lunch."

Cai agreed, "Yeah, getting it on there was no big deal, but it didn't get us much. Hud, these guys are no joke."

Sage chimed in, "We literally saw the unit track the car back to their house, and then five minutes later, we lost the signal."

"You lost the signal, how?" Hudson wasn't sure what that meant, but he had an idea.

So did Cai. "They must have found it back at the house. Perhaps they scan their cars for trackers after each trip."

"Do you think they are that sophisticated?" Sage was wondering.

Hudson was nodding his head, "I guess we shouldn't be surprised when I tell you guys what I found. Grab a drink and some snacks, and I'll give you some background on the Beale family.

After a minute or two of preparation, Hudson began his presentation. He had his digital projector Bluetoothed to his tablet, and he started his slide show. The opening slide said, 'Operation: The Beales.'

"I spent a few productive hours digging into the history of the Beale family, and let me tell you, they go back. Way back."

"Like how far, Hudson?" Sage was munching on a cracker.

"At least to the Middle Ages, if not even further. Just from doing some online genealogy research, I have traced their family back to the famous Robert de Ros of England, who died in 1227."

"Holy shit, Hud, that is old school!" Cai was shocked; she had never heard of families that were that old. All of her ancestors were kidnapped from Africa and had their histories and cultures destroyed, so everything she knew in terms of family history was relatively new.

"Yup, and this was no regular guy. He was one of King John's top men. Responsible for implementing the Magna Carta, which was a kind of bill of rights for rich barons at the time. But it gets even more interesting when I dug into this guy a bit more. A little research shows Robert was a Knight Templar from at least 1212 on, and was buried as a Knight Templar in the Templar church when he died in 1227."

Cai interrupted him, as she knew Hudson would not stop for twenty minutes if you did not force your way in. "Hud, didn't we learn something about the Knights Templar in school the other day?"

Hudson thought about it. "Sorry, don't remember, that place bores the hell out of me." He thought about it a little more, "Nah, this is too interesting. If they had mentioned it, I would know."

Cai just shrugged. Why argue with him, she thought. Hudson was a bit of a know-it-all, if Cai was honest with herself. Well, no one was perfect. Even the great Hudson. She smiled to herself.

Hudson continued reading his notes on Robert de Ros, while showing images on the projector of his tomb, estate, house, and Templar flags and symbolic imagery.

"In historical accounts, he is known to have been a 'munificent benefactor to the Knights Templars.'" Hudson was laughing; he thought the old word "munificent" was hysterical. Old words made him laugh like that. He looked at the girls, and apparently, for them, not so much. He regained his composure.

"What that means is he gave way more than he had to. This guy gave it all to his church and order. Robert de Ros donated the manor of Ribston, the village and mills of Walshford, and the town of Hunsingore to the Knights Templar in 1217. This property eventually became the Ribston Preceptory, a priory of the Knights Templar.

Sage was literally on the edge of her seat. This was so interesting, medieval castles and kings and barons! "Hudson, he gave pretty much everything he had to his church and order. Is that normal at the time?"

"Yeah, actually, for a Templar. That was a requirement of being a Knight Templar; you had to give all your wealth and property to the Templars, which was a religious military order, or a church army. So, the knights were supposedly poor, but the church was rich. In reality, they all just lived off the church money, so they looked poor, but they lived in luxury. Very tricky."

"Now this Ribston Preceptory will need some more investigation on my part. But from what I could find during the trials of the Templars, when their order was outlawed, and they were all rounded up, there was testimony and evidence from multiple people about suspicious secret practices and rituals being performed by Templars at the Preceptory."

"Hud, that is so wild!" Cai was blindly reaching for some nuts. "What are you saying? Are they witches or something?" Cai made a grimacing face.

"I am going to have to read into it more, but I don't know yet. Ok, so moving on from Robert for now, the family gets even more interesting, if you can believe that. This Wick kid is not from the Smith family down the road, if you know what I mean."

It then became a little dark outside as a rain cloud moved across the sun, blackening the room.

Hudson stopped for a moment, then continued with his voice a little lower, "A few hundred years after the founder of the dynasty, we have an odd duck in the family, but a famous one at that. It turns out that a descendant of the de Ros line, a carpenter, married a famous English witch named Ursula Southeil, also known as Mother Shipton, the Witch of York.

Just then, thunder burst, and lightning flashed outside, stopping everyone for a second. Hudson turned back, his voice a little quieter now, even with the growing storm outside.

"She was born in a cave in 1488 to a young girl during a violent thunderstorm. The cave has a pool shaped like a skull that, if you put something in it, turns things to stone. You can still visit the cave to this day." Hudson looked outside to the rising storm, then leaned in to Cai and Sage, quieter still.

"Ursula was born deformed and hideous, with a large hunchback, crooked legs, and bulging eyes. There were rumors in the community that Ursula was the spawn of Satan, and her mother was a witch herself."

Both Cai and Sage were so transfixed with both fear and fascination; neither was moving, eating, or drinking, and they were holding on to Hudson's every word. He had become quite a good storyteller lately, and he could keep people on the edge of their seats.

"Aside from this woman being an herbalist and healer, she was known to have made prophecies. In 1666, some random recorded in his journal that while surveying the damage to London caused by the Great Fire of 1666 in the company of the Royal family, he heard them discuss Mother Shipton's prophecy of the event."

Sage shuddered. "Holy freaking cow, this lady was seriously bad-ass." Sage then backed down, being a bit embarrassed.

Hudson and Cai burst out laughing. Sage was usually such a sweet, empathetic hippy-dippy type that you never heard her swear. Or cheer on a witch!

"It's ok, Sage, this is pretty exciting stuff. A lot more fun than a psychotic doctor with a God complex, right?"

Sage looked down a bit, and Hudson realized he had made a mistake. He was joking, as was his way, but sometimes he didn't consider other people's feelings. After all, it was Sage who was kidnapped by the good Doctor Dedorius almost a year prior, and he nearly removed her finger in a deranged attempt to keep his deceased family alive with fresh body parts. Sage was continually recovering from the incident, but trauma like that scars you for life.

Cai looked at Hudson disapprovingly, and Hudson knew he had done wrong again.

"I'm so sorry, I didn't mean anything."

"No, no, it's fine, I'm strong, like a female bull." Sage was laughing. Cai and Hudson joined in.

Hudson continued, promising himself to be more mindful of other people's feelings. He had never had so many real-life, aka non-digital, friends in his life, and he didn't want to lose them.

"Finally, and I will need to do some more digging on this final item, there does seem to be an ongoing vein of criminality in the family line, from smuggling to trafficking and things like that. I can't put my finger on anything specific, but there is some shade on parts of this family, that is for sure."

Just then, there was a knock on the door, and everyone was on their toes immediately. Who the hell could that be, Hudson thought, definitely irritated. If someone wasn't invited, they shouldn't be knocking on his door. He went down as his two partners stayed in the room. Hudson was ready to give his best mean face to let whoever was there know they were disturbing him, when it was Hudson who was to be bowled over. Standing there, looking just like he did the first time he saw him, was Wick.

"Hey, Hudson, what's up?" Wick flicked his long black hair back from his eyes, somewhat languidly.

Hudson was surprised, but not enough to ask a question. "Hey, Wick, where you been, man? We were talking about you and kinda getting worried."

"Nah, no big deal, just been dealing with some family and other stuff."

Hudson could tell he was not going to get more from Wick, so he stopped pushing. He stepped aside to let Wick in.

"Oh no, sorry, I am not here to stay. Believe it or not, I have an invitation for you and the other two." He motioned up the stairs to Hudson's room with his head while he pulled out something from his pocket and handed it to Hudson.

"My parents are having a party, and you and the Club are invited. They want to meet you, believe it or not."

Hudson was having trouble believing it. He never got any indication that they gave a crap about Wick or anything in his life, but he knew enough to be polite here and not commit on the spot.

"That's cool, thanks, man. Well, let me talk to Sage and Cai, and we will get back to you."

Wick seemed satisfied, having performed the task he was appointed, and he nodded to Hudson, flicked his hair back, and sauntered back to the sleek black car with dark-tinted windows that Hudson was now sure was a brand-new Bentley.

Chapter 10

Cai and Sage were just as shocked as Hudson to get an invitation to the Beale manor. They didn't think they would see Wick again, much less get an invite to his house for a get-together. Sage, the most social and outgoing of the three, was excited to meet some new people. Hudson and Cai, not so much. It took some convincing from Sage that this would be in both their best interests as investigators.

For Hudson, being able to build his behavioral analysis by directly interfacing with the family was enough to convince him to attend. For Cai, it was enough that the other two were going, and she wanted to be there to protect them. And if Wick was suffering from ongoing abuse, physical, emotional, or mental, she wanted to help him. She didn't need to like him to have compassion for him.

Once it was agreed that they would be going, the Serial Club had to decide what to wear and how they would get there. The latter was easy; once Hudson and the girls told their parents about the invite, they were only too happy to make sure the kids got there safely. After all, this was the family that owned much of the town, so being on good terms with them was in everyone's best interests. Brody, Hudson's big, seventeen-year-old brother, who now had a license, was recruited to drive the kids there and then pick them up in two hours. He did so without much fuss, as any excuse to drive was a welcome distraction to him.

The Serial Club had been invited to what was called on the invitation a 'garden party.' None of them had any idea what a garden party was, but they guessed it would be outdoors and in or near a garden. Hudson didn't have much in the way of clothes beyond t-shirts, shorts, or jeans. So, he was forced to wear his Sunday church clothes, which he hated as they were incredibly uncomfortable. Sage looked adorable as usual, and dressed up her usual look with some nicer jewelry and crisp Native American patterns on her clothes. Cai, like Hudson, had little else to wear but her Sunday church clothes, which consisted of black shiny shoes, a pleated dress, and a white blouse. Hudson almost laughed when he saw Cai, but quickly stifled himself as he knew she did not like to be made fun of. Besides, Hudson was a little afraid of Cai.

As Brody drove them up the winding, hilly roads leading to the rich area of town, he blasted his music, which seemed to be some grindcore-technical death metal-melodic groove hybrid metal that everyone but him in the car hated. That made Brody like it even more. When he saw Hudson getting irritated and uncomfortable, he just turned it up louder.

Soon, the houses got fewer and fewer, and the roads got nicer and nicer. No more potholes or broken signs. Then they saw a row of beautiful, ancient oaks lining the road, growing from smaller to larger and more formidable trees, creating a sense of majesty and impending doom as they proceeded. Soon, it felt like they were passing through a tunnel of trees, back in time to a mystical land. The grinding death metal music sounded fitting for the scene, and they marched silently into a future and past unknown.

Then there was a light ahead, and it grew and grew until it was blinding. It took a moment for everyone to adjust their eyes, and then they saw a stone wall and a massive gate, with two stone pillars flanking it, each bearing a statue.

"What the hell are those?" Cai just blurted things out; it was her way.

As they got closer, Hudson was making them out. "Holy shit, those look like Egyptian sphinxes. Look, they have that weird King Tut headdress, and they are lying down with their paws forward, and their bodies look like a lion, or a dog."

Sage and Cau could see precisely what he was saying. Yup, those were sphinxes, like the one in Egypt.

"What in all the name of weirdness does an old American and British family like this have Egyptian sculptures guarding their house?" Sage was perplexed. She never saw anything like this in the States.

"And look at that gate, what is that design?" Hudson was alert now.

Cai said, "I'm not positive, but it looks like a two-headed eagle, with each head facing the opposite direction."

"Yeah," Hudson put that down on his mental notes to research. He didn't need to write it down; he would remember.

As they approached the gate, they could see the seriousness of the surveillance. There were at least two heavy-duty cameras in protective boxes, and a metal pole with a control panel right before the gate. Even Brody, typically an in-your-face teenager, was intimidated. He turned the music down and sat up straight. Everyone did for some reason.

Brody pulled up to the gate. He saw the box but didn't see any controls. Then he heard a voice.

"Please state your name and reason for visit." It sounded almost robotic. Maybe AI.

"Brody, dropping off Hudson, Cai, and Sage for the Beale Garden party."

Then, without reply, the gate began to open slowly almost immediately.

After they went through the gate, it was similar to the road they had come down, but was now fully manicured. Giant oak trees lined the road, while one could see off into the distance a rolling and winding driveway, without a main house in sight. The size and scope of the compound were enough to impress any person, regardless of their vanity. Brody let out a breath, and they drove up to the house in silence, in awe of the wealth that they never knew one family could have.

Eventually, the driveway straightened out, and the now semi-enclosed tunnel of oak trees suddenly opened into light and brightness, revealing a truly spectacular scene. It was not a house, one could call it a mansion, but perhaps manor would have been the more appropriate term. A grand English country manor that looked like it came right out of the Renaissance. A majestic estate towering to the sky, built of stone and brick, with exquisite grounds and hedges to make the scene right out of a picture book or the TV show Downton Abbey.

And right in the middle of the circular driveway, on a grass area, was a most peculiar object, not what one would expect to see in front of an English manor. A large monolithic stone edifice, tall, four-sided, and with a pointed top, similar to what the Washington Monument in D.C. looks like.

"What the hell is that, Hud?" Cai really hadn't a clue, just that it looked out of place.

It didn't take Hudson long. "It looks like the Washington Monument. But I don't think that's what it is. Probably Egyptian, based on the sphinx."

Brody pulled the car up and parked near the steps leading up to the front door. Hudson and Cai jumped out of the opposite side so they could see the stone pillar up close. As they approached, they could see faint writing on its side, in a language they didn't recognize. And there appeared to be a plaque on the bottom, with something written on it. Hudson walked by as close as possible to take a picture of what it said on his phone. Once he did, he kept walking to the door.

Cai asked him quietly, "What did it say?"

Hudson showed her his phone. The plaque read, "netjer nefer men-kheper-re di ankh - The Good God, Thuthmosis III given life."

Cai looked at Hudson and mouthed "WTF!" to him. He shook his head, not understanding why some wealthy English family would be so interested in Egyptian relics. Maybe they were just eccentric. Who knows.

Brody and Sage waited for them to come back around the car, and they all walked up to this massive estate, up a stone staircase to a stone platform, and two large wooden doors with intricate carvings on them. They looked antique and might have been from the Middle Ages. There were all sorts of weird, mythical characters involved in strange and unknowable acts. To the left and right of the doors were two tall columns, with strange symbols running up their sides and golden globes sitting atop them.

It was all so much for these four regular kids to take in; they were just in awe of the wealth and scope of it all.

"Check that door out!" Sage was blown away, like everyone, at the antiquity of it all. It felt like they were in medieval Europe, not Old Springs, Nowhere, USA. She tried to make out some of the details, but the more she looked at it and tried to make sense of it, the more confusing and mysterious it became.

Just then, before they could ring the bell or knock on the door, the giant, dark wooden doors began to open, and a very smartly dressed young man stood inside.

"Greetings, would you please follow me to the back patio for the garden party?"

Before anyone could respond, the young man turned around and began walking briskly. The Serial Club hurriedly followed him, while Brody quickly turned around and took his exit, happy to be out of this uncomfortably pompous place.

"I'll be back in two hours," he said over his shoulder as he retreated from the front steps to the safety of his father's car.

Chapter 11

The Serial Club didn't feel the same way Brody did. Sure, they were intimidated, but they were also fascinated. What a weird and interesting place they were in. The hallway floor, which stretched into the distance, was a black-and-white checkerboard pattern, and as they progressed, they encountered an assortment of antiquated, expensive-looking paintings and statues. Most of the paintings were of rich-looking old people from years gone by, like one they saw for some guy named Saxo Grammaticus, but the statues were more interesting. They could see Greek statues, and some looked Egyptian for sure. The kids saw what seemed like a small pyramid, or maybe it was a recreation or miniature of a real one. Then they saw another obelisk like the one they had just seen on the front lawn, but this was a fragment. And it had markings on it, too. This one looked very real.

The hip butler had gotten pretty far ahead of them, so the team had to hurry along and miss some details they wanted to take in. As they reached the end of the hallway, they came to a large panoramic window that stretched from the ceiling to the floor and extended in both directions, offering a spectacular view of the main grounds. Right outside the window on the patio, a party was getting going, but beyond that, there was a scene of a stream cutting across rolling fields, framed by rows of trees and low rolling hills, in a feast for the eyes that just kept escalating the experience. It took everyone's breath away as they walked out on the patio following the butler.

Before the kids had time to wonder about what to do next, the butler formally announced them to the gathering crowd. Immediately, several people approached them, and the kids could see that their friend Wick was one of them. The Club was about to say hello to Wick when an older, taller, and exceptionally well-dressed man in a suit pushed his way to the front and made sure everyone knew who to talk to. With him was a gorgeous woman dressed in a lovely black dress with very high-end jewelry and diamonds. The kids didn't know much about fashion, but they could bet his suit, her dress, and jewelry cost more than most of their homes.

"Why hello, young people. Welcome to Beale Manor." The man's smile was wide and genuine-looking, and his voice had a mix of American and English accents. He did not stoop to shake hands with anyone.

The woman now inserted herself only after her husband had finished speaking. "We wanted to invite you to our home and to thank you for welcoming Wick into your home. He has only the nicest things to say about all of you." Hudson, Cai, and Sage doubted that it was true; Wick had barely interfaced with them.

The woman continued, "This is my husband, Lord Faustus Beale, and I am Wick's mother, Lady Elizabeth Beale. We welcome you to our estate." Lady Elizabeth gestured to the expansive grounds beyond the patio.

The kids didn't know if they were supposed to bow to them or something. Sage curtsied in her sundress. So far, Wick had said nothing to the team. He hung back a bit behind his mother and father, off to the side, not included in the conversation.

"And I assume you would be Hudson?" Lord Faustus looked down at Hudson with a bit of a smile on his face.

"Yes, I am. And these are my two friends, Cai and Sage."

Lord Beale completely ignored Cai and Sage; it was almost like they weren't there to him.

"Wick says you produce a podcast on serial killers, Hudson. I find that very interesting. What drew you to that area of investigation?"

Hudson couldn't believe this sophisticated and educated man was talking to him as if he were an adult. Adults never spoke to him respectfully. They always condescended to him. Hudson was so flattered by Lord Beale that he didn't even notice how rude he was being to his two partners. But Cai and Sage noticed, and they did not like Lord Faustus Beale at all. To them, he seemed arrogant and elitist.

"Well, we began investigating some cases of child abuse and neglect, which led to an investigation of our local psychotic doctor, who kidnapped Sage. He is what started my interest in serial killers. How can a person be so delusional that they think they are a good person doing good things when they really are a monster?"

Lord Faustus's eyes widened a bit. "That is a wise observation, Hudson." Just then, Lord Beale motioned to another man, this one a bit older and gruffer in appearance, with an unkempt beard, but somehow very imposing and regal at the same time.

"Hudson, I want you to meet my brother, Ricimer Beale. Ricimer, Huson was just telling me about a podcast he does on serial killers. Isn't that interesting?"

Ricimer immediately perked up. "Is that right? At your age? Do you do it all alone?"

"Well, my two friends Sage and Cai help me." Just like Lord Faustus, Ricimer didn't even look at the two young girls. "And Wick helped us produce the last episode, and it looked amazing. The best production values we ever had."

Wick's mother immediately shot a look back at Wick. "I didn't know you helped your little friends on their project?" Wick just cowered under her critical gaze and didn't reply. His mother turned back slowly.

"Well, I will be sure to check that out, as well as some of your past episodes," Ricimer replied to Hudson in a very respectful and adult tone. Even though he looked a little dark and intimidating, Hudson liked him immediately. No one usually paid Hudson any respect.

"Oh, that would be great. I did one recently on a behavioral analysis of famous serial killers that was unlike anything we had produced before."

Just then, Lady Beale inserted herself, "Cai and Sage, why don't you come with me, and I can show you around the grounds. Let the boys have their conversation. This talk is too gruesome for respectable young women."

Neither Sage nor Cai was sure what to do in this situation. No one had ever tried to split the Serial Club up before, and they were very protective of Hudson. But they figured this was a safe space and that they would be picked up in a few hours, so what was the worst that could happen? Besides, these two pompous asses didn't think much of women, so why bother letting them condescend? They willingly followed Lady Beale away.

Ricimer continued talking, barely noticing the women had left. "You know, Hudson, we have an extensive family library here that dates back, well, to the Middle Ages. I'm sure we could arrange some time for you to access it for research purposes."

Hudson was floored. He didn't know what to say. He was trying to respond when Lord Beale jumped in. "We are very encouraging of educating young people about our family and history. We would have no issues with you accessing whatever you want. Of course, you might need to know some medieval Latin!" The Beale brothers laughed heartily. Hudson wasn't sure of the joke.

"I don't know it, but I will learn." Hudson was serious; he didn't understand they were having fun with him.

Lord Faustus looked at Ricimer, then back at Hudson. "Well, I am sure we are going to enjoy getting to know you, Hudson. You seem like an exceptionally bright and quick-witted young man."

Hudson was beside himself with pride. To have such wealthy, intelligent, and powerful men think he was smart and special meant the world to him. His Dad was a decent guy, but he didn't understand Hudson at all. His brother Brody was mainly a goon. Hudson just stayed out of his way. But these Beale brothers were intelligent, worldly, and rich, and they liked him.

Ricimer said, "Look, Hudson, I'm Wick's uncle, so you just call me Uncle Ricimer. That's my nickname around here. Here is my card. When you want to schedule a time to use the library, my assistant can help you. Anytime you want." Ricimer smiled and showed his too-perfect teeth that Hudson realized were probably fake.

It was then that Hudson realized Wick was still there, hiding behind and to the side of his father and uncle, staring off into the distance or at the ground, barely aware of the conversation.

Chapter 12

During the next after-school session at Hudson's house, the impressions of the Beale Garden party were being expressed candidly.

"What a bunch of assholes." Cai wasn't mincing words. She had seen enough bigotry in her life to know what it was.

"And the way the two men just ignored Cai and me, like we weren't even there." Sage was equally insulted.

Hudson was perplexed. The Serial Club was always in synch about things, about what was right and what was wrong. Comfort and security came from knowing that two other people in the world saw things as you did. But this time, he didn't understand where they were coming from.

"I don't know, guys, they seemed alright to me." Hudson wasn't trying to disagree with his friends; he didn't understand.

Both Cai and Sage were shocked by Hudson's naivete in this situation. He was usually level-headed and down-to-earth. How could he be so blind?

"Hud, for real? Look, those two guys wouldn't even acknowledge mine or Sage's existence. That is what people do when they think they are better than you. They dismiss you."

"Hudson," Sage was a little more empathetic to Hudson's limited perspective, "those two men did not like me and Cai because we are women. Or she is African American, and I am Native American, take your pick. And his wife wasn't any better. Patronizing us like we couldn't possibly understand the men's conversation."

Hudson was confused. How could he be so wrong about this? Yes, the men were a little rude to his friends, but maybe that was because they were so impressed by Hudson himself? Hudson didn't usually think of himself as something special, but perhaps he had more going for him than he realized. Maybe it just took some mature, intelligent people to see him for what he really is.

"How should I have reacted differently?" Hudson was trying to be understanding here.

Cai replied, "Well, first off, there were times when you said 'we' in terms of the Club's work, but then retreated to 'me' statements when they started complimenting you. It became 'I' did this, 'I' researched that, etc. It's not the way a team leader would normally talk. A team leader supports his members, even when someone else is trying to undermine them."

That made sense to Hudson. He didn't think the Beales were trying to undermine them, but he would take the suggestion to support his friends better publicly.

"Ok, I get it. I'm not sure they were trying to undermine us as a team, but I will watch myself in the future and ensure I talk as a 'we' rather than a 'me' in relation to Serial Club matters. Fair enough?"

Cai was somewhat satisfied. Yes, Hudson agreed to modify his behavior, but he didn't really acknowledge the main complaint. Sage was a little more patient; she knew breaking

Hudson free of his biases would take more than a five-minute conversation.

"So, what are the next steps here, Hudson?" Sage wanted to diffuse this situation and keep the mission moving forward.

"We continue our research into the family and its history. They offered to give me access to their family library; I should take the offer."

"Do you want some company going over there, Hud?" Cai was always looking out for Hudson's well-being, whether they saw eye to eye on something or not.

Hudson thought about it for a second. 'Nah, it's OK, Cai. It's just me going over and reading books and taking notes for a few hours in a library. I can have Brody drive me."

Cai didn't like it, but what was there to argue with him about?

Chapter 13

Hudson was so excited to do research at the Beale family library that he bugged his father and Brody about it for days straight. Brody, who usually would be up for a drive anywhere, was not happy about going back to the Beale estate again.

"Why do you want to go back there, Hudson? It was stuffy as shit."

Their father immediately shot a look at Brody, "Come on, watch your mouth, he's too young."

"I am not." Hudson hated it when adults treated him like an infant. He was smarter than most of them, and he was just as competent, aside from the fact that he was fifteen. "If I could drive, I would go there myself; I don't need anybody."

"Stop it, Hudson. Brody, please. This is for his business and podcast, and let's not forget Hudson is starting to bring some real money into this house."

It was true. As the podcast series grew in traffic and followers, revenue from podcast subscriptions and sales from his merchandise store began to bring in not hundreds, but close to a thousand dollars in profit per month. Hudson was becoming a bread-winner in his own right.

Brody didn't have much of a choice. Besides, any chance to take his father's car out was a good enough reason for him. He backed down, and they reached an arrangement in which he would drive Hudson to the Beale house once a week for about a month, until he completed his research.

Hudson was beyond thrilled. The chance to dig into some real information, not online dreck that had been stepped on and polluted with misinformation and disinformation for decades. He assumed that any book from any time period would be biased by the personal and cultural limitations the author was bound by, but this material would be closer to the source. To read books dating back hundreds of years. What kinds of mysteries and hidden gems of information would he glean?

He knew that before he delved into a library of old manuscripts, he would need to understand how to disseminate the material effectively. What languages would they be in? Could he use some online translators to help him with parts he couldn't learn? Immediately, Hudson began taking online language courses in Latin, French, and Italian. He found some reference books on old medieval and Renaissance manuscripts and learned about how to read them and what to look for. He couldn't become an expert; he just needed enough background to research the family's history and try to find out what was going on with Wick. But Hudson figured if he had the luxury of time to do a bit of extra research on topics that would be attractive to him, he would.

When Hudson made an appointment with Uncle Ricimier's assistant, he was told that the library hours for guests were weekdays from 7 to 11 p.m. Hudson was a little put off by this. He really did not like to be out of the house after dark. But the lure of secrets and hidden mysteries and information was too much for him to resist.

The way up to the Beale house felt very different this time. It was dusk, and the tunnel of oak trees on the way in went from creepy to downright ominous. Until they reached the gate, there were no lights, and it felt like they were traveling back in time to before the advent of electricity. The gate was scary in a different way. With the spotlights and high-end cameras in metal casings, it had a militaristic vibe. Not welcoming at all. Past the gates, the area was now lined with lights, all illuminating the perfectly spaced oak trees. As they approached the main house, the Egyptian obelisk in the driveway circle was lit with a soft, white light, making it look in place with the rest of the more conservative mansion.

Brody pulled up to the front steps but did not get out of the car.

"Ok, dude, you can go the rest. I'll be back in two hours."

Hudson was a little intimidated. He had to walk up alone, and it just felt weird. But why should Brody walk him up? He wasn't a little kid anymore. Hudson retrieved his bag with all his equipment and left without thanking Brody. It wasn't on purpose; Hudson was feeling nervous. Brody figured that, so he forgave him.

At the door, Hudson was greeted by a different butler than the first time. This butler was creepier for sure. He barely looked down at Hudson or acknowledged him at the door before he turned around and started walking. Hudson assumed he should follow him.

It wasn't a few hundred steps down the main hall, underneath the painting of family historian Saxo Grammaticus they had seen prior, that there was a large oak door. Above it, Hudson could see a very intricate hand-carved wooden relief of an owl perched. The butler opened the door, clicked on an old-style light switch, and a harsh overhead light in a metal cage came on, revealing a stone spiral staircase leading down below. The sight terrified Hudson. He had no idea that this library was located in the basement or lower level.

"Excuse me, I thought we were going to the library?"

The butler only turned his head back a bit. "This is the way to the library. This is the original library of the house, dating back to the sixteenth century. They used to put important things underground back then, so they didn't burn in a fire." The butler turned around and started down the stairs.

Oh well, Hudson thought, too late to back out now. He took a deep breath and started down the steps into the waiting darkness.

Chapter 14

The remaining two members of the Serial Club still met at Hudson's house when he went to do his research at Beale Manor. Their parents continued to work late, so the need for a safe after-school space with some minor adult supervision remained. This was a good thing, as Cai and Sage rarely had the chance to interact without Hudson present. He was the glue that held the three of them together, as much as Sage or Cai was. All three of them were as important as any of the others for the integrity of their group unit.

Cai and Sage were talking about the Beales and Hudson. They were worried about him being alone over there, even for just a few hours, and were discussing what, if anything, they could do to support and protect him. In the middle of this tense conversation, they heard something hit Hudson's back window. They ignored it, figuring it was a branch of something. But then they heard another clicking sound and knew it was not natural. Cai got up with Sage to look out the window. It being past dusk made it difficult to tell who was out there trying to get their attention. All they saw was the light from a smartphone flashing. Then, it was gone.

"What the hell is that, Sage?"

"Someone is trying to give us a message. But why in person, and why not get in touch digitally?"

"I don't know, but it creeps me out."

"Well, we need to go down and see who or what that is. I mean, we are investigators. Do we just let a mystery sit unexamined?"

"Sure, but I am not going to do something stupid and put myself at risk." Cai was thinking hard about how to do this safely.

"Look, we have Brody here. How about one of us goes out with a flashlight, the other stays on the porch and watches them, and we can call Brody if anything looks funky."

Cai thought about it. "Ok, but let me go. If it looks shady, I'll bounce out of there."

Sage agreed. It was more Cai's area to deal with this type of situation, so she didn't push back.

Cai turned on the flashlight feature on her smartphone while Sage turned on all the outside lights, waiting for her on the back patio, the door open and the lights all on. No one would be moving around out here without seeing them. Cai slowly walked back the way they had seen the shadowy figure. As she approached, she saw what looked like a yellow note stuck to the tree. She grabbed it without reading it, didn't see anything else in the immediate vicinity, and retreated quickly to the safety of the house.

Back up in Hudson's room, Cai and Sage sat down at the meeting table and put the note on the table. In a printed hand, it read: 'I must speak to you both about the potential danger your friend, Hudson, is in. Go to Town Park at nine p.m. tomorrow night and wait at the gazebo.'

Cai looked at Sage in astonishment. "Is this person kidding us? What kind of whacko wants to meet us in dark park in the middle of nowhere?"

Sage felt the same way. "I'd feel much safer talking to them online or through some secure chat app. What do you think this is all about?"

"Well, there may be a reason he doesn't want to get in touch with us digitally. Maybe we are under surveillance."

Sage looked at Cai with her head cocked. "Really? I hadn't considered that. Maybe we tapped into some sensitive things in our research?"

"It's obvious it has to do with Hudson based on the note. Unless they are using that to draw us out."

"I don't know about you, but if Hudson is in danger, I want to know about it. End of story." Sage was never going to let one of her friends down. Especially Hudson.

Cai wasn't either. She had already decided before Sage said anything. "Ok, so we meet this person. How do we make it as safe as possible?"

Sage was furrowing her brow; it only took her a few moments. "How about we tell Brody we have to go on a scavenger hunt, and one of the locations is finding something at the park tomorrow night. He waits in the car while we go with flashlights and some protection to find out what the deal is."

"Yeah, why not? I mean, how good of an excuse can we come up with to go to a park at night on a weekday? I hope he'll buy it."

"Yeah. And let's hope he doesn't tell our parents, I'm not sure they would buy our lame excuse."

Chapter 15

Neither Cai nor Sage had ever been to a public park at night, and neither of them had any idea how scary it would be. Brody pulled up to the pothole-pocked parking lot, where one dim street lamp flickered under a sign that said, "Park Open from Dawn to Dusk."

Brody looked at the two girls, somewhat concerned. "Are you two sure this is OK?" He looked around. The place looked dark and creepy to Brody. "Do you want me to come with you? Or wait here?" Brody secretly didn't want to go, but he didn't want to appear cowardly.

Cai thought about it; they couldn't have Brody seeing whoever wanted to talk to them. "No, it's OK, we are just going to look around that gazebo there." Cai pointed to a structure that was only a few hundred feet away.

Sage jumped in. 'We will have flashlights and be in view of you from the car; it should be OK. We need to find an item that is supposed to be hidden here."

It all sounded good to Brody; he wasn't their parent after all. He turned some music on and sat back to wait for them.

Cai and Sage got out, each bringing a flashlight. Cai had an extendable police baton she had gotten from her mom's boyfriend, and Sage had some pepper spray, just in case. They walked slowly to the gazebo. The shadows cast by the car's headlights and the single street lamp were schizophrenic, jumping around at unnatural angles, creating a menagerie of light and shadow.

As they approached the gazebo, they walked up the steps, and the inside was empty. It looked like it hadn't been cleaned in years. They started walking around the inside perimeter, and when they got to the far side, the side farthest away from the light and parking lot, they heard something. They stopped and leaned against the railing to listen.

Beneath them, in the shadow, was a man leaning against the gazebo, with his back to them. He spoke softly, ensuring no one but they could hear.

"I am glad you came. I know this seems strange."

"Who are you?" Cai didn't like playing games with anyone.

"At this point, I can't tell you. That is for your safety and mine. Let's say I am a researcher working with a group that investigates individuals involved in certain nefarious activities. What that is, I can't exactly tell you right now."

"Why couldn't you contact us online?" Sage wanted to know what this was about.

"Simple. Online and digital communication can't be trusted. It's vulnerable to spying."

"Are you saying we are under surveillance?"

"I am saying we all are under surveillance. Certain subjects and communications should not be discussed digitally."

"I thought software like WhatsApp was encrypted and private?" Cai had learned a lot from Hudson.

"Nonsense. Anyone who matters, aka our handlers, has direct access to the backbone of all digital communication technology. It's been compromised since day one."

This was freaking Cai and Sage out a bit. Is this guy saying nothing is private anymore? Who was he?

"Look," he said, looking around before continuing more hurriedly. "This is meant to be a heads-up for you two. As part of the group I work with, we have eyes and ears on a certain aristocratic family you met recently. Well, these people may not be quite what they seem."

Cai's eyes widened. She knew there was something up with the Beales.

"One of our operatives saw your friend Hudson going to the Beale manor at night alone."

"Yes, sure, he's going to do some research in their library. They invited him." Sage wanted to be clear that Hudson was a good guy.

The man paused for a moment. "Interesting. At this point, my goal is to inform you and, if necessary, warn you. Hudson may be fine, I'm not sure. You need to get educated on people like the Beales, and make sure you know who your friends are associating with."

With that, he reached into his coat. "Here, take this." He tossed something wrapped in a brown paper bag up, and it landed on the gazebo floor. Cai quickly picked it up.

"Read that, study it. It'll give you an idea of what you are dealing with and what type of situation your friend is in. I'll be in touch if anything changes."

Sage bent down to ask another question, but the man was gone. All that was left were the distorted shadows and the uneasy sounds of wind pushing its way through the creaking, paint-chipped gazebo.

Chapter 16

The next meeting at the Serial Club HQ was to present Hudson's findings from his research at the Beale mansion. As was his way, he delivered an elegant and informative presentation that explored various elements of both the family history and the cultural and political forces that contributed to their evolution. He had snacks and drinks prepared and was using his portable digital projector connected to his tablet.

Sage and Cai had discussed whether to tell Hudson about the meeting with the mysterious stranger at the gazebo, and decided there was no reason not to. Being honest and authentic with your friends is one of the most rewarding things you can do, so they felt being open with Hudson was the right way to go. They decided to let him give his presentation first, then inform him about their meeting and the package they received.

Hudson began, "First, let me say how interesting the last few weeks have been. There is so much information at the Beale Manor that I could easily spend the rest of my life doing research there and barely come up for air. What was most fascinating was the variety and scope of material. History books, books on the family, yes, for sure, I expected that. However, there were also books on medicine, science, and older subjects such as occultism, alchemy, and magic. I found books that date back to the 1600s, and I bet there are even older manuscripts hidden somewhere. Of course, I can only read and interpret so much, using some basic online language courses and digital translators, but I have found enough to begin to tell a story."

"Wait one sec, Hud, occultism, alchemy? What are you talking about here exactly?" These were totally new words to Cai.

"I'm so glad you asked, since that is what a lot of my presentation is about. Well, not really. Let me explain. This Beale family is part of the old aristocracy, as you know. On paper, they go back to a famous English Templar Knight, and based on some other rare documents I found, they may go back even further."

"How far back, Hudson?" Sage thought this was way more fun than school.

"Maybe back to ancient Roman family bloodlines. Like the Templars and groups that followed them, they are a continuation of a tradition that dates back thousands of years. And it's all wrapped up in aristocracy and their family bloodlines; it's all connected. Generations of a family will belong to a group like the Templars."

"Hang on, Hud. Weren't they outlawed in like 1307 or something?" Cai was listening in school, unlike Hudson.

"Yes, but from what I am reading, they lived on in various incarnations until the present day. For instance, according to one book I read, when the Templars went underground, some of them, who had ships and one of the largest navies in the world, went to the high seas and made their living as pirates. They flew the skull and crossbones, one of many Templar symbols. That is how they continued to operate incognito, in secrecy, with secret handshakes, codes, symbols, and the like. I am still learning the background, which is really complicated and full of dead ends and detours meant to confuse you. It's almost like playing with a Chinese puzzle box, or a Russian tea doll set."

Neither Sage nor Cai knew what a Russian tea doll set was, or a Chinese puzzle box, but there was too much information, and Hudson was rolling. You never stopped him when he was rolling. They let it go and kept quiet. Everything was being recorded in case they needed to listen again.

"Well, we see that the Templars, once on the run, are involved right away in criminal activity like piracy. They were indeed on the run, but they left with all their wealth intact, so they were not broke. After an initial period of criminal activity, until they got themselves back up and running and secure in their new countries, why did the Templars continue operating underground afterward?

"The answer is surprisingly simple. Former Templars formed secret societies in places like England and Portugal so they could continue worshipping their freaky pagan god without being attacked by Christians, that's why. That's the big secret I learned! The Templars are not Christian; they pretend to be. They are really pagans, and they worship this winged demonic deity called Baphomet. No shit!" Hudson then projected an image of an artist's interpretation of the winged demon Baphomet, a goat-headed, human-fusion horror-thing with horns, wings, hooves, and more.

It freaked out Cai's Christian sensibilities more than Sage's. Sage was a Shuar, a native American people from South America, one of the original native Americans who never willingly gave in to the European invaders. She was familiar with and comfortable with the concept of multiple gods, not just one. And there were both good and evil gods, some nice and some mean.

"Well, let's not condemn them just because they are pagans. There are bad pagans, and not bad pagans, no? Just like there are good and bad Christians." Sage wanted to defend her people. It had been some time since anyone in the Americas had engaged in old pagan activities like human sacrifice, as far as she knew.

Hudson thought. "Well, as paganism developed, they replaced human and animal sacrifice as a religious rite with more tame forms of worship, like giving food, flowers, effigies, or offerings to the gods. Not actual people."

Cai's mouth was almost hanging open. "Are you trying to say that stuff was real, people used to sacrifice other people as part of some whacked-out religion?"

Hudson was nodding his head. "Oh yes, and not just sacrifice adults, they would sacrifice children too, they were considered purer and better for the rituals. They would sacrifice someone to ensure a plentiful wheat harvest, or to honor their gods, or something like that. Like, let's burn these children in a whicker man effigy, you know, like the one they use today at Burning Man."

"Yeah, but no one has done that for like, hundreds or thousands of years?" Sage didn't think a modern human could do such things. It was barbaric.

"Maybe some crazy cultists still do this stuff? Who knows. But we are getting off track. That is history. Pagans, after Christianity conquered them, either converted or went underground, and worshipped in secret, joining secret societies, with all sorts of names, like Knights Hospitaller, the Rosicrucians, Knights Templar, Rose and Cross, and more recently, Freemasonry."

Sage dropped her glass on the ground, and it smashed, almost in slow motion, in front of the whole room. It was eerie. Cai looked at her and then back at Hudson.

"Which leads us to what we wanted to talk to you about, Hud." Cai took out her bag and handed an item wrapped in brown paper across the table.

Hudson went to open it, and out came a ratty book that looked decades old. He read the headline aloud to the team. "Born in Blood: The Lost Secrets of Freemasonry." Hudson was awestruck. What a bizarre coincidence. "Where did you guys get this?"

Cai looked at Sage. "Believe it or not, Hud, some creepy guy threw a rock at our window and gave it to us. He gave us this message, too." Cai handed it to Hudson, the message telling him he was in potential danger with the Beales, but giving no further details.

At that point, Hudson wondered whether he should fully reveal to his best friends how much he really knew about the whole affair, but he decided it was best to hold back certain information. To protect his friends at the very least. He wasn't sure they were ready for it, yet.

Chapter 17

The Serial Club spent the subsequent sessions strategizing about their next steps. It wasn't immediately clear to them the direction to take. Hudson could spend years researching information in the Beale library, and he planned to do a lot more, but it wasn't necessarily getting them closer to understanding what was going on with Wick. They needed a clearer direction to move in, so Hudson could narrow down what he was looking for. Plus, none of them had seen Wick since the garden party, so they didn't have a chance to probe him for more details.

In the middle of this intense conversation about the future of the current mission, there was a weak knock at the front door. The team had to stop talking to hear a faint scratching and knocking. It sounded so strange that all three of them went down to the front door to investigate.

When Hudson opened the front door, there was Wick, alone as usual, dressed in black, but this time he was covered in something else—blood. Mostly on his hands, but there were blood splatter and streaks on the rest of his body. Wick was in an obvious state of shock, shaking, pale, and barely cognizant.

Sage was the first to act. Instinctively, she put her arm around Wick, blood or not, and led him into the home and the bathroom so he could get cleaned up. It was Cai who interjected some more hard-headed common sense.

"Sage, wait one sec. Before you clean him up, he could have been involved in some violent crime. We would be destroying evidence."

After he came out of his own shock, Hudson was nodding in agreement. "Yeah, I want to help this kid, but I do not want to be complicit in whatever he did."

Sage understood what they were saying. She took Wick into the bathroom, and they examined him to see if he had cuts or defensive wounds. They could see none; he was totally uninjured except for having blood on him.

Sage tried to talk to him, "Wick, are you there? Can you hear me?" She snapped in front of his eyes, clapped in his ears, but he did not acknowledge her. He was mumbling a bit, but they could not make out the words.

"I'm not sure, guys, he has no injuries. I doubt he stabbed someone, or else he would have knife wounds and whatnot on him." Hudson and the team knew their forensics from watching way too many true-crime TV shows.

"Look, I don't feel comfortable turning him over to the police yet," Sage said. "They won't help him. If anything, they give him back to his parents, who are doing God knows what to him. We need to find out what is going on with this kid and then make a decision."

Hudson agreed. "Yeah, I don't like doing anything major until we know the playing field. We could be ending this kid's life, and what if he is innocent?" Just then, it struck Hudson, and he had a plan to move forward.

"Holy shit, I've got it. One of the books I found at the Beale house is about mesmerism, or, as it is more commonly known today, hypnosis. It allows you to put someone into a trance so that you can tap into repressed memories, or alter someone's memories so you can control their mind."

Sage was unsure. "Is that safe, Hudson? Like this is new for you, and this is a pretty big deal."

"Well, I don't know, but we need to get some information out of him, or we have to turn him in. He could have done something really horrible, and it wouldn't be right to keep him from justice."

Everyone agreed. If they found out he had committed a crime, they needed to turn him in. But if not, their mission was to help Wick, and that was just what they planned to do. First, they decided to clean him up, but not without saving some blood in case it needed to be tested for DNA later.

Chapter 18

Luckily, Hudson had already spent some time studying the old book on mesmerism before Wick showed up covered in blood. While at the Beale library, he would regularly scan pages from books with a portable scanner he had purchased, then use the digital copies later for reference. Hudson had written down some basic steps for the hypnosis process and other tips he could use to ensure a successful session while they prepared Wick. Hudson had also set up his phone to record all video.

One thing he read in his book was that some people were more susceptible to hypnosis than others. And it really comes down to consent. If someone resists being hypnotized, the process becomes more challenging. For the very suggestible person who wants to be controlled and directed, they are much easier to put into a trance because they are more willing. In short, they give their willful consent by more easily giving in to the process and the manipulation.

It was clear to everyone that Wick was in terrible shape. Could he even consent to the hypnosis? Hudson didn't know, so he had the girls sit Wick down in one of their chairs. Wick followed their instruction without pushback. He almost seemed like a robotic automaton, going through the motions and doing what he was told. Wick was still dazed and barely coherent.

Hudson started by trying to get Wick to relax, if that was possible. He talked to him in a calm, reassuring voice, attempting to get him to relax his muscles and posture and slow his breathing. Wick did seem to react positively to Hudson's soothing voice. He calmed down a bit, and his breathing seemed more normal and less rushed. Once he was satisfied, Hudson then moved on to the visualization phase of the hypnosis process.

"Wick, I want you to think about your bedroom. Imagine every detail in the room. What kind of things are on your walls? What do the windows look like? What does it smell like?"

Hudson could see that Wick was thinking about his bedroom and was reacting to the different images in his head as Hudson talked. After Hudson felt good about having completed this phase, he went on to the next—picking a room Wick was less familiar with.

"Now, Wick, I want you to visualize your dining room. What does that room look like? What do the windows look like? How does it smell?"

Hudson could see that Wick was struggling to recall the details of the dining room. It was no surprise to Hudson, given his doubt that the Beales spent much family time around the dinner table. Due to this searching confusion and conflict, the book told Hudson that Wick was now open to suggestion.

"Wick, can you tell me how you are feeling right now?"

For the first time that day, Wick spoke in a clear and intelligible voice. "Wick is not here. How he feels does not matter."

Sage and Cai's mouths were wide open. Hudson was floored. It looked like there was something to this hypnosis thing. He knew not to ask leading questions or to suggest to

Wick anything that would change his memories or perceptions. Hudson just wanted to know what was going on, not to use hypnosis to modify Wick's behavior.

"Who are you?"

Wick did not hesitate. He spoke clearly. "I am the Star Child."

Hudson and the team were taken aback. This sounded like when Wick was dreaming.

Hudson decided to go with it. "What is your purpose?"

"To complete the great plan."

"What is the great plan?"

The Star Child looked toward Hudson with a sideways tilt in its head. "That is not for the profane."

Hudson didn't know what this Star Child was talking about. He wanted to get more out of him, but it was like deciphering a puzzle.

"Explain your purpose."

"I am the keeper of mysteries, a servant of Thoth. An adept of the mystery schools."

Hudson paused for a second and then tried again. "Please explain your purpose, keeper of mysteries."

The Star Child reflected for a moment. "My purpose? What is the purpose of the sun that is born and dies each day? Of the wheat that is reaped in the field? The wind blows. The wind is. I am one, for all time. A servant to the great plan."

Hudson did not know what to make of this. He expected to get a response about Wick being abused or something, not to talk to some other being about deep mysteries that he had no idea what they were about. Hudson looked to each of his partners for some direction, but both were as flummoxed as he was. How do you communicate with someone and get answers when all the responses are strange riddles?

Hudson whispered to his friends, "I don't know, guys, I think we need to figure out who this Star Child is, and what some of these things he is talking about mean. I can research them, but it may take time. I don't know if we have that time. Someone may be hurt, or dead, and we shouldn't sit on that."

Hudson then told Wick he was going to clap his hands to wake him up, and he did, and Wick seemed to come out of his trance and shock somewhat. As he sat there recuperating, the conversation between the Serial Club continued.

Sage was the first one to come up with a solution. "What about getting help from the mysterious man who tried to warn us about the Beales? He said he worked with a clandestine group investigating certain nefarious people. He may know what Wick is talking about with his Star Child babble."

"Do you think we can trust him?" Cai was always careful around people they did not know well. "This guy could be a cop, or a fed, or some other shady character."

Hudson thought about it, "I think we will know more when we see his response to what we recorded of Wick. We see if this guy is straight with us, and if not, we move on. We don't tell him about the blood we found on Wick, so he has no reason to rat us out."

"That makes sense, Hud. Sage and I will leave him a note and meet up to see if he can shed light on what Wick was talking about. If we get nothing, we move on from him and do the research the hard way."

"What do we do with Wick in the meantime? I'm not turning him in until we know for sure he did something." Sage was emphatic on this point.

Hudson couldn't think of many options. "I guess drop him off at home. We tell his parents we are dropping him off after a normal session at my house, and mention nothing." He figured that was the safest path to avoid escalating things.

It was agreed that Wick would be cleaned up a little more, and Brody would be contracted for a ride out to the Beale manor to drop him off, with a few extra bucks from Hudson to make it worth his while.

Chapter 19

The next day, on the way to school, Cai and Sage walked together and dropped a note on the far side of the gazebo at the town park. It said simply, "We have information. We need direction." On the way back from school on the same day, they checked behind the gazebo, and their note was gone.

"Wow, this guy must be really on top of this; he checked it almost immediately." Cai wasn't sure if that was a good thing or not.

That night, while at Hudson's soon after dusk, they heard a crack on the window as they had before. Cai rushed downstairs while Sage waited on the porch. Cai returned in a few seconds with a note, telling them to meet the next night at nine at the same spot in the park. This time, they decided to take Hudson with them. Maybe he needed to hear some things about his new friends, the Beales, directly from this guy.

Another lame excuse, from Hudson this time, and a few extra bucks got them a ride from Brody again. Brody pulled up in the dim parking lot, put some music on, and took out his phone. Hudson set his phone to record audio. He wanted to see if this guy was legit or just yanking their chain.

The Serial Club walked the short walk to the gazebo. Hudson hated being outside at night, especially in the woods. The wind was blowing strongly, and a light mist hung in the air. The gazebo's three steps creaked as the group ascended them, the dirt-covered gazebo floor showing their footprints from the previous visit. Apparently, this gazebo was not very popular.

They reached the far side, looked down, and did not see anyone. So, they turned and waited, and within thirty seconds they heard a breathing sound. They turned, and their mystery man was there, still in the shadows, but a bit more exposed than before. He looked like a middle-aged man to them, like one of their teachers. No one knew what to say, so they waited for him to start.

"You said you had some information for me?"

This guy is not one for chit-chat, thought Hudson. So, he jumped in. "We have a friend of ours who we are worried about. I think you know the family; you warned my friends about them."

"Yes, the Beales. My group has had our eye on them for some time."

"What group do you belong to?" Cai wanted more information from this guy.

He hesitated for a moment. "For now, let's say we are a group dedicated to investigating certain nefarious organizations and individuals."

"And you know for sure the Beales are nefarious in some way?" Cai was trying to get what she could out of him.

"Not for sure, we are still investigating. Once we saw your presence at their house on several occasions, we decided to contact you, hopefully before they compromised you."

"Compromised how?" Hudson wanted to know what this man was talking about.

Another pause. "It's hard to explain. Give me the information you have, and I will try to help."

Hudson took out his phone and played the recording of Wick's hypnosis session. After it was done, there was a long pause; everyone was shaken. Hearing it again, now detached from the actual event, it was even spookier.

Finally, the stranger spoke up. "I'm sorry, I can see that must have been…concerning." Again, the stranger paused, as if searching for the right words. "Do any of you know what secret societies are?"

Hudson replied first. "A little bit, they are like men's clubs or something?"

The stranger snorted and then suppressed a sarcastic laugh. "Oh yes, they are men's clubs all right. Have you read the book I gave you?"

"Not yet, we wanted to talk to you about Wick first." Sage didn't want to get lost in the fact that they were here to help Wick, not the other way around.

"Based on some of what he said, I would say Wick is involved in something that may be over his head. But I'm not sure this is something you can change."

Sage wasn't having it. "We owe it to him to try and help. If we can't, we can't. But we will try. Can you help us?"

Another long pause. Then, in a low voice that they could barely hear. "The Brotherhood of the Golden Serpent." Then, as the man turned around to walk away, he said, "And my name is Marlow."

Chapter 20

Hudson had spent the next few days engrossed in both the book on the history of Freemasonry that Marlow had given them and in researching the Brotherhood of the Golden Serpent. The former was the easier effort; the latter required more time and thought.

As was his way, Hudson prepared an excellent presentation in two parts. The first concerns the history of the Knights Templar and the Freemasons, and the second concerns what he found about the Brotherhood. Cai and Sage usually sat back while Hudson did his research phase. Neither of them was sure he wanted them involved in it, regardless.

Snacks and drinks were prepared and laid out, and the whiteboard had the cover slide projected onto it. It said, "From Knights to Freemasons and Brotherhood". There were a bunch of creepy symbols and emblems below the title.

"What do those weird symbols mean, Hud?" Cai had never seen these before.

"Ah, good question. I will explain as we go along, but these are examples of Masonic symbology and crests. They help trace back the influences of the organization to the Middle Ages."

"They go back that far?"

"Oh yes, in fact, they may even go back further. But let's start with the first subject, which is what the book Marlow gave us is all about." Hudson went to the first slide, which showed a timeline from the Middle Ages to modern times, with a series of groups and events listed.

"As we know from school and general history, the Templars were criminalized in France in 1307, and they went underground and traveled to Britain, Portugal, and other places, and onto the high seas to engage in a life of crime and piracy beyond the law. Then, in Britain, due to pressure from the Pope, they were fully criminalized in 1312.

"In response, the Templars, already hiding underground in Britain, created another secret society to continue their pagan worship and criminal activities. An organization that was supported in secret by the British Government itself. This society is called The Order of the Garter, and it was established in 1348. According to the book, this is the first organization to carry on Templar activities under a different name. One way the author says that you can trace these organizations through time is their repeated use of universal twilight language, or symbology."

"What the heck is twilight language, Hudson?" Sage was settling in and really enjoying the presentation.

"It's a system of non-verbal cues and symbols that has been around for thousands of years. In fact, before people could read or write, they relied on symbols to convey information and provide direction. Like when you see a barber pole, you know that's a place to cut your hair. The Templars had a variety of ancient traditions, symbols, secret handshakes, and secret words that the author argues became the foundation of what became the Freemasons."

"What are you saying? That Freemasons are Templars? They are directly related?" Cai was getting into this, too; it felt like they were really onto something interesting.

"Yes, that is the central thesis of this book. And let me tell you, after reading it and some supporting literature, I am pretty convinced. The two organizations seem very closely related. More importantly, the book provides an understanding of what these organizations are. They call them religious military orders. So, they are a religious army, but it is not a Christian army. It's a pagan army that worships a demon deity called Baphomet."

"Well, that is really messed up, Hud. My Mom is a pretty devout Christian, and she would not be too crazy about anything pagan-related." Then, thinking about being a bit more tactful, she said, "Sorry, Sage, no offense."

Sage just smiled. None taken. Christians had a big bug up their butt about paganism, Sage knew. They imagined all Mother Earth-based religions were about blood sacrifice or something, but that was not how Sage saw it at all. To her, it was about nature, and how all things were interrelated, and how everything had a spirit, and all acted in concert to make up what we know as the natural world. Humans were an integral part of the natural order, not above it or in control of it.

Hudson continued, "It gets even more disturbing. In 1381, a Peasants' Revolt, also called the Great Rising, occurred in England. At the time, 100,000 English people revolted and marched on London. The mob destroyed things in a supposed uncontrolled rage, burning down houses, opening prisons and letting prisoners loose, and killing anyone who tried to impede them. But no one ever knew how it started and who organized it.

"The book argues that revolt was actually organized and executed by the Templars in response to having all their lands taken by the Pope and being given to a competing religious military organization called the Knights Hospitaller, now called the Knights of Malta. Rebel leaders confessed to being agents of what they called a 'Great Society', which was based in London, and that they deliberately targeted the Knights of Malta's properties before harming anything else."

Sage was shaking her head. "What complete scumbags! Are you telling me they didn't like a ruling from the Pope or King, so they burned down half of London? Nice people."

Hudson jumped in. "You can see, though, that they were being attacked and repressed…like tortured and executed in masse? And now that they were underground, all they had left was some property, which the state was taking away. I would be pissed to."

Now Cai was getting in the mix, "Sure, Hud, but that doesn't justify mass murder and wanton destruction. Maybe they should have gone after the King or Pope, not their rival organization and the public."

"Yeah, Hudson, that is what terrorists do." Cai paused, thinking. "So, the Tempers are essentially early terrorists?"

Hudson was considering, "Interesting perspective. They certainly over-reacted. But as Baphomet-worshipping pagan occultists, they must have been involved in some pretty disturbing stuff to have wrought the anger from the Church and State. They clearly considered them a significant threat.

"However, it seems the Church, even with the assistance of nefarious groups like the Jesuits, was unable to stop the Templars, as the group continued to grow and morph underground until it was formally unveiled as the Freemason society in 1717. After that, Freemasonry grew like crazy, probably because it was already well-developed underground. Guess what famous people are Freemasons?"

Both Sage and Cai just looked at Hudson, like, come on, tell us, we don't want to guess.

Fine, Hudson thought. No one was any fun. Oh well. "Most of the founding fathers, from George Washington to Benjamin Franklin. Then on and on. From Andrew Jackson to Theodore Roosevelt, Harry S. Truman, you name it. Of course, so was British royalty, like King George VI and Prince Philip, Duke of Edinburgh.

"But look, mostly what I wanted to communicate from this book is that the Templars were a pagan secret society that eventually became the Freemasons, who are also a pagan secret society. Funny that so many prominent people in a Christian nation like the USA and the UK are, in fact, secret pagans. Which leads us into our more focused discussion: The Brotherhood of the Golden Serpent.

"When I tried to find information about them, it was not easy. The first thing I found that sounded related was a group that dates back thousands of years, probably part of the whole Templar/Freemason timeline, but before it, called The Brotherhood of the Snake. This was an ancient secret society, a serpent cult, that predates the Templars by at least several thousand years.

"In the mythology of the ancient world, the serpent is universally the symbol of the sun. So, the serpent was considered the source of all life and was said to be the great enlightener of mankind, which is why it's their symbol. In other words, these guys go way, way back—all the way to ancient Sumer and Mesopotamia, some of the first human cultures.

"Just like the Templars, they had a secret initiation, hidden symbols, twilight, and language. They wore snake headbands, just like the pharaohs of ancient Egypt. And some of the most famous thinkers and magicians in history were supposedly part of it, including Aristotle and Socrates. Many believe this is the foundational secret society from which other groups emerged, such as the Templars and Freemasons, which continue to survive in various forms to the present day.

"I would guess that The Brotherhood of the Golden Serpent, if it exists, is an offshoot of other mystery school projects, and may even trace its history back to the first and original secret society. Or, it could be some Johnny-come-latelies who just borrowed the name to give their group some cache.

"I assume Marlow told us that name and gave us the book on Templars/Freemasons to imply his group thinks the Beales may be involved in either group. Freemasons are pretty secretive, but have been known publicly since the 18th century. But this Brotherhood he referred to is totally hidden. I could only find references to the original Brotherhood of the Snake, nothing about the more recent offshoot. I may be able to find out about them in the Beales library. Now that I have something specific to look for, I can dig in deeper."

"Are you sure it's safe to go back there, Hudson, until we know what these people are up to?" Sage was worried about her friend, and for good reason. Secret societies were known to engage in all sorts of criminal behavior, and she wanted Hudson as far away from such people as possible.

Hudson thought about it, "I think it's safe for now. I mean, no one there even talks to me, I am just let in and let out."

"Still, I think I should go with you next time." Cai wanted to keep a closer eye on Hudson, if possible. Sage agreed with her, and Hudson realized it would be too hard to fight back. So, he gave in.

Chapter 21

After their session on the Freemasons and the Brotherhood, Sage and Cai decided to leave a note for Marlow at the gazebo, to let him know what they found and see if he had any more direction. So, like they did the first time, on their way to school, they left a quick note with a few details, indicating they wanted to meet again. Then, like before, on their way home from school the same day, they swung by the park to see if the note was gone as quickly as before. But this time it wasn't. It sat there tucked into the back of the gazebo wall, untouched. The girls figured Marlow was busy and would get to it later. But when they stopped by the next day and a few days later, the note was unmoved. They weren't too concerned until about a week later, when they checked again, and the note was still there. At this point, they decided to pick it up so no one would find it and discuss it with the team.

Back at the HQ, the Serial Club was discussing next steps in light of Marlow's disappearance.

"How do we react to this?" Sage wasn't sure of the right direction. "Was this guy Marlow for real, or is he some shady character trying to mislead us?"

"And is he really in trouble, or not? Like, do we try and find out who he is and try and help him?" Cai knew that this was the whole purpose of the Serial Club: to find justice and support for those who had none.

Hudson wasn't sure about this Marlow guy. "He gave us some information, but nothing I couldn't really find online.

This Brotherhood, which I haven't found much about yet, seems to be the direction we should take the investigation, unless we find reason not to. Maybe as we probe into that, more about who this Marlow guy is will come to light."

This made sense to Cai and Sage, who had no leads or clues to point the team in a different direction.

"Fine, so we continue our research at the Beale manor," Cai said. "But this time, Hudson, I am coming with you. You need protection, or at least an extra set of eyes."

Hudson had already reluctantly agreed for Cai to accompany him, but it didn't mean it felt any less emasculating to him. He could take care of himself and was pretty sick of everyone thinking he needed their help. He was fifteen, for God's sake!

About two to three times a week, as before, Brody drove Hudson up to the Beale manor for his nighttime research session, and this time, Cai was included. Cai didn't like this place much, like Brody. Both found it elitist and creepy. Hudson felt differently. To him, it was knowledge and learning that he cared about, not who thought they were better than whom. If these rich people would let him learn and absorb their valuable material, then why should he not take advantage of it?

The night butler didn't even acknowledge that Hudson was there with a partner, but followed his instructions to lead Hudson to the library door and then pick him up several hours later. Throughout that time, Hudson was entirely on his own in the Beale library, able to read and research whatever he wanted. He was never given any rules or restrictions on what he could access. Hudson had never even considered venturing into other parts of the house.

Once he saw the first pile of old books, he was hooked and dug into them for all they were worth.

Cai wasn't as into books and learning as Hudson was. It's not that she wasn't intelligent and inquisitive; she was, she just wasn't bookish like he was. She lived in a more complex world than the sheltered Hudson and had to apply her smarts to survival and safety. With Hudson, she felt like she had someone to protect other than herself, and she liked it. She enjoyed being his substitute big sister. Of course, Hudson thought he was the more mature one. That made Cai laugh a bit.

To Cai, the library was interesting, but creepy. It was dim, with ancient-looking lights to read old manuscripts. After about thirty minutes of browsing through a few books and exploring the rather extensive library, she sat down next to Hudson. She used her phone while he delved into manuscripts, searching for references to a brotherhood or a serpent. He had notes with him on his phone, including the Latin, Italian, and French words for brotherhood and snake, and he would scan pages and relevant text for these references. If he found something, he would scan the page with his portable device, then study the pages in depth at home later. He tried to make the most of his time at the library to gather the information she needed, then do more in-depth research at home.

But this search was proving to be challenging. The books he encountered were fascinating, but none delved into the bizarre and exotic realm of secret societies. They were on more tame subjects, such as mesmerism, history, and biology. Suddenly, it occurred to Hudson that they may be looking at the wrong section of books. He naturally gravitated to what was closest, considering the vast size of the collection. So, both he and Cai spread out and began looking through the larger book collection to find areas of knowledge and mystery that were unknown to them.

The basement library, which had been in the house for about four hundred years, was larger than either of them thought. The stacks of books and tall cases curve back, constantly extending and winding endlessly into the darkness. In the walls were sepulchers, or holes containing little statues and figures which looked ancient and strange. Near them were yellowing light fixtures, now electrified, that looked grimy with centuries of age.

On and on they searched, never really finding what they sought. Then they finally came to what seemed like the end of the long hall, and on Cai's side, she saw something that Hudson did not see on his side. A small door, one that must have been half a millennium old, caked with years of grime and almost petrified from encrustation. On the front of the door, there was what looked like a hand-made sigil, or magical symbol— a five-pointed star, a pentagram. But this one was inverted, upside down. Cai texted Hudson to come to her; she didn't want to enter this dark place alone.

When Hudson saw the four-foot-high door, he let out a small gasp. He kept his voice low when he talked to Cai, "That is wild. An ancient door with an upside-down pentagram on it. We may have found our mysterious room."

Cai did not want to go in there at all. Something about the pentagram made her very uncomfortable. She could not say what, but it offended her Christian sensibilities in a way she had not encountered. It seemed unnatural to her. Unholy. She couldn't explain it to Hudson, much less herself, so she kept quiet. She was there to protect Hudson, after all.

Then Cai noticed something else, "Hud, look up there."

Above the door, inscribed into the stone by ancient hand, were the words, "Omne datum optimum."

"That's Latin." Hudson was getting to know the basics of this old language, but he couldn't read it yet. "Lemme take a picture of it, I can decipher later. It sounds familiar, though."

Hudson went to open the door before considering whether they should go in. No one told Hudson he could not explore the whole library, so why shouldn't he? That was how straightforward Hudson's thought pattern was. He just did. He pulled on the circular door handle, which Hudson now noticed was shaped as a wreath. Like a Roman laurel wreath. Interesting, he thought.

Inside was a smaller room, and it looked considerably more ancient than the main library, if that was possible. The room looked like it had been hewn from solid rock; the walls looked like they had been chipped with old stone tools. There was an old oak table in the middle of the room, and on it was a lit candle in a lamp, a human skull, a square ruler, and a compass. Around the table were stacked scrolls and books that looked like they came from the medieval period or earlier, arranged in what appeared to be handmade bookshelves and cubbyholes. Right away, it dawned on both of them that this was what they were looking for—a hidden room, hopefully with knowledge of the great hidden mysteries of the world.

Chapter 22

Hudson and Cai approached the old oaken desk with large iron clawed feet in the center of the stone cave-like room. It glowed from a single candle, shedding spectral light upon the darkest corners of the room. On the desk were a variety of items that perplexed the two young people. They had no idea why a skull or compass would be here. But more interestingly, on a platform for examining books was an ancient-looking book, easily from the Renaissance or the Middle Ages. It attracted Hudson's attention immediately. The book looked special. There was only one wooden stool to sit on, and Hudson, not thinking about his manners, jumped down immediately so he could examine the book. Cai didn't mind at all; she knew Hudson didn't think about that stuff as others did. She stood while he opened the book.

Hudson could see from the cover what it was. Right away, he was shocked. "Holy shit, Cai, do you know what this is?"

Cai hadn't a clue; she knew Hudson's question was rhetorical. Hudson didn't wait for a response.

"This is one of the more infamous books in modern history. It's called The Malleus Maleficarum in Latin. This translates to "The Hammer of Witches" in English. Written by some German nutjob priest named Henricus Institor in 1486, I shit you not. It is the best-known book in the world about witchcraft and demonology."

"Really, witchcraft. Like, how to be one?" Cai hadn't a clue about this stuff.

"Oh no, it's a book about how to persecute and convict and torture women for witchcraft. And of course, then burn them alive at the stake. Nice people back in the day, huh?"

"Were people really witches, or was this just some excuse to terrorize and subjugate women?" Cai had been around the block and knew this type of anti-women bigotry was historically prevalent.

"That's hard to tell. Most likely the latter, but I am sure there were and still are people practicing the pagan black arts who Christian inquisitors legitimately convicted. Who knows how much of it was real versus persecution, but the methodology they used is wholly unscientific and biased. For instance, women who did not cry at their trials were immediately convicted of being witches. Even the Catholic Church condemned this book as not in line with church doctrine and unethical.

"What this book did was make people who did witchcraft or sorcery, or magic as we call it, criminals who were guilty of heresy. It suggested using torture to gain confessions, something that was common at the time, and the execution of guilty witches being burnt alive at the stake. This book was used as legal justification by courts at the time to hunt down people and murder them in witch hunts during the sixteenth and seventeenth centuries."

Cai was not smiling at all. This horrific persecution of women, disguised as a Christian hunt for pagans, was sickening to her. She believed in compassion and decency, the things her mother taught her. This she did not believe in. This was not a Christian act, but one of terror and repression.

"How many Hud? How many women did these psychos torture and kill in their witch trials in the name of Christianity?"

"No one really knows. Just as in the Catholic Inquisitions of centuries earlier, the numbers are deliberately hidden. Modern experts say that some 50,000 people were executed for witchcraft, the large majority being women. But some people say the real number is much, much higher."

Cai didn't doubt it. Those in charge liked to modify the past to make their actions look better.

Hudson continued, "But this book was one of the first ever that got widespread printing after the invention of the printing press. And it's incredibly misogynistic. Hear what this guy thinks about women. This is from my notes:

'All wickedness is but little to the wickedness of a woman. What else is woman but a foe to friendship, an unescapable punishment, a necessary evil, a natural temptation, a desirable calamity, domestic danger, a delectable detriment, an evil nature, painted with fair colours? Women are by nature instruments of Satan — they are by nature carnal, a structural defect rooted in the original creation.'"

"Jesus Hud, what a nasty bigot! He sure hated women."

"Oh yeah. You did not want to be a woman or a minority or an atheist back then, that is for sure. And this wasn't that long ago; this is what historians consider the beginning of the modern era."

Hudson finally opened the book. The book was a spectacular copy, with handwritten notes and inserts by owners over the ages, to hand-drawn inscriptions and images gleaming with gold inlays. Hudson made sure to be very careful and only touch the edges of the paper. He felt the book almost vibrating with dark energy.

"Cai, do you know how valuable this must be? I can't believe someone just left it sitting here."

"And with a lit candle next to it." Cai finally caught on. "Who do you think lit that Hud?"

She made the gear click in Hudson's head. Oh, someone was here right before them. Perhaps they should hurry before whoever came back. Hudson started taking digital pictures of as many pages as he could, but he wasn't sure this was the information they were looking for. It was fascinating, sure, but it wasn't on secret societies. Or was it?

At that moment, Cai noticed something, being the observant and inquisitive person that she was. "Hey, Hud, take a look at that crest up there. Isn't that like what we saw on the front gate on the way in?"

Hudson looked up to the left, and in a dark corner, above a hand-made bookcase filled with tattered books and scrolls, was a double-headed eagle crest, precisely like the one they saw on the external gate. Hudson knew this was where the family information on the Beales would be.

Hudson reached up and took the book right under the double-eagle crest to start. It was bound in some animal skin, definitely not leather. Eww, thought Hudson, who knows what this is. Maybe sheep skin. He took it down, moved The Hammer of the Witches to the side, and looked at the cover. On it, aside from the Latin text he could not decipher immediately, it said in large words, "Fraternitatem." He typed into his Latin-to-English translator, and it said, "Brotherhood." He looked at Cai with glee in his eyes.

"This is it, Cai!" Then he remembered to keep his voice down, as someone who lit that candle might be nearby. Hudson immediately started taking digital pictures of the book; he didn't know how much time they had here, or if they were even supposed to be here. He got about halfway through when both of them heard a sound that made their blood turn ice cold. It was crying—the mournful, soulful crying of someone in deep pain and torment.

Cai looked at Hudson and mouthed the words, "What the fuck?"

Hudson, literally shaking in his place, looked down to the left, where the sounds were coming from, and there, in the dark corner that neither of them had noticed when they came in, was a trap door in the floor. On the front of the trap door was a gold flaked emblem from centuries past. Something both children knew well. The death head symbol. A skull and crossbones.

Chapter 23

The natural inclination for both Hudson and Cai, upon hearing a distressing sound in a place they were not supposed to be, was to run. They were already freaked out being in this bizarre old library cut from the natural stone, amid books on witchcraft and sorcery. Now, a man's faint howls of pain and torment came up to them through the floor, and they were frozen in time. They wanted to run, but could not. Run to where? Back into the library to pretend they didn't hear anything until it was time to go? The idea sickened both of them. Cowards, the Serial Club was not. The sobs continued for a few minutes, and both kids continued to be frozen in place.

After it became clear the sound would not stop, and the kids would either need to leave or investigate, Hudson whispered to Cai, "I'm not sure what to do here, Cai." Hudson was confused. He usually knew the right thing to do instinctively and just went and did it. But here, he was in someone else's house, a guest. Did he have a right to go sneaking around their property and poking his nose into things?

Cai listened for a moment. "It sounds real, Hud. Like this guy is in pain."

Hudson considered that. If someone were in pain, they should help, no? Perhaps someone had broken their foot and needed help. They had no way of knowing. But the fact that it was coming from a trap door with a skull and crossbones on it made it more conspicuous that something shady was afoot.

"Maybe we just pop down there for a moment, Cai, make sure they are OK, and then come right back up. Either that, or we leave and pretend none of it happened." Hudson thought about it for a second. "I'm not sure I can do that, Cai. It seems wrong."

"I hear you, Hud. Pretending something isn't happening to make yourself feel better isn't what we are about. That is delusion plain and simple."

Cai's words rang true to Hudson. "Right, we can't ignore someone's cries of pain. If we can help, we should try. If we find it's none of our business, we hightail it back up here asap. Then we pretend nothing happened." Cai smiled at that.

Hudson was about to ask who would go first when Cai took the initiative and grabbed the trap door handle. She tried to pull it up, but the trap door was too heavy for her to lift by herself. Hudson had to help, and they finally got it open. Below, they saw a spiral stone staircase leading into the waiting black. They turned on their phone lights and began to go down.

It was damp and musty going down the ancient spiral staircase, which seemed as old, if not older, than the house's foundations. The wetness and mustiness grew as they descended, becoming the stale smell of years long gone. When they got to the bottom of the stairs, there was something more substantial in the air that neither of the two young people could put their finger on. Something denser and more grotesque than simple mustiness.

As their eyes adjusted to the lower light, they could now see down a stone hallway, with a worn stone pathway that looked like it had been in use for a millennium. As they slowly walked down the hall, listening for the whimpering of a solitary individual, they could see that, as upstairs, there were sepulchers in the walls, but instead of mystical beasts residing in them, there were human skulls. As they continued, the pockets in the walls grew larger, and more bones and skulls were piled up in them, some more neatly stacked than others. You could clearly see the skulls, arranged with thigh bones in a cross, in some of them, looking like the death's-head Jolly Roger.

Eventually, the piles of bones and skulls turned into full stone coffins, then into more ornamental stone sarcophagi with elaborate designs and carvings. These more advanced burial plots bore inscriptions, unlike the anonymous graves that preceded them. Hudson stopped to read one.

He brushed some of the dust from the nameplate and read it aloud, "Thomas Bradbury (1610-1695), Great Migration Immigrant 1635. 12th Great-grandson of Robert de Ros. Damn, this is some old school shit, Cai."

"Yeah, looks like we are in the family tomb. This must go back to when they first came to the Americas from England."

More such tombs appeared on the walls, and a glance showed the dates increasing until more recent burials were found. It was then that they heard the soft sounds of crying again. They had heard nothing for some time and were thinking it was about time to turn around when those sad sounds again pierced their ears and their hearts. It was quiet, but heart-wrenching. The person making those sounds was not a tough man accustomed to such conditions. They were of a soft man pleading for his life.

The sounds were getting louder, and it was clear they were coming to the end of the tombs. Now, instead of spaces in the walls for bones and stone coffins, some doorways led into what looked like prison cells. The cells were only large enough for someone to lie down in, and were covered in grime and filth from decades, if not centuries, of misuse. In front of each one was a massive iron gate that looked like it came right out of a medieval torture dungeon. As they walked down the lonely dungeon hall, the crying got louder.

Finally, in the last cell, they found the source of the sound. Each peeked around the corner of the cell door to see who was in there before showing themselves, and both Hudson and Cai almost shouted in exclamation when they saw who it was. For in the cell, chained up, pale and shaking, covered in bruises and cuts, with black bags under his eyes, was Marlow, their connection from the gazebo.

As soon as they saw who it was, they came into full view of the cell. Marlow looked up in shock, as if what he was seeing wasn't real. He took a moment to focus, still not sure who he was seeing. Cai decided to speak up.

"Marlow, it's us, the Serial Club." She saw no recognition in his face. "Cai and Hudson. You gave us the book on Freemasonry at the gazebo."

That clicked something in his head. "The…serial…club. Yes, yes, you are investigators. Like me." He could barely speak, stumbling over his words and slurring as well.

Hudson realized he may be heavily drugged. He spoke to Cai in a low voice, "Cai, this is messed up. This guy looks like he has been tortured." Hudson was getting scared. Anyone who would do this to someone might do it to them. Violence was not something Hudson wanted to have anything to do with. "I'm not sure we should be here."

Cai nodded. "I know, Hud, but we can't leave him here." She looked at Hudson, letting him know they would not run from their responsibilities. Hudson wasn't about to argue with Cai. He looked around, and right on the wall was one of those iron keychains you see in the movies. He grabbed it, inserted a skeleton key into the lock, and clicked it open. Marlow barely seemed to realize what was happening. After Hudson had used the keys to unlock the chain around his neck, wrists, and ankles, he started to come to—now, looking at his two young friends as if he had known them all his life.

"How did you find me here?" Looking around in shock, Marlow was as confused, if not more, than the kids.

"I was doing research in the Beale library, and we heard you down here and followed it. How did you get here?" Hudson had to ask, but he didn't really want to know.

Marlow looked around, unsure if he should talk freely. "I can't tell you that now, the all-seeing eye is everywhere." He looked around with a wild, paranoid glance around the room. "I must get out of here now." He looked like a caged animal who just wanted out, in any way possible.

"You can come up with us through the library. That is how we got down here." This made sense to Hudson. Go the way you came.

Marlow shook his head, "No, no, no. They will see. I can't get you in trouble for helping me." Marlow looked down the hall both ways. "I will go out the back way, the way I came in through the catacombs. Go back up and finish your work. You were never here."

Hudson and Cai couldn't think of a better plan. It would be best if they just went back to their routine and pretended like they never came down and found Mr. Marlow. Before they could say anything or suggest an alternative path, Marlow was up and out of the cell and limping out past them to an exit only he was aware of. He shook Hudson's and Cai's hands weakly as he left, his hands chapped and covered in grime, sweat, and blood.

Chapter 24

It took Marlow some time to regain his senses. He did not go straight home, worried that someone might be waiting for him, so he reached out to his Christian faith volunteer group, the Star Crusade, for some money, clothes, and a place to crash until he could get well. As he was recovering, it dawned on him how long he had been a prisoner in the Beale catacombs. He thought he was there for a few days, but it turns out he had been gone for weeks. He could not, for the life of him, remember large chunks of the time he was imprisoned. Who knows what devious methods for torture and mind control they had been using on him? He had no idea what information he gave them, if any. His mind was nearly wiped clean about his time there.

After much heated discussion with the team's core leadership, it was decided that Marlow had to report the incident to the authorities, if for no other reason than to document it. But no one thought going to the local police department would be the right move. They lacked the skills for behavioral profiling and handling more complex cases, as evidenced by their mishandling of the Doctor Pretorius case. If it wasn't harassing some kids at a park, the local cops didn't want anything to do with it. After much debate, it was decided that Marlow needed to report the incident to the FBI. They had experts on the occult and serial killers, and could provide the support and direction they would need.

The next day, Marlow, newly cleaned up and rested, walked into the local FBI office to speak with an available agent. He deliberately didn't call ahead of time so as not to tip anyone off to the investigation, just in case. Inside, he sat in a waiting room for the next available agent. Marlow brought some pictures of himself taken by his group showing his injuries to provide some evidence of his kidnapping, as well as the doctor's report. After about a three-hour wait, he was called into Interview Room Number Six.

Waiting for him was Agent Dale Johnston, FBI Special Investigations Unit. If a case sounded weird or abnormal, Dale was the specialist they would bring in to determine if it was significant and authentic, and where to direct the investigation. Dale spent most of his day talking to whackos and nutjobs. People who were barely holding onto reality, and who thought there was an international criminal conspiracy around every bend. So, every meeting he took was with a grain of salt. He was polite and professional, but aware that what he was dealing with was probably paranoia, not a federal crime. He motioned for Marlow to sit down.

"Nice meeting you, Mr. Marlow. We appreciate you taking the time to express your concerns to the FBI Special Investigations Unit. Now, please start at the beginning. I hope you don't mind us taping this conversation?"

Marlow wanted this on record, so no, he said, it was not a problem. He then took a deep breath and began his narrative, one he had prepared well beforehand.

"My name is Jonathan Marlow, and I am a history teacher at Old Springs Academy. Or at least I was until I disappeared for the last two weeks. I am not sure if I still have my job there. I live an uneventful, staid life, like most teachers. In my spare time, I try to contribute to worthy community causes. As a practicing Christian, I joined the Star Crusade, an activist Christian group, a few years ago. A dramatic name, I know. The focus of the group is to root out evil-doers across society that the police may not be equipped to deal with. Mostly, we focus on the occult, and crimes committed against decent people by purveyors of black magic and witchcraft."

Agent Johnston almost rolled his eyes, but his years of experience ensured he had more tact than that. He couldn't count the number of times he had nearly had this exact conversation before, but "the Star Crusade" was a new one to him. He wrote down their name to check up on them and ensure they were not involved in anything that crossed the legal line.

"Please continue, Mr. Marlow."

"Some time ago, my group began investigating a very well-known family in town, the Beales."

This name made the agent's ears prick up a bit. After all, they were the wealthiest family in town. He was surprised the city wasn't named after them. Now, he was paying attention. Were these whack doodles harassing the Beales?

"We believe that the Beales are a leading family, what's called a Star family, in an insidious pagan cult, the Brotherhood of the Golden Serpent."

Oh, this was getting good now. Agent Johnston felt like he hit the jackpot. This would be fun to tell the others at lunch. "Please go on." He was writing notes down mostly in jest; everything was recorded.

"This cult goes back thousands of years, perhaps back to ancient Egypt, but at the very least, Ancient Greece. They have been in the background, mucking with society and people's minds, for longer than any of us know."

"When you say mucking with society and people's minds, what do you mean exactly?" The agent couldn't wait for the response to this one.

"We believe they use criminal methods, black magic, hypnosis, torture, and mind control to terrorize the God-fearing Christian population. One of the tactics they use, we believe, is to manufacture killers and turn them against the public."

"What do you mean, killers? And turn them against the public, how?" This was sounding a little more interesting.

"They make serial killers, and have been doing it for some time. They make them from birth, and they program and condition them and turn them into remorseless psychotic killers. That's where all these serial killers in the USA are coming from, they are being made, deliberately."

"I don't get it. Why would anyone want to make serial killers? What is the purpose?"

"To terrorize the general public. To make them mentally ill with fear, and then the same people sell us drugs, alcohol, and program us with entertainment to relieve the pressure from the mental instability they cause."

At least Agent Johnston was getting a direction here, and he knew how to position the case. "Ok, but how do they make them? Give me an example."

Marlow looked down and spoke softly. "Torture. At a very young age."

The agent stopped for a moment. Even though this sounded ridiculous, he could now refer the case to the Serial Killer Behavioral Profiling Unit, or to the Child Trafficking Unit. He doubted anything would come out of it.

"Ok, well, how do we get from you investigating this family for un-Christian activities to you being kidnapped?"

Marlow knew he would have to fudge the truth just a bit. If he told the real story, he might get arrested. "As part of our duties for the Crusaders, we do recon on certain suspects, all from public areas, to see who goes in and who goes out of key locations. All very legal, we do not do anything that is not permitted." This was a lie, but Marlow knew they bent the rules sometimes to do what was right.

"As part of my responsibilities, I was observing the entrance gate to the Beale estate from the nearby woods for several recent events, a garden party and a formal evening ball. I had a digital SLR camera with a zoom lens, which allowed me to take pictures of guests and their license plates as they came and went. During the evening ball, towards the end of the event, as I was waiting for people to leave, I was struck on the head from behind and woke up in a stone cell in the basement of the Beale estate. In that cell, which I thought I was in for days, but I was really there for weeks, I was abused, drugged, interrogated, tortured, and denied sleep and food. I am unsure exactly what happened or what they or I said; most of my memory of the event has been wiped clear. But I did bring these pictures as proof of my ordeal, and a doctor examined me, and here is his report. I luckily escaped from the Beale catacombs because of their carelessness. But I have been in hiding ever since, afraid to go home or back to work."

Agent Johnston was now finding this much more interesting. Yes, this Christian group sounded like a bunch of whackos, but they might have gotten into an altercation with Beale security, and things got out of hand.

"Mr. Marlow. Do you mind if I bring another agent into the conversation? He specializes in these areas, and I would like him to hear this story from you."

Marlow figured he was in deep now, all of his deepest secrets being recorded for all to see, so why not? The more the merrier. He sat and waited, drinking from his paper cup of water. Within about ten minutes, Agent Johnston returned with someone. A tall agent with immaculate, cut blond hair and unmistakable, rounded glasses that were very unique. The glasses were so distinctive that Marlow recognized him instantly, from the night he was abducted and from the garden party at the Beale manor, where this agent was a guest at both.

Marlow began to panic. His mind was racing. He didn't know what to do. He was cornered. This was one of their operatives—or at least an accomplice.

Agent Johnston began, "Mr. Marlow, this is Dick Peters, a special investigator who works on occult crimes and child endangerment cases. I'd love for you to retell him some key points of your story, and he may have some questions."

If Special Investigator Peters knew Marlow or suspected him of knowing he was an associate of the Beales, Marlow could not tell; he had a perfect poker face. In fact, all these FBI guys did.

"Nice meeting you, Mr. Marlow. Why don't you tell me what brought you here?" Peters was cool, calm, and in complete control.

Marlow knew he was done. If this was their occult investigator, the FBI was compromised, no question about it. They already had all this on one tape; it was time to go. He could decide what to do later with the group.

"I feel terrible about wasting your time, gentleman." Marlow hastily gathered all his photos and documents. "I am realizing now that I had a critical business appointment that I must go to. I will call and reschedule with you, ok?"

Both agents were flabbergasted. But honestly, happy to get rid of this nutjob, at least Johnston was. All he would be bringing them is more paperwork and nonsense. Before either of them could respond, Marlow was up out of the chair and out the door, walking to the exit. Neither agent tried to stop him; he was there voluntarily. The agents looked at each other and shrugged.

Chapter 25

Wick was as comfortable as he ever was in Uncle Ricimer's study. He found the place both comforting and oddly disturbing, sometimes both at once. He wasn't sure why. There was so much in his uncle's office that intrigued him. Ricimer had an incredible collection of rare mechanical devices and ancient medical gear, much of it, he called, quackery. He proudly stated he owned a part of the famed Antikythera mechanism, an ancient Greek analog computer that could predict the movement of the heavens decades in advance. It was a way to track the Zodiac, he had told Wick once, the ancient magical belief system of the stars, the sun, and the moon, and time immemorial. His small fragment of a single gear with a partial symbol for Saturn etched on it was encased in plexiglass and stood proudly on his desk.

Also, Wick just liked talking to his uncle. He was so intelligent, so educated in the vast mysteries of the universe, you could sit and talk to him all day and never run out of insights or clever stories and parables. He had something to say about anything, and his conviction was second-to-none. Ricimer knew something about everything. At least a few times a week, Wick came down for his chats with Ricimer, and when he left, he felt more refreshed and focused than before. His uncle helped to provide Wick with direction and substance. He felt like he was learning so much here from this wise and learned scholar.

While Ricimer felt a certain affection for Wick, his focus was more on the task at hand. He had a job to do, and he did it without question or guilt. What could be more critical to the future of their family and clan than the development of their youth? Wick's training and programming had been going well. These were tactics and methods developed by members of his society over hundreds, if not thousands, of years. Helping to trigger in a young individual what may be the key to opening their more sensitive areas of sensory experience was a specialty of his. A combination of coercive physical methods, as well as ongoing hypnosis bolstered by administration of a custom drug regimen, had been successful in promoting a particular desirable trait in their youth, as well as their ongoing compliance to repeated suggestion.

This made sense to Ricimer. How else could they ensure young people would keep their eye on the Brotherhood's goal of completing the Great Plan, one that has been in place and their core objective since, well, since before time began. Imagine putting thousands of young people who had the keys to the kingdom out there without the proper conditioning, they would run amok and destroy what their families had built up over generations. No, it was best to remove as much chance and randomness as possible from the equation and ensure young people took up the mantle of protecting their family bloodlines.

These sessions with Wick began with some light conversation to put him at ease. Then he would slip Wick into a light hypnotic state, sometimes a deeper one depending on what he needed to accomplish. Today, he wanted an update on his relationship with the Serial Club, specifically with that bright, young Hudson boy whom Ricimer and Lord Faustus Beale found so intriguing. In light of the whole Marlow affair, he needed to get up to speed so they could plan their next steps. Ricimer wasn't concerned at all. He was just being thorough and doing his job. The role he was bred for and trained to do, since birth, like all the rest of his family and brothers. Just like Wick. They were all pawns in some fantastic game beyond anyone's control, weren't they, Ricimer joked to himself as he was preparing Wick for the session.

"Can you hear me, Wick? How do you feel?" Ricimer spoke in a soft and comforting tone.

Wick did not respond. "I can hear you. I am the star child. I feel fine." Wick, the star child, sounded almost mechanical. Perfect thought, Ricimer, that's precisely how he should be acting.

"Excellent Star Child. Servant of Thoth, Keeper of Mysteries, relate to me your last interaction with the child called Hudson." Ricimer didn't waste time; he went right to the issue at hand—no need to confuse the hypnotized subject.

"Wick, the vessel, was put under hypnosis by Hudson. During the session, I, the Star Child, was revealed."

Ricimer was floored. This little kid actually put his subject under hypnosis? What a scamp! Ricimer loved it, such initiative and intelligence in that one. He would make a useful servant to the Order.

"What did you tell him, Star Child?"

"That I was a servant of Thoth, the Keeper of Mysteries, a follower of the Great Plan. Nothing more."

Ricimer was satisfied. That would mean nothing to anyone who mattered. In fact, he wanted people to go out and expose their top-level secrets, which would make them look like conspiracy theorists and fools. Without context and reference points, it was all just a big house of cards. A Russian nesting doll set, always one more hidden contained in another, forever obscuring sight into the deep areas of the unknown.

"Excellent, you are a worthy servant for he who brings both light and night, our father Osiris. Star Child, you are to go back to Hudson's home. There, you will plant this listening device in his bedroom. Ensure it is well-hidden and cannot be found. You will then convince Hudson to come and visit me, and the three of us can talk. Wouldn't that be nice?" The Star Child didn't react; the word 'nice' had no meaning to them.

Ricimer then clapped his hands and brought Wick out of his trance. Wick felt wonderful, as he usually did after his talks with his uncle. When he left Ricimer's study, it felt as if he could take on anything in the world, and that everything was possible. He walked out, excited for his day and to reconnect with his new friends. Funny, at first, he didn't care for Hudson too much, but now, he was growing on Wick. He wondered if Hudson would like to meet his Uncle Ricimer? Two such intelligent people must have a lot to talk about. In fact, Wick felt an overwhelming urge to go and talk to Hudson about it right now and set up the meeting.

It wasn't that difficult for Wick to convince Hudson to go with him to the Beale manor to meet with Ricimer. He began telling Hudson about all the cool antique medical and mechanical items in his study. Once he mentioned he had a real piece of the Antikythera mechanism, Hudson was sold. He loved history, but also had a fascination with technology, and he had read a lot about the famous Greek analog computer.

Once at the Beale manor, Wick led Hudson to Ricimer's study, which to Hudson was even more impressive than it was to Wick. The walls were stacked to the ceiling with books of every type and every age, with strange medical devices and mechanical oddities scattered throughout. There were automatons too, old-school robots that Hudson was immediately transfixed by. The complexity and skill that must have gone into them were mind-boggling. Ricimer could see that Hudson's eyes were lighting up as he took in all of his proudest acquisitions, and nothing pleased him more. Oh, he liked this young man all right; he was a smart one. Very useful to the Brotherhood.

"Thank you so much for coming, Hudson. Wick has nothing but the nicest of things to say about you." Ricimer lied. Wick didn't even mention Hudson.

Hudson was surprised to hear that. He and Wick hadn't really gotten on that well. Maybe he was wrong about him. He had misjudged Sage, too, when he first met her.

"I appreciate you inviting me, Mr. Ricimer. Your study is fascinating. I've never seen most of these things before." Hudson motioned around the room. "And I heard from Wick that you had a piece of the Antikythera mechanism. Honestly, I really wanted to see that. I read all about it in my research."

Oh, Ricimer likes this one, alright, what fifteen-year-old is doing research for heaven's sake! What a character. "Well, please take a look." Ricimer passed the device fragment in Plexiglass to Hudson, who looked at it transfixed, in a sort of trance. Once Ricimer saw Hudson was open to suggestion due to his fixation, he began.

"I have to say, Hudson, I am really impressed by your overall intelligence. You have to be one of the smartest young boys I have ever met." With years of training and decades of research, Ricimer knew that the secret to beginning mind control on a subject was straightforward. It started with flattery and with building the subject's confidence.

Hudson was floored that this wealthy, intelligent, and experienced adult would not only recognize Hudson's intelligence but also admire him for it. Hudson was used to getting mocked and dismissed for being smart. This was a first for him.

"Why, thank you, sir." Hudson was almost stuttering a bit, embarrassed by the overt compliment. The emotional honesty and directness of it were not something he dealt with. His intelligence was a subject to be avoided at all times with his family; here, it was being lauded.

Ricimer knew he had him. How easy it was. Obviously, the younger they were, the more effective the programming and conditioning could be. Also, the more severe the programming was, the deeper it needed to be embedded into the child's brain. With Hudson, at his advanced age, Ricimer would have to see how he could mold the child. It all depended on his willingness.

"Hudson, few people in the world can really understand the deepest secrets of the universe, the great mysteries that surround mankind. Intelligence is not just about raw brain power, but the willingness to explore. You have to be open to all kinds of information and directions that you never knew even existed. Do you think you have that kind of adventurous spirit, Hudson?"

It was like music to Hudson's ears. For the first time in his life, he felt like someone really understood him. All Hudson wanted to do was learn and find things out, and the more things the better. "Of course, sir, I am open to all forms of knowledge and enlightenment. I want nothing more than to know. The more I know, the better decisions I can make with that information."

Oh, this kid was perfect. If only he had a difficult or damaged upbringing, that would be even better. Much easier to exploit their emotional weaknesses. "Are both your parents still alive and well?" Ricimer knew how to get right down to the nitty-gritty and shock the subject.

Hudson bowed his head down, obviously psychologically injured by the quick about-face Ricimer pulled on him. From compassion to pain, in quick succession, another tool of the mind controller. "My mother is dead, sir. I live with my father."

Oh, good, the mother, that was definitely something Ricimer could work with.

Now the compassion again. The programmer provides the pain and discomfort, and then the relief, making the subject more reliant on them for soothing. "I am so sorry to hear that, Hudson. I am sure she was a wonderful woman who loved you very much." That love, or lack thereof, between mother and son was something Ricimer could exploit psychologically.

And now, the final carrot: the offer of wealth or knowledge, while the subject is disoriented, under a trance, and open to programming. "Hudson, I feel that you are a very special person. You have a level of intelligence and insight that I have rarely seen in an adult, much less a fifteen-year-old boy. What if I told you that I was part of an organization dedicated to preserving exotic knowledge, which some might call esoteric or hidden information? As you have seen, we have an exquisite library that I know you are very familiar with." Could Hudson see a slight smirk in Ricimer's mouth? He wasn't sure. "We are looking for someone to help us with a variety of tasks, from finding lost books, to interpreting and decoding certain passages, to the preservation of material. Does that sound like something you would be interested in?"

Again, Hudson was on cloud nine. It was everything he had ever dreamed of: learning, being respected, and being around others like him. It was all too much to take in. He tried to stay calm and not seem a rube. "Why, yes, sir, I would be very interested. I would be something I would have to discuss with my dad, of course."

Ricimer wasn't worried; the father worked for the family doing lawn maintenance. He could be controlled easily. "Not a problem at all, Hudson. This is a young person's organization within our larger group. We call them the Children of the Sun. In fact, Wick is a member."

Hudson couldn't believe it. Was Ricimer asking him to join the junior version of the Brotherhood? He wasn't sure, but he knew this would be a fantastic way to do research and gather information for their cases. And what better way to find out what is going on with Wick? Hudson then looked to the right and saw Wick sitting there, looking very serene, with a blank stare, gazing off into space.

Chapter 26

"HUDSON! ARE YOU KIDDING ME!" Cai was up out of her seat, and it was frankly making Hudson uncomfortable. "Are you trying to tell me, tell us, you want to not only go back to that freaky Beale house, but join some weird Nazi club for kids? You have to be FUCKING KIDDING ME!"

Cai was pissed, that was for sure. Hudson wasn't sure why she was overreacting so much. But he tried to be patient. "Cai, I am not talking about really joining them. I want to get in for long enough to get the information we need, then bail out. Before anything goes too far."

Sage wasn't having it either. "And how do you know when that will be. What kind of initiation process will you have to go through? Do you have to sign anything? I have to agree with Cai, I'd be careful here, Hudson."

Ugh, now Sage too? Hudson loved his friends, but he thought they were both being a bit of a worrywart. Hudson could handle the Beales. Like any old family, they have some shady history and characters that many families would want to hide.

"All he said so far was that it was a youth group, I think called the Children of the Sun, that was connected to their family group, which, yes, I assume is the Brotherhood. Now, he told me they want me to look at documents and decipher things, and that is all I am doing now. So far, so good. Honestly, you two, he seemed really nice. Smart. Supportive. It seems relatively safe to me, at least to see what it is all about. Then, if it looks dicey, I bail, before I take any blood oaths or anything!" Hudson was trying to make a funny face, but the girls weren't buying it. They both stared at him, not getting his point. He tried again.

"Maybe I can get access to deeper material than what we saw, which was already, frankly, incredible. Right, Cai?"

Cai looked down. "Sure, Hudson, right before we found the guy who was tortured, and we let him go. What if they finger us for that?"

"If that was the case, Ricimer would have said something, or implied something about it. I sensed nothing about that at all. It was wholly about trying to get me in this group."

Neither Sage nor Cai liked the sound of that. Why did they want Hudson so bad? This was not a rich kid. What did he have that they wanted?

"What about our case. Aren't we supposedly trying to help Wick and find out what is going on with him?' Sage wouldn't let that go.

Hudson felt some shame. He had made this about acquiring more knowledge for himself, rather than helping someone in need. That was selfish of him. "This would also be a potential way for me to get closer to Wick and find out what is going on. How else am I going to get that close to him? I never see him at the library, and I can't just roam around the house at will."

The fact that Hudson and Cai had released a captive from the Beale's tomb was enough to stop both girls from agreeing to any situation in which Hudson went back to that house again, without a police SWAT team for backup. Who knows what people like this would do?

"Look, Hud, just wait for a little bit. We should talk to Marlow about this. This is too big, man. You can't go in there alone. Please."

What was Hudson going to say? It looked like Cai was about to cry. He looked over to Sage, and she seemed equally distressed. "Ok, fine. No worries. Ricimer didn't give me a deadline to reply or anything; it was very cordial. You are right, considering what we found in the basement. We need to check in with Marlow on this."

And so, the next day, on the way to school, they left a note for Marlow, this time at a new location, on a walking path in the woods. Within a day, he responded, and they set up a meeting at a Crusader safe house, one of several strewn across the state. They went on foot to ensure no one followed, including Brody.

Once inside, they were sitting around a kitchen table when ex-professor Marlow came in and sat down with them.

"I would ask if you want coffee, but I think you may be a little young. How about some water? Juice?"

A no, thank you from everyone. This cloak-and-dagger stuff made them nervous. They wanted to get out of there asap.

"No problem. Now tell me. What happened when you went to see Ricimer, Hudson?"

Hudson was shocked. "You know? How?"

"Our organization, the Star Crusade, has the Beale home under surveillance. We are an anti-occult Christian group that fights against those who perpetrate crimes against nature through pagan rituals."

The kids were all shocked. What the heck was this guy talking about? Marlow could see their confusion, so he backtracked a bit. But he didn't have forever to grow these kids up; they were going to have to do that themselves quickly.

"I was investigating the Beales for potential crimes when I was abducted by them and held and tortured in their dungeon. Thank you, by the way, both of you. I may not be here if not for you." This Marlow guy looked sincere and genuinely thankful. Hudson made note of it. He seemed trustworthy.

"And I am sure Hudson has done his research on them, much like I have. Hudson, did you come up with the Robert de Ros genealogy connection?"

Hudson was taken aback. This guy knew what he was talking about. Well, it was public genealogy knowledge. You just had to look.

"Oh yes. We established the connection between the Beale family and the de Ros Templar line. This was further confirmed with visual evidence of an early descendant in their catacombs."

Marlow liked this kid. He was quick. Smart to not believe everything he reads.

"Good. Well, this isn't just about the Beales, although they are the focus right now, especially after our encounter." Marlow rubbed his bruised side. "This family, from a Templar line, is powerful. Really powerful. For instance, I went to the FBI to report my kidnapping and assault, and a special agent came in who was focused on the occult, and I IDed him as a Beale associate from several gatherings. That is how powerful they are, their agents are in the government itself!" Marlow looked dead serious, so the kids took him at his word. If Marlow was trying to mislead them, none of them thought so.

"This de Ros bloodline, it practically dominates our modern world in the United States. As you probably found in your research, Hudson, the de Ros family gains access to royal bloodlines by marrying three of their great-granddaughters to Henry the Eighth. Once his great-granddaughter, Elizabeth I, takes over the British Empire, they are in charge of what would become the world's largest empire. Then, they came to the US, as evidenced by the early descendant you found in the tomb, and they are the ones who really founded our country. In fact, George Washington is their direct descendant, the 15th great-grandson of Robert de Ros."

All the kids were floored. They had never heard anywhere that George Washington was directly related to Queen Elizabeth and to Templar bloodlines. But they all went to public school, and no such factual information was ever presented to the majority of American children.

"It gets weirder. They are still in charge today. Across all of politics, business, entertainment, anywhere that control against the mob needs to be deployed. For instance, they may be a little old for you three, but both George W. Bush and Barack Obama, the Republican and Democratic Presidents, are direct descendants of Robert de Ros. They are direct blood kin. The 23rd and 25th great-grandsons of de Ros himself. Don't you think it's interesting that it is not mentioned anywhere in the US media?"

The kids were getting the feeling that what they were reading in the news and in history was not the whole story, but rather a carefully tailored narrative created by those in charge. And it seems the same people, or group of people, or more accurately family of people, have been in charge and mucking with the system and people's minds for a long, long time.

"I could go on and on. Bill Gates is his 24th great-grandson. Allen Dulles, who founded the CIA, was his 22nd great-grandson. But, aside from all the famous politicians, industrialists, actors, and revolutionaries that make up the de Ros family members, some of the most interesting should be of particular interest to your group, as they are serial killers."

That really caught everyone's attention. That was the Serial Club's specialty: hunting and profiling serial killers.

"The famous Lizzy Borden was Robert de Ros' 22nd great-granddaughter. She supposedly hacked up her mom and dad with an ax back in 1892. She was never convicted. The jury couldn't believe that she would do it—such a lovely young girl.

"But the one I think you should really look into is Dr. H.H. Holmes, the Devil in the White City, the 20th great-grandson of Robert de Ros. His activities have an occult air to them, and I would not be surprised to find him at the center of this portion of the conspiracy."

Hudson knew that name very well. He had profiled him in his serial killer exposé and had never once, in all his research, found any connection to de Ros or the Masons. This was one of the most famous serial killers of all time, and along with Jack the Ripper, really kicked off the serial killer terminology and craze that continues to this day.

"Is it possible that this is coincidental, that so many famous people come from this one bloodline? Or are they stacking the deck?" Sage was thinking aloud.

Smart kid, thought Marlow. "It's not coincidental. This family and their Brotherhood are up to something. They have been inserting mind-controlled family members into various key roles and positions for centuries. Their operations go far and wide, well beyond anything we, as a group, could handle.

"What my group is interested in is the occult aspect, and crimes being committed while they engage in their pagan activities. I assume your group is interested in the serial killer angle. We think there is something there, which is why we are talking."

Hudson was the first to ask, "What kind of serial killer angle?"

"It's hard to say. You may know more about it than we do. We think they engage in brainwashing and mind control of their own kids and others, like Wick, for instance. And seeing as they have a history of famous serial killers in their family, including the most famous of all, The Doctor of Death, along with the UK's Jack the Ripper. It seems relevant. For instance, is there an occult ritual/serial killer connection or angle to their operations? That would be my advice for where to direct your research next.

"Look, I am trying to impress on you the kind of people you are dealing with. At your age, and considering their strange attention on you and your group, my strong advice is to stay far away from the Beales." He looked and wasn't sure he was making enough of an impression on Hudson. "No, I need to implore you, Hudson. I see you are a talented and competent young man, but these people are over your head. Trust me. Look what they did to me."

Hudson thought to himself, in their defense, you were spying on them. They are inviting me, which might be a little different. Besides, Hudson was brilliant. More intelligent than most people, adults included. He thought he could handle it.

"Well, I do research on serial killers for a living, even though we may be young. Are you asking us to drop this case?" Hudson didn't like the sound of this at all.

"No, no, not at all. Please do your research, but do it remotely. You are not safe in that house, with those people, even with protection around." Marlow looked to Cai and grimaced, then back to Hudson. "They are pure evil, Hudson. They will act as if they genuinely like and respect you. But they respect nothing but themselves, their own kind, and their superiority over other people. They don't see you as an equal. They see you as below them. Something to be used, and then disposed of." Marlow didn't want to be too harsh with this kid, but he needed to get the message across. This was not playtime. This was a real-life-or-death type of game.

Hudson was listening, but not really taking it in the way he should have. He liked this Marlow; he seemed compassionate and decent. A little too religious for Hudson, but he wouldn't hold that against him. But again, like so many adults, this Marlow totally underestimated Hudson. The only adult who didn't underestimate Hudson was Ricimer. Hudson remembered that as well. Besides, Ricimer had things to offer: knowledge, secrets, and answers to the mysteries of the universe. These were things that Hudson wanted very, very much.

Chapter 27

The next few weeks at the Serial Club HQ, aka Hudson's bedroom, went on as usual for the majority of the Serial Club. As far as Cai and Sage were concerned, they had successfully stifled Hudson's desire to join the Beale's Children of the Sun youth organization and were hoping Marlow's speech made as much of an impact on him as it did on them. They got into this, reporting on crimes against young people, as a way to do what was right and to investigate cases the authorities weren't interested in. Neither of them ever had any intention of putting themselves in danger for a side hobby.

But Hudson took the podcast and his research much more seriously than his two friends. And based on his limited real-world experience, he wasn't aware of the actual danger that the world might contain. Cai had been around the block. At her young age, she had been exposed to things that children should not see. But it hardened her. Made her more street-wise. When silver-tongued con artists like the Beales came around, she knew exactly how to catch them in their deceptions. But for Hudson, being sheltered, bookish, wanting nothing more than to learn, their syrupy compliments and vague promises more easily took him in. These con artists know how to dazzle the mind with supposed secrets and delights, opening a vulnerable young person's mind up to suggestibility and manipulation.

While Cai and Sage continued their podcast research and production, Hudson, for the first time, was operating on the side in a secret capacity. His father, once pressed by his boss to allow Hudson to attend day sessions of the youth training programs, readily agreed and seemed positively exuberant to see Hudson potentially secure himself a better place in the world than his father could ever offer. Brody, who was contracted to bring Hudson to the library at night, now brought him during the day three times per week. As far as the Serial Club knew, Hudson stopped going to the Beales altogether. Hudson's father and brother knew enough not to badmouth the people who put bread on their table.

On the first day of the Children of the Sun kickoff, Hudson was surprised to find that he and Wick were alone in Ricimer's study again. Ricimer started by showing Wick and Hudson some of his new mechanical acquisitions, speaking to them in a soothing, comforting tone. After that, it was like starting school all over again. Ricimer began with a history lesson, or, as he called it, a hidden history lesson. And if Hudson had attended the same prestigious school as Wick, he would have likely heard many of the same things Marlow had told his classes on numerous occasions. For Hudson, hearing someone with intelligence talk with passion about a fascinating subject was enthralling. Public school felt so intellectually below him. This was something he could latch onto. He felt as if he were hearing a lot of information for the first time, and the massive data dump of new ideas was intoxicating. And Uncle Ricimer talked about everything, from science to religion to history and art, all at once. He made connections and drew parallels that wouldn't be apparent on the surface. He called it pattern recognition, and he thought students like Hudson had it in spades. It was one of the things Ricimer found so intriguing in Hudson: his ability to see deep patterns underneath the distorted, opaque surface.

"If you listen to modern historians, laughably, they would tell you that human history and civilization only go back five thousand years, but nothing could be further from the truth." Ricimer was on a roll today. Talking about these subjects was almost as exciting for him as hearing them was for Hudson. If one were immensely perceptive, one could almost hear in Ricimer a very slight stutter that had all but been eliminated by speech therapy over the years.

"Our civilization goes back at least ten thousand years, at least to the early days of ancient Sumer. Yes, there were perhaps many more before that, like the island continent of Atlantis, forever wiped from existence due to cyclical planetary-wide catastrophe. In ancient Babylon, the greater Zodiac was developed. There, in the mystery schools, the ancient mystery religion was formed and spread throughout the world. All the way to the New World, this ancient religion spread and guided mankind through tumultuous eras, aiding in man's spiritual and cultural development.

"Respectable scholars would tell you civilization sprouted up, magically, in five separate places, with five distinct cultures. Well, this is nonsense. One master civilization started it all, based on the ancient mystery religion, the first form of structured paganism for the learned elite. All cultures, civilizations, and peoples in the world originate from the glorious kingdom of Nimrod, the architect of the Tower of Babel, located in Babylon. It is this kingdom that has given rise to what we know today as civilization. Without it, we would be like animals in the woods, engaged in barbaric practices and sleeping and living in our own filth."

Hudson was writing notes as if there was no tomorrow. There was so much information, without any context, that

he would have to look things up later on his own. He didn't
know the Bible very well; his family was not a religious one,
but he would become familiar with it to ensure he knew the
terminology. He wanted to ask Ricimer questions, but for
some reason, he didn't. He was at peace, taking in
information openly without wanting to question it or dig
deeper. Interesting, he thought, that wasn't like him.

Ricimer knew that the combination of soothing speech that
escalated into moments of hysteria, complex, unknowable
terminology, and pointing to unknown and unseen mysteries
would help reduce the children to a moldable trance,
making them more susceptible to suggestion. After all, this
process was time-tested and reflected the regulations and
rules that formed their Brotherhood. In fact, this process
was the working plan for how to spread their faith, the true
faith.

Ricimer also knew that the first rule of being a missionary
for the faith was to be an expert in human psychology. This
allowed him to select suitable people for admission into the
organization. Those who would prosper under their
tutelage, and not crumble as unworthy. Ricimer was
reminded of his own training from his senior missionary and
the critical aphorism that was driven into his head: 'Cast no
seeds upon rocks.' Hudson was a good seed. Just a little old.

As far as Ricimer was concerned, that was all he did here
anyway, suggest things to people and lead them toward the
light. To Ricimer, they took the action on their own. They
gave their consent as he was nudging them, victims of their
own true human nature. Oh sure, Ricimer made sure their
drinks were laced with their latest psychoactive drug
cocktail, so subtle and targeted that the patient never knew
they had been dosed. It opened their mind just enough and

lowered their defense just enough to make the process almost seamless.

But this Hudson child was lucky to be the age he was. If Ricimer had gotten a hold of him when he was two to three years old, then he could have really programmed him for something special. But alas, this was a young teen, and Ricimer's process could ensure at least a dedicated follower. It was only a matter of time and effort. Sometimes, a little patience. Not with Hudson, though; this was a rare kid that Ricimer actually liked a little. He felt good about bringing him into the light.

"The first worldwide religion was before written language, before people could read or write. So, it was communicated by symbols and numbers, and each symbol had an exoteric meaning, meaning a public one, and an esoteric meaning, which was hidden or secret. These symbols from the ancient world are still around today. If any of you have seen the movie The Da Vinci Code, while it is a fictional hoodwink, it does explain symbology and the sleight of hand of the mystery priests fairly well. I would recommend it to you. At your age, I am sure it will seem slow and/or pretentious, especially given Tom Hanks' dreadful acting, but try to be patient with it.

"For your assignment this week, I am going to present you with a book of symbols and codes and expect you to learn it. You can bring this home. Hudson, these books are not just valuable; they are important pieces of our family history and sacred artifacts in their own right. I expect you to keep its existence private and to yourself."

This was always a good way to gauge how well the programming was sticking, by giving the subject an assignment to deceive their friends and see if they wouldn't spill the beans. Having Hudson's bedroom bugged for both video and audio made it easy to track his progress. This subject had achieved such high response rates and tested so well that Ricimer thought he could fast-track Hudson's training to 3 months, not 6. The faster he could get him in and through the initiation process, the better. No turning back for the youngster after that, Ricimer thought sarcastically.

Hudson looked at the book presented to his care with astonishing delight. It looked like it was from the Renaissance. Gold gilded. Hudson couldn't believe something of this age and value was being entrusted to him. He knew he must care for it well, and as instructed, secretly. This did not feel good to him, hiding things from his best friends, but lately, they didn't understand him as well. They felt more distant, interested in pedestrian criminal cases, while Hudson wanted to pursue the big picture. He liked doing the serial killer profiles and the behavioral profiling the most, and getting inside their heads and trying to figure out how to decipher why they became that way. It was a human mind puzzle. What complex set of elements and circumstances leads someone to have such intense rage and fury? Hudson looked over to Wick, not forgetting that once he came to their house with blood all over him. Wick was looking forward, transfixed on everything Ricimer was saying, with a glazed look in his eyes. Huh, could he be a killer, Hudson wondered? A serial killer? Hudson was having trouble seeing it.

In the end, this is the project Hudson had been developing in his mind for some time. His grand vision—to find out where serial killers come from. To discover how they are being made and who is doing it. How did serial killers come about in the late 19th century and thrive until the present day? Were they born that way? Or were they being created another way? Either through indirect environmental factors that contribute to a dysfunctional society, or through deliberate programming by nefarious actors. After all, Hudson reflected, if serial killers were born with a genetic anomaly, then they should have been around way before the 19th century, again.

What Hudson was becoming surer of was that the acts of serial killers had a specific, ritualistic overtone that was different than mass murderers of old. There was something repetitive and coordinated about their activities, and Hudson felt he was now on the right track to understanding what it was all about.

Chapter 28

Once home, Hudson spent considerable time trying to figure out where to hide the book so it would be safe and where no one could find it, including his family. He did not plan on squandering the trust that had been put in him for shepherding this rare book. He wrapped it first in a brown paper bag, then in plastic ones. Then, to ensure no water got in, he wrapped it in plastic wrap. It took some time, but he eventually discovered a tucked-away air vent in his closet. After removing the casing with a small screwdriver, he was able to slip the book into the air vent and rest it there. Once the metal cover was back in place, the book was totally hidden.

Soon after, both Cai and Sage arrived, and the three of them went to work producing this week's episode. Within a few minutes, all of them were shocked to hear the downstairs door open, and Wick come up to the bedroom. He was dressed in his usual black outfit, but he seemed a bit more chipper this day, as if he genuinely wanted to be there working with them. He brought his laptop pre-loaded with all his video production software and seemed primed to work.

It was one of the best work sessions they had ever had, and in the end, they put together a great episode on a local child disappearance case, their bread and butter. Hudson, by far, enjoyed working on the serial killer material more now, but these local-interest cases were what drove much of the viewership and interactions. So, they dedicated about 75% of their podcast to true crime cases people could engage with, and the remaining 25% to serial killer exposés and profiling studies.

Wick's production work was, as his previous efforts, exceptional. All of them recognized he had real talent in this area and would probably end up in TV or film production in some capacity. It was natural for him to take all the disparate elements and weave them together into a tantalizing narrative, sure to keep you guessing and engaged until the very end.

With Hudson's insights, Wick's production, Sage's human interest stories, and Cai's no-nonsense asides, they had something special now with their independently-produced podcast. All of them were happy they had never sold out to corporations when they first came calling, trying to buy off the Serial Club. But Hudson and team saw the corporate snakes for what they were: users. They had something significant here, and they were not going to let just anyone come in and mess with it. After they were done, they relaxed for a few minutes before their parents and drivers came to pick them up. The club then discussed what their next episode would be about.

"I really want to do another historical serial killer exposé. This one on H.H. Holmes, the Doctor of Death." Hudson glanced over at Wick to see if he would react, knowing the famous doctor was from his family's bloodline, but if he did, they didn't notice it. Wick seemed placid and nonplussed. "If possible, I want to look into how and why H.H. Holmes became a serial killer, as well as any possible occult connection. Like was discovered in the 1970s in the Ripper case."

None of the team wanted to spill anything to Wick about Marlow or what they found out about Wick's family history, so they kept that detail out of view, for now. Hudson knew he would make the episode factual, and he would point out the de Ros connection plainly when the time came.

"Cool, Hud, but I do worry about you getting in too deep with that stuff." Cai was looking at Hudson with empathy. "Just don't spend too much time messing around in serial killers' heads, you don't want to start thinking like them. We like you how you are."

"Right, if in fact being a serial killer is learned, and not genetic and inborn, that would be possible. One could catch being a serial killer from others engaged in it as a normal activity." Sage was now always an active member of their talks, not letting Hudson and Cai dominate as much as in the old days.

Hudson considered what they were saying, "I can't help but feel it makes sense for it to be a blend of heredity and environment. A balance of the two, forever mixing and shifting to form something uniquely destructive and unnatural."

Cai and Sage had noticed that Hudson and Wick were interacting more during this session, and it was clear that their initial mismatch was turning into something more collaborative and productive. It sure seemed to happen fast for both of them. Not that they didn't want Hudson to have some male friends, they did. However, the sudden shift in Wick's attitude, combined with his improved relationship with Hudson, caught the attention of our two female investigators, who noted the anomaly.

Neither of them voiced any concern to the other, but both were aware of a rapidly changing situation that neither could quite put their finger on. Not that they wanted to, this was one of the best production sessions for the podcast they had had, and everyone wanted to keep that going. It hadn't dawned on either of them that Hudson would lie to them and was developing his relationship with Wick while under the watchful tutelage of Ricimer Beale. And it was his and Wick's common situation, being under hypnosis and burgeoning mind control from Ricimer, that was leading towards their common shared viewpoint.

Chapter 29

The sessions with Ricimer and Wick proceeded like clockwork as the weeks went by, with them now having at least a half dozen educational-hypnosis rounds under their belts. This was all a matter of course for Wick; he had already been through this training. He was there mainly to help Hudson feel comfortable and to keep Hudson's eye off what was really happening here, that he was being brainwashed.

A lot of what Hudson had learned over the past few weeks was an alternate retelling of world and cultural history as seen through the eyes of the ancient order of The Brotherhood. Most of what he heard made a lot of sense, and he wasn't sure why it would be considered so heretical or secret to know. Well, maybe in the Middle Ages it would have been dangerous information, with the threat of torture and death by Catholic inquisitors.

He saw the evidence from Ricimer that human religion and culture came from a single source, and Hudson agreed that it was a most likely scenario. He couldn't say for sure that ancient Sumerian and Babylonian cultures were the source of the mystery religions, as Ricimer did. Still, they were the oldest known civilizations, which would make sense. However, all this was based on supposition rather than scientific evidence. In short, Hudson knew, causality does not equal correlation. Just because things seemed similar didn't necessarily mean they came from the same source. You must track the chain of cause and effect over time, and then you can formulate a scientifically valid hypothesis based on real data.

Hudson was bright enough to be aware that the information he was listening to wasn't real science, but a form of pseudoscience—an interpretation of certain cherry-picked facts integrated into a convenient narrative to come to a pre-determined solution. He didn't know at this point what that was, just that there was some pre-existing belief present in this cultural alternate history he was hearing. He wasn't disagreeing with it, though, and he was finding his time here was well worth the effort. He was learning the kind of things he hoped he would—all sorts of fascinating hidden mysteries. Hudson loved to learn.

He was enjoying this so much and was so dedicated to his new studies that Hudson had no time to work on his thesis about serial killers. He was ostensibly keeping an eye on Wick, looking for serial killer cues that he had read about, like perhaps abusing animals or something, but he saw nothing like that in him. But he would say that Wick was detached and withdrawn. In fact, he always had been. It was interesting to note that lately, Wick seemed a little less withdrawn, while Hudson felt a little more drained. He found Ricimer's workload significant and sometimes dozed off for a second or two during his training sessions. Sometimes he would snap back in to hear Ricimer in mid-sentence about a subject he didn't know about. It could be a little jarring.

Ricimer had been increasing the dose in Hudson's drink with each session, which was standard protocol for initiation. As the deeper secrets were revealed to the initiate, they would be put deeper and deeper into hypno-sleep. This enabled them not only to absorb significant amounts of esoteric information but also to accept it readily and without question. It all depended on the subject's will. Ricimer could see Hudson absorb information like a sponge, but he still harbored a lot of independent will, and that needed to be adjusted. Only the most dedicated servants of truth could hold the immaculate knowledge. Ricimer could read Hudson's face when he was questioning or pushing back too much on the programming. So, he would nudge up the dose and help to put Hudson into a deeper trace to accept the programming without reservation. The deeper the trace, the lower the subjects will—simple science to Ricimer.

Another fascinating anomaly that interested Ricimer was that the deeper you send a patient, the more complete the programming, but also the more socially dysfunctional they become. They could become whacked-out psychopaths, for instance, a useful behavioral trait that the Brotherhood had leveraged many times in the past. When Ricimer worked with really young kids, like 2- to 3-year-olds, the programming is so deep and terrifying that, as an infant, the programmer effectively splits their personality into multiple parts. Lighter programming splits an individual into two personas; the heavier a person gets programmed, the more they are divided into dozens of shattered personas. It's how their psyche deals with the trauma. To break into a thousand pieces.

None of this bothered Ricimer; those who had programmed him from infancy had ensured that he lacked empathy, allowing him to continue his work for the Order in this critical capacity. He made the necessary adjustments to ensure a successful outcome, as any good scientist would, and recorded the results until he felt Hudson had fully completed the initiation process. Of course, it wasn't truly over until Hudson did the final ritual with all members in attendance, in all his glory. But each day, Hudson became theirs more and more, first internally, then finally externally.

The next part in the process Ricimer enjoyed quite well. So far, he had been building the subject up, emotionally and intellectually, and he knew he had established The Brotherhood as a primary source of truth and knowledge in the subject's mind. Now it was time to use that belief to undermine the subject's safety and mental composure. By presenting Hudson with knowledge that was far beyond his current conception, it would shock and cast doubt in his mind, and allow them to then further mold his mind into one of their servants. It also helped establish the subject's subservience to the programmer. However, they needed to be far enough along in the process for it to take effect; otherwise, the mind would reject that knowledge, and you could lose the subject and have to start again. If the programmer wasn't careful, this could be a time-consuming process, and the longer it went on, the greater the risk of damage to the subject's brain.

Regardless, Ricimer was getting antsy and wanted to move Hudson along, so he decided to give it a shot. He not only refreshed Hudson's drinks with a higher dosage but also deployed an aerosol for full epidermal penetration. Ricimer felt that not leaving things to chance, or the fact that a subject may not always be thirsty, was prudent thinking.

"Excellent, my children. I hope you are both well today. Wick, how are you and Hudson getting along?"

Wick was surprised; he and Hudson were getting along quite well. It seemed like an odd question for his uncle to ask.

"Just fine, Uncle. I am sorry, was there some concern about us?" He looked over at Hudson, as if it were his best friend. They were getting along just fine, but he exaggerated a bit for Ricimer.

Ricimer picked up on the exaggeration but saw the truth behind it. "Oh no, I only wanted to make sure you both were feeling a sense of cohesion and being part of something larger than both yourselves. You will need that support today and forever. The one is never stronger than the several. The few are never stronger than the many.

"Today is a special day. I will reveal to you ancient and secret information, highly guarded gems of knowledge that few initiates or adepts are ever made aware. Why am I telling it to you? To convince you, Hudson, to join our order and see the value of brotherhood to mankind. Wick, you are a lucky participant in this ride. Only the top priests of the Order are aware of the most glorious insights."

Wick noticeably picked up his attention on hearing these words. Hudson was feeling amped, too; he was ready to have his mind blown with some new information. He had his notepad prepared to go. He had to take manual notes as Ricimer would not allow any electronic recording device in his study. It seemed odd to Hudson, but to each his own.

Ricimer continued, "I have told you much about the history of mankind. How a single glorious culture begat all the other cultures of the world, and spread its wings across the globe, seeding all parts of the world, from the old to the new. All cultures, from those in Europe, the East, and the Americas, ultimately derive from a single source. We can infer this because all these religious and cultural systems originate from ancient mystery schools, and their symbology and numerology can be traced back to that single source. This is why I have given you so much esoteric knowledge on codes and symbols; it is how we, those who are not profane, transmit information and ideas across the millennia. This is the secret language of the shepherds of humanity.

"Now, it would lead towards a logical conclusion that the mystery schools find their foundation in Persia, migrating to Babylon and being formally structured there. But this is not the truth. The hidden story is that of a lost civilization, from which all other civilizations are said to have sprung. This is the keystone culture that has shaped everything we know about modern humanity. We in the Brotherhood call this ancient civilization, Atlantis."

Hudson had heard that name before, but he thought it was a myth. He didn't say anything, but waited to hear more from Ricimer.

"In the story of human pre-history, now only told in parable and myth, before the great flood that wiped out much of humankind nearly ten thousand years ago, there was a great, highly advanced civilization. This civilization reached heights that would be considered futuristic even by today's standards. Do you think the idea that man could regress from previous heights is a fanciful one? I say to you, look at this Antikythera mechanism, at least a two-thousand-year-old highly advanced mechanical device that couldn't have been developed before the scientific and industrial advances of the nineteenth century. How did the ancient Greeks build this without modern tools, science, and metals?

"I will then point you towards South America. Recently, scientists discovered that metal alloys were used as pins to hold stone blocks together thousands of years ago. A metal alloy process that was not developed in European culture until the nineteenth-century Industrial Revolution. Yet, thousands of years ago, these supposedly primitive people were millennia ahead of the white man.

"How is this possible? How did this universal culture, with similar belief systems and rituals, permeate the globe and then become divided? Was it really a land bridge that the native Americans supposedly came over through Alaska to the Americas, or was there another large land mass that they could have migrated across? One that was wiped out and disappeared during the great flood.

"And as we think about it more, don't the pyramids in Mesoamerica look strangely like the pyramids from Ancient Egypt? It seems odd that they would have developed independently, rather than from a common religious and cultural source. And what are pyramids, regardless? Are they tombs as historians would like you to believe? Or are they ritualistic? Centers of prayer and ceremony to please the gods of the sun, moon, and the harvest. Where sacrifices would be performed to curry the favor of Mother Earth and her servants. Indeed, in the Americas, this is what they were used for; why not in Egypt?

This was out-there stuff, thought Hudson, who was a pretty down-to-earth type of person. It made some sense to him, but, like many things, it lacked objective evidence. It sounded like supposition to him. Ricimer could tell the information was not being taken in by Hudson fully, so he turned up the aerosol drug cocktail to open his mind and take down his resistance. Immediately, Hudson seemed more at ease and pushed back less on what he was hearing.

"And where was this great civilization of old? What is the name of one of our largest oceans? The Atlantic Ocean. Atlantic. Atlantis. Do you understand now?"

Hudson got it. How could he not have seen it before? It seemed so obvious to him now, so clear.

"The great flood of Noah came, recorded by every world religion. The flood represents a natural ecological process in which the world's magnetic poles shift every 10,000 years or so, and when they do, the sun gets hotter, the world gets warmer, continents move, and sea levels rise. Great earthquakes and typhoons destroyed much of what was modern society before our recorded history began. And the great civilization of Atlantis, in all its glory and splendor, was wiped from the face of the earth and buried beneath the sea for all time. And when this happened, the old world and the new world were forever separated, and the landmass connecting Central America to Africa was forever severed, allowing the now distinct civilizations to flourish in solitude."

Hudson's mind was blown. He had never heard anything like this before, from anywhere. Ricimer was so knowledgeable, so intelligent, that Hudson doubted that anyone could pull the wool over his eyes. So, if Ricimer was convinced, that was almost good enough for Hudson. Until he heard some alternate retelling that made sense to him, this was solid history.

Ricimer could see the programming was taking. It always did. Give it enough time, hypnosis, and meds, and you could make anyone believe anything. And if not, there were other ways to produce their compliance. But that wasn't Ricimer's area. They had lower-level mobsters who handled that dirty work for them.

"For the mystery schools begat Babylon, they begat Egypt, and they begat the Olmecs. These things are not in debate. But how did it permeate the world? Through the Far East? Please. They migrated across the Atlantic, which once contained a large island continent, Atlantis, now buried beneath the sea for miles, destroyed by the Great Flood.

"And the antediluvian Atlanteans, like their brethren the Egyptians and Greeks that came after, had glorious technological inventions that were the wonder of the world. They were so advanced that some of their technology would be seen today as magic, perhaps from another world, for they had perfected the science of magico-scientific toponomy—a scientific, magical, and geographic system that has been lost to time eternal. Well, perhaps lost eternally to the profane." Ricimer suppressed a little laugh. "Among the technologies they pioneered, the Atlanteans had mastered the art of electro-magnetic manipulation, allowing them to create flying vehicles that dotted the skies for hundreds of years."

Ricimer took a good look at Hudson's face to ensure the programming was having its intended effect. He seemed engrossed in the information, and Ricimer did not see the look of distrust or confusion a non-controlled subject typically displays when hearing either unsubstantiated or outright false information. Sure, Ricimer had both subjects remotely monitored for all their vitals, and he could review them minute by minute later, but he preferred to rely on his own innate senses. They picked up things in a subtle way that the machines could not. He knew when he had a fish on his line, and he had Hudson hook, line, and sinker.

"But how, how did the Atlanteans develop such technology? Was it the process of evolution and trial and error, or did they have contact with another civilization, one much older, from much farther away than even theirs? Is it possible that the Atlanteans, like the Egyptians and Greeks who followed, were just one in a long line of ancient civilizations lost to time?

"This is what I want you thinking about until our next session. Think of the possibilities. Who knows how many civilizations and cultures there have been across the globe? Who knows what level of technology and science they have achieved? You have seen evidence of lost technology in Greek and American cultures that was not rediscovered for 2,000 years until modern times. Who is to say there were no other lost technologies from thousands of years prior that got buried by time and ignorance?"

Hudson was thinking about that. The Greek mechanism lent credibility to the idea that advanced technologies can be developed and lost, perhaps for thousands of years. Who knows what crowning achievements humanity had achieved before the cruel hand of Mother Nature smote them down? Hudson could see that the Earth was a lot like an individual living being, and he could understand why the Brotherhood saw it as an entity. It ebbed and flowed, built up and crashed down, kept itself in stasis and equilibrium for eons. Just as the earth, so is the greater universe, so down to the smallest molecule—a self-sustaining and self-replicating system.

Hudson had a lot to think about that night.

Chapter 30

The last episode of The Serial Club had done incredibly well online. It was their best-performing episode ever, both in terms of traffic and new member sign-ups. Hudson sold sponsorships and ran cost-per-click advertising to promote hard-copy versions of the podcasts, along with merchandise such as t-shirts and stickers. Everyone was so pleased with its performance, naturally, they wanted to get started on the next one asap.

"So, Hud, have you been doing any research on H.H. Holmes, the Torture Doctor?" Cai was excited to listen to one of Hudson's expert presentations. She knew this Holmes special would perform exceptionally well if they could tie it to broader trends in serial killers in the U.S.

"I haven't had enough time, Cai, way too much going on." Hudson was oddly lacking in enthusiasm for Cai's inquiry. He normally jumped at the chance to display his knowledge on a subject that was of this much interest to him.

Cai wasn't sure what he was talking about. They were doing the same old stuff.

"What else is going on other than the podcast?"

Hudson stopped briefly, realizing he wasn't a very good liar. He would need to work on that. He needed to come up with something, quick.

"Oh, just that my dad has been having me help around the house more while he is working, that's all." Phew, that was pretty good. Not too easy for them to confirm that; they never talked to his father. "But I plan on getting started very soon, I promise."

"Wow, Hudson, you are promising us to research serial killers? We usually have to hold you back!" Sage was picking up on the fact that Hudson wasn't being totally honest with them. He wasn't too hard to read. When someone is as authentic and direct as Hudson, any variation from that is incredibly noticeable.

"Uh, yeah, sorry, I'll get to it soon." Hudson had his head down a bit, like he didn't really want to engage with the subject. His hair was falling into his eyes, hiding them a bit.

Sage looked over at Wick, who was next to Hudson, and she saw the similarity. Wick's head was tilted down as usual, and his black hair was hanging down over his eyes. Hudson was slouching in his chair more than normal, just like Wick was.

Cai never knew Hudson to be at a loss for words. What was going on with this kid? Look at him, he looks pale, and he doesn't want us to see his eyes or the fact that he is lying. The meeting was so uncomfortable that Cai made sure to arrange to walk to school the next day with Sage so they could talk about Hudson.

"What is going on with him, Sage?"

"I don't know, but he's not acting like himself. He seems withdrawn and is self-isolating."

"It's weird. And did you see how he is starting to look and act more like Wick?"

"Yes, that is what is so freaky about it. Are they hanging out separately from us? I mean, they can, but why wouldn't he tell us?"

"Sage, maybe we should do some light recon of our own. How about we put a tracker on Brody's car shuttle? See where he is driving Hudson and what they are up to?"

Sage considered it, "I have to be honest; I don't like betraying Hudson's trust. But, if he's not being honest with us, and we are trying to make sure he is not in danger, then I think we can bend the rules."

"Sounds good, I'll make sure to put it on their car when I know everyone is out. As far as I know, Hud doesn't have security cameras on his house, so we should be good there."

"Cai, I'm worried about him. What if he is hanging with Wick back at the Beale place? We have to get him away from those people. I trust the stuff Marlow told us, don't you?"

"Completely Sage. Those bigots only want to use him for his brains. They don't respect anyone from the wrong side of the tracks, like us."

"OK. Let's give it a few days and see what the data says, and then decide. But what if he's going back to the Beales? What do we do about it? Talk to his father? He works for them."

"I think our first stop should be Marlow, if it involves him. But let's not jump to conclusions."

However, conclusions should have been drawn, as the tracker results showed the girls that Hudson had, in fact, been going to the Beale house regularly, about three times per week. What was most interesting was that he was no longer going at night, but was now there on the weekends and once during the week. Neither Cai nor Sage could figure out why that would be. However, it clearly showed both of them that Hudson, once their best friend and closest confidant, was now lying to them regularly.

It was also clear that Hudson was not getting to the bottom of what was happening with Wick, but was instead falling prey to whatever was being done to him. They were becoming twins both visually and in their attitudes. Hudson had taken on an air of smugness that he never had before. He was more dismissive of his partners and their opinions, leaning on Wick to support him and bully the other two rather than building consensus within the team.

On another walk to school, Cai and Sage talked about what they should do next.

"I guess we can talk to Hudson directly about it. See what he says?" Sage did not want confrontation under any circumstances.

Cai was shaking her head, "No, it won't do anything but put his guard up. He's already lied to us, to our faces, multiple times. He must be doing it for a reason."

"So, we go to Marlow and his Crusaders, see what they say. Come up with a plan."

But what kind of a plan? If Hudson was there by his own free will, and nothing illegal was going on, what right did they have to do anything? But they had to do something. They couldn't abandon their friend.

Cai responded in kind, "Yep, let's talk to Marlow."

Chapter 31

The sessions with Ricimer and Wick had taken on a different tone since more hidden, esoteric information had been released to them. It was more serious, for sure, and Hudson was taking it just as seriously. Ricimer's tone had changed from fatherly to a sterner, authoritarian one. He was almost barking out information at times, reaching a fever pitch when discussing more exciting subjects. It was helping to excite Hudson in a way that made him uncomfortable. Then, just as he was feeling disconnected and wanting to get out of his seat, the discussion would shift to a more empathetic tone, temporarily alleviating Hudson's discomfort. He would settle back in, begin absorbing and learning, and the process would repeat.

This was all textbook to Ricimer. They had formalized these studies on unwitting American citizens during the CIA's MK-ULTRA mind control experiments, which were in high swing back when Ricimer was still making a name in field research. He recalled this exact process being used on one of their star subjects, soon to be known worldwide as the Unabomber, Ted Kaczynski. Ted was an MK-ULTRA test subject while he was a graduate student, unbeknownst to him. During this time, he was experimented on by a CIA scientist who eventually turned his mind into mush. One of their favorite tricks was to ask test subjects to write an essay on their more deeply held personal beliefs, and then the programmers, who had built rapport with Ted, would mock him and tear down his ideas during hundreds of hours of bright-room interrogations. The subject never knew they were under programming, how could they? That would ruin

the experiment. They would keep a subject like Ted on the
see-saw, giving him encouragement and support, then
tearing him down, over and over, until he was theirs to
mold into whatever they wanted.

This was also an essential part of the initiation process for
the Brotherhood of the Golden Serpent. In fact, it had been
long before the CIA formalized its mind control techniques.
Programmer Ricimer had filled Hudson's head with all sorts
of real and false information, to the point he had no idea
which way was up anymore. To insert into that now
exposed mind breach that he had created in Hudson's mind,
the discomfort of not being sure what he really knew,
Ricimer would insert the Brotherhood's belief system. They
would be his new source of truth and light. If Hudson felt
sad, misdirected, or lonely, he would look to the
Brotherhood for support. He would reject and toss aside
his old family and friends to join his new family for all
eternity. This was why this level of initiation was so
important. Hudson needed to be tested to see if he was
truly one of them, or just acting as he thought Ricimer
expected him to.

"Children of the Sun, you have completed many hours of
exhaustive learning. You are now educated in the ways of
our forefathers and know of the glories of the father,
mother, and son. I speak to you the words of Hermes
Trismegistus — 'The Sun is its father, the Moon is its
mother, the Wind has carried it in its belly, its nurse is the
Earth.'"

Ricimer then pressed the button under his desk, and the
Eye of Horus bas-relief behind his desk now emitted a
warm, glowing light. Just enough to look authentic to the
doped-up test subject, like he was really having some

mystical experience. Ricimer and his kind have been pulling this con on mankind for millennia.

Ricimer stood up, his figure towering over the two young boys, backlit in an eerie glow. "All hail our father Osiris! All Hail Isis! She who weaves magic and is of the serpent and horns. All hail Thoth! Ancient Keeper of the Mysteries, God of science and mathematics, master of knowledge. All hail Sirius, the Dog Star!"

Ricimer was keeping a close eye on Hudson, especially with the religious cult programming; you had to be sure. If he were faking it, not really being fully programmed, it would be a problem. Ricimer needed a fully compliant slave. He wasn't sure he could get Hudson to take the lead in a serial killer case, but he could act as support or fall guy when needed. After all, there was no way the family would let Wick take the fall for something they could easily get a stooge for.

This was easy enough; they had done it hundreds of times. He remembered when they had to kill those two pain-in-the-asses back in San Fran. The mayor, Moscone, and that gay leader, Harvey Milk. The guy they got to take the fall, Dan White, was just a patsy like Oswald. They brainwashed him and had him open the doors for the real mechanic, an unworthy craftsman, who did the deed, and White takes the fall. So simple.

No, Hudson would not be a Son of Sam or Jack the Ripper; that was reserved for the special few, the Star Children, and you were only born into that role, typically from a keystone Star Family. Born and molded to be a ceremonial assassin for the ancient order of the Brotherhood. That was the role Ricimer knew was laid out for Wick decades, nay, centuries in the past. Soon, Wick would go into the eye of the storm and look beyond the conventions of man, beyond good and evil, and become what his destiny always had been. A servant in the rite of perfection. He would take his place in the Novus Odo Seclorum, the New World Order, as a Star Child, the progenitor of a new race of man. To Ricimer and the Brotherhood, servants like Hudson were just there to assist in the apotheosis of their bloodline class.

But that was not for Hudson to know, now, nor ever. He, like so many initiates into the order, was nothing more than a useful idiot to the Brotherhood, as smart as they may think they are. They were there to serve the goals and objectives of the Order, and their personal feelings or needs were wholly irrelevant. In short, all that mattered was The Great Plan, and Ricimer had an essential part in that. He was key to creating and maintaining their army of Star Children and support soldiers, who were ground troops to induce terror in the population, in which separate elements of the Brotherhood then alleviated that terror through technological wonder and sophisticated illusion. To create a fascist order from induced chaos is the goal of The Brotherhood of the Golden Serpent.

Now it was crucial to secure Hudson's commitment to the cult. First, Ricimer would administer the oath, which would be repeated until the final rite of initiation, sealed with a blood rite. "Students of the light, you must now take an oath. This is the first of many oaths you will take to protect the secrets of the Brotherhood from the unhallowed gaze of the profane. Raise your hand and extend your arm straight." This was the traditional Roman salute they had kept in favor for so many years, with slight variations.

"I promise never to reveal any of the truths revealed to me, to anyone outside the Brotherhood, for fear of punishment and death."

Hudson did not hesitate to repeat the phrase without hesitation or inflection. He had little of his own will or personality left; he was now a near-empty vessel waiting for more cult programming. Perfect, thought Ricimer.

"Now that you have promised your good word, of which I know is solid, Hudson. There is another secret I must bring to your attention. Our organization, as you might expect, is an incredibly powerful secret group that has been helping shepherd humanity since ancient times. Almost all the most important people in history, across all areas of leadership and counter-leadership, are our brethren—from the great Robert de Ros to his descendants, like Star Family member George Washington, and psychopaths like H.H. Holmes. We are the Brotherhood. And soon you, too, Hudson, will be part of something bigger, something that matters."

Hudson was beaming! To be part of something. To matter. It's all he ever wanted.

Ricimer then spent the next hour or so testing Hudon on everything he had learned for the past few months. He wanted to ensure that he had not only absorbed the historical and technical information presented to him, but also accepted the programmer's opinions as fact. What was important here was to attach the subject to the programmer's ideas, so that he was the source of truth and light for the dependent. After monitoring Hudson's vitals and responses for an adequate amount of time, Ricimer was pleased and convinced that Hudson was now entirely reliant on him for direction and enlightenment. The initiation process was almost complete. The final stage of initiation, the blood ritual, would be next.

"Sun children, it is important for you to remember that the strength of our Order exists in the fact that we manifest ourselves under many different names and many different faces, and sometimes even seem to oppose ourselves, in delightful contradiction. But at the highest level, we are of one mind. One goal, one objective. I welcome you, brethren, to a higher level of being."

Chapter 32

Cai and Sage followed the standard procedure for scheduling a meeting with Marlow. They were given the address of yet another safe house and a specific time to get there. When they did arrive, for the first time, Marlow was accompanied by several other members of his anti-occult Christian action team, the Star Crusade. One was an African American man in his thirties, and the other was a young Asian American woman. They were on one side of the kitchen, while seats were left for the two remaining members of the Serial Club.

"Cai, Sage, these are two members of our organization, they are here since I am sure you have some significant and troubling news for us. This is Grant, and Michelle." Both the girls nodded in affirmation. Grant and Michelle did not nod back. This was serious business.

"I assume you are here to talk to us about Hudson? Please, update us." Marlow waited patiently.

Cai looked to Sage, and since Sage did not start, Cai jumped in. "We are seriously worried about Hudson. He is repeatedly lying to us about going back to the Beale house. He goes multiple times per week, now during the day."

"We have witnessed this during our surveillance," Grant spoke up for the first time.

Sage chimed in, "He is starting to look and act like Wick Beale. He is pale, keeps his head down, and isn't being open and honest with us. It's like he is turning into a different person in front of our eyes."

"We don't know what to do," Cai's voice was starting to shake a bit. "In only a few months, we have watched our friend disappear, and we don't know how to stop it. We don't even know if we have the right to stop it. Is he doing this of his own free will? What are they doing to him?"

Marlow took a moment to weigh his words. "Your friend is being initiated into a cult, and what you are seeing is him going through the initiation process."

Cai and Sage didn't reply; they needed time to digest that. A cult? Hudson?

Marlow let them absorb that, then he continued, "The initiation process of the cult is a brainwashing process. It's the beginning of a longer, more sustained mind control program that they will continue to develop in Hudson until he is fully under their control. Once he is, then they will direct him and use him in some capacity."

"What kind of capacity?" Sage did not like what she was hearing.

"That is hard to say. He's not one of them, meaning he was not programmed and conditioned from birth, which makes them easier to control. And he is not of their blood, so they think of him as a lower order of life. Something to be used and exploited, nothing more. No offense, please. It's important to realize these people, the Beales and their kind, do not see the rest of us as something even remotely equal. They see us as barnyard animals, to be shepherded, and culled, if necessary."

"What do they use their own kin for, the ones programmed from birth?" Cai needed more information to make sense of this. She didn't get it.

This time, it was the woman, Michelle, who spoke up, "We believe that the Beales run the Brotherhood's cult serial killer program. The brother of Lord Beale, Ricimer, whom we believe Hudson has been seeing three times a week for at least three months, is their main programmer. He runs programs for the family's children, as well as all the cult's kids and random strangers they pick up for experimental testing. They also use strangers as fall-guys and patsies." Michelle could see that the young girls didn't really get it. She didn't worry; it would take time and education.

"For instance, Oswald wasn't the actual shooter of JFK, but he was a patsy who was mind-controlled and set up to take the fall. That is what we think they might use Hudson for. Not to kill someone, he isn't under enough stringent mind control, but to take the fall for someone else's kill." She paused for a second. "Maybe for Wick."

That made something click in both Sage and Ca's minds. That would explain why Wick and Hudson were getting so close and why they started looking alike. The cult was linking them together during the brainwashing process.

"Are you trying to say that this cult programs their own kids to be…. serial killers?" Cai was astounded. This was the most anti-Christian value she had ever heard. To not care for one's children and to use them as a disposable commodity.

"Yes, we believe so, but it is hard for us to get verifiable information." Marlow reflected. "Once someone gets involved in the initiation process, you can no longer trust what they say or think. They are having their very personalities changed into being a mind slave for their new masters."

"I'm sorry, sir, but Hudson is brilliant. I can't believe he wouldn't see through what they are doing to him and resist it." Sage knew Hudson was made of sterner stuff.

"Believe it or not, intelligent people are more, not less, susceptible to brainwashing and manipulation." It was clear this was Michelle's specialty. "They tempt and tease someone like Hudson with hidden information and knowledge, and lead him down a bunch of rabbit holes, giving him glimpses of knowledge without any depth. Then they awe him with their power, their history, and their extensive membership. After they have him in their grip, they undermine his trust in anything but them. They separate him from friends and family, and the cult becomes his new family. Then they will leash him to his programmer, which may be Ricimer himself, which would point to our inclination that they consider Hudson a fairly high-priority target."

"How far is Hudson in the process? Is there anything we can do?" Cai almost didn't want to know if it was too late.

Marlow weighed his words again. He began slowly, "Normally, the initiation process takes at least six months. But if they need to use Hudson for a specific operation, they could accelerate it. And that again would point to Ricimer's direct influence. He would be the only programmer expert enough to increase the speed of standard initiation." Marlow thought momentarily, "It might also mean that Hudson was easily being programmed, and they didn't need to take as long."

Grant jumped in, "We think they are preparing for Hudson's final initiation ritual. He has gone through the full initiation process, but he has not been formally initiated into the cult. Once that happens, there is no coming back for him. It is for life, like the mafia.''

Marlow looked sternly at the two young girls, "We don't have a lot of time. If they initiate Hudson, he is lost, and who knows what atrocity they will get him involved in. Maybe pin the assassination of a President or celebrity on him.''

Marlow then leaned over his shoulder and spoke to someone around the corner and out of sight, "Can you come in, please?''

Just then, to Cai's complete shock, her mother, La'Shell, came around the corner. She ran over to Cai and hugged her. Cai and Sage were beyond words.

La'Shell talked quickly, seeing the confusion, "Honey bunny, I am so sorry to deceive you and not come out earlier. I did not want you ever to be involved in something like this, but now it seems we have no choice." She was kissing her head and looking at Cai warmly. "I am a member of the Star Crusade, and I have been working with Marlow on tracking anti-Christian pagan activities for years. I want you to trust me when I say we are not criminals. Beyond some minor privacy violations, most of what we do is legal and above board. But these people, if we don't stop them with your friend, you may never see him again until he is on the evening news.''

Grant, who seemed to be the operational specialist, always took over when it came to the next steps. "We have to get him out of there, and that means tomorrow night. We are sorry to drop this on both of you. We are not sure exactly which day the final ceremony is, but we know it has not happened yet, and tonight is almost over. We have talked to the larger group, and tomorrow night is a go."

La'Shell added, "We have a team of a dozen Christian warriors who are ready to put their lives and freedom on the line to save your friend. Make no mistake, this is a life-or-death situation for Hudson. And no one is going to appreciate us going into the Beale family's residence, much less the police or the FBI, so we should expect no assistance there. If anything, their ranks are rife with Brotherhood cult members."

"We will be armed, and none of us thinks that you two, courageous young people, should be anywhere near this situation." Grant was in charge again. "It simply wouldn't be safe."

Cai wasn't going to hear this. "That is our best friend. We are not going to let him down and not show up, period." She looked at her mom, pleading, "Seriously, we don't need to be on the front lines; let us sit in a car in case you need us. What if you need us to talk Hudson down or something?"

La'Shell thought about it. She looked at Marlow. "What do you think? In the backup car, not anywhere near the action, just in case we need them? I think it would be ok."

"Look, Cai and Sage, what we are doing tomorrow will be technically illegal. There could be serious consequences if we are caught. Are you sure you don't just want to stay home and let us relay to you the action?" Marlow did not want these kids to come along and perhaps get deeper in something they knew nothing about.

"We simply cannot do that, Mr. Marlow." Sage was almost in tears. "We have to do anything we can for Hudson, but most of all, we have to be THERE for him, not sitting at home. Please, let us be there for our friend."

Marlow looked back at Grant, then at Michelle, then at La'Shell, and finally back at the kids. "Ok, tomorrow you get ready, this will be a night mission, so dress in dark clothes. Bring your phones so we can text you and keep you updated. We can set up a live stream so you can watch the operation too. Our goal is to go in quickly and quietly, and take Hudson home, hopefully peacefully, by force if necessary. He and they may not want him to go, so we must be prepared to take the steps necessary to liberate him."

"What happens when he comes back? Will we be able to get him back to normal?" asked Cai.

"It depends on how deep his programming went, and how far along his conditioning is going," Michelle said. "The good news is that if he is only three months into initiation, that bodes well for the deprogramming process. If we can get him out safely."

"We go in tomorrow, so get a good night's sleep. Especially considering what tomorrow is." Grant had a crooked grin on his face, the first of the night for anyone.

Almost in unison, Cai and Sage said, "What's tomorrow?"

La'Shell looked at them compassionately, "Why, honey bunnies, it's Friday the thirteenth, Black Friday. The day the Knights Templar were arrested by the King of France in 1307, and their blasphemous, demonic order was first put down, only to rise time and again to pollute the decent Christian world with their skullduggery."

La'Shell looked up and spoke to the room, loudly and clearly, "Tomorrow, true Christians of faith will reclaim the title of crusader, and we will show the cult of Osiris that their power is not unlimited, and that Christ's light cannot be darkened by their heathen blood rituals. We will save this child of light from the horror of the stars above."

Chapter 33

Hudson wasn't exactly excited for his initiation ritual, but he was surprised at how little agitation he felt. Usually, being put into a situation where he would be on stage and in front of others would have had his anxiety through the roof. But today, he was calm and focused on the task at hand. He had no doubt he could attribute that to Ricimer's training. Hudson had already learned several methods for reducing stress and anxiety, and he found Ricimer's voice omnipresent in his head, offering helpful advice and suggestions. Hudson felt he finally had a father figure he could lean on intellectually to help him learn about the world.

Oh sure, Hudson knew Ricimer and the Brotherhood wanted something from him, but he wanted something from them too—knowledge and experience. Hudson hoped that once he became a full initiate, he would gain access to the family library's deeper areas, which would aid him in completing his thesis on the creation of serial killers. Something he knew he was far behind on. But there was so much to learn about the Brotherhood and the Beale family's history that he forgave himself for this little detour from his primary goal.

For a moment, Hudson was aware of how lonely it felt not to have any of his friends or family here to celebrate. But he knew that this was a secret society, and their words and rituals were not for the profane. Unless his friends and family became initiates, he could never discuss some of the things he had learned with them. This was not something Hudson relished, thinking he was above or separate from other people. But Ricimer had made it clear that to violate any of the Order's rules was strictly forbidden, and secrecy was rule number one.

Hudson did not like or connect with any of the religious stuff the Brotherhood was trying to program into him, just like when the Christians tried to program him years prior. So, he played along so he could get to the parts he really wanted access to, their hidden and esoteric knowledge. All the metaphysical stuff just went right through or over him; it seemed so ridiculous. Hudson would remind himself that these people were still obsessed with an ancient religion, one that did not conform to modern laws or values. And so, he tried to look at it more from a historical or cultural perspective, rather than actually worshipping their silly Greco-Egyptian gods or pyramids. Oh man, how they loved their pyramids, like the Christians loved their crosses.

Hudson wondered briefly if he was being overtly affected by their programming, but quickly dismissed the thought. No, he could see where they were trying to influence him, and by being aware and in control during the process, Hudson felt he was keeping his general sense of self and purpose. But to be fair, he did not have a close independent voice to air any concerns to. But how could he, in this secretive process? He could only lean on Ricimer or Wick, and he knew Ricimer was trying to 'sell' him on being a member, and Wick was impossible to get anything out of sometimes. Once in a while, though, Wick was talkative and engaging, and they had a genuinely good time together. But then Wick went back to being a zombie, and Hudson forged ahead, alone, as was his way.

All of this was perfect for Ricimer. He did not need to read Hudson's thoughts to see that his programming was working and taking hold. He did not need the initiate to believe everything he told them right now, just that he opened the door in their mind to subtle manipulation and guidance that the subject was hardly aware was happening. Then, after several months of ongoing conditioning, the subject could be easily put into a trigger-based trance that would at least allow them to be in the right place at the right time, when needed. Yet again, Ricimer yearned to get this promising young boy when he was under two, then he could have really done something special with him. But, given the late age at which he was indoctrinated, at best, he would be a convenient dupe for a true Star Child, like Wick.

Ricimer was particularly excited for tonight's initiation ritual. He knew Hudson was blessed to be initiated on such a momentous day for their Order. Ricimer had spent some time preparing his standard initiation ritual potion, which he would apply to the initiate at the appropriate time. Hudson was far too early in his programming to be required to take the necessary steps, so a little extra nudge to help him along was sufficient.

Currently, Ricimer was in the process of putting together some of the standard initiation items needed for the ritual. On his study desk, he had all the traditional ceremonial items from the Beale family vault, dating back at least five hundred years. A handbound book with rules from the Brotherhood of the Golden Serpent in Latin and a translation in English. Then, a ceremonial dagger, a scepter, a balance, a crucifix, and the Order's traditional amulet bearing the crest of the two-headed eagle. On the other side of his desk was the Brotherhood's ceremonial candelabra from ancient Rome, with the required seven black candles. Next to the candelabra stood an old stone bowl, its origins dating back far before the Beales, possibly to the ancient Greeks, soon to contain the requisite human blood. Ricimer knew that all the items were necessary, but none mattered more than the blood. This was a blood ceremony after all.

Hudson hadn't a clue what kind of ceremony he was about to go through. He had been christened in a church, so he figured it would be something like that. But the stuff he had been given was nothing like what he got in church. First, there was the black robe. That wasn't that weird in of itself; it was kind of like a college graduation robe, but made out of black satin. The odd thing was that it came with a matching hood that was pointed on top, no brim, and had slits for the eyes. He remembered seeing something like this while researching the Spanish Inquisition and the priests' attire there. When he put it on and looked in the mirror, it looked positively frightening, like some way-too-real Halloween costume. Finally, he was given a pair of red leather shoes to wear, almost like dress shoes. It seemed like such a bizarre addition to the outfit. Weird, why the hell would they want me to wear those?

Hudson then put it all to the back of his mind. Just get through the day and go through the motions, then it will be over, he thought to himself, which was precisely how Ricimer had programmed him. If a disturbing thought entered his mind that did not align with his daily tasks, Hudson was now trained to automatically compartmentalize that information so it did not disturb his psychological equilibrium. Hudson set the black robe and hood aside, focusing on preparing the rest of his items and reciting the necessary rituals and chants to prepare for his big night. It would all be over soon, and he could get back to his usual routines and his podcast.

Chapter 34

The night was the blackest any of them could remember for some time. The moon was shrouded behind a sea of clouds, providing the approaching Crusaders with cover from encroaching eyes. They had come through the deep forest on the back side of the house, equipped with the necessary tools to scale walls, cut wires, and accomplish any task required to gain access to the target.

The Star Crusaders discussed in depth how they would approach and penetrate the Beale estate. With the information provided by Marlow during his first abduction, they planned to go in through the back entrance he previously escaped from. While there were security checkpoints on the way, they had been assured by their inside person in the mansion that security cameras would be off or set to ignore critical areas during the raid. The Star Crusade had an insider planted in the Beale operation for some time, which was where they got their best information from.

For the twelve-person action team, the focus then was on avoiding or neutralizing live security guards and cult members, ideally without lethal force, as they followed the plan to liberate Hudson. They would be receiving live updates, or at least near real-time, from their inside person, so they hoped that would ensure a quick and efficient operation. However, one never knows how randomness infiltrates the cleverest plans, sending them spiraling off into unknown and unseen directions.

The only one who was armed with lethal force was Grant, who was a licensed private investigator permitted to carry a firearm. He had a Glock 9 equipped with a silencer. The silencer was not legal. The rest of the team was equipped with a variety of defensive weapons. Everyone had a high-power taser gun as their main armament; each had a fifteen-foot range and two shots before they needed to be refilled. The stun gun would immobilize an attacker completely for five seconds with total neuromuscular incapacitation, giving the rest of the team enough time to secure and subdue them. Each team member also carried a nightstick as a precautionary measure, in case they needed additional protection beyond the stun gun. Every action team member also had duct tape and zip ties so that any guard could be neutralized for the duration.

They would all be equipped with headsets networked into a group chat server, enabling real-time communication among the action team, the Beale insider, and the surveillance van, which Michelle, Sage, and Cai manned. Michelle had the entire estate on a digital map in front of her and could direct the team step by step. She would update the map with security positions, so everyone had a live, dynamic map of the raid. They needed to be in and out in about thirty minutes, ensuring they had time to escape before any police or feds could be summoned to the residence.

Grant was the point man for the warriors, with Marlow in second as strategic lead. Cai's mom, La'Shell, was in the third position, and she was responsible for acquiring Hudson and sheltering him until he could be extracted. The other crusaders provided support and would follow the direction of the top three leaders. Each was prepared to lay down his or her life to free Hudson from the clutches of this deranged elitist cult.

The team's cars, along with the surveillance van, were parked in a residential neighborhood on the other side of the woods, from which they approached the main house. Grant had led the team through the dense woods, and it took them nearly an hour to cross. Grant and Marlow were both equipped with night-vision goggles, which were very similar to those used by police departments. This allowed them to lead the team through the black woods and into the edge of the clearing near the back of Beale Manor. Once there, Grant paused the team as he looked across the open field to the first stone wall, which they would need to climb with a rope.

Within a minute, a lone security guard was seen coming around the corner of the house and began walking near the team through the open field on patrol. As he passed, Grant fired a stun bolt from the wooded area, hitting the guard in the back and dropping him like a sack of flour. Two crusaders quickly ran out and zip-tied the guard's hands and feet, and duct-taped his mouth shut. They dragged him back into the woods, while Grant and Marlow proceeded to the wall and threw a rope with a grappling hook to the top, hooking it onto the barbed wire. Marlow pulled a small pad out of his backpack, went up the ladder, and laid it across the wire. Grant then signaled to the team to take to the ladder, as he and Marlow went over and landed in the courtyard. As they did, another guard on his rounds came around a corner, and before he could raise an alarm, Grant downed him with his second taser round. Quickly, the rest of the team was over the wall, and several members zip-tied and gagged the courtyard guard, like they had the first.

Michelle was watching all of this and keeping the team apprised of everything happening out of their line of sight. Cai and Sage sat there listening to Michelle and watching on a small LCD screen, and could hardly believe they had gone from common public-school students to Christian crusading warriors raiding a pagan cult within a few days. They could see a lineup of all the headcams on one of the monitors and saw that the team was heading around to the back of the mansion to access the lower passage to the dungeon area, where Marlow had gone in before.

Marlow took the lead, being as this was a repeat of his previous incursion, and he was looking to see what was new versus what he had seen during his first run. He walked slowly around the inner courtyard towards the back of the house and peeked around the corner, only to see a video camera pointed right at them. That was not there before. There was no way to tell if the camera was on or off. Marlow made sure to point it out to Michelle, who was in touch with their inside person, and she communicated back to Marlow and the team that the camera was switched off.

Around the corner, almost hidden in ivy, were a set of small concrete steps leading down into a grimy area that resembled a basement or storm shelter. Marlow confirmed to the group that this was the secret entrance into the Beale tomb, and the team proceeded slowly and with caution. LED headlamps lit the way, and the surveillance van captured the video clearly. As Cai, Sage, and Marlow had seen once before, the familiar hallways and gloom of the ancient tombs of the Beale family extended off in several directions. Luckily, Marlow knew the way back to his cell, which they retraced. After a few minutes, the action team found the hallway of cells where Marlow was kept, now all abandoned with no jailer in sight.

From this point, Marlow turned the group around and, instead of heading back the way they had come or to the upper library area from which the kids had rescued him earlier, he led them to another hallway they had not yet explored. Marlow assumed this would lead to the ritual room where Hudson's initiation was being conducted. It finally dawned on Marlow that on such a big day, Friday the Thirteenth, and a new initiation, there was shockingly little security that they had encountered so far. This was feeling a little too easy overall.

The team descended a long and dark passage, dripping with condensation and reeking of decay. Along the walls was dim illumination from ancient sepulchral lamps embedded in the walls. Also along the wall were cavities and burial chambers in which the bodies of the dead lay in unperturbed slumber. Finally, after what seemed like a long time, they came to a burgeoning light at the end of the hallway. Grant pushed his way into the lead ahead of Marlow, knowing they might come upon a dangerous situation soon. As he approached the opening, Grant signaled to the group to stop with a hand gesture. He quickly peeked around the corner and was shocked to see what he found. Or, to be clearer, he was shocked not to find what he wanted.

For beyond the opening was a large hall, big enough to accommodate hundreds of people. The walls of the hall were all draped with black satin, and on the satin cloth was a variety of golden and sparkling inlays, some of stars, some of drops of water, like tears. In the middle of the room was a large circle on the ground, with the very edge made of white crystalline powder. Marlow and the team knew this to be a magic circle, where black magic rituals were performed. The circle had strange markings around the outside, something more experienced members like La'Shell knew were signs of the Zodiac.

In the middle of the circle was the infamous magical sigil that sent fear into the hearts of every team member—the pentagram. Around the points of the pentagram, equidistantly around the circle, were black candles, all unused. In front of the room, Grant also saw a series of seven steps leading up to a red-draped platform. Upon that platform was a throne, lined with black satin that was accented with red, and in front of it was a table also covered with black satin. On top of the table, Marlow could make out an actual human skull with crossbones below it, the Death's Head. He shuddered.

Surrounding the throne was a variety of statues and imagery. Two stone lions to the left and two to the right, along with four stone eagles perched on wall platforms looking down to the throne. Between those, and behind and above the throne, was a large statue of an angel, but this angel had six wings, not two. Finally, on the walls to the east and west of the throne were large, old, chipped images of a sun and a moon, respectively. Connecting those two on the back wall was a large mosaic of a rainbow. This bizarre collection of imagery had little meaning to Cai and Sage, who were watching from their safe and warm car, but it meant volumes to experienced researchers and activists like Marlow and La'Shell. These were the symbolic representations of a cult of pagan witches whose goal and intention were the subjugation of the human race to their sick will.

The most extraordinary thing of all, which completely shocked Grant, Marlow, and the team who were now filing into the hall, was the fact that this ritual room was empty. There was not a soul to be seen. But the echoes of the monstrous rituals that were performed in this room reverberated through the imaginations of the more educated members of the Crusade. Marlow could smell the blood and death, whether it was still here or not.

Chapter 35

Hudson couldn't wait for the initiation to be over. He had already spent several hours preparing, and the process seemed to go on and on. It was exhausting, frankly. But he told himself that he only had to do this once, and then he would reap all the benefits of being a member of the Brotherhood. Just go through the motions and get it over with —that is what he kept telling himself.

With his robe on and hood donned, carrying his copy of the rules of the Brotherhood, and having remembered all his call and response lines, Hudson was as prepared as he was going to be. Just then, Ricimer, fully dressed in his black and red satin priesthood garb, with a circlet around his head that had a small snake on it, and with a large golden sun medallion around his neck, entered the room with two brothers in tow. They were both dressed in black hoods and robes like Hudson. He took Hudson by the hand without a word and led him out of the preparation room and into the ritual room, where at least a hundred brethren were waiting in silence.

Ricimer led Hudson to the top of the steps, before the throne, and then spoke in a firm, enunciated tone that was easily projected throughout the large hall, "Beloved brethren, we are all agreed to receive this young man as a brother. If there be any among you who know anything of him, on account of which he cannot lawfully become one of us, let him say it."

Not a word was spoken from the throng of black-hooded figures in the great hall. With no objections being spoken, aspirant Hudson was sent back to the small room he had come from, along with Ricimer and his two accompanying servants.

Ricimer then continued with the initiation script, one that they had refined over several millennia. "Brother, are you desirous of being associated with the Order?"

Hudson knew his response to each question. "I am prepared to embrace the trials and tribulations of being a servant to the true faith. For the sake of God, I am willing to undergo anything to remain in the Brotherhood for life."

One of Ricimer's subordinates said, "Are you married, or have you a betrothed?"

That was an easy one. "No, I am alone, ready to serve my new masters." God, this stuff was creepy. Well, it's what they wanted to hear.

The other subordinate then said, "Have you made any vows to any other order or group?"

"No, I have not."

Ricimer now. "Do you owe more money than you could pay back to your lenders?"

"No, I do not."

Back to the first subordinate. "Are you of sound mind and body?"

"Yes, I am."

The second subordinate. "Are you a servant of any person?"

"No, I am my own man. A servant to no one."

Upon this, Ricimer and his men seemed satisfied that Hudson had responded in the appropriate ways. They led Hudson back into the ceremonial hallway, where the Brotherhood awaited him.

Ricimer, the puppet Master, spoke to the hall in a forceful tone, "Brothers, are you willing that this aspirant should be brought in, in God's name?"

The hooded figures all answer in unison, "Let him be brought in, in God's name."

Ricimer looked again at Hudson. "Do you still desire entry to this Order?"

Hudson knew not to vary from his assignment. "Yes, I do." He then folded his hands and got down on his knees, as he had been instructed to do.

"Sir, I have come before God and before you for the sake of God and our dear Lady, to admit me into your society, and the good deeds of the Brotherhood, as one who will be all his life long servant and slave of the Order.' Ugh, Hudson didn't like these words at all. But they meant nothing to him; they were just words after all.

"Beloved brother," answered the puppet Master, "you are desirous of a great matter, for you see nothing but the outward shell of our Brotherhood."

The first part of the initiation being done, Ricimer handed Hudson the golden chalice from the satin-covered table, with a special mixture of mind control potion that would keep him compliant and manageable for the more strenuous parts of the ceremony.

Chapter 36

Cai, Sage, and Michelle, following the action team closely from the surveillance van, were just as shocked as everyone else when they didn't see anyone in the Beale ceremonial hall. It was clear to all that this would be the proper place for any initiation ritual, and their person on the inside had never indicated it would be held elsewhere. It was a confusing situation, and would require a regroup and assessment. Michelle was pulling up a digital map of the estate and a diagram of the tombs to help guide Marlow and the team. However, this was unknown territory; they had planned for contingencies, but not for the ritual to be held anywhere but in the main hall.

"Where the hell is everyone, Marlow?" Michelle was flummoxed. "Do you see anything in the hall to indicate it was recently used. Are we too late?"

"Not sure. The candles weren't even used; they were brand new." Marlow was looking around, as perplexed as Michelle was. "I can smell some incense and smoke from more recently, and the stink of dried blood and decaying flesh from longer ago."

Sage and Cai didn't know what he meant. Why would there be dried blood in a ceremonial hallway? They looked at Michelle questioningly, but they couldn't get her sight line. She was too engrossed in finding a new direction for the team.

"I am not seeing anything on my map that would indicate a better place for the initiation. They always had them in the same spot, as far as we knew." Michelle was scrolling down the hallways, looking at which rooms in the manor could accommodate a large gathering.

La'Shell, who had been nearly silent so far, allowing Marlow and Grant to lead, finally spoke excitedly up, "Wait one second! What were we thinking? This isn't a normal day, so this isn't going to be a standard initiation."

Marlow got her point, sort of. "Right, it's Friday the 13th, a special day for the cult around the world, I am sure. But what place would be more appropriate than the main hall that the Beale family has used for centuries? Where would they rather be doing a blood ritual with a new initiate than in the safety of their own home?"

At that very moment, both Michelle and Marlow realized exactly where the initiation ritual was being done. How could they not have seen it before? It was such an obvious oversight; one they made because they were not thinking like their enemies were. They needed to think like Pagans, not Christians.

Before Michelle could signal to Marlow her realization, one window of the surveillance van was smashed in, and then another, in a series of deafening and shocking crashes. Multiple hands reached in and opened the locked doors suddenly, and before Sage could release herself from the paralyzing fear she was feeling, a pair of arms grabbed her hard and yanked her from the vehicle. Michelle barely had time to react before a canister of gas was thrown into the car, incapacitating her almost immediately. Cai, unlike the other two, reacted immediately, throwing open the door closest to her and launching herself out of the van before the gas got her. She ran into the woods as fast as possible, without looking back. She disappeared into the woods, unsure if anyone was following her, and continued running, deeper into the woods, navigating by pure instinct and adrenaline-driven fear.

Marlow and the entire team could hear through Michelle's headset, so they were privy to everything that transpired in the van. Michelle's muffled screams, the commotion from the windows smashing, and the scuffle to grab Sage had everyone on the action team panicked and looking at each other for reassurance. Grant and Marlow looked at each other in complete confusion, never expecting their surveillance van to be in any danger whatsoever.

"Marlow, we are compromised. Should we abandon the mission?" Grant was panicked, looking at the exits and planning a retreat plan in his mind.

Marlow wasn't so sure. They still needed to find out what was going on with Hudson's initiation, and now they needed to ensure Michelle, Cai, and Sage were safe. They could go back to the van and then try to trace the cult's steps from there. Or, they could continue on the mission, now more alert and aware that at least part of the operation had been blown up.

"If we go back through the woods to the van, and then try to trace them back, it could take us hours, and I am not sure we could track them through the woods." Marlow considered their situation. "It makes more sense to continue to the initiation, and if they took people from the van, we may find them there."

"Ok, Marlow, fine, but where is the initiation? It's not here, so where?" Grant needed to be pointed in a direction.

"I figured it out right before our cover was blown." Marlow looked at his map and nodded towards an exit from the ceremonial hall they had not yet taken. "This is the way. For they are initiating Hudson under the grace and protection of their Moon Maiden tonight."

Chapter 37

After drinking from the chalice, Hudson felt much less anxious than before. He thought that things were what they were, and he just needed to hang in there and put up with it until it was over. Hudson had learned to tolerate many annoying things throughout his life. This didn't seem any different. He settled into the process and gave in.

Suddenly, the lights in the hall dimmed, making all present nothing more than a series of vague forms and shapes. The black satin draped the room, only intensifying the effect of darkness and loneliness. All that could be seen now was the very faint light of the sepulchral lamps emitting a yellowing glow around the edges of the hall, and the sparkling of stars embedded in the black satin fabric. Hudson was faintly aware of a very dank smell right now, almost that of decaying flesh.

Hudson could now make out movement in the room. What looked like corpses, shrouded in rotten linen, moved about the room, brushing up against Hudson and stinking in their death and decay. Suddenly, two ghouls appeared on either side of Hudson, and they tied a ribbon smeared with blood around his forehead. The blood dripped down Hudson's face, giving him a horrific look right out of the movie Carrie. The mind-control mixture Ricimer had given Hudson made sure he had no concerns whatsoever. He didn't even know it was human blood dripping down his face.

Ricimer then handed Hudson a crucifix from the table and hung the family's double-headed eagle amulet around his neck. At this point, to what would have been shocking to a sober Hudson, but not a doped-up one, two members came up from behind him and took his robe off his shoulders, exposing his bare chest and upper frame. This all seemed perfectly normal to him, and Hudson just regarded it with gentle good humor and a silly ritual he needed to put up with. Then, upon Hudson's shirtless body, Ricimer dipped his finger into the stone bowl on the table and drew crosses on Hudson's body made from human blood.

As Hudson stood there, shirtless and exposed, with blood dripping in his eyes, and bloody crosses blazing on his tiny teen frame, he heard blood-curdling cries and guttural sounds from the distance. Soon approaching him were five horrific and blood-covered figures, who soon surrounded him, threw themselves down on the ground, and then convulsed while speaking some ancient prayer that sounded like Latin. For more than what seemed like an hour, these figures mumbled prayers around Hudson. At times, Hudson thought he was going to pass out, but Ricimer would steady him, and he would stay resolute. Just a bit longer, and it will all be over, he told himself.

Finally, the five figures dispersed, and Hudson slowly noticed the lights were a bit brighter. He could make out that he and Ricimer were now alone in the hall. The smell of blood and death was prevalent, and Hudson felt so weak and overwhelmed from all the shocking activity that his brain was trying to calm itself down.

Ricimer looked at him gravely. "The initiation process has now moved into its final stage. Because you are so unique and special, we are conducting this ceremony on a most auspicious day, the day when our forefathers were unfairly persecuted by the state, the church, and the mob, who became three of our mortal enemies."

Hudson felt an overwhelming sense of pride and accomplishment. How many people had been initiated into such a prestigious fraternal society as the Brotherhood of the Golden Serpent at the age of fifteen? Even though he was only a junior member, it sure seemed like a full ceremony for an official member. And to be initiated on such an important day in their history, he must be an exceptional recruit, which he knew was true for sure. Hudson was beaming.

Ricimer was pleased. Hudson was going to be a very moldable and effective servant for the Order. He could see the programming taking place as planned. Ricimer's methods, at this point, were almost foolproof, with failure on only a small fraction of initiates. It was all about choosing the right material to mold. Cast no seed upon the rocks.

"Follow me initiate, for tonight we celebrate your joining of our Order underneath our mother, the Moon Maiden. And by the glory of our father, he, too, shall bless your rebirth into a more advanced being."

Hudson did not doubt what Ricimer said. He was growing and changing; he could feel it. Becoming something bigger. More complete. He didn't know what was happening to him, but he liked it.

Chapter 38

Cai finally had to stop. She ran and ran, never once hitting a tree or branch, somehow psychically navigating her way through the pitch-black wooded terrain. It was her years of experience that had honed her senses and reflexes to the degree that she could handle this challenging situation almost effortlessly. When Cai finally stopped running, she was walking in circles, breathing slowly, when the cold hit her. For the first time, she realized she had no coat on, and certainly wasn't equipped to be walking around in the woods at night, no matter the time of year. Cai had run in a straight line, so she knew approximately where the van she had run from was. Although she wanted to go back and help her friends, Cai did not think it was a good idea to try to confront anyone who might be armed and dangerous. She knew getting out of there to find help was the right thing to do, but it still bothered her, like she was running out on Sage and Michelle.

So, she took a moment to get her bearings and decide on the next steps. The shock of the unexpected event was beginning to wear off. It was clear to Cai that the operation was compromised, most likely by the cult. Police would never have just attacked like that, without announcing themselves and following their standard procedure. Also, they knew what they were looking for; they grabbed Sage before even dealing with Michelle, so it seemed to Cai that Sage was the intended target. But why? What would these people want with her, and why alert the action team to the operation by attacking the surveillance van rather than the team themselves? Or maybe this was just the first part of the counter-operation, where the cult was silencing the communications before attacking the team inside the compound. Either way, this did not bode well for anyone involved. Who were they going to go to for help? The police? The FBI? Please. Marlow had made it quite clear, and the experience of the Serial Club confirmed this, that the police were primarily interested in public relations and career advancement. At the same time, the FBI was likely partnered with, and had members within, the Brotherhood itself. No, they would be getting no help from the authorities, that was for sure.

Well, first things first, Cai knew she needed to get out of there and to safety, and then get help. Most of the people she knew from the Star Crusade were already here and involved, so she wasn't sure what assistance would look like, but she had to find something. But, which way to go? By this time, Cai's eyes had begun to adapt to the darkness quite well. And it seemed like the clouds were clearing up somewhat, and the moon was emerging, so there was more light seeping into the dank woods than before. With it, Cai was surprised to see what looked like a clear yellow glow straight ahead of her. The more she focused on it, the more apparent it became. Was it the lights of the downtown area? No, that was too far off. Maybe a street fair or something of that sort? Whatever it was, Cai didn't have many options. Either walk off to the left or right into the darkness, or proceed straight ahead to the yellow glow. Going back to the van was out, so straight ahead it was. Cai started moving again, this time at a more deliberate pace. Feeling her way around the trees and branches step by step instead of at full speed in panic and fear.

Chapter 39

Grant and Marlow made sure to tighten the group up, given the good chance that the cult was well aware of the infiltration of their headquarters. Marlow continued to try to get through to Michelle, and he knew the lack of response did not bode well for her and the kids. The worst part of it was that he had allowed Sage and Cai to sit in the surveillance van. What a fool he was. He should have had them stay back at the safehouse; this was no place for innocent kids. Now, he put them in danger, and he did not know where they were. He looked over to La'Shell, who looked positively petrified.

"I am so sorry, La'Shell, this is my fault. I never should have allowed them to come."

La'Shell wasn't the type of person to put blame where it wasn't deserved. "No, no, don't put this on your head. I could have stopped them, too. I am her mother. I never wanted her involved in any of this, and now she is. I am to blame, no one else."

"This isn't about assigning blame, but addressing the anomaly and adjusting our strategy to accommodate the changes." Grant was always about the operation and moving from point A to point B as efficiently as possible. Having someone like him around who didn't get caught up in emotional issues was critical to ensuring a successful operation.

Marlow knew what he was talking about and got refocused. "Right, we need to reassess and reacquire the target. Most likely, Sage, Cai, and Michelle should be with the larger group, and I'll bet when we find Hudson, we find all of them. As I mentioned before, since this is a special occasion for the Brotherhood, they are holding the initiation ritual at a special location. And when you think like a pagan, not a Christian, they celebrate their gods and beliefs outside and in nature, typically in some grove. That is where they will initiate Hudson, underneath the protective light of their Moon Maiden, their female Isis. So, we must go into the woods and find them. According to my maps, the hallway we have started down leads towards the back of the estate and then drops off the map. We head down this hall and look for an exit to the outside, and hopefully we will find our target."

Grant now came to life as the lead, "OK, team, everyone walks in a straight line, with the two people in the back looking rearwards periodically to ensure no one sneaks up on us. Stay close to each other, no stragglers. Keep either your stun gun or baton out and handy, this could get hot any second."

While the entire tomb complex they had been walking around in felt old, the hallway they had started down felt even more ancient, if that was possible. It was almost like they were heading out of the near past, a few hundred years back, into the deep past, beyond the memories of modern man. The hallway began inclining down slightly, then more steeply. The walls transitioned from smooth stone to more jagged rocks, with moss and water dripping between them. The hall got danker and wetter the farther they went. Their feet no longer felt like they were walking on stone, but centuries of padded down muck and mire. Their boots began to sink into the muck, then became more stuck, pulling them down. As people pulled their boots out, there was a sucking sound.

Grant looked back at the team to make sure they were all moving along. The water was up to their ankles, and it was clear they were no longer walking on solid ground, but on silt. He was feeling increasingly confined as the hallway narrowed and descended into the unknown depths. Leading a team into the waiting darkness without knowing what lay on the other side was the nightmare of all tactical team leaders. This was how entire teams got slaughtered or captured. Grant put all this in the back of his mind as he advanced, more slowly now, feeling more vulnerable without concrete information about what was ahead of them.

The water kept getting deeper; first it reached their ankles, then their knees. Once it reached their waists, the team leaders grew nervous. How deep was this going to get? It was ice cold, too. If Grant didn't get the team out of here soon, they could be looking at hypothermia. But he didn't want to rush them, lest anyone got stuck in the mud or fell into the freezing water, they would be in trouble for sure. The water kept rising until it reached the shorter people's chests, and they were holding up any electronic or sensitive equipment over their heads.

At this point, everyone began to panic a bit. They had no idea how much longer they had to go, and if the water went any higher, they would have to turn around. Could they even do that? They had been walking for thirty minutes now, and to go back through that cold water again? No, they needed to go forward. Grant knew they were in a pickle, and they needed to save Hudson and everyone before it was too late. There was no going back.

It was then that, for the first time, La' Shell felt something strange against her leg. It wasn't dirt or mud, that was for sure; it was harder. Maybe it was a rock or something she walked by, so she ignored it. But then, she felt it again. Something rubbing up against her, something strange. It was hard to tell with how cold the water was and the fact that their legs were starting to get numb.

At that very second, someone a few spots behind her screamed, "What the fuck! Something bit me!" Everyone began to panic and thrash around in the water more. With that, multiple people started to scream. "Ouch!", "What the fuck is that?", "Something is on my leg!" Grant had long rubber boots on, so he felt nothing, but he could see fear starting to take over the group. He needed to do something.

Grant screamed, "EVERYONE! WE ARE ALMOST OUT! FOLLOW ME QUICKLY NOW!" Grant was lying; he had no idea how much longer it would take until they got out. However, he needed to motivate everyone to move forward quickly. They needed to get out of this water. And whatever was in it.

Grant double-timed it, and everyone followed suit, and that seemed to alleviate some of the attacks, except for one team member, who kept crying out that something was on him. After a few minutes, the water began to drop, and the prevalence of slimy water things no longer nipped at their feet and shins. Grant had no idea what those things were, but was happy they were moving past the danger. Except for team member Lopez, he seemed to have one of them on him.

Finally, they were out of the deepest part of the water enough for them to take a look at Lopez and his leg. He went to pull up his pants, while Marlow shone an LED light on him, and there, underneath the pant leg, was a long, black, scaly, eel-like creature. It almost looked like a giant leech to Marlow, but he had never seen a leech that was a foot long. And yes, it looked hooked onto Lopez's leg, and they were going to have to get it off.

"Does it hurt?" Marlow knew the answer already.

"Fuck yeah, it hurts! This thing is latched onto my damn leg! Help me, for god's sake!"

Marlow looked to Grant, who kneeled and looked at Lopez's slimy new companion. "Well, like anything alive, a shock should loosen its jaw and resolve. Hold on, Lopez, I'll turn the stun gun down so you don't get too hurt." Lopez didn't care; he would do anything to get this thing off him.

Grant turned the gun down to twenty-five percent power and held it to the blood eel. The shock forced it to loosen its grip instantly, and it dropped back into the water and slithered away before anyone had a chance to kill it.

La'Shell kneeled with her medical kit and looked at the wound. It was bloody, but it appeared to be a surface wound. Unless the animal is poisonous, it would not be a concern. She cleaned up the wound and bandaged it. Lopez seemed strong enough to continue, but he was no longer able to move as well. He was limping pretty badly. So, they moved along, trying to have him keep up in the rear.

Finally, they got out of the water, and the stones on the walls turned into packed earth with wooden posts at intermittent distances, both horizontal and vertical. It almost looked like they were in an old mining shaft. It felt to Grant like they were emerging from the foundation of the home, and hopefully, they were now moving out into the woods. He looked at his compass, and it was due west the whole time. Based on his estimation, they should be past the yard and open area and into the woods now.

Marlow wanted to get the team out of there as soon as possible. Recently, he had seen a few tunnels going off to the right and left, and had no doubt these were still in use to some degree. It would be the perfect way to move people and supplies underground, keeping them out of sight from the ground or the air. He wondered how far and deep the tunnel complex went. He did not doubt that, under any of these secret criminal organizations, there would be a wide array of tunnels used for smuggling contraband. What better way to move children and other trafficked individuals to be used in their sick blood rituals? He shuddered at the thought.

The incline had been building for some time. They seemed to be coming to an area that opened up from the narrow tunnel they had been in for some time. From Grant's perspective at the front, he thought he smelled a very slight scent of smoke. He signaled to the group to stop and quickly turned off his LED headlamp. Grant could see a faint orange glow from the end of the tunnel. He hand-signaled to move forward again, but slowly this time.

As he got closer to the opening, he could see it was a wide, round area at least ten feet across, and in the middle was the base of a metal ladder going up. Just then, Grant realized not only did he smell smoke, but he could hear chanting—the dark and sinister words and mumblings of the blackest magic. Grant shuddered, knowing all too well what was on the other side of that ladder. He checked his Glock, made sure his stun gun was fully loaded, and signaled down the line for everyone to prepare for an assault. They all did the same, as Grant took out a stun grenade, and Marlow took out several smoke canisters.

The team fanned out into the circular room, covering the entrance to it while Grant prepared to ascend the ladder, with Marlow right behind. As Grant put his foot on the ladder, a switch triggered a mechanism that lowered a steel gate behind them, locking them into the circular enclosure. Grant realized the mistake he had made. He was too confident. Too arrogant. They were onto them the whole time, just leading the team here. And they fell for all of it. Jesus, they could kill us all right now, and there is nothing we could do about it.

Almost on cue with that thought, three canisters dropped down from the opening above the ladder, and within seconds, the entire team was completely unconscious and incapacitated.

Chapter 40

It had taken Cai almost an hour to navigate her way to the yellowing glow through the dense woods and overgrowth. Luckily for her, the emerging moon and the yellow light gave her enough sight to move forward safely. She felt, as she moved closer, that the wind was blowing more strongly through the woods, and she hoped this meant she was getting closer to the edge of the forest.

Cai was thinking about getting out of the woods as she began to smell smoke—a faint hint of a bonfire, like the kind you have on the beach. She thought she had heard something too, but it was strange, unlike anything she had ever heard before. Was that chanting? A low guttural hum that rose and fell somewhere in the back of her ears. What the hell was that? Oh, wait, now she could hear someone speaking, and it was louder and clearer than those other voices. This sounded like a man making a speech or something. Oh, Cai was so happy. Finally, civilization and assistance!

In her excitement, Cai wasn't paying as much attention to where she was stepping, and she stepped over a branch only to get her foot caught in a knot of a prone tree. Her forward motion took hold, and she fell head over heels, down into a hidden ravine and gully, falling and rolling at least twenty feet, banging and scratching herself on rocks and sticks on the way. Finally, she stopped moving and came to rest on the bottom of the gully, on what felt to her like a large pile of rock and stones. Things were sticking to her back and sides, and it was incredibly uncomfortable. Nope, it was downright painful! Cai was hoping she wasn't hurt seriously, but she needed to get on her feet to check herself out. Every time Cai tried to stand up, the ground was so uneven and stacked with rocks and other pointy things that she couldn't get her footing. When she put her hands on the ground, it was so sharp that it hurt her hands too much to lean on them.

What Cai needed was more light; it was too dark down here in the gully, and she had no phone or any way to light things up. She sat for a moment, hoping something would help to light her way on how to get out of this predicament. Then she heard a rising commotion from the glowing area, as if there were some climax to the proceedings. Then, the normally dim glow that had been helping her to see became significantly brighter, and for the first time, Cai could see the ravine she was in clearly. Now she could see that it was not rocks and sticks she was sitting on, but bones.

Cai looked all around her, and the ground was covered, in all directions, with thousands and thousands of bones, of all kinds—bleached bones of all sizes and shapes. But most of these were bones Cai recognized. Right next to her, almost touching her side, Cai could see a human skull. Then, looking more closely, she could see leg bones, rib cages, and more. Cai was sitting in a pit of death, and as it dawned on her, all the color drained from her face, and she scrambled to get herself away from the bones, painful cuts be damned.

She rolled herself off the pile and got to the side of the pit and tried to gain her composure. What was she sitting in? Why would human bones just be scattered across the ground and dumped here so unceremoniously? Didn't these people bury their dead? It seemed so disrespectful. Cai could not understand it; there was something wrong here.

With that thought, Cai's mind made the connection to a conversation with Hudson from months earlier. They had been discussing pagans, and Hudson made the point that ancient pagans used to commit human sacrifice to honor their gods and ensure a good harvest, among other benefits. And they liked to use children, virgins in fact. It was then that Cai realized that the skull sitting next to her was not a man's skull, but a child's. Cai shuddered, thinking about the pain and torment that child must have gone through. What kind of people were these Beales and their kind? Cai was starting to understand why her mother, La'Shell, was fighting against them. Anyone who could do this to a pure child needed to be stopped. After all, it was the Christian thing to do. Plain and simple.

Chapter 41

Ricimer Beale, high priest of the Brotherhood of the Golden Serpent, puppet Master of the Star Children, began the regional grand convocation of the priesthood of the mystery schools, including hierophants, adept masters, and priests on this day, Friday the Thirteenth, the year of our Lord the light bringer.

Under a clear sky, the bonfire beneath the grand edifice of their beloved Baphomet warmed and lit the glade, and the congregation, garbed in traditional black robes and hoods, cast eerie shadows that seemed to bleed into the surrounding woods. The area, circled in torches, along with the woods, had a primeval feeling to it. A glade cast into the earth so long ago, both integrated with and separate from the natural world around it.

The adepts and priests all stood in concentric arcs, facing the grand stage, below the bonfire and the towering statue of their Order's primary god, which stood a formidable twenty-five feet high. The image would be familiar to those knowledgeable about esoteric mysteries. Still, to others, it would seem a beast more than a god—a goat's head, with a pentagram embedded in its forehead. The being is winged, and has the breasts of a woman, and the lower half of a man, with the hoofs of a goat. Its right hand is elevated with two fingers extended; its left is lowered with two fingers extended. A horror to any Christian, it should need no explanation—the Beast.

Upon the stage stood an altar, one built of human bones. It would not take one much to surmise that this was, in fact, the bones of sacrificial victims, children most likely. These things would not be of concern to anyone in attendance, as they were here to serve their god, and their god demanded sacrifice for all he provided to the members of the Order. For under his guidance, their fortunes have increased, and their lives improved immeasurably, which means they must give him even the slightest of donations, that of a pure virgin child. For this is to be done on both solstices and equinoxes, so that Orion and Sirius should receive their souls unfettered during the proper alignments.

Their lord Baphomet was to be honored on other special days, such as Friday the 13th, a landmark day for the Brotherhood, as it is for many secret societies around the world connected to the Grand Templar Order through heritage or allegiance. So, while an initiation was not usually an occasion for such a prestigious event, Hudson would be honored with seeing his entrance into the Brotherhood connected to the blessing about to be conferred on their patron.

As required, the sacrificial victim lay still on the bone altar awaiting liberation. Their consciousness was managed with Ricimer's special potion, this time to a near catatonic state. The victim was wrapped in black satin; their face and head fully covered. Next to the altar was a stone pedestal and a stone bowl. On the pedestal was a ceremonial dagger, one that dated back to the earliest days of their kind, used to honor the strongest and most potent of gods, our father/mother.

In front of the altar stood Ricimer in all his glory, his black gown and red sash flowing in the wind. When he raised his arms, golden scepter in hand, one could make out his red leather shoes, similar to the ones he had given to Hudson.

In fact, standing a few feet away from him, to the right of the altar and facing the crowd, was Hudson. He looked in a similar state to when he was in the main ceremonial hall, now more heavily drugged up, his shirt and robe lowered down, and his upper body covered in bloody crosses, his forehead wrapped in a linen soaked in blood, dripping down his face in a macabre horror. On the other side of the altar stood Wick, dazed and immobile as usual, dressed in the standard black cloak with hood in his hand. He looked out at the crowd into the distance, almost through them, seemingly completely unaware of the ritual taking place next to him. A zombie would be the best way to describe how Wick looked right now, totally out of it.

None of these sights of ancient blood rites were ever intended to be seen by the profane, those untrained and undedicated to the mystery schools. But today they were, as all the members of the Star Crusade, disabled, zip-tied, gagged, and some still unconscious, sat in the back behind the main throng of worshipers, just out of Hudson's sight, a few feet where the ladder from the tunnel world had emerged.

The Crusaders never had a chance; the Beales were part of a broad, high-level network with too much surveillance and too many resources to stay under their radar for long. As soon as they had an inkling about the Crusades' intentions, all their moves and communications were monitored. At any second, the Brotherhood could have plucked each member off the street, but this was simpler, cleaner.

All in all, they take out the primary anti-occultist Christian group within this region of the US, and they could pretty much do anything with them they want. They were trespassing, and most likely, anyone who knows they are at the Beale estate is already here. Ricimer had decided to hold off on dealing with them for now, as the ritual was on a timetable. And no, he was not talking about Hudson's initiation. That was a minor affair to Ricimer. Ensuring that his god, his light, his beacon of truth, power, and glory would have the soul-nourishment it needed to blossom into its eternal divinity was his primary concern. His love for his god and his religion was total for Ricimer. After all, he had been bred that way, like all high priests. The role was too important not to have the most devoted followers to the cause.

Ricimer spoke with a commanding tone. No amplification was needed; his words rang clear, true, and deep for all the attendees. The wind seemed to die down as he spoke, and the fire blazed up a little more. Ricimer felt all the power and glory from his god, whose massive artifice crowned the skyline behind him.

"We who are the Guardians of the Secrets of the Ages, All hail Baphomet! Our father, our mother, our light, our darkness!"

"All hail Baphomet!" The gallery responds in perfect unison, like in a church.

"He descended from the heavens to deliver unto us wealth and power, and advanced technology with which to slay our enemies, and defend our colonies and interests!"

"All hail Baphomet!"

"We repay him with the souls of the pure through a blessed sacrifice!" The high priest turned to gesture towards the sacrifice victim, still immobile and fully covered with black satin on the human bone altar.

"All hail Baphomet!"

"We will serve him until the end of time, and until we establish his new order for the ages, his glorious novus ordo seclorum!"

"All hail Baphomet!"

"Look how the Moon Maiden has blessed us this night!" High priest Ricimer looked up, arms spread. "She is strong and bright and has graced us all with her divine presence!"

"All hail Isis!"

"Soon, she will be joined by her one, him whom one may not name, Osiris of the mysteries, who springs from the returning waters!"

"All HAIL OSIRIS!" The gallery of adepts and priests of the Order was getting more aroused. But the fact that the sun god Osiris commanded a larger response than the god for whom the ritual was performed would be insulting to any god. These arrogant brethren should mind their place in challenging the glory of Baphomet, Baptist of Wisdom.

As if to signify this gross insult to their own deity, five figures came out from the left and right, all covered in blood, mumbling to themselves, and walking around in circles. The high-priest put his head down as the drama proceeded. The figures started to coalesce around Hudson. As they had done before in the crypt, they threw themselves down around Hudson and began chanting a guttural prayer in a dialect that was beyond the understanding of most in the glade. They spent a long time in prayer. Hudson and Wick were so heavily medicated with time-release serum that Ricimer wasn't worried about their coming out of their trances, so they held strong through the hour.

Finally, from somewhere unseen, echoing from the deepest parts of the forest, came the sound of a lone person crying. One of the bloody figures got up and took hold of Hudson's shirt and shoes, and then threw them in the fire. At that time, the funeral pyre began to increase significantly in intensity and size. In front of the flames, all five of the bloody ghouls went into severe convulsions. Soon they calmed.

It was then that the high priest spoke again, "Stand in the box, initiate!" Ricimer pointed to the standing coffin just behind Hudson that had been in the shadows, completely unseen until that moment. Hudson did what he was told and stood, then leaned back in the nearly vertical standing coffin.

"Speak these oaths after me, initiate." Ricimer looked back at Hudson a bit. "In the name of the crucified one, I swear to sever all bonds which unite me with mother, brothers, sisters, wife, relatives, friends, mistress, presidents, superiors, benefactors, or any other person to whom I have promised faith, service, or obedience."

Hudson, leaning back in the coffin, crossed his arms across his chest like a vampire, repeated every word, clearly and without any slurring, in perfect repetition of what Ricimer said, "In the name of the crucified one, I swear to sever all bonds which unite me with mother, brothers, sisters, wife, relatives, friends, mistress, presidents, superiors, benefactors, or any other person to whom I have promised faith, service, or obedience."

The high priest continued, "I denounce this land in which I was born. Henceforth, I live in another dimension, which I will not reach until I have renounced the evil globe which the heavens have cursed."

Hudson repeated this, slightly modified. "I denounce Old Springs in which I was born. Henceforth, I live in another dimension, which I will not reach until I have renounced the evil globe which the heavens have cursed."

Ricimer then looked back at Hudson and said to him, "For now, onwards I shall reveal to my new chief all that I have heard or found out; and I shall also seek out and observe things which might have otherwise escaped me."

Hudson subconsciously understood this meant he should submit fully to his new master, Ricimer. "For now, onwards I shall reveal to my new chief all that I have heard or found out; and I shall also seek out and observe things which might have otherwise escaped me."

Ricimer was pleased; Hudson was his, entirely. He was a conductor, a psychiatrist, a programmer, and an alchemist, and this was his work, his art, and his destiny. He continued, feeling closer to his lord with every word, every thought.

"I honor the use of poison; it is a quick and essential medium of removing from the earth, through death or robbing them of their wits, of those who oppose truth, and those who try to take it from our hands."

Hudson, usually repulsed by any thought of violence and death, agreed without nearly a delay. "I honor the use of poison; it is a quick and essential medium of removing from the earth, through death or robbing them of their wits, of those who oppose truth, and those who try to take it from our hands."

Ah, another killer, always valuable for the Order, Ricimer thought.

"Lightning will not strike as rapidly as the dagger, which will reach me, wherever I may be, should I betray my initiation and what I have now heard."

Hudson, not really knowing what he was agreeing to, not only a life in this demonic organization, but the threat of torture and death if he betrays them, repeated the line. "Lightning will not strike as rapidly as the dagger, which will reach me, wherever I may be, should I betray my initiation and what I have now heard."

It was then that a figure in black emerged and placed a large golden candelabrum with seven black candles in the center of the stone table, next to the bone altar and the stone bowl. Ricimer lit the candles while engaging in a sacred prayer in Latin.

He then spoke clearly to the candidate formerly known as Hudson. "Come now, initiate, and wash yourself clean of your past and your sins."

Hudson came forward from the coffin and walked in a trance-like state to the stone table. There, he put his hands in the bowl and brought out two handfuls of human blood, and began to smear it on his body. All over his face and neck and arms and torso, he covered himself in a deep slathering of fresh blood.

Ricimer then spoke again. "Now initiate, DRINK, drink, and be clean."

Hudson, without pause, began to drink the human blood from the stone bowl. He took several good gulps. At that point, another black figure came out, moved the coffin

Hudson had previously been in to the ground near him, and then took the headband off Hudson's head and guided him back into the coffin, now lying down. The figure then brought several buckets of warm water and began to scrub and clean the blood off of Hudson, while he lay in the coffin.

When the process was complete, and Hudson was floating in a warm bath, as a newborn babe, the high priest finished the initiation. "With this initiate clean of his past, and his family, and commitments, and now being reborn as a member of The Brotherhood of the Golden Serpent, I give him his new name, one that he will be known to all others in the order."

Ricimer looked down at Hudson in the coffin and spoke now more loudly and forcefully. "ALL HAIL BAPHOMET! ALL HAIL OSIRIS AND ISIS! ALL HAIL ORION! ALL HAIL SIRIUS!"

The crowd again chanted in perfect unison, "ALL HAIL BAPHOMET! ALL HAIL BAPHOMET!"

'I now welcome to the Order, a servant to the great plan and to our master's will, he who will walk the righteous path in between light and dark, he who will liberate his trapped divine spark from our flawed material world, our newest member, Jubelo, the unworthy craftsman!"

Chapter 42

Cai was cold and in pain. She was wearing jeans and a long-sleeved shirt, which wasn't enough for this late-season weather. Her fall in the ceremonial bone pit gave her scrapes and minor cuts all over her body, but mostly on her hands, arms, and face. She didn't know this then, but Cai was fortunate not to have been hurt worse. She easily could have had a random rib bone protrude into her skin for a deep cut, and there was no emergency room anywhere nearby. After a few minutes of licking her wounds and sitting on the ground trying to decide what to do next, the sounds Cai had been hearing in the distance had gotten a lot closer, and she could now make out some of what was being said, although none of it made any sense.

"ALL HAIL BAFOME!"

What the hell were they saying, all hail who? What was a Bafome? Cai hadn't a clue, but whatever it was, it sounded creepy as hell. The whole tone of what she was hearing was not of some nice block party or family cookout; it sounded much more sinister and insidious. The talking continued, but it made little sense to Cai without context; it sent shivers down her spine, that was for sure.

Cai was now fairly certain she was nearing the pagan rites ceremony the Star Crusade had been looking for. She had no idea what else this could be; it was totally foreign to her. Cai decided to proceed to the light and sounds, but slowly and with caution. It was close now; she began to feel warmth from the bonfire, which she was incredibly thankful for. For the first time in hours, Cai was not freezing and shivering. She crept closer through the woods to the lights and sounds, making sure to keep herself near larger trees to shield her approach.

Finally, she saw light. But not artificial light. She could make out a line of torches near the edge of the woods. Torches? What year was this? Weird. She crept a little closer, going from tree to tree, edging up to the commotion. She kept hearing chanting and prayers, all in unison, which reminded Cai of a church. However, this didn't feel like any church she had attended. Eventually, Cai was close enough to be able to see a large portion of the opening glade emerging in front of her. Her mind had trouble perceiving what was in front of her.

There was a clearing in the forest, one that looked very old and almost natural. On the edge of that clearing, a series of torches lined the entire perimeter. Then, towards the back of the clearing, was a giant statue of some sort. Cai thought this thing was butt ugly and just plain bizarre. It must have been a few dozen feet high, and was that the head of a goat? What was it made out of? To Cai, it looked like real fur was used to make the head. She could see a woman's body as its torso, and it looked to her like it was made from real skin, too. Gross! The more Cai looked at the giant taxidermic figure, the more disgusted she became by it.

In front of the monstrous creature was a large bonfire, now blazing very high. And in front of that, Cai could see a stage, and on that platform, she could make out a few people in black robes and what looked like a table, but at this distance, she couldn't make much detail out. Standing in front of the stage, in a series of concentric arcs, were what looked like a hundred or so attendees, all seemingly enraptured by the events. Cai couldn't tell really how they felt, of course, as they all had black robes and these weird pointed black hoods on. What was up with those! They looked like inverted Ku Klux Klan members to Cai; that was where she had seen hoods like that before, on old videos her mom had shown her.

It was difficult for Cai to get a good perspective from her vantage point, as she looked at the gathering from the side. She decided to sneak around the perimeter and head toward the back so she could at least see head-on what was going on the stage. She slowly crept around, tree to tree, around the perimeter of the forest clearing. She did not think anyone would notice; they all seemed completely transfixed by the strange events taking place before them. Cai really wanted a better vantage point to try to formulate a plan of action. Finally, after a few minutes of creeping, Cai came around to the back of the glade. There in the trees, she found a variety of cut stumps among the mature trees. So, she saw a larger stump near a fully grown tree she could use for cover, and she climbed onto it for a better view. And boy, did she get one.

Once up on the stump, Cai could see over the throng of black hoods and could now see the stage, bonfire, and that giant goat-headed demon statue behind it all. On the stage, Cai could see what looked like some table or altar, and it looked like it was made from…bones? Jesus, were those human bones? Cai's brain was having trouble making sense of something few humans had seen in thousands of years. This didn't look real. Maybe it was a play or something? But it looked all too real, all too authentic. No, this was the real deal; this was no joke.

Upon that realization, finally, Cai's brain began to put the pieces together. It dawned on her that she recognized the people on stage. That nut-job in the middle in the black and red gown, that was Uncle Ricimer Beale, that bigoted windbag Cai had been dismissed by at the Beale Garden party. He looked like some wizard out of a fantasy book or something, with a scepter and golden medallion and all. To his left was Wick, looking just as out of it and disconnected as always, in a black robe, looking into the distance. As Cai looked to the right, her knees began to give out. She had to do a double-take to make sure what she was seeing was real. There was Hudson, standing there looking like Wick, like a zombie, with his shirt off, his head wrapped in a bandage and dripping with blood, and his body covered in blood and bloody crucifixes. Oh my god, what were they doing to Hudson? How far had he fallen to become a tool in their sick game?

Cai then began to panic. She instinctively knew she needed to try to help Hudson, but how? There were a hundred cult members here, who knows what they would do to her for ruining their ceremony? She took a better look around the open area. She only saw black-hooded members; no obvious security guards were in sight. Finally, she looked down, which she had not done prior, being so interested in the exotic sights, and there, in the back of the throngs of worshippers, she saw about a dozen people all sitting on the ground. As she focused on them, she could see they all looked restrained, as their hands and feet were all connected. With unbound happiness and joy, Cai saw the back of a head she recognized, and that was her mother, La'Shell, seemingly unharmed and sitting fairly close to the woods.

Without overthinking, Cai immediately jumped down and crawled over to the edge of the woods where her mother was sitting. She just wanted to be near the warmth and security of the one person who loved her unconditionally. Lucky for Cai, there was a good amount of noise, chanting, and prayers coming from the clearing, so she was able to move without giving herself away.

"Mom," she whispered so softly. "It's me, Cai."

Her mother didn't stir. Was she unconscious? Cai wasn't sure; everyone who was tied up seemed immobile, but it was tough to tell in the dark. She moved a little closer and tried again.

"Mom, can you hear me?"

Still nothing. Cai then moved within a few feet of her mom, picked up a stick, and then poked La'Shell's back with it. This finally produced a response, as her mom stirred, but minimally. Cai wondered if the monsters had drugged her mom and her friends to keep them quiet during the ritual.

"Mom, it's me, Cai."

La'Shell replied weakly without trying to turn her head. "Is that you, honey bunny?"

"It's me, Mom. What the hell is going on? I was in the van with Michelle and Sage, and someone grabbed them. I ran into the woods to escape, but didn't know where to go. I saw some light, so I headed in that direction. This is where it led me."

La'Shell shook his head a bit. "I am so sorry, sweetheart, this is my fault. I should never have gotten you involved."

"No, Mom, we were involved way before I knew you were part of the Star Crusade. This has to do with the pagan freaks that brainwashed our friend, kidnapped our other friend, and terrorized our family and neighbors. They are to blame."

La'Shell did not respond. Her shame was total and would not be assuaged. She had gotten her daughter into a life-or-death situation and was not sure she could get her out. Things were looking bleak for the Star Crusade. They were all zip-tied up, drugged, and were totally neutered. What hope did they have, honestly?

When her mom didn't respond, Cai knew it was up to her to be the adult now. She needed to take on her mom's role because her mom was unable to. Cai was not going to let her or her friends down; that was for sure.

"Mom, you don't fret. I am here and will take care of things. What do I need to do? I need to get you out of here."

"No, no. If you try to get me out, they will see and blow your cover. We have to get Hudson and the others out of here, too, not just me and you."

"Ok, Mom, I get it. But I need to help you get loose, and then I can try to free Hudson. I am not leaving you here tied up."

"Yes, I understand. Look for something sharp to help cut these zip-ties. If you can find me something, I can help free the others." La'Shell was coming out of her daze now, with some hope for freedom, her mind started working overtime. They may not all die here after all, that was the first time she allowed her mind that luxury.

Cai heard loud and clear, and now she had a goal and a mission. "I'll be back, Mom."

Cai crawled back into the woods and began looking around the perimeter for something that could cut plastic. She wanted to find something like a box cutter, but good luck finding that in the woods. As she walked back and forth searching, Cai stepped on something and heard a crack. She then looked down and saw she had stepped on a piece of sheet glass, breaking it. Huh, she thought, maybe this is something I could use? But how, without cutting myself while trying to hold it? It then dawned on Cai that if she picked up some green leaves and wrapped them around the end of the glass shard, she could use it to saw through the zip-ties and protect her hands.

Well, there was only one way to find out. She made it back to her standing stump and then crawled back over to La'Shell and began cutting at the zip-tie. It cut through very easily, and when her mom's hands broke free, Cai felt a sense of hope and elation she had not felt before.

La'Shell was much more alert now, keeping her hand behind her so no one would know she was now free. "Honey bunny, I need you to cut the ties on Grant and Marlow, right next to me. Then you leave the glass for us."

La'Shell was well aware that the only reason there were no security guards on them right now was that the ritual was private and only for cult members. The prisoners were allowed to watch since they would probably not live much longer. But, if they made too much movement or commotion that would raise an alarm, so they needed to move silently, but quickly. Hudson's initiation was almost done, and the sacrifice would take place right after that. If they were not out of here by the time that was done, they were done.

"Cai, when you are finished, I want you to back off and sit in the woods until we can get Hudson free and get out of here. I do not want you in danger anymore." La'Shell knew her headstrong daughter wouldn't listen, but she had to try, as a good mother.

"No way, Mom." Cai wasn't having it. "You don't have weapons, and there are A LOT of them. You need my help."

La'Shell knew she was right; it was what it was. If one of them lived, they all lived. Hopefully.

"While I talk to Marlow about what we will do, why don't you sneak around the perimeter and try to get around the back of that goat thing. There may be some tools or a stash of our weapons dumped somewhere. It's a long shot, but we should try. Hurry, but be quiet. We don't have much time. We need to get out of here, but we can't leave Hudson. What we need is a distraction so we can slip him out of there, and then we all disappear into the woods. OK?"

Cai agreed and started back through the woods, circling now the other direction, looking for anything that would be of use.

Chapter 43

The tension had been building throughout the night. The once stoic gallery was becoming increasingly aroused. The black-hooded figures began writhing and moving about more excitedly, slithering and pulsating in an awkward dark dance of primal passions. The glory of their god, only a representative, a mere contrivance, for their true gnostic belief, worship of the earth, the father sun, and the moon mother.

The high priest spoke in both Latin and English, sometimes vacillating between the two, in a form of symbolic language only the adepts trained in the secrets of Babylon could fully penetrate. To those in attendance, the dark priest seemed to be in communication with powers far beyond the limitations of others bound by space and time. As he spoke, the fire burst into larger flames, his speech reaching an increasingly fevered pitch.

"When our forefathers came to this land, they called it Amaruca, Land of the Plumed Serpent. And from the priests of the great cultures of Amaruca, we begat our divine providence, for Quetzalcoatl himself paved the way for our order to take the new world into our governance."

The priest spoke like a being that witnessed such monumental changes in person, a continuous form passed from one high priest to another, down through the ages, dying and being resurrected over and over again, just as their god Osiris is yet born each day anew. An eternal dance, of light and dark, of life and death, from above, to the pit below.

"So, in the father sun we find the analogous being, the snake. In all its glory, the serpent is our glorious fire God. For the sun is the great enlightener of the physical world, and the serpent is the enlightener of the spiritual. It is from this serpent we receive all knowledge, all light, all seeing."

The high priest, Ricimer Beale, was walking slowly across the stage, back and forth, stalking his audience for powers unseen, channeling the old ones in his mind and spirit.

"This is why we are the Brotherhood of the Golden Serpent. We worship the light-bringer, he who brings us out of the darkness, into the golden illumination of knowing. We stand naked in the sun, drenched with sweat under the moon, dancing our fair dance before the winds carry away our fate into the hands of another—the great, benevolent earth."

The priest then gestures with his scepter toward the stars, the moon, the earth, and the wind.

"The great intelligence that we live within and upon will ensure our actions are only undertaken on those who agree to our domination. For their consent drives us towards further and greater heights, and we take their dark energy and transfer and transmute it towards the satiation of our glorious Baphomet!"

Just the mention of his name sent the crowd into a sexualized frenzy. "ALL HAIL BAPHOMET!" The crowd grew increasingly excited as they chanted, pulsing in throngs of dark intent. "ALL HAIL BAPHOMET!"

The high priest continued to work the crowd, get them all excited, then bring them down, then up again, constantly shifting subjects and tone, over and over, creating an uneasy sense of religious fervor among the goers, making them all pliable to his suggestions and manipulations.

"We reach our gnosis through alignment with the Zodiac's twelve signs that govern our daily lives. And when the sun and the serpent enter each heavenly house of the Zodiac, in the thirtieth degree, and leave at the thirty-third degree, so it can be said that our god, our Father, the Sun, the Serpent, too began his ministry at age thirty, and he shall perish by age thirty-three."

To Ricimer, this occult-based babble made total sense. It was all connected into a glorious, simple plan that only seers like himself and the great gods of antiquity could fathom. He could only deliver small crumbs to the slovenly followers who could not grasp such sophisticated magical concepts.

"Can it be no wonder or cosmic coincidence that the human spine has but thirty-three segments? For this is the vehicle of the fiery ascent of the serpent force, which resides in all our human forms, delivered through the space seed that gave man his divine spark of pure thought."

The knowledge the high priest had could only be obtained from the rarest and most valuable alchemical manuscripts from the Middle Ages to the Renaissance. His followers hung on every word, perhaps today would be the day they received a new hint, a new secret, on which to unravel their lives.

"Can it be a mystery why we are of the golden serpent? What higher plane could a man hope to attain? But that of as close to our father, the sun, as possible."

The high priest looked gravely across the multitude. His stern gaze penetrated the walled veil of the gathering.

"When Isis resurrected Osiris from the dead using the words of power, to be born again yet another day, his light shone across the world, but it was not to be eternal. Each day, so the light comes, so must the dark and the underworld come."

Ricimer, for the first time, looked down and addressed the figure covered in black satin on the bone altar.

"To foster this transition and show honor to our great benefactors, we perform the rite of perfection. We cleanse this spirit of this earthly body so they may ascend and join our lord in delight and glory for all time."

He then reached down and ripped the black satin cloth away in a dramatic motion, and there was Sage, lying drugged and unconscious, with but a loincloth on, prostrate on the human bone altar. Hudson and Wick stood flanking her, looking straight forward, seemingly unaware that their best friend was lying next to them, about to be ceremoniously murdered.

Ricimer gestured towards Sage again, "And this pharmakos shall be the vessel to make the ascent to godhood. For pity not this child, but praise them, as they are our lord incarnate, awaiting to be reunited with his companion in the great beyond."

"ALL HAIL BAPHOMET! LORD OF WISDOM! ALL HAIL OSIRIS! HE WHO SHALL NOT BE NAMED! ALL HAIL ISIS! SHE OF THE SERPENT AND HORNS!"

"ALL HAIL BAPHOMET! ALL HAIL BAPHOMET!" Shouted the crowd in near delirious unison.

With that, Ricimer put his scepter down and picked up the ceremonial dagger that had been passed down through the generations, from the great temple of Solomon itself. He held it aloft to show the adepts gathered. They oohed and aahed in reverence and glee.

"Behold the blade of the Temple, the blood letter, the Gebel el-Arak!" The knife was so old, ancient Egyptian, in fact, that it had an ivory handle and a flint blade. It was a prized treasure of the Beale family, and priceless. How many human and animal sacrifices had it performed over the millennia? It was incalculable.

Ricimer felt the power of all their gods and the whole of the earth, sun, and moon in his hand with this historical and mystical blade. Few men had ever held it, and only an ordained priest could use it as it was always intended. To cut the heart out of a living human victim and set that heart afire for their gods. Ricimer had no sense of guilt or shame for this act; in fact, quite the opposite. This was a traditional religious ceremony, and he was their lord's assigned representative. This was his birthright.

With that thought, Ricimer moved in front of Sage with his back to the gallery. He gripped the knife, on its ivory handle, with both hands, and raised his arms into the air, in a theatrical motion, and paused at the top of the arc, ready to plunge the dagger into Sage's chest.

Chapter 44

Cai was getting increasingly nervous. She kept circling the clearing, now to the right, looking for anything that could help them either release Hudson or cause a distraction. So far, she had found nothing but more stumps and broken branches. Cai hoped that when she reached the back of the stage, there would be some tools she could use. Maybe a saw or an axe or something used to help build the support for their freaky goat god, towering high over the bonfire.

What was really disturbing Cai was what was happening during the ceremony. The things Ricimer was saying were totally bizarre and made little to no sense to Cai. What religion was this? It was not Christianity-based, that was for sure. It seemed like a bunch of unrelated pseudoscience and metaphysics that was mashed together into a phony magic pie, or at least that's what it seemed like to Cai's supposedly unsophisticated fifteen-year-old mind. How anyone could take this nonsense seriously was beyond her. So, she tried to block it out of her mind, but hearing them chant and babble and writhe around was downright disturbing to Cai's conventional sensibilities.

She kept sneaking and moving, and Cai was almost around the back now. As she came around and got behind the stage, Cai could now see that there was a black hooded figure there sitting on a tree stump, and he was working a bellows, an old wooden air pump device. He would pump the bellows, and it would, in turn, shoot up the bonfire flames more when Ricimer spoke. Ah, thought Cai, this was how they were creating that effect.

Seeing this person manipulate the fire actually made Cai less afraid than before, when she had thought the proceedings might be authentic. These were a bunch of hucksters, just like other religious frauds, who use religion and faith as a way to manipulate others to their will, just like those horrible megachurch pastors who drive around in Ferraris while they fleece their poor parishioners.

This person controlling the bellows had their back to her, so Cai was able to at least scan the area for tools or weapons from the edge of the woods. There was nothing to see, and the presence of a cult member made it impossible to search any closer to the stage. Cai was getting really nervous now. Ricimer seemed to be getting more excited, pacing across the stage and lecturing the crowd about some nonsense involving wacky gods and the Earth and Sun. She felt like she was running out of time and needed to hurry and get back to her mother and friends.

Cai went back the same way she came, across the woods along the edge of the pagan glade, sneaking from tree to tree to maintain cover. She doubted anyone there would notice at this point; they were all out of their minds, dancing around and gyrating like a bunch of drug-addled hippies. They were hailing Baphomet, and Ricimer was ranting and raving in some half-Latin language diatribe that probably made sense to no one but him.

The fire was getting higher, and the sounds were getting more disturbing. Cai stopped for a moment, found a stump, and got up to see what was happening. Ricimer was getting the crowd into a state of complete delirium. He himself seemed to be on another plane, channeling something from beyond the fabric of their reality. Cai saw Ricimer face the figure on the altar, grab the black satin covering it, and pull it away in a dramatic motion, like a magician working a Las Vegas crowd. And there, lying on the horrifying bone altar, was Sage.

Cai almost fell off the stump. It had never occurred to her that Sage was in immediate danger. She figured she was one of the group that was tied up in the back and would be freed soon. But no, not only was Sage not safe, she was apparently to be the next victim in a pagan sacrifice, and there were a hundred black-hooded cult members in Cai's way. Well, not totally in her way. Aside from the one figure behind the stage and Ricimer doing his bit, the whole gallery was engrossed in the ritual, facing the stage. From where Cai was on her stump, she was directly in front of the right side of the stage, and could make a beeline there without being molested. But what good would it be? She could not take on Ricimer alone and carry Hudson away, so what would be the point of running up and exposing herself? She was considering whether to go back and join her mom and others when Ricimer continued the ritual.

He said some more stuff that was incomprehensible to Cai, "Behold the blade of the Temple, the blood letter, the Gebel el-Arak!"

Cai couldn't help but roll her eyes, even in such a precarious and dangerous situation. This guy was a grown man playing pretend like he was living in ancient Babylon on top of a stone pyramid five thousand years ago. Grow up, little man, that's what Cai was thinking to herself. You are another shyster in a long line of fakers who play on people's fear and suspicions for personal gain.

It was then that Cai saw him put his scepter down and pick up a long, creepy-looking knife. The crowd began to beat their chest like apes, crying and mourning. Jesus, she thought, is this it? Is he really going to kill Sage in front of all these people? This has to be a play. Or a joke. But something told Cai, deep in the back of her brain, maybe in the brain stem, that this was real. It was not a play, or a put on, but a sick religion still practicing its deviant beliefs within a decent Christian society. It was unholy, plain and simple. And there was no one, not one person in the world, but Cai, who was close enough to do something to stop what was about to happen.

Cai's animal and protective instincts kicked in, and the realization that Sage was about to die, within microseconds, triggered something in her. Her adrenaline flew into overdrive. She launched herself off the stump, right out of the woods towards the stage, not caring or even thinking if anyone could see her. She went full speed to the side of the stage, saw the steps going up, and jumped up them two at a time until she hit the stage still running. If anyone had seen her so far, one wouldn't know; she was so fast, and everyone was so whacked out that no one moved to intercept her.

On the stage now, she ran at top speed towards Ricimer, who had not seen Cai and was raising the dagger in one of his more memorable moves, plunging the dagger into the chest. Now, as people saw her closing in on him, some members close to the stage began to advance, and Ricimer finally saw something out of the corner of his eye. As Cai went to jump at Ricimer, who was much larger, she wailed a scream so horrifying and blood-curdling that Ricimer froze, and Hudson, now standing in a black robe, seemed to snap out of his trace, if not for a moment. Cai hit Ricimer with her two feet in a kick and knocked him off balance, dropping the knife, and Cai bounced off to the left. Cai was so much lighter than Ricimer that when she hit him, she lost her balance, and while going left, she got so close to the edge of the stage that a few sets of black satin-covered hands came out and grabbed her.

Ricimer was shocked by the whole event, but also amused, given that the young girl was now subdued. He had to respect her initiative. If only she had a weapon, she might have stopped him. Hmm, perhaps she would make a good subject in his experiments. After we get rid of her mom, she will be available for programming. But Ricimer digressed, back to the ritual at hand, and then he would deal with the girl and her friends in the back. All things in good time. He chuckled to himself. This would be a fun story to tell at the next convocation.

Ricimer then bent down to pick up the dagger, and Cai started yelling loudly. "HUDSON! NO! IT'S SAGE! CAN'T YOU SEE HER? HELP HER! HELP!" Cai was yelling and screaming and howling, kicking and biting at the increasing number of hands trying to silence her.

Hudson, having already been shocked into coherence from Cai's screaming jump kick at Ricimer, could now see what was going on. He was having trouble processing it. There he was, standing on what looked like a stage, at night in front of a bonfire, next to a table made of bones with Sage lying on it. His best friend in the world was lying there unconscious, and then he realized Ricimer was standing there, with a dagger, and was raising his arms, as if he was actually about to kill his friend. It didn't look real, like some ridiculous play about pagan witch times. But like Cai, his brain knew differently: this was real, and he was part of it.

Not dissimilar to Cai's surge of adrenaline, Hudson now saw his friend's life in immediate danger and reacted, from a primitive level of fight-or-flight. Live or die. With his building adrenaline, Hudson gripped the side of the coffin and launched himself at Ricimer, the high priest of the Brotherhood of the Golden Serpent. Ricimer was not watching for Hudson and was totally shocked and surprised by him. He was also surprised at what Hudson did, which was to immediately grab the dagger out of his hand, before Ricimer could get a good grip after picking it up, and then pull at his priestly garb, putting him off balance.

Leaning back to the right, Hudson pulled Ricimer, who was already off balance, towards the bonfire right behind them. When they were close enough, Hudson swung the knife at Ricimer, and Ricimer leaned back, and fell over the railing and into the bonfire flames, knocking flaming pieces of wood to the left and right, in front and back. Several flaming pieces hit the dry base of the goat god Baphomet, and the hair on its hoofs caught fire immediately. Ricimer jumped out of the flames and tried to put himself out, while the flames rose from the statue in all directions, setting the clearing afire in an even brighter and more hellish light.

At that moment, somewhere deep in the crowd, a loud amplified voice bellowed out, "THIS IS THE POLICE! EVERYONE STAND WHERE YOU ARE AND PUT YOUR HANDS ON YOUR HEADS!" Other unamplified voices repeated that this was the police and that no one should move. This was a mass arrest. The entire area froze into silence for one second, and then burst into chaos as black-hooded members began running back and forth, into the woods, and scattering wherever possible.

Hudson took this moment, while looking at Ricimer, who was patting his flames out in anger, to gather all his strength and rush at Ricimer, with the ceremonial dagger leading the way. Hudson lunged at Ricimer, slashing at him with all his might once again. This time, Ricimer could not lean back, and Hudson found his target every so slightly by slicing the puppet Master's throat open into a crimson grimace. In shock at the blood gushing out of his neck, Ricimer began to panic and instinctively tried to retreat, only to fall into the flames once again. This time, though, Ricimer couldn't get out. He grabbed at his throat and struggled helplessly as he lay there immobile, bleeding out and burning. Ricimer howled and screamed in pain. His hands continued to grasp his throat while gasping for air until he stopped moving, literally cooked alive.

Meanwhile, the crowd, seeing the high priest burning in the fire, and hearing sounds of the police closing in, had all freaked out and were trying to get out in any way possible. Many of them were losing their hoods, which exposed them to Cai and Hudson, as well as anyone else who had the time and wherewithal to look. Actually, some of the first people who lost their hoods were the ones holding onto Cai near the front of the stage.

When the megaphone with the cop's voice started, and Hudson slashed Ricimer with the dagger, Cai started kicking and fighting even more violently. Her foot kicked off one of the hoods, and she almost went into a state of shock seeing who it was, for she recognized that face, all too well. It took her a few seconds to place it, but they realized she was looking at the Mayor of Old Springs himself. The mayor seemed to look right at Cai when she recognized him; he panicked, let go of her, and ran off into the woods.

At that moment, Cai saw Marlow and her mom, La'Shell, come running up from the back, and began grabbing at the people holding Sage, pulling at their hoods and robes. Eventually, another hood came off, and Cai saw a beautiful blonde woman beneath it. Well, what was once a lovely woman. Even after years of excessive plastic surgery, Cai recognized this face almost instantly. She knew her well – Kelly Martin, celebrity newswoman, conservative firebrand, and disgraced media mogul who was the subject of an earlier Serial Club investigation into the disappearance of her disabled son Dylan. The Where is Dylan? movement was a national sensation, and Kelly had disappeared from the headlines some time ago. Well, it was now clear to Cai how Kelly got her success, for it certainly wasn't for her talent. Just as horrified as the mayor was to be exposed, the second Kelly's hood came off, so did her arrogance. Her mask of anger and superiority now melted away into that of a sad, deranged, and washed-up semi-celebrity scrambling for her scraps of freedom and dignity. She ran off into the distance, whimpering and trying to shield her face from recognition.

There was only one person left trying to subdue Cai, and Marlow grabbed them from behind and yanked off all their black coverings. And there, standing in front of Marlow, was FBI special agent Dick Peters, one of the two agents who laughed him out of the headquarters for trying to report the Beales for occult crimes. Peters was equally shocked to be exposed, but not as much as the others. He used his elbow to clock Marlow on the side of his head, knocking him down, and then ran off into the distance. Fine with Marlow, he thought as he lay on the ground dazed, that agent probably had a gun; he didn't.

During all the commotion, the group of now freed Star Crusaders continued to frighten the scattering throng of Baphomet worshipers, yelling that the cops were coming, and to run and take cover. It worked like a charm, making everyone run in all directions without much thought, dropping candles and their hoods along the way. Members of the crusade identified at least a dozen prominent figures in government, business, and society whom they could now track and pressure. We know who you are, and we are coming for you, Marlow and La'Shell thought as they made mental notes of certain people.

Running like a bunch of cockroaches exposed to the light of Christian decency, everyone ran into the woods or went down the well or other secret exits. Everyone but Ricimer Beale, his flesh satiating the air as it burned uncontrolled on the massive bonfire, the twenty-five-foot effigy of Baphomet now entirely in flames, never to stand again over rituals of such venomous intent. Today, your god received his blessing and sacrifice, Ricimer; it was simply a different one than originally intended. Even Wick disappeared, most likely with his parents, whom the Crusade leaders just assumed were in the crowd somewhere and slipped out unseen.

Still on the stage were Hudson and Sage. Unaware of the declining chaos around them, Hudson gently put the black satin cover over Sage to protect her, still unconscious on the altar. He kissed her forehead and prayed to God that she would come out of this all right. Tears were streaming down Hudson's face, him feeling such a deep sense of shame and disgust with himself that he could barely be in his own skin. He then, for the first time, noticed that he was covered in blood and fell over onto the stage floor, shaking, and began retching and heaving, uncontrollably coughing up red blood and black bile.

Chapter 45

No member of the Serial Club had been to Hudson's home since the ritual a few weeks prior. Hudson had not really been there, either. Instead, Hudson had spent the last few weeks in a medical facility trying to be deprogrammed by a variety of doctors and psychiatrists. The facility was procured through assistance from the Star Crusade's lawyers, who made sure the institution had no connection to any Beale or Brotherhood business interests. This was harder than it looked on the surface, as the Beales and their kind were heavily invested in medicine, psychiatry, and pharmaceuticals. Really, anything that was used to deceive, manipulate, and control people is the business of the Order.

For the first time since the incident, the remaining members of the Star Crusade and the Serial Club met at a safe house to discuss the fallout from the operation and next steps in pursuing the remnants of the Brotherhood in Old Springs. Sage had recovered well, seeing as she was drugged quickly and did not have to witness any of the horrific things done to her, or the fact that she almost became the latest sacrifice in a long line to pagan gods. She still had PTSD from the incident with Dr. Dedorius, but it was further exacerbated by the kidnapping in the surveillance van, so treatment and therapy were going to be on her menu for some years to come.

For Cai, it was not going to be so simple. Yes, Cai was made of sterner stuff than Sage, mostly from her tough upbringing, but she was not a machine. A young girl like her can take a certain amount of stress and tension, but even the strongest and most resilient can only take so much. The things Cai saw and heard will be with her forever, burnt into an area of her mind that will not diminish over time. The horrific sight and feel of falling into the human bone pit, the goat-headed statue bursting into flames, the high priest ranting and raving about gods and destiny, those monsters in their black hoods and cloaks, and the fact that she almost witnessed her best friend getting murdered by one of these psychopaths. If Cai had not done what she did, which was run at Ricimer to delay the sacrifice until it could be stopped, she could never have lived with herself. But Cai did what was right. She followed her instincts. She put herself in danger to save a friend's life. To do what had to be done. All the horror melted away for a few moments when she thought about how she launched into Ricimer with both feet, ruining his perfect ceremony.

Many members of the Star Crusade quit after the botched operation. People felt like they put their lives on the line, only to get bad intel and be put at risk by poor planning. Marlow, La'Shell, and Grant knew better. The Beale family and their network were much more powerful than they had initially thought. Once the cult was onto the Crusade, they were so heavily infiltrated in the police and feds that it was easy to track all the Crusade members, and they soon knew their plans in detail. There didn't need to be a mole in the Crusaders; technology and the all-seeing eye were enough to ensure total exposure.

This day, the meeting at the safe house was attended by Sage, Cai, Marlow, Grant, and La'Shell. They all sat around a kitchen table, sipping coffee and iced tea and engaging in small talk until Marlow officially began the meeting.

"Thanks, everyone, for coming. I know the last few weeks have been crazy, but I thought it was important to update everyone on where things were at and what the next steps will be." Marlow was all business as he spent the last few weeks dealing with the police and other authorities.

"First, I wanted to update you all on Hudson. The good news is he is recovering. His vitals are getting back to normal, and they will begin the deprogramming process soon."

"Hang on one second, they haven't begun deprogramming him yet?" Cai wanted to see the authentic Hudson, their Hudson.

La'Shell jumped in, "No, honey, they needed to get his body stabilized first and withdrawn from the drugs they were giving him; he was under extreme conditions of malnutrition and other ailments. They make their subjects weaker physically so they can control them mentally."

Marlow continued, "The deprogramming will take some time, most likely months or years. It's hard to tell how far gone he is, and we are not sure how honest he is being. They essentially had converted him into a cult member, and now we need to convert him back to being one of us. The good news is that this process is proven to work, but it will take time and effort from Hudson. He has to want to come back."

"When can we see him?" Sage was hurting. Hudson saved her life, and she wanted so much to hug him and tell him how much she loved and appreciated him.

Marlow shook his head side to side, "Not for a while, sorry. He needs to be brought back down to reality first. When the doctors feel like it's time for him to have visitors, you will be the first they call." He smiled at Sage sympathetically, "Maybe in a few months. Next up, the departing members of the Star Crusade. We lost about three-quarters of our membership from this botched operation. Yes, thanks to Cai and Hudson, it was successful, but it was a fluke. We were in over our heads, and that was all too clear."

"I feel horrible that we put people in danger. We should have known more about our opponents before undertaking such an aggressive operation," La'Shell replied.

"I agree. It was all about intelligence. We had bad intel, which caused us to overplay our hand," Grant inserted himself for the first time.

"Well, I don't blame people for quitting. The real question is, what is the mission of the remaining elements of the Crusade, if in fact we do continue? But let's talk about that after we finish debriefing the current situation." Marlow didn't want them to get sidetracked, like any good leader.

"The mission was successful, thanks to Cai's quick and decisive thinking, Hudson's silencing of Ricimer Beale, Grant's idea to create a make-shift megaphone from cardboard, and the general chaos and confusion caused by LaShell's idea to impersonate the police. It turned what would have been a dire situation into a total win. Saving Hudson without losing a life, other than that deviant monster Ricimer." Grant looked around the room earnestly. "Please pat yourselves on the back, we saved a life, and hopefully put a dent in a very sinister organization. I am sincerely impressed with you, especially the Serial Club. You have been amazing partners, and a partnership that I hope will continue and grow in the future." Marlow held up his coffee to cheer the Serial Club and Star Crusade partnership.

Both Cai and Sage were so flattered to be treated like and considered adults by these adults whom they respected so much. Their concern for Hudson quickly turned into pride for their role in the events.

"Let's go over next what happened with the enemy, and what the official response has been so far. Believe it or not, we are lucky they came and attacked the surveillance van and took Sage, as that was not on their property, and it was kidnapping. We have multiple witnesses, and it is a tight case; it's just questionable who actually kidnapped her. There were so many hooded and unknown figures throughout the night. But what we told the cops was that they took Sage, and that caused our members to converge on the house and ritual area in the woods to recover her. So that explains what we were doing there—nice and clean.

"The police investigated the ritual area and found the bone pit in the woods. It will be a massive police and federal operation to try to identify those remains. There were perhaps hundreds of sacrificed victims, dating back maybe hundreds of years, left to rot in that pit." Marlow was disgusted by the poor treatment of the most likely Christian dead. Those bodies deserved to be buried, not desecrated.

"The rest of the stage and statue were completely burned down, as well as much of that bone coffin. I am sure they will be able to get some DNA samples from it, and I would suspect that it was made from sacrifice victims, too. I would also, without grossing out everyone too much, assume that the Baphomet statue was, in fact, made with real hair and real skin. Human or goat, we will never know."

It was disgusting, but at this point, even though they were traumatized, Sage and Cai were also desensitized and numb. That these sick monsters used human bones, skin, and hair to make creepy effigies didn't surprise them one bit. Especially Cai, she saw everything that Sage was only hearing about. Who knows what else they did behind closed doors?

"After the cops found the human bone pit, that gave them the ability to get a search warrant for the Beale manor, as the pit and the ritual glade were both on the edge of their property in the deep woods. But by the time the cops got there, the house was pretty clean, with the place being wiped down and anything of criminal value being removed. They did find a network of tunnels below the house and into the woods, but that, while being suspicious, is not a crime.

"Before the police even got there, the Beale family was on a plane and headed to London; the kid Wick and his parents, Lord Faustus and his Lady Elizabeth. Their high-priced lawyers now shield them, and they will have to answer some questions from the UK. Do I think such a wealthy and connected couple will see justice in this case? I want to think so, but I have a feeling some fall guys will be coming. We fed a bunch of names to the police, and hopefully, it will trigger some criminal investigations.

"Some of the names we fed to the cops are important people. And that includes several very notable people we saw in person at the event who were trying to restrain Cai. The mayor of our fine town, caught red-handed manhandling her, has already resigned. He is going down, as the opposition will use this to rake him over the coals. I would expect criminal charges to be coming." Everyone felt very good about that. Who wanted some nutty pagan blood worshipper running the town?

"Next up is another good potential fall guy, Kelly Martin, TV woman extraordinaire, now not so much. She already has a horrible reputation as a woman who sold her kid out to cover up some bad PR. This is the final nail in the coffin of her career, and maybe a prison sentence along with the mayor.

"Finally, FBI special agent Dick Peters, with whom I had a run-in." Marlow rubbed his chin, which still hurt. "He has been put on paid leave pending an investigation, but I don't expect much in the way of punitive treatment. As everyone knows, the feds and police are heavily infiltrated by the various cults under the umbrella of the mystery religion. Whoever replaces Dick will surely be just as compromised and corrupt. So, we will hope for some exposure and punishment for him, and consider that a bunt for us.

"There are at least a dozen more names that we identified, but no confirmation from other witnesses at the scene. Given that there were at least a hundred people there, and the few we unmasked were all the elite of Old Springs society, the majority of those in attendance are still, and probably will remain, unidentified. But we can assume the rest were in equally impressive positions, using the apparatus of the state to drive and protect their sick blood rituals."

Marlow looked around and saw people looking a bit forlorn, perhaps feeling like they didn't entirely stop the occultist menace in its tracks.

"Listen up, everyone. What we accomplished is incredible. The Beales have been run out of the country, for now. That has never happened in their hundreds of years in the US. It's a public and private humiliation. Sometimes, for rich people, the best you get is humiliating them. We have probably sent the cult even deeper underground, at least for a while, and that is something no one has done in hundreds of years. In short, we have made a significant impact on their activities and worship, causing a PR nightmare for them and the family. This helps to elevate our cause in exposing criminal occultists, as the Beales are a high-profile target. So, in the end, while we may have lost a lot of followers, thankfully, no one on our side was mortally wounded.

"We can rebuild, if we want to. What say all of you? Should we continue? Not just as one organization, but as two? We both serve an essential function. The Serial Club researches and broadcasts on child abuse and serial killer cases, while we conduct investigative and operational work to bring these same people to justice. Also, we are over eighteen adults, and can access things and get around stuff you as minors cannot.

"If it is amiable to everyone in the room, we could continue operating as two separate groups while collaborating behind the scenes to pool resources and information. This, to me, makes a lot of sense. What say all of you?"

Marlow stood there waiting for others to acknowledge their desire to continue, only a few weeks after their tragic events. Cai and Sage felt guilty agreeing to anything without Hudson, whom they still considered their leader. But he was going to be laid up for months, maybe longer; it only made sense for them to keep the podcast and supporting machinery going until Hudson got back.

"I'm good with doing that, if it's ok with my mom?" Cai was the first to indicate a desire to continue the crusade they had begun.

La'Shell looked at her, then back to Marlow. "Why, you stinker, I knew you would work on her before I could talk to her about it."

Marlow grinned. "No, I presented it to the group as a whole; everyone has the opportunity to continue or not. What say all of you?"

"I'm in." La'Shell stood up out of her chair. "Anywhere my daughter goes, I go. Together forever, right, angel?" Cai couldn't have felt prouder and safer than at that moment.

Sage jumped up out of her chair, "I'm in too!" Sage had come too far and been through too much to give up now.

"You know I'm in, I don't think anyone else would want me anyhow." Grant's acerbic wit never missed.

Marlow looked around the room at each person, now delighted that the rebirth of their organization was going to happen.

"I want you all to join me in christening this new collaborative organization, one that researches, reports on, investigates, and holds accountable all those who would attack the decent populace with their occultist horrors, be they the serial killers they manufacture or other forms of terror and repression.

"How about we call this new organization," Marlow had to think only for a few seconds, "the Serial Crusade? What say you?"

Everyone shouted in unison, clicking their glasses together, "All hail the Serial Crusade!"

Chapter 46

It was several months later when Hudson was on a day pass during his recovery. He had been progressing so well that the doctors thought that time with his friends, planning for the future, would be of great benefit to him. The Serial Club, soon to be merged with the Star Crusade into the Serial Crusade, was in their old HQ, Hudson's bedroom, discussing how they would relaunch the podcast and what type of operational procedures they would establish with their new partners.

"Having these types of resources at our disposal will really take us to the next level as investigators." Hudson was visibly excited about joining up with the Star Crusade, something both Cai and Sage were pleased about. They worried for some time that they were undermining Hudson's leadership by agreeing to the partnership without him present.

"We now have real on-the-ground investigative support, with Grant being a licensed private investigator. Marlow is a serious intellectual and researcher, and his providing directive insights, along with what I glean, will be invaluable. And of course, La'Shell is all about grass-roots Christian community-based support. And if the Serial Crusade is going to succeed in our new, expanded mission, we're going to need broad support from the activist Christian community.

"Most importantly, we need to start educating Christians and others about the dangers of occultists in their communities. We need the right language and messaging to get this out of conspiracy theory land and into the world of evidence and facts. And as you both know, there is plenty of evidence of occult pagan conspiracy globally. We need to bring it out and make it consumable for the average Joe."

"I couldn't agree more, Hud," Cai, as a Christian, knew this message would resonate, if only they could make it palatable. "Christians get too hung up on end of days and Satan and all that stuff, but what they really need to understand is that these people they oppose are pagans, and they abuse and murder children to practice their occultist blood rituals. I feel like with the new podcast, educating and informing Christians about the occult needs to be priority number one."

"Agreed, I think we need to make sure the focus is on the elite too, not the random high-school kid practicing witchcraft." Sage was much savvier than people gave her credit for. "We saw who was at that blood ritual. The mayor, a leading newswoman, an FBI agent, the wealthy Beale family, in other words, the cream of the crop of our society. Their owned and controlled media apparatus likes to shine the light downstream on perpetrators; it will be our job to refocus it upstream on the real criminals running the show—the elite."

That was music to both Hudson and Cai's ears. They wanted to see the master criminals get their comeuppance. They knew, all too well from their already extensive experience dealing with the adult world, that these types of elitists rarely, if ever, saw any form of punishment. At best, it was usually humiliation and social exile, never jail time in an actual prison. They would find a few fall guys, like the mayor and Ms. Martin, and throw them under the bus, while the actual criminals that run the scam, the Beales, walk scot-free. It reminded Hudson of the Sackler family, who unleashed the opioid epidemic on the American public, only to walk away without any jail time, nary a slap on the wrist. At the same time, street-level minority drug dealers went away for life.

"What about Wick?" Sage wasn't going to let him disappear that easily. "I feel like we failed him. We wanted to get him away from that family and help him heal, and now they took him away, and we will probably never see him again."

"I feel the same way, Sage, but we couldn't kidnap him from his family." Cai knew they did what they could, and saving Hudson had to be enough. "They would have come after us with lawyers and money, and I don't think Wick would have supported running away anyhow. He is too deep in."

"From birth, that is how they breed their young and their serial killers." Hudson didn't want to talk about the Beales, but he knew he had to face it sooner or later. "Wick is programmed from birth to be what they want him to be, a serial killer. I was being programmed to be his fall guy, like Oswald was for the real JFK killers."

"I'll never understand how they can do that to their own kids?" Sage didn't get it at all.

"They use kids like commodities, tools, things to be exploited for the parents' benefit. They wrap it up in ritual and tradition as a way to provide moral justification to the parents for being monsters and users. Simple as that." Hudson was so disgusted by the Beales that he felt nothing but shame for ever idolizing them in any way.

Just then, there was a knock at the door. Hudson and his two partners in tow went downstairs to answer it.

Standing on their doorstep was a slightly overweight middle-aged man with a crumpled, untucked dress shirt, jeans, a five-o'clock shadow beard, and what looked like an old briefcase in his hand. He put his hand out and offered a greeting.

"Why hello, you three, nice meeting you!" He had a broad smile and looked genuinely excited to meet the Serial Club. "You don't know me, but my name is Brandon Levinson, and I am the owner of Apathy Production Studios, a film and TV production company. You must be Hudson, Cai, and Sage. It is wonderful to meet you in person!"

The kids looked at each other, and seeing as this guy was at least trying to be friendly and considerate, they were as well, and each shook his hand in turn.

He continued, "I am not here to waste your time, as I have nothing but respect for what you are all doing in terms of your investigations and podcast. And I also know that you just came through a very traumatic and difficult situation, and I in no way want to impose or impede on your recovery."

The Serial Club was listening; this Mr. Levinson was saying all the right things. Hopefully, he meant it. He never asked to talk to their parents, which was a win for him from their perspective.

"That being said, I do have a business proposal for you three. Briefly, I believe what you are doing would translate wonderfully into a feature-length movie, which is what I wanted to talk to you about. And that would be just to start, I could see this being a TV series, kids solving crimes about other kids and serial killers. It's perfect. Honestly, I think the story and its authenticity would translate well into video games, perhaps an entire franchise." Mr. Levinson got all amped up as he talked, creating a genuine sense of enthusiasm among the three young kids.

"You guys are amazing, and I believe the Serial Club brand could be leveraged into a multi-billion-dollar business for both my company and you guys. We would both benefit significantly from this."

Hudson liked that this guy was at least being honest about how he would benefit from it, not just painting it as some magical gift he was giving to the Serial Club. Hudson wasn't sure if he trusted him, and that was a good thing. If there was one thing Huson learned from his experience with Uncle Ricimer, master puppeteer, it was not to trust an adult who seemed knowledgeable and offered him golden prizes and secrets. Beware those who bear such gifts, Hudson reminded himself.

"Look, Mr. Levinson, that is very nice of you to say. But I am not sure we are interested in licensing our name for anything. We have a good little business here, and it's independent. No one tells us what to cover, and what we can and cannot say. Freedom and justice, not profit, that's what matters to us." He looked to both of his partners to make sure he was not speaking out of line for them, and they both nodded vigorously in the affirmative. This wasn't about fame and fortune for any of them. The Serial Club was made of more significant stuff.

Surprisingly, to Hudson, Mr. Levinson seemed to understand. "I hear you, Hudson, and I want you to know I am not in any way suggesting we use your name or have you do anything you would not normally do. I propose that we take what you are doing, as you are doing it, and, with your participation, translate it into another medium.

"In short, Hudson, Cai, and Sage, I want to give you complete creative control over your material. Keep doing your podcast, and we will make the Beale story into a feature-length film. You all will serve as creative consultants on the film and will retain complete story control, with the help of some screenwriters, of course."

Mr. Levinson, who was getting pretty excited himself, couldn't really get a read on these kids. They were stone-faced.

"Well, what do you think? Does that sound like something you would want to discuss further?" Mr. Levinson looked nervous, as if this were a deal he did not want to blow.

Hudson looked to Cai, then to Sage. Slowly, he looked back at Mr. Levinson.

"Come on in."

Hudson opened the door.

www.ingramcontent.com/pod-product-compliance
Lightning Source LLC
Chambersburg PA
CBHW020336180726
47991CB00020B/1724

Speak Your TRUTH

MARIE SOLEIL

Contents

To my Nova,
May you never hesitate to speak your truth.

Prologue

EIGHT YEARS AGO

I leaned into Lucas, feeling the warmth of his body pressed against my side. It was a welcome contrast to the cold, metal bleachers under my legs. A shiver ran through my body. Lucas sat frozen for a moment, his eyes darting over to me. I rested my head on his shoulder, watching the sun rise through the peach and pink clouds.

"I can't believe we stayed up all night," I whispered, trying not to break the sanctity of the moment.

Lucas chuckled under his breath and relaxed, leaning his body into mine. "Yeah, I never imagined my first all-nighter would be the night after high school graduation."

Adrenaline pulsed through my veins. Like Lucas, I had never been awake for twenty-four hours, either, and I was getting delirious. Maybe this next move was a little reckless, but I thought I was being bold. I sat up and looked Lucas in the eye.

"Lucas, you've been the best part of senior year for me," I said.

He swallowed, his Adam's apple bobbing in his throat. "I

feel the same way about you." Slowly, he took my hands in his trembling fingers. He kept his eyes on our locked hands, and my heart started racing. "I thought moving down here would be terrible, especially during senior year. But meeting you, and being your friend, has been incredible."

Taking my hand from his grasp, I gently rested it against his stubbled cheek. It was rough against my hand, but I didn't mind because my touch brought his eyes to meet mine. "I don't want to just be your friend," I said.

His eyes widened slightly, and he leaned into me, resting his forehead on mine. "I don't either."

This was it. My moment of truth. I closed the small gap between us and pressed my lips to his, maybe a little too hard and with puckered lips. It was my first kiss, after all. Eighteen years of fairy tale stories about princesses built up the anticipation for this moment. It was sweet, but out of nerves, I pulled back an inch after a gentle moment. Still, the electricity that passed between us was startling.

"Amy," he breathed, then took his hand and wrapped it around the back of my head, crashing his lips against mine.

I couldn't breathe, but only because it was the purest joy and love I had ever felt. He kissed me like I was his lifeline, and my heart beat out of my chest. Wrapping his other arm around my waist, he pulled me as close to him as possible. After a few moments of the most intense emotion I had experienced in my life, he slowly decreased the pressure and gently kissed my lips once, twice, three times. He leaned his forehead against mine again, breathing heavily.

"I'm in love with you," he sighed.

Tears sprang into my eyes. It was like my own fairy tale come true. "I love you, too, Lucas," I whispered.

He pecked my lips again, then pulled back. Uncertainty clouded his blue eyes. "Maybe...you should come with me to New York."

I pulled back. "Wait, what?"

He chuckled, emboldened and more sure of himself. He picked up a hand and pulled on a strand of my long, brown hair. "Come with me to New York. Forget about your parents. You can pursue your dreams with me, instead of worrying about what they want you to do."

Stunned, I looked back at the sun rising through the clouds. I tried to picture my life with Lucas, across the country from the only home I'd ever known here in southern California. A life away from my parents and their perpetual disappointment. A life where I could find my own passions and make my own way.

Terror coursed through me. What repercussions would come from my parents? From my brother, Scott? How would I even manage on my own?

Trembling, I shook my head and turned back to Lucas. "I can't. Not yet. I wish I could, but..." I trailed off, unable to find the words.

His eyes flickered back down to his hands, then up to the sky. "But what?"

"My parents...and my brother...I just have everything set up for me here. But that doesn't mean we can't—"

He shook his head slightly, his eyes sliding back down to his hands. "No, Amy. We can't."

"What? But we love each other!" I reached for his hand, desperate to stop him from the path he was following. "Lucas, come on."

He shook his head again, more determined this time.

"We'll be on opposite sides of the country, living separate lives. We'll drift apart. I saw what that did to my parents, and I don't want to go through that with you." His eyes turned back to mine, pleading with me. "Please, Amy. I'm begging you. Come with me. We'll have each other, and that's all that matters. We can figure out the rest together."

Hot tears welled up in my eyes for the second time, this time streaming down my cheeks. I shook my head to shake off the dread and despair that overwhelmed my senses. "I can't, Lucas."

He closed his eyes tightly, just for a moment. He held my face in both his hands and kissed me, fiercely and firmly, then pulled away. "I love you, Amethyst King. I hope I'll see you again."

He stood up and jumped down the bleachers. My body instantly missed his warmth and shook from the cold morning air. Or maybe it shook with the sobs that wrenched through my core. Either way, he was gone, and I was all alone.

One

NOW

Will I continue waking up at four every morning? The answer is a hard no. I definitely achieved some benefits, like a regular window for exercise and mindfulness, but the negative effects on my work productivity cannot be ignored. And being ready for bed at five is a major killer to my nightlife, even if that just means getting drinks with the girls after work. If you're a morning person, it's definitely worth a try! But I'll be reverting to my six A.M. wakeup (and getting the satisfaction of feeling like I'm sleeping in).

I clicked *save* and sighed with relief as I pulled my sweater a little tighter to fight the frigid office air. Another "thirty-day" article done for Women in the Workplace, the most prestigious blog with advice for women navigating today's business world. Although the past thirty days of waking up at four were not as difficult as the thirty days of drinking celery juice every morning (that was pretty disgusting), I was relieved to be done with this past month. It was always hard doing something out of my comfort zone, but in the end, my job performance had spoken for itself. My name was starting to become known, slowly but surely.

I sat back in my office chair and took in a deep yawn (did I mention that I'd been waking up at four for the last thirty days?), then settled in to proofread while picking at the split ends of my long brown hair. I wished I had worn my cute dress pants today instead of a pencil skirt. The cold air was on full blast today. My smart watch buzzed with a text alert from my best friend and roommate Ivy.

IVY

Girl! Google your name and celery juice!

A slight buzz ran through my body. My celery juice article had been up for about a week. Maybe it was picking up traction. A viral article would be worth the thirty days of digestive torture I had endured. With trepidation and shaky fingers, I pulled up my web browser and searched "Amethyst King celery juice." There it was, right at the top! I clicked my article on the Women in the Workplace blog and saw hundreds of comments.

"Holy biscuits," I breathed.

Wavy brown hair and copper skin popped over my cubicle partition. "What's going on?" Farah whispered.

"My celery juice article took off," I whispered back. "I thought the celery juice fad was over, but I guess not."

Farah giggled behind her hand. "How are the comments?"

I scrolled to the bottom and read a few. "Mixed, as I would have expected. Kind of a bummer."

"People online are brutal." Farah reached over and rubbed my shoulder. "In this world, any kind of comments are good for internet traffic. No wonder you're getting so much traction! We should check the Facebook page."

Since our company blocked Facebook on our work computers, I pulled out my phone and checked Facebook, getting more and more excited. There it was. My post on our company's page had been shared 3,000 times.

"That's amazing!" Farah said with a smile, but it didn't reach her eyes.

"Thank you, Farah," I said, meeting her eyes. "You never know which article will take off! I'm sure one of yours will go viral soon, too."

She smiled a little wider. "I appreciate it. Congrats!"

Farah waved as she disappeared back into her cubicle. I was really grateful to have a good friend at work, especially considering how cutthroat some of the others could be. I took in a deep, shaky breath, excited about what this could mean here at work. I texted Ivy quickly.

ME

I cannot believe it! Drinks tonight with Hannah to celebrate?

I glanced at the clock: 4:46. Only fourteen minutes left, so I figured I could start packing up now. I wasn't going to be very productive after that bit of news. Ivy's response came through then: *Yes! I'll make reservations at Mike's!* My mouth started watering already, thinking about our favorite restaurant right across from the beach in our small hometown of Canyon Cove.

With a small smile on my face, I placed the last of my items in my bag. *Click, click, click.* I heard the distinctive footsteps of our tiny but intimidating boss, Gia Lee, and I frantically unpacked the contents of my bag back onto my desk. She arrived at my cubicle as I had my sunglasses in my hand, and gave me a confused look.

"Is it too bright in here?" she asked.

I laughed, a little shrill. "Oh, you know, just...rearranging some stuff in my purse."

"Ah," she mused, nodding and glancing at the items sprawled across my desk. She didn't fall for it, but she moved on anyway. "Well, I wanted to congratulate you on your latest article! I hope you saw how well it's doing."

"Yes, thank you! I can't believe celery juice is creating such a stir."

Gia smiled. "You never know these days. People get all up in arms about interesting things. But there's no such thing as bad press, and your article is bringing tons of traffic to our site. We'll be able to reach so many more women now with our message."

I beamed. "That's great. I'm happy to help with your vision."

She tilted her head. "*Our* vision, Amy. It's not just about me."

I silently berated myself for that mistake. "Of course. *Our* vision."

"With articles like this, we're working one click at a time to bridge the gap between men and women in the business world." Her eyes gleamed with excitement. If she didn't have such a noble cause, she'd make an incredible villain. Or a dictator of a small country. Her drive and enthusiasm for her cause were almost frightening.

"I hope you're right!" I tried to match her fervor, but fell short. I could never get as excited as she did.

"I think this could mean great things for your future here. I have an article in mind that needs someone with full commitment, and I think you could really nail it."

I perked up. "Oh, really? What is it?"

She glanced at the clock. "It's almost five. Let's just wait until Monday. I still haven't fleshed it out completely. But it could really change the direction of the website and our company."

What in the world did that mean? Maybe she really was a villain in disguise. Celery juice was hard enough. What torture did she have in store for me now? But I had to put on a brave face. "Sounds good, Gia. Thank you!"

She waved as she walked away. "Enjoy your weekend! We'll talk first thing Monday morning."

I packed up my things without fear of reprimand, but a little less peppy than before. I really admired Gia. She truly wanted the best for all women in the business world—equality in both pay and treatment. And while I admired her thoroughly for it, that didn't necessarily mean it was my purpose. To be honest, my purpose was a whole lot less admirable. But parental approval can be a powerful force. Shaking my head, I cleared those thoughts from my mind and allowed myself to feel excitement over seeing my friends tonight.

Two

"Ah, there's our celery juice star!" Ivy's loud voice rang all the way from the entrance of Mike's. Ivy was one of the most energetic people I'd ever met. She was the perfect balance to my more laid-back personality. I went up on my tiptoes to see her hand frantically waving at me, her blond hair piled on top of her head in her signature bun. Short with long, lean muscles, she looked like a dancer wherever she went. And rightly so—she was the award-winning choreographer at our local dance studio, The OC Dance Project.

I gestured to the hostess that Ivy was calling to me, and she nodded me back. I wove my way through the crowd to the table where Ivy and Hannah were waiting for me. "Thank you, thank you," I said with a silly bow.

Ivy laughed out loud. "You are on fire! I'm so proud of you. By the way, my parents said that you should have juiced their celery instead of the junk at the grocery store. It would've been free and tasted better."

I wrinkled my nose. "I don't know about that. Their

produce is usually extra pungent. I've had their celery; it tasted like feet."

Ivy tilted her head, thinking. "Yeah, you might be right."

"How's their farm?" I asked.

"The summer veggies are coming in like crazy. I keep telling them to sell the extras, but they just want to give it away to friends and keep it as a hobby."

Ivy's parents, Brent and Rachel Jones, were the most lovely couple. I spent more time at their house in my high school years than at my own. They always wanted to have a plot of land with a farm, but that wasn't exactly feasible in our small town in southern California. Instead, they made do with what they had and created a microfarm in their suburban home, turning their front yard into a vegetable garden and their backyard a home for their chickens and mini goat. Ivy and her three younger sisters had the coolest childhood. And now that she had moved out, they made sure to load her down with extra produce to give away.

I turned to Hannah and gave her a hug. "Hey, Hannah! How was work today?"

Hannah gave me one of her quiet smiles. "Pretty good. I had very sweet patients today, and thankfully it wasn't too busy."

"Good, I'm glad," I said. Hannah was the direct opposite of Ivy. Delicate and petite, she had long black hair that was silky smooth and straight. She still lived at home with her parents, immigrants from Japan who taught her refined poise and manners. She was the image of perfection, with a heart of gold. It was only fitting that she was a nurse in the ICU, and everyone's favorite in the whole hospital.

I sat and looked over the menu, even though I always got

the same thing. "So, Hannah, how are the wedding plans going?"

She brightened. "Really good! Only three weeks to go, and I think we're basically ready." She fingered her engagement ring, a classic round solitaire. "Evan needs to get the guys fitted for their tuxes, and I have one last dress fitting left, but otherwise, most of the details have been completed."

"That's great!" I said. "You never hear of brides being so relaxed right before their wedding."

"Yeah, that's because Hannah is super organized and amazing." Ivy squeezed Hannah's arm. "And you have the best bridal party ever," she added with a wink.

Hannah laughed. "That's for sure."

"I still cannot wait to see your dress on you," I said. "You are going to look so stunning."

"Evan is definitely going to go crazy," Ivy added, wagging her eyebrows.

Hannah blushed. "Well, enough about my wedding," she said. "Tell us all about this article."

I sat up a little straighter. "I can't believe it's going viral. Kind of embarrassing that I was mostly talking about my bowel movements. I thought my article about dressing in business wear 24/7 was going to be more popular."

Ivy cackled with an evil grin. "I still remember you waking up in the mornings with your work skirt on. That was hilarious."

"Well, not hilarious enough for a viral post. I guess celery juicing is still a popular fad," I said.

"I'm really happy for you," Hannah said. "You've been working so hard. Have you told your parents yet?"

"No, I was going to wait until family dinner tomorrow. You know they don't have Facebook and I doubt they're googling 'celery juice' on a regular basis. But hopefully they'll be a little proud."

Ivy dramatically flopped her head on her arms. She hadn't even had a drink yet. "I still can't believe you care so much about what they think. You're a successful writer at a popular and renowned blog. You graduated top of your class in creative writing, got your MBA—"

"But not where it matters," I cut in. "You know it was USC or bust."

"Oh, they can get over themselves," Ivy said with a wave of her hand. "They're too much and you know it."

"Ivy, they paid my entire tuition," I reminded her. "I can't just ignore that. It was a lot of money."

Hannah asked softly, "Are you doing all of this for them? Do you really care about your job?"

"Of course I do!" I exclaimed. A few nearby customers' heads snapped over. Maybe I overcompensated. "I really like my job. I feel like I'm helping make a difference."

"I'm glad to hear that," Hannah said. "I would hate if you were killing yourself at your job just for your parents. I know you have a lot of extra talents and passions."

"Like what, calligraphy?" I asked. "That's just for fun."

Hannah gently touched my arm. "Amy, you are so talented. My wedding invitations were a work of art. You could really make something of that."

Ivy smooshed my cheeks. "Amethyst King, Hannah's right. The world is your oyster. Women in the Workplace is an awesome job, but you don't have to work there for anyone but yourself."

I shook myself free of Ivy's grasp. "Thanks, girls. You know I love you both, and your opinion means the world to me."

"But not as much as your parents'," Ivy sighed.

"You know what happened between my mom and Aunt Linda. If she won't speak to her own sister after her dog pooped on the rug, she'd disown me for following my own path." I shrugged, trying not to show how much their feelings affected me. "Well, Gia said she has some exciting new project for me to work on, but she won't tell me until Monday what it's all about."

Ivy's eyes widened. "Ooh, I can't wait to find out what this one is going to be. Maybe you're going to run a marathon."

I groaned. "Don't even joke about something like that."

Hannah laughed. "Or maybe you're going to volunteer somewhere. Like my hospital."

"That would be amazing," I agreed. "I'm dying of suspense, but I'll have to wait to find out."

The server came to get our order, which was a good time to switch topics. "So, Ivy, how's the dance team going?" I asked.

Ivy beamed, her eyes glowing with excitement. "So good! Their national competition is next month. They're going to kill it."

"Or they're going to blind the competition," I said. "You've been going crazy with the rhinestones."

"Don't knock it! The judges love the bling," she exclaimed. I guess she would know better than I did, but our kitchen table had been covered with the costumes for weeks and even I was having trouble seeing because of all those bright stones.

"Katy is so excited about her first national competition. It's all she would talk about today in rehearsal," Ivy added.

"I bet she gives you a hard time," Hannah said.

"Yeah, it's been a little rough coaching my little sister, but she's doing better than I expected. She brings the sass for sure," Ivy said. Ivy's youngest sister, Katy, gave her parents quite a surprise by being conceived seven years ago. Even though Ivy and her two other sisters were already in middle and high school, they all joined in and rallied around the newest member of the Jones family. She was a feisty little fireball who always said what she was thinking.

"Aw, I miss her," I sighed. "She's so fun."

"I'm babysitting her Monday evening. Maybe I'll just bring her to our place for dinner and you can hang out with her," Ivy suggested.

"Ooh, yay!" I clapped my hands with excitement.

We eventually ordered some food and passed the time laughing and catching up. After dinner and dessert, we headed down to the beach. It was a quick walk across the busy main street of Canyon Cove and onto the sand. Hannah and I linked arms as Ivy clicked away on her phone, probably messaging some dance mom. Soon we were on the sand. We dangled our shoes in one hand and walked slowly, listening to the waves crashing. A warm breeze was blowing, since it was the end of May, and we couldn't resist dipping our toes into the freezing water. No matter how warm it was outside, the water was always frigid.

I sighed. "There's nothing like the beach. I couldn't live anywhere else."

Ivy tilted her head. "I could live in the mountains. You know I love snowboarding. And it's just a couple hours from the beach. I could head over here if I needed to."

I opened my eyes in mock surprise. "Don't you dare leave me!"

She laughed. "I would never. It's just hypothetical."

"What about you, Hannah?" I asked.

Hannah paused for a moment to consider. "I do love the ocean. But I don't think I need it the way you do."

I nodded my head. "There's something about the sand in my toes and the sound of the waves that just...grounds me. I can think more clearly here."

Ivy slapped my arm playfully. "You should make a wall print with that line. That's pretty good."

I laughed and grabbed the foldable mat from my purse. I always carried it around for moments like this. You never knew when you needed to sit on the sand in work clothes. I spread it out on the sand, and it was just the right size for the three of us. We huddled together, enjoying the bright and beautiful moon reflecting on the waves below.

Ivy's phone buzzed, breaking the silence. "Oh, Lucas is going to come say hi!"

I blinked a few times, trying to rewind what she said. Did I hear that correctly?

Did she just say *Lucas?*

My head turned sharply in alarm. "What?"

Hannah looked at us. "I heard he came back to Canyon Cove. I haven't seen him since graduation."

"He's back? I didn't know about this." My breathing turned shallow.

"Yeah, I ran into him at the dance studio today," Ivy said

casually, avoiding my eyes. She was standing on treacherous ground, bringing Lucas here without warning me. "He wanted to see if we needed a piano accompanist for the ballet classes. I guess he's looking for work now that he's back home. He asked what I was doing tonight, and when I told him we were having dinner he said he'd love to see you... Both of you."

My pulse thumped in my ears. I was sure the girls could hear it over the roar of the waves.

"Maybe I should've warned you..." Ivy murmured. "I'm sorry. I thought ripping the bandage off would be easier than thinking about it all evening."

"You might be right," I admitted.

Hannah gave me a reassuring hug. "You'll be fine. You guys still talk, right?"

"Not since graduation," I said. Did Facebook stalking count? Probably not. I decided to keep that to myself. The last I knew, he was still in New York City teaching music at the local elementary schools. I had no idea he moved back home. I zoned out for a minute, flashing back to the first time I met him.

It was the first day of senior year, first period AP English. Ivy and Hannah were in different classes, and I knew some people in this class, but no one I knew well. I took a seat next to a boy I had never seen before. He was strikingly handsome, with blond hair that curled at the nape of his neck and the most incredible clear-blue eyes. His skin was perfectly sun-kissed. I would've bet my mom's wardrobe that he was a surfer.

"Hey, I'm Lucas," he said with an easy smile. "I just moved from NorCal."

"I'm Amy," I said. I pulled out my binder. He put his hand on the cover, and I jumped.

"What is that?" he asked.

Confused, I looked down at my binder. "What is what?"

"That writing. It's really cool."

"Oh, it's calligraphy. I'm just learning. Have you ever read The View from Saturday?"

"I love that book! About the kids and the trivia contest right?"

I grinned from ear to ear. Cute and well-read? This was too much. "Yeah, remember how Noah learns calligraphy? I always wanted to learn after I read that book. I've been teaching myself."

His eyes analyzed the writing, then peered deep into my own. I felt like he was reading my soul. "That's incredible. I love it." He reached into his binder and pulled out a piece of loose-leaf paper. "Do you think you could write this in calligraphy?"

I skimmed the paper. "Is this a poem? 'Rows of flowers on the ground, you're the coolest girl around'?"

"It's song lyrics. I want to be a songwriter. But it would be really cool if you could write these up for me."

"Okay, sure!" I exclaimed. I cleared my throat and tried again. "I mean, yeah, I should be able to do that. It would be good practice."

"Awesome." His smile lit up his whole face. "I think this is going to be the start of a beautiful friendship."

"Here, I'll invite Evan. It'll help break things up a little." Hannah's voice pulled me from my daydream, and she pulled out her phone to text her fiancé.

"When will Lucas be here?" I asked.

"He said he lives up the street, so just a few minutes," Ivy responded.

A few minutes? I wasn't surprised he chose to live next to the beach, but this did not give me enough time. My mind drifted off again, thinking about living on the beach with Lucas. How would things have been if he'd stayed here in Canyon Cove and we had tried to make things work? In the mornings, I'd watch him surf while I worked on calligraphy. And every evening, we'd watch the sunset snuggled up together.

Pull it back, Amy. What was it about Lucas that made me a lovesick puppy? I needed to remind myself that I was a twenty-six-year-old woman, not eighteen anymore. I took deep breaths in and out, trying to calm my nerves. I didn't want to look like a complete mess when Lucas showed up.

"There he is!" Ivy called.

Oh, biscuits. Too late.

Three

Lucas crossed the sand, guitar case in hand. I tried to get my first look at him in eight years without being a creeper.

Facebook stalking didn't do him justice. The light breeze blew his wavy, sandy blond hair that swept across his forehead and curled at the nape of his neck. But where he had been tall and lanky as a teenager, he was now fit and toned. His teal shirt fit him just right, showing the years of change in the best way. His forearm muscles strained under the weight of the guitar case, and I nearly fanned myself but held back before I completely embarrassed myself.

"Breathe," Ivy whispered at me.

"You better sleep with one eye open tonight," I whispered back.

Ivy's eyes widened as she barked out a laugh. She waved Lucas over and he set his guitar down next to our setup.

"Hey ladies," he said with an easy smile, his clear blue eyes lighting the way in the darkness of the night. He knelt down and reached for Hannah, giving her a warm hug. "Hannah! Congratulations on the wedding."

"Thank you, Lucas! It's so good to see you. Evan will be coming soon."

"That's great. I'd love to see him." Lucas turned to face me. "Hey, Ames," he said softly. He knew he was on treacherous ground.

I tried to paint a big smile on my face, then toned it down. *Act casual, Amy.* "Hey, Lucas. It's good to see you."

He reached for me and pulled me into a hug. My whole body zinged at his touch. It clearly never forgot the electricity that had passed eight years ago. He pulled away quickly, and my body sighed with disappointment. Maybe the last eight years had put enough of a hedge on his end.

"So, what are we up to?" Lucas asked as he sat back cross-legged.

"Well, tonight we were celebrating Amy's viral article," Ivy said, bumping her shoulder into mine.

"Oh, really?" His blue eyes pierced mine, his full attention on me.

I pulled my long, brown hair over my shoulder and started picking at the ends. I couldn't look at those eyes without getting lost. "Yeah, I write these articles for Women in the Workplace. It's a blog for businesswomen. I spent thirty days drinking celery juice and apparently it struck a chord with a lot of people."

Lucas laughed. "That's awesome!" He put his hand on my knee, and I looked back up at him. "You've always been a great writer. I'm happy for you."

"Thanks," I said with a smile. "What about you? I didn't even know you were coming back home."

Lucas brushed the sand with his fingers. "Yeah, New York was awesome, but it was time to come home. I really missed some things about here." His eyes flickered up to me for a second, and my heart skipped a beat. "Like...the beach," he added quickly.

"Are you living around here?" Hannah asked.

Lucas pointed toward Mike's. "Just up the street there. I'm living with Nate, remember him? He works in internet security now."

Ivy's eyes widened. Nate was Lucas's best friend in high school, but they made another hilarious pair of opposites. Where Lucas was a heartthrob with easy smiles, Nate was a classic nerd with a massive crush on Ivy.

"How could we forget?" I asked, choking back a laugh.

Lucas cleared his throat. "He's moved on, Ivy. Don't worry."

"I sure hope so," Ivy said with a straight face. "But living here must be awesome, even if it's with Nate."

"It is," he agreed. "I can walk down to the beach every morning and surf. It's pretty amazing."

Visions of Lucas surfing floated across my vision. I had to change the subject. "Ivy said you were at the dance studio today," I said.

"Yeah, I'm trying to find some work now that I'm home. The dance studio said they would love to have a piano accompanist for the ballet classes, so I'm going to start there. I have some private lessons in piano and guitar that should start up soon. And I'm still working on my songwriting. Being closer to LA might help me get some connections in the music industry, so I'm keeping my options open. My

YouTube channel is starting to get some traction, which is pretty cool."

My heart sank a little. I didn't know why I hoped that he would have found a stable, secure job that my parents would approve of. I knew he wasn't completely broke when he lived in New York, but my parents' expectations for whoever I chose to date and eventually marry were the same as they had always been. Which was the same reason why I never pursued anything long-lasting with Lucas in the first place.

Before I could say anything, Evan walked across the sand. Hannah squealed and ran up to him, dropping her usual poise and composure. She led Evan back to our spot, their hands joined as usual. Evan reached out and gave Lucas a fist bump. "Good to see you, man."

"Thanks, you too. I haven't seen you in a while. Didn't you graduate a few years before us?"

"Yeah, I'm the same age as Amy's brother, Scott. Hannah and I reconnected in college."

"That's great. Congratulations on the wedding. When is it?"

"Three more weeks." Hannah rested her hand on Evan's chest. "We can't wait." She looked up at Evan with a sparkle in her eye. "Didn't your college buddy just say that he's stuck in Africa and can't come? We can use his spot for Lucas!"

"I don't want to be a burden," Lucas said. "I know it costs a lot to have a person there."

Hannah waved her hand at him. "Not at all. It was already paid for. You'd be doing us a favor. We'd love to have you there." She looked over at Evan, and he nodded in confirmation.

"Well, in that case, I'd be honored to be there," Lucas said. "I love weddings."

My heart picked up again. Weddings were the best. I loved the lights, the music, the flowers all around, the cake, and most of all, I loved the love. A wedding for one of my best friends was bound to be my favorite of them all. But a wedding with Lucas there? Combine the romance in the air with the way I reacted to seeing him, and I was destined for major trouble.

Lucas took his guitar out of its case. "Anyone want some music?"

"Do you know Ed Sheeran's 'Perfect'?" Evan asked. "That's our wedding song."

Lucas strummed the first few chords on his guitar and nodded. Evan and Hannah settled in, Hannah between Evan's legs, her back against his chest. Lucas played the song and sang, while we all sat and enjoyed the sound of the crashing waves mingled with his amazing voice. He was already an incredible singer when we were eighteen, but now his voice had matured and deepened, and its smooth tones lulled me into the most confusing mix of relaxation and nervous energy. I didn't listen much to the lyrics, just studied his face with his eyes closed, fully absorbed in the music, his features lit by the moon. His jawline was marked with stubble, highlighting the perfect curve of his nose.

How on earth was I going to stay away from him? I wished I didn't have to worry about that, but my parents' expectations had been ingrained in me from a young age. Get a degree, a prestigious career, then marry someone with an equally impressive upbringing and lifestyle. I was still working on the career part, and Lucas's outlook on life didn't fit my parents' philosophies at all. I couldn't let myself give in to these feelings that I'd been suppressing.

I changed my focus to the crashing waves and tried to tighten my resolve. We could be friends. This would all work out.

Lucas finished the song, and we sat and chatted a bit more about our plans and lives. Around nine, I yawned and stretched. Lucas turned his attention to me.

"Tired?" he asked.

"Yeah, I've been waking up at four for the last month," I said.

"Another viral article?" he asked.

"Hopefully." I smiled. "Maybe a couple viral articles will make my parents proud."

His face sobered at the mention of my parents. He probably remembered our conversation on the night of graduation. "Do they know about this one yet?" he asked, a slight twinge of bitterness in his voice.

"I doubt it. But I'll see them and Scott tomorrow for our weekly family dinner," I said.

"Say hi to Scott for me. I always liked him." Lucas paused, tapping his fingers on his leg. "Any other plans this weekend?"

"Um, not really," I said. "I have to spend the day getting ready for dinner. Sunday will probably just be a day of recovering physically and emotionally." I giggled, a ball of nerves. *Pull it together!*

"Well, I'd love to grab lunch some time to catch up. I got a new number when I moved back home. Can you put your number in my phone?" He pulled his phone out of his pocket and handed it to me.

"Oh, sure." I typed in my name and number. "Same number since high school."

"That makes it easy." His eyes twinkled. He stood up, then held his hands out to help me up. I put my hands in his, feeling the calluses on his fingers from years of playing guitar and piano, and felt another jolt of electricity. I hopped up and pulled away quickly, rubbing my hands on my pants to hide my reaction to him.

"I'll see you around," I squeaked. Ivy looked up at me with a glint in her eyes. I glared at her until she calmed her face.

"I'll come home, too," she said. "It was so good to see you all."

We hugged and exchanged goodbyes, then headed home separately. As I drove in my car, I tried to forget the unsteadying effect that Lucas had on my body, and I touched my lips, remembering the morning eight years ago when we realized our lives were heading down different paths and there was no chance for us.

He was everything I wanted, but nothing I needed. He was kind, generous, and compassionate. But he never wanted any part in my parents' world. He didn't want to see them, be part of their social circles, or participate in any of their schemes. And I couldn't see my life without them, not when they had supported me all this way.

I drove home without thinking of the path, walked into my apartment, and crashed on my bed. I tried not to think about Lucas, my parents, work, or anything. I just wanted to sleep and pretend nothing was happening. Tomorrow would be a new day.

Four

I never thought sleeping in on a Saturday would mean waking up at six. But after thirty days of waking up at four, I felt incredibly rested. Ivy wouldn't be up until at least eight, so I decided to have a nice calligraphy session to myself. I made myself a cup of tea while Waffles, our gray cat, rubbed herself against my legs.

"Good morning, little lady." She purred as I petted her head. I relished every moment with her, my very first pet in my whole life. I grabbed my tea and supplies and headed over to the couch. Today was a brush pen kind of day. Sometimes I would get really involved and bust out the dip pen and bottle of ink, but I just wanted a snuggly morning on the couch. Waffles curled up next to me as I set my tea on the little purple table next to the couch.

Ivy let me have some fun decorating the apartment we rented in Park City, the town just outside of Canyon Cove. Park City was a cookie-cutter town, full of the perfect families and perfect businesspeople. Ivy wasn't thrilled about living here, but being the amazing best friend she was, she agreed to be close to my work. But when it came to decorating, I went crazy with rebelling against my parents' all-white ideals and couldn't wait to add color into our lives. The kitchen was all teal, including our stand mixer. The living room was bright yellow with splashes of purple. The couch was the coziest for watching a Hallmark movie, and we had the best royal purple throw blanket tossed over the edge. My mother would throw up if she ever saw our apartment, but thankfully it was beneath her to visit. I always came to her house, just like I would be doing for tonight's dinner.

I started slowly, practicing my basic strokes that were the building blocks for every letter in the alphabet. With my fingers used to the repetitive motions, my mind wandered to Lucas last night. You'd think eight years would have been enough to get over the guy. But seeing him last night brought all the feelings back. He was a distraction, and that worried me.

I tried to focus on the smooth feel of the pens against the paper and the varying pressure of my hand. After a few minutes of that, I flipped through my notebook and surveyed my previous projects, usually quotations from The Office. Half the fun of calligraphy was taking ridiculous quotations and making them beautiful.

Bears. Beets. Battlestar Galactica.

I just want to lie on the beach and eat hot dogs.

But other times, I liked to take truly meaningful words and let them speak through the calligraphy. There was one that I kept coming back to. The line Jim said to Pam when she worried she wasn't enough for him.

Not enough for me? You are everything.

I had attempted this line so many times, but never

seemed to capture the right feeling. I figured I'd give it another go. Using my pencil, I sketched out the letters to see if I could get it this time.

As I sketched, I thought again about the quotation. How would it feel to have someone say that to me? No matter who it was, I felt like I was never enough. I was never enough for my family, that's for sure. They never approved of my choices. I didn't take enough AP classes in high school, but Scott did. I didn't get into the right college, but Scott did. I majored in creative writing for my bachelor's. At least getting my MBA placated them for a period of time. My career was mildly acceptable, and getting a viral article would probably help. But they'd find something else to be disappointed in. That was the exact reason why I used Rent the Runway every time I had to go for a family dinner—I didn't make enough money to buy clothes that were acceptable, so it was easier to rent a designer dress for the night and make sure I had a different outfit (outrageously out of my budget).

I must have lost track of time, because the next thing I knew, Ivy's voice came from over my shoulder. "It's getting there."

I jumped, startling Waffles. "Gah! Next time, a little warning would be better than a creepy voice in my ear."

"I've been up making coffee for the last five minutes." She laughed, rubbing her eyes. "Didn't you smell it? Or hear me?"

"I guess not. Kind of lost in my thoughts," I said. "Just give me five more minutes and we'll get started on breakfast."

"Sounds good. I need some coffee and music anyway,"

she said. In true dancer fashion, she always wanted music and a beat to move to, even when she was half asleep. She turned on Britney Spears and danced around the kitchen. I looked down at my progress. It was almost there, but once again, "not enough." I snapped a quick picture and put it in my Instagram stories. My calligraphy account was doing surprisingly well. I had about 1500 followers, and sometimes they liked to see that my work wasn't perfect and sent encouraging messages back.

I sighed, picking up my supplies and putting them away on the bright purple shelf on the wall. So close, but still failing. It was like the story of my life.

"Stop being so disappointed. You're doing an amazing job," Ivy called from the kitchen, interrupting my thoughts. I had to love that she could practically read my mind, but it was a little annoying, too.

"It's just not good enough. But you're right, it's getting there." I tried to sound positive so she'd let it go. I must have been convincing, because she focused on making and eating breakfast.

We went our separate ways for the day—Ivy headed to her parents' house to help with the garden, and I spent the day getting ready for my family dinner. As expensive as it was, I still had fun getting all dolled up for the evening. I hated the pretense of my family's motivations, always trying to please other people, but I loved making myself feel beautiful. Unfortunately, there was always a damper on the festivities, because there would be something to criticize.

At 5:00, I unhooked my purse from its spot on the wall and gave myself one last look over in the full-length mirror we hung by the door. I was happy with the result overall—

my long brown hair had been blown out and curled softly at the edges. I had been practicing makeup to accent my plain brown eyes, and settled on a muted purple. I smoothed down my fitted black dress, the long sleeves helping elongate my look. It was classy and formal, my mother's favorite combination. Hopefully it would be enough.

I climbed into my car and drove the twenty minutes to my parents' house. The drive went too fast, and I pulled into the driveway before I was mentally prepared. I got out of my car and circled the ornate fountain in the front yard. The sound of the water in the fountain was more irritating than calming, and I wiped my sweaty palms on my dress, then remembered it would probably show on the fabric. My hands shook slightly, and I took a few deep breaths in and out to calm my nerves.

The huge glass and wrought iron door loomed ahead of me. One last deep breath, and my shaky hand rang the doorbell. You'd think I'd be used to this by now, but it was always overwhelming.

Marta came to the door. "Ms. Amethyst, I'm so happy to see you," she said. Her hair was graying now, still in a short, wavy bob. She was shorter than me and pleasantly plump, which made her hugs so comforting. Being wrapped in her arms reminded me of my childhood and the few good memories I had with her raising me. I was so glad my parents kept her on for cooking and cleaning.

She swung the door wide open. My mother had ordered a new chandelier for the grand entrance. The house was wide open, with a huge curving staircase to the right, and the kitchen was straight ahead. The smell of fresh roses wafted over me, a familiar scent from my childhood. Sometimes I wonder how I even survived in here at four years old without breaking every trinket and muddying up the perfect white floors.

Marta guided me left to the sitting room, where my family was gathered, waiting. Another open space, with ornate sofas that no one ever wanted to sit on. But we had to, because heaven forbid Ruby King's family sat together around the kitchen or in the living room. No. Guests had to sit in the sitting room until they were called to dinner.

At the end of the room was a white grand piano on a stage. Yes, a stage. And guess who played the piano in our family?

No one. Not one of the Kings played the piano.

It sat at the end of the room, dusted semiweekly by Marta, for no one to touch.

Well, no one except Lucas.

Our senior year of high school, we partnered on a project for English class, and I invited him over to our house. Lucas was awed, but what really got him excited was the beautiful piano. He walked to it slowly, gently touching the side panels.

"You have a Steinway Model B?" he asked. His voice quivered with reverence I had never heard applied to a musical instrument.

"I guess?" I said. "No one plays it. It's just for show."

"No one plays..." His voice faded out. "This is a travesty."

I laughed. "Not to my mother. It's the statement piece she needed in this room."

"Are people allowed to play?" he asked.

"I think so. Only Marta is home now, so it should be fine."

His eyes lit up as they met mine. He pulled out the bench, sat down, took a deep breath, and started to play Debussy's Clair de

Lune. It was the first time I had heard the piece live, and just those first few chords gave me chills.

"Amethyst! So glad you're finally here." My mother's voice brought me back to the present. I felt goosebumps on my arms from reliving his magical playing and silently thanked myself for wearing a long-sleeved dress.

Of course she would say I was *finally* here, even though I came right at 5:30. But in Ruby King's eyes, nothing I did was ever good enough. Especially when Scott had gotten here first.

Speaking of the devil, he stood up and came to give me a hug. "Hey, little sis," he said, ruffling my hair. I smiled tightly and smoothed my hair back down. I didn't pay for this blow-out to last only the first five minutes of seeing my family.

Dad leaned against the piano, talking to someone on his phone. He glanced my way and halfheartedly held up his hand in greeting. I returned the gesture, smoothed out my dress, and sat down on the rock-hard couch.

My mother's brown hair was in a sleek French twist, not a stray hair out of place. She wore a pale pink business suit, in the style of Jackie O. On the outside, my mother was the most elegant and classy woman I had ever met. But on the inside, there was a lot left to be desired. She had work done over the years, and her face had been pulled and filled to the point that she was not recognizable.

"It's good to see you, Mother," I said. She pursed her lips. "How's the Foundation work going?"

"Oh, just wonderful. We're going to put on a gala in four weeks. Lots of celebrities will be invited. It will be our best event to date."

I painted a smile on my face, just like she taught me.

"That sounds wonderful. I'm happy for you." Not really. But I had to be polite.

Scott took a sip of his drink—whiskey on the rocks, just like Dad. He looked a lot like our father did in his younger years: tall, dark, and perfect. Even objectively, I could agree that my brother was handsome, which wasn't really fair. I got to be average, and he got to look and act like a Greek god.

"And what about you, Amy?" Scott asked. "Anything new?"

"Yes, actually," I said happily, shifting in my seat with excitement.

"Stop wiggling," my mother scolded me.

I sat up straighter and put my hands on my lap. I looked over at my father, who was still on the phone. "I did want Dad to hear this, as well," I said hesitantly.

Scott glanced over at my father. "He should be done in a second. I'll tell you my news then—I've been promoted to partner!"

Well, biscuits. There goes my big news. Once again, Scott eclipsed my exciting news with something bigger for himself. Maybe I had a viral article, but that didn't mean I earned more money or a promotion. But Scott now would make more money, with a prestigious position—the most important things to my parents.

"That's great, Scott!" I tried to muster up as much fake enthusiasm as I could.

"Thanks, Ames," he said. He took a sip of his drink and casually sat back, crossing one foot over the other knee, with his arm on the back of his stiff seat. I slumped down in my chair, disappointed again.

"Yes, we're so proud of you, Scott." My mother beamed.

He was her pride and joy, the one to carry the King name to Mount Olympus so everyone knew what a success her family was.

"What are we proud of Scott for?" asked my father.

"My promotion," Scott said.

"Ah, yes. I heard about that from Nicholas," he said. As in Nicholas Taylor, the president and owner of Nicholas Taylor Investment Banking. Husband of Rhonda Taylor, from the True Trophy Wives of Orange County television show. My father and Nicholas were golf buddies, which had helped Scott secure the position in the first place. But Scott had proven himself to be the employee they all envisioned and worked his way up on his own merit.

I had a hard time being angry with Scott. It wasn't necessarily his fault that he was perfect. But every time I had something to be proud of, he had already one-upped me. It was impossible living in his shadow.

"Well, Amy had something to share, too," Scott said. *Thanks, Scott. Perfect timing.*

I channeled my proudest self. "Yes, I was excited to tell you all. I've had an article do very well. It's driving a lot of traffic to the website and has been shared on Facebook over 5,000 times."

"That sounds...exciting," my mother said flatly.

"Did you get a promotion?" asked my father.

"Um, possibly," I fibbed. Hopefully Gia would include something about that in our meeting on Monday. "I have a new special assignment coming up."

"Hopefully that will lead to a raise, then," he said. "Maybe you can move out of that place you have with Fern and get your own apartment."

I furrowed my brows. "Fern?" I asked. "Do you mean Ivy?"

He waved his hand, ignoring my question and ending the conversation. He pulled out his phone and started checking the news. My mother took a sip of her wine, and Scott shrugged at me.

Well, that was disappointing.

Marta came in and told us dinner was ready. We walked silently to the twelve-person dining table, my father at the head and Scott to his right. My mother sat on the other side of my father, and I sat next to her. Eight empty seats greeted us, but enough food filled the table for twenty. My setting was accented with a glass of red wine, which I hated but pretended to enjoy, because that's what I was supposed to do.

We ate our meal, with my father and Scott talking about business and my mother chiming in with people she knew who were related to the businessmen they mentioned. I stayed quiet, with nothing really to add to the conversation.

"Oh, Amethyst, I almost forgot to tell you. I ran into Ethan yesterday," my mother said to me.

I choked on my wine. My mother glared at my impeccable table manners. I already couldn't stand the taste of wine, and any mention of Ethan Taylor (son of Nicholas and Rhonda Taylor) made me want to vomit. He was exactly what my mother would have loved in a child—the image of perfection, with a heart of ice. "That's nice," I said, even though it was anything but that.

"Yes, he said something about you and celery juice. I couldn't really understand what he was talking about."

Sigh. He was most likely mocking my article and its "success," but my mother didn't understand if it didn't involve lots of money and appearances.

"I gave him your phone number. He said he'd like to take you out sometime," she added casually.

My eyes widened. "I highly doubt that," I said.

She narrowed her eyes at me. "Ethan is successful and influential. You would do well to go out with him."

I neutralized my facial expression and looked back at my plate. "Yes, Mother," I said. I doubted he would contact me, anyway.

She changed the conversation back to my father and brother, more chatting about the gala and how beautiful and expensive it would be. The more I sat there, the more I felt like I was dying inside, but I stayed and finished the conversation. As soon as we were done with dinner, my mother gestured everyone to retire to the sitting room for coffee and dessert.

"You know what? I'm not feeling very well. I think I need to go home and rest," I said. Being around my family always made me sick, and the thought of Ethan having my phone number made it worse.

"Fine," my mother replied with a straight face. "We'll see you at dinner in two weeks." She leaned in for air kisses and a faux hug. I reciprocated, said goodbye to my father, and gave Scott a halfhearted hug.

"Sorry about earlier," he said. "I didn't mean to steal your thunder."

My frustration with him deflated like a balloon. I knew he wasn't trying to make me look like a failure in my parents' eyes, but he definitely wasn't helping. "It's not your fault that I suck," I told him.

He pulled back but held onto my shoulders. "You don't suck," he said firmly.

I rolled my eyes, trying to hide the tears that formed. "Okay, big brother. Thanks for the pep talk."

He dropped his hands, shifting uncomfortably. He didn't do well with emotional discussions, something he inherited from my father. "Your time will come, Ames. You'll see."

I shrugged, ready to change the subject. "I almost forgot," I added. "Lucas Carter is back home. He said to say hi to you."

Scott narrowed his eyes. "I hope you're not getting any ideas about him, Amy. I know that was hard for you senior year."

I shook my head. "It won't be a problem. I know how Dad and Mother feel about him."

He nodded and patted my arm one more time. "Good. I'll see you later."

I drove home in silence, repeating my determination. I had to keep trying. I was almost there. Monday would come, and I'd have a new assignment that would change everything.

I hoped.

$Five$

"Amy, it's time to get up!" Ivy's frantic voice rang through my door.

I rolled over in alarm and checked my phone. It was 7:45 on Monday morning, and I needed to be at work at eight. "Oh, biscuits. Thank you, Ivy!" I shouted back at her. Apparently my body was still in recovery mode after thirty days of waking up at four. Besides, I had stayed up way too late the night before. I tried to keep Lucas out of my mind, but failed miserably, especially when he texted me Sunday evening.

LUCAS

Hey Ames. It was so good seeing you again yesterday. I'm really proud of you for your article. How was dinner with your family?

It was so hard to write back without giving away any feelings, but I remembered what Scott said and kept it friendly and neutral.

ME

Hey! It was great seeing you, too. Family dinner was the same as usual, a bit of a disappointment. But it's all good.

Hoping he wouldn't text back (but at the same time hoping he would), my mind raced through my memories of him. All the classes in senior year where he passed me copies of the lyrics he was working on and asked me to draw in calligraphy. I pulled up his YouTube channel on my laptop and checked for any new songs. He hadn't posted anything in the last few weeks, which meant my secret collection of his beautiful words was up to date. My phone buzzed again.

LUCAS

I'm sorry to hear that. Hopefully, I'll give you something to smile about when we have lunch this week.

I pressed my phone to my chest and leaned my head back on the couch. This boy was trouble. He always was. So I spent the rest of the night rewatching his old videos and allowing myself to fully enjoy his incredible music, without worry of what anyone else would think or say.

But now I was late for work, so I sprinted to the bathroom, brushed my teeth and did the fastest makeup of my life. I pulled my long brown hair into a messy bun on top of my head, threw on my easiest work clothes (black slacks and a green long-sleeved sweater), and bolted out of the door. I glanced down at my phone: 7:52. Thankfully we lived one street from my office, so I would be able to make it only a few minutes after eight. On my lock screen, I saw a text from an unknown number, and just glancing at it, I saw the words "Ethan Taylor" and "celery juice."

"Ugh!" I groaned out loud.

"Is everything okay?" Ivy peeked her head out of her bedroom. She didn't have work today, but it was a miracle that she was awake to get me out of bed.

"Ethan flipping Taylor. But I can't deal with this now," I said.

"Oh, girl. We will definitely discuss later. Dinner with Katy tonight, remember?"

"Yes, I can't wait. Your little sister always cheers me up." I blew her air kisses and ran out of the apartment. Of all the days to be late, it had to be the day that Gia had a planned meeting with me. I could only hope that she wouldn't be looking for me right at eight.

I made it to the office in record time. I still had to park in the parking structure, walk to my building, and take the elevator up to the eighth floor. When I walked into the office, the clock above the door read 8:10. Not terrible. I scurried back to my desk and Farah waved me over.

"Hey," she whispered. "Gia asked if anyone had seen you yet."

"I should've known," I whispered back. "I slept in."

Farah giggled behind her hand. "You probably needed it. I wonder how many hours you missed from the last month."

I sighed. "Let's see what new torture she has in store for me. Thanks for letting me know."

She waved with a smile, and I headed to my cubicle to set my things down. The second I was settled, Gia appeared. She popped her head up over my cubicle partition and smiled when she saw me.

"Amy, I've been looking all over for you," she said.

"I must have just missed you," I said quickly.

She hummed. "At least I found you now. Come to my office and we'll talk about your new project."

I followed her to her huge and spacious room, with huge windows overlooking Park City. Not that there was much to see. Even though we were only eight miles from the beach, it looked like any other corporate city. Gia's awards covered her walls; she had accomplished a lot for the sake of women in business and was well acclaimed for her efforts. Her desk was huge, with three computer monitors and a well-kept orchid in a pot. I could never keep those things alive.

"Have a seat," she said. Unlike my parents, she had super comfortable chairs. I had to hand it to her: at least she had an appreciation for the comfort of your seat.

"So what is this new assignment?" I asked. "Regular exercise? Or drinking more water?"

"I had a more mental exercise in mind this time," she said. "I've been waiting for this particular assignment, because I think it needs someone who has the skill to write another article that will have an impact. And with your celery juice article, you've proven that you have the skill to write something that people will read and think about."

I started to get those cold sweats, the ones that send shivers down your spine. The ones that come from the combination of freezing cold air and intense nerves. I only hoped my underarm sweat wasn't showing.

"Can I ask you something?" she asked suddenly, sitting forward in her chair and clasping her hands together on the desk. Visions of Gia as a tiny dictator started running through my head again, a map on her desk with tiny figurines that she moved around as she plotted battles.

"Um, sure," I said.

"What are you thinking right now?" she asked.

I hesitated. "I think that I'm really excited about this opportunity."

"That's not what you're really thinking. Tell me what you're *really* thinking."

What in the world? My hands started to shake a little. I didn't like telling people my exact thoughts. My mother had trained me to always put on a calm, collected front, no matter what. But this was my boss, so I had to answer. "I…I think that I'm a little scared of what exactly you're asking me to do, and I'm not sure I'll be able to live up to your expectations."

"Exactly." She sat back in her chair with a big grin on her face, like she had finished her proof. "As women, we hesitate to speak our minds. To speak our truth. We're so worried about what others will think that we lie or sugarcoat our true feelings."

"I wasn't lying," I protested, worried that she was trying to trap me.

"No, I wasn't implying that," she said with care. "But that's exactly what I'm getting at. We subconsciously hide our truth because we worry that we'll hurt our image or hurt others' feelings. And I want you to do the opposite of that."

"The opposite?" I repeated. This sounded dangerous.

"Yes. For thirty days, I want you to speak your truth. If you're asked what you're thinking, you have to answer truthfully. Give your honest opinion and feelings. And at the end of the thirty days, you can write about what it has done for your relationships and your work life."

Stunned, I wasn't sure what to say. This wasn't just celery juice or waking up early. This would change my whole life. "Oh, Gia," I said. "I don't know if you understand what you're asking me to do. My family…" Lucas…

She sat forward again, with sympathy in her eyes. "I do understand. This could make or break certain relationships. But don't you think it's important to have relationships that are built on honesty and truth? If you're never able to reveal your true self, do you think they are relationships worth keeping?"

I didn't think she understood my family. Honesty and truth didn't matter one bit to them. "I get what you're saying, but I'm not sure I'm the right person for this."

"I know it's daunting. Just think about it for today. You don't have to give me an answer yet. But Amy, I *know* you're the right person for this one. You have the skill and the ability to implement consistent changes in your life. I truly think you are the best for this assignment, and you'll do a fabulous job." She paused. "And if this article does as well as the last one, I think there may be a promotion in store for you."

"A promotion?" I repeated. She must have thought I was so dumb.

She smiled at me. "Someone with your skill should be writing articles more meaningful than 'Thirty Days of Drinking Celery Juice.' We can consider this a trial assignment."

That changed things. Maybe it would be worth the effect

on my relationships for the sake of my career. I stood up. "I will definitely get back to you tomorrow with my decision."

"Thanks, Amy," she said, standing as well. She walked around her desk to pat my shoulder, which felt awkward with her tiny size, but I appreciated the gesture. I walked out the door and back to my cubicle in a slight daze. I sat in silence for a few minutes.

Farah popped over the top. "Hey. You look upset."

I shook myself from my daze. "Gia just offered me another assignment...but I'm not sure I want to take it."

"I have to know what this one is," she said. She came around and sat on my desk. "Spill. You look like you need to discuss."

I turned my chair to face her. "She wants me to say exactly what's on my mind for the next thirty days."

Farah laughed. "Wait, what? Is that really so bad?"

"You have no idea what goes on in my head most of the time."

Farah's eyes widened. "Oh..."

"Nothing about you! I swear!" I exclaimed. I was already getting myself into trouble. "I'm mostly thinking about my family." And Lucas.

She drummed her fingers on my cubicle partition, looking off into the distance. "I guess I can see where you're coming from."

I sighed. "I just don't know if I can manage changing up my life like that. It could ruin relationships."

"Are those relationships worth keeping?" Farah asked.

"That's basically what Gia implied. I think she wants me to shake my life up a bit."

Farah nodded thoughtfully. "That's really tricky. I have to admit, I can't wait to see what happens when you do it."

"When?" I repeated. "I haven't decided if I'm going to do it."

"Oh, you will," she said with confidence. "I know you want to make your parents happy, and this will be another viral article."

"If only they cared about the last one," I muttered. But then again, maybe Farah was right. The last article was about celery juice. If I wrote something with more substance and full of emotion, maybe I would have something to be proud of.

Farah gave me a quick squeeze on the shoulder as she disappeared back into her cubicle. I decided to put off thinking about the new assignment and focus on editing last week's article about waking up at four. Thank goodness that assignment was over.

That was the point, right? It was only thirty days. Maybe I could repair any relationships that were affected after the thirty days were over. Like on The Office, when Pam finds out that Jim had a crush on her, and he played it off like it was in the past, but not that second (even though it was). Maybe I could make this work.

I busied myself with the first draft of my article, reading through and making edits. Before I knew it, the morning was over. I checked my phone to see if I had any calendar invites for lunch and saw the unopened text again from Ethan. Ugh. Time to face reality, I guess.

Hey Amethyst.

He would use my full name, even though hardly anyone called me that.

> I ran into your mother last week. She's such a lovely woman.

That was already a point in the wrong direction.

> I would love to take you out to dinner and tell you about my latest accomplishments.

Seriously? That's his pickup line?

> How's dinner this Saturday at 8 pm?

That was a little late for this grandma.

> I'll pick you up and we can go to Magistra's. Don't worry, I'll cover the tab.

The nerve to imply that I couldn't afford a dinner at Magistra's! Granted, he was right. I couldn't spend seventy dollars on a steak, and then pay for sides separately, but that had to be the worst text I'd ever received asking me out.

What choice did I have, though? My mother would absolutely flip her lid once she found out that I said no. I'd have to go and hope that my personality would be enough to turn him away.

I paused, thinking about Gia's assignment. If I decided to accept, what would that mean for a situation like this? Would I have to write him back and say, "No way, buddy"? Maybe it wouldn't be so bad to have an excuse to speak my mind.

Regardless, I hadn't accepted the assignment yet. And current Amy would say yes. I texted him back.

> Hi Ethan! Nice to hear from you. Dinner on Saturday sounds great.

Great? That was definitely a lie. Oh, well.

He texted back a minute later.

> Fantastic! Send me your address and I'll see you then. Make sure you're ready right at 7:30, I don't want to be late for our reservations.

Ugh. So demanding. And I was never late. Well, except for this morning.

I slunk back in my seat and closed my eyes. What a weird week this was turning out to be.

Six

I walked into my apartment to the smell of fajitas on the stove. "Hey ladies! I'm home!"

A tiny blonde rushed over to me. "Hi Amy! I'm Katy. Katy with a Y."

I gave a confused look over her tiny blond head to Ivy cooking in the kitchen. She smiled. "My parents just showed her the original Anne of Green Gables movie. She found a *kindred spirit* in Anne, especially how she makes sure to tell everyone that her name is 'Anne with an E'."

I laughed, remembering when Ivy had first shown me that movie. I could see why Katy loved Anne's character. She was feisty and opinionated, just like Katy. "Well, Katy with a Y, I'm so happy you're here this evening. What are your parents doing tonight?"

"They have a date night," she replied.

"On a Monday?" I looked at Ivy again for clarification.

"When you have four kids, you take a date night whenever you can get one," Ivy explained.

"I guess that makes sense," I conceded. "So what did you two do this afternoon?"

"We got our nails done!" Katy flashed her hands in front of me. Each nail was painted a different color, with a rainbow on her thumbs. She started taking off her socks. "My toes too! Ivy let me do whatever I wanted."

"The nail technicians were very amused by her," Ivy added. "She was very sweet, but she made sure to tell them when they used the wrong shade."

"Well, it had to be right! And now I love them!" Katy exclaimed.

"Silly girl," I said, smoothing her hair. "It's a good thing everyone who meets you loves you." I walked towards the kitchen, a big whiff of spices and chicken leading the way. "Dinner smells amazing," I told Ivy.

"Thanks," she said. "It's basically done, chicken fajitas with black beans. Not pinto. Katy did not want pinto beans."

Katy shrugged and skipped to help her sister set the table. "Pinto beans are gross."

"Katy girl!" I laughed. "You have to give your sister a break. She's making a delicious dinner for us."

Katy would have no problem fulfilling my assignment; she already lived her whole life speaking her truth. What would I have done at her age? I wouldn't have said anything, and would have just skipped the beans. Or my mother would have forced me to scarf them down.

Ivy and Katy set the food on the table and we settled in. "So, do I get to finally hear about this mysterious assignment?" she asked.

I sighed. "It's not what I expected. But I did want to discuss it with you tonight."

"Spill," she said, with a mouth full of fajitas.

I sighed. "Gia wants me to say exactly what I think, to anyone who asks, for thirty days."

Ivy spat out a laugh, and some food flew out of her mouth. "Ew, gross. Sorry about that. But that doesn't sound so terrible. You're acting like someone ran over Waffles."

I gave her a blank stare. "Come on, you know it's going to be impossible for me to do this around my parents."

Ivy's eyes widened as she realized the implications. "And Lucas..."

I motioned towards Katy and gave Ivy a quick "Shh!"

"Amy. We all know you're in love with him." Katy said as she took a bite of her beans.

"Katy!" I exclaimed. "How on earth would you know anything about that?" I turned sharply to Ivy.

Ivy had the decency to look bashful. "I may have mentioned to my parents that he was back in town, and the conversation went a certain way..." She let her voice trail off, then stuffed her mouth with chicken and gave me a shrug and a grin.

I put my fork down and sat back in my chair. "This is so embarrassing. Katy, please tell me you won't say anything to him."

"Of course not. I'm only seven," she said casually.

"Maybe it won't be as bad as you think," Ivy said. "When do you have to make your decision?"

"Gia wants me to give her my answer tomorrow."

Ivy set her food down. "Okay, here's what I think. Let's test it out. You can say whatever is on your mind all night tonight. And if I still love you, then you have to do it."

"That's not fair! You promised that you'd love me forever, no matter how awful I am."

"I never agreed to anything like that. But I think this is the perfect testing ground."

I rubbed my forehead. A trial run might not be the worst idea. Then I'd have something concrete to base my decision on. And Ivy and Katy were probably the least likely of all my acquaintances to get their feelings hurt. "Ok, fine. We'll try it out tonight."

"Yay!" Katy said. "I'll help you. I always say what I'm thinking."

Maybe she was right. I could learn a few things from her.

Ivy's eyes twinkled with mischief. "So, Amy, what do you think of the dinner?"

"It's delicious!" I said. That was easy.

"Hmm...how do you like my nails?" she held up her hand. She had painted her nails lime green with yellow polka dots. Very Ivy.

"They're very 'Ivy'," I said.

"That's not what I asked. How do *you* like them?"

I sighed. "I don't love them."

Ivy hummed. "I guess I'll take that."

Katy chimed in. "What about my nails?"

"I love them on you."

Katy shook her head. "No. I want the same thing you said to Ivy."

I laughed. "I really do love them on you! It's not the choice I would make for myself, but I think they're perfect for you."

Satisfied, Katy beamed and went back to her food.

Ivy kept chewing and staring at me, like she was trying to

come up with a trap for me. She looked around our apartment, then grinned. "What do you think of the dance costumes I'm working on?"

I smirked at my friend. "I think you already know how I feel about them."

"That should make this easier."

"Fine. I'm glad the judges like them, but they're way too sparkly. And too mature for the girls' age."

Katy gasped. "Amy! You don't like the costumes?"

Biscuits. These were Katy's costumes, too. "Sorry, Katy girl. But I don't dance or coach like your big sister, and she knows exactly what she's doing. I'm just giving my opinion."

She eyed me warily. "Then you're wrong."

"Maybe." *Crisis averted.*

"Don't worry, Katy," Ivy said. "I win a special costuming award every year. Amy will come around." She winked at her sister, then went for the fun stuff. "All right, Amy. What do you think of Lucas?"

I glared at her. "I think I don't want to talk about it."

"Too bad. It's just practice. Besides, Katy and I already know. You just have to vocalize it now."

"I've never actually put it into words. I don't let myself think about it. It's not an option."

"Okay, let's try this a different way. Let's say an alien came right here to this apartment and said, 'Hey. I heard you have this friend, Lucas. Tell me about him before I go back to my spaceship and never come back to Earth again.' What would you say?"

"You're ridiculous," I said, shaking my head. "But fine, I'll play." I paused for a second and played with the ends of my hair. I pulled up the memory of Lucas in my mind, smiling at me and playing the piano in the sitting room. "Lucas is the best-looking guy I've ever seen. His hair is perfectly golden, his eyes are crystal blue, but the best part is that you can see his joy through them. I don't know that I've ever met someone who is so genuinely happy. He loves life and he follows his passions. He's considerate, thinks of others before himself, and wants to share his joy through music." I looked down and pushed my food around my plate. "I don't think there's anyone I'll ever love the way I loved him." I looked back up. "How was that?"

Katy and Ivy both stared at me with wide eyes. "Yowza," Katy said.

Ivy glanced at her sister before looking back at me. "Okay, I knew you had a crush on him, but I didn't know it ran so deep."

I laughed sarcastically. "Well, you asked!"

"Did you ever try to talk to him about this?" Katy asked. *Was she really only seven years old?*

I flicked my eyes over to Ivy, who knew what happened between Lucas and me that morning after graduation. "Uh, kind of. But there's no way my parents would ever approve of him. It's pointless. I just keep trying to move on, but no one compares. And instead, I get to go on dates with Ethan Taylor."

"Whoa, whoa, back up!" Ivy sat back and waved her hands at me. "Since when are you going on a date with Ethan Taylor?"

I pulled out my phone and showed her the texts. Ivy's eyes gleamed with laughter. "What is wrong with you?" she asked. "This is the worst idea ever. He's the biggest narcissist I've ever met!"

"My mother ran into him last week and apparently he knew about my celery juice article, but she had no idea what he meant. He must have seemed somewhat complimentary, because she gave him my number."

Ivy set my phone down on the table and fixed me with a steely gaze. "If you take the assignment, you're going to have to tell him exactly what you think. The whole night."

I reached back across the table for my phone and nodded slowly. I flipped the phone around in my fingers. Telling Ethan what I thought could spell disaster.

Ivy clapped her hands. "It's decided. You're taking the assignment!"

I laughed out loud. "And why is that?"

"Someone needs to set Ethan in his place. I can't wait to hear how this all goes." She tapped her fork on her plate like the decision was official.

I rolled my eyes but smiled. The good news was that I didn't care for Ethan, so a bad date with him wasn't the worst idea in the world. I could tell my mother that I went, and she would just be disappointed in my inability to secure a second date. Not that she would be surprised, though.

I stood up and cleared the plates, since everyone was done. While I washed the dishes, Ivy sent Katy to go draw a picture and stood by me at the sink. "So, what are you most worried about happening?" she asked quietly.

I slowly scrubbed a plate, trying to formulate my words. "With you, Ivy, it's not hard to speak my mind. I basically already do. You got the worst thing out of me when you asked about Lucas, but everything else I feel is pretty much open to you. I do worry about my relationship with Lucas, but I might be able to spin that to protect myself. But my parents...I don't know if there's any way to protect that relationship. And I don't know if I can risk that right now."

Ivy nodded. "I can't say I understand why you need to protect that relationship. But it would be a risk."

I turned off the water and faced Ivy. "I know they're not the most loving and supportive parents. But they're still my parents, and I want to make them proud."

She drummed her fingers on the counter, thinking. "Well, maybe you can make it work. Maybe you can train your thoughts from now until the next time you see them, so you can still say what's on your mind but not say anything that will get you in trouble."

I considered her suggestion. "That might work."

"Okay!" Ivy said, with a slap on the counter. "You can do this! I think it's going to be so good for you."

I wiped my hands on the nearby towel. I felt like I was going to throw up. Although I wasn't shy and reserved like Hannah, I still had a protective wall around my thoughts and heart. I wasn't sure I'd come out whole at the end of these thirty days. I looked at Ivy, and she knew right away how anxious I was feeling. She wrapped me up in a big hug. "You can totally do this. I believe in you."

If only my parents felt the same way. I squeezed her tight. "You're the best, best friend. Thank you."

She smooshed my cheeks. "I've got your back, always." She glanced over at Katy, who was absorbed in tracing her hands and recreating her manicure on a piece of paper. "My parents will be here soon to pick her up."

"I want to craft with her. How much longer do we have?" I asked.

She checked her watch. "About ten more minutes, so that's perfect," she said. "I'll get her things together."

I walked over to where Katy sat on the couch. "Can I sit with you?" I asked.

"Yes!" She patted the spot next to her. "Are you going to do your fancy writing?"

I smiled. "Yes, I wanted to work on something, too." I pulled out my supplies from the shelf and sat next to her. Using my pencil, I sketched the words, "Speak Your Truth." I added bounces and flourishes, and when I was satisfied, I took out my brush pens. Katy sat watching, mesmerized. "I love when you do this."

I smiled at her. "I think you're my biggest fan."

"No, I think Lucas is," she said with a giggle.

I put down my pen. "Katy. I don't know what you think, but Lucas doesn't feel that way about me. And I am begging you, please do not repeat anything that you heard tonight."

She gave me a hug and a kiss on my cheek. "I promise, Amy. I won't tell anyone that you're in love with Lucas."

I sighed. This was going to be an interesting month.

Seven

Katy and I were deep in concentration when a knock sounded on the door. Katy groaned. "I don't wanna go home!" she cried as Ivy opened the door to greet their parents.

I smoothed her hair. "It was so much fun having you over. I don't want you to go home either. But I'll save your project, and you can work on it the next time you're here." She shrugged. "Your drawing looks awesome. I know how it feels to put a project down when you're not done."

She nodded in agreement and gave me a hug. "Thanks, Amy. I had fun with you. And I think you should speak your truth next month. It's a lot of fun, and you won't be so scared all the time."

Before I could ask what she meant, she bounced off the couch and ran to her parents, giving them a big hug.

"Did you behave?" Rachel, her mom, asked.

"Yes!" she exclaimed. "Amy, tell her."

I walked over to the door with a laugh. "Yes, she did. She was a sweetheart."

Rachel smiled at me, and my chest warmed. She gave me the motherly feelings that I never got from my own mother. "Thank you for watching her," she said. "She was so excited to spend time with the big girls tonight."

"I love having her. Feel free to go on another date night whenever you want," I said.

"Not whenever," Ivy interjected. "Let's not get crazy here."

Her dad, Brent, nudged her on the shoulder. "Don't worry, Ivy. I know you've got a wild social life."

"Not so much. But I do like my freedom," Ivy said.

"Well, it's time to get you home, Katy," Rachel said, gathering her things. "It's a school night, and you're exhausted."

"I'm not tired," Katy said with a huge yawn.

"Mm-hmm," her mom mused, as Brent gathered Katy up in his arms and carried her out the door. Rachel gave Ivy a hug, then wrapped me in her arms. "Thank you," she whispered into my hair. "I'm so glad you're part of our family."

My eyes misted over. "Me too," I whispered back. She squeezed me one more time and headed out the door.

As Ivy finished cleaning the aftermath of Katy's art supplies, I snuggled with Waffles and spent a little more time finishing up my project. I was really proud of this one. While I worked on my lettering, I let my mind wander through the different scenarios that might arise while speaking my truth.

The first, and most obvious, was a catastrophe with my parents. I held back so much when I was with them, even the fact that I hated red wine, but I still choked it down every two weeks. But maybe if I tried to use the next couple weeks thinking about their strengths and positive points, I'd be able to make it through another family dinner. And I rarely saw them outside of family dinners. There was an occasional phone call from my mother, but we didn't run in the same circles and they never bothered to come see me in my apartment. Once this article went viral (because it *had* to), I'd have my promotion, and I'd finally have something to make them proud of me.

Then there was Lucas. My whole world had turned upside down since he'd been back. I couldn't get him out of my mind, knowing that he was just a few miles away. Sure, I still thought about him when he was living in New York. Probably a little too often, considering how often I looked him up on Facebook and watched his YouTube videos. But now that I'd see him more often, I had no idea how I would keep these feelings to myself. How would I get through a conversation with him when I kept picturing him shirtless, gliding across the waves while serenading me with a waterproof guitar?

Hey, it could happen.

Even my job could be compromised. I deeply respected and admired Gia. She had such drive and vision, and she truly wanted the best for all women—to be treated fairly and with equity. But it wasn't *my* vision. Sometimes I felt like rolling my eyes in our meetings and wondering if it was really my place. At least Gia would know what was behind my outspokenness, but it could really put everyone off. I could alienate coworkers, and worst-case scenario, destroy my career. Gia wouldn't offer a promotion to someone who didn't have the same feelings towards the vision of Women in the Workplace, that's for sure.

But when I weighed the risks and the benefits, I still felt

like it was the best option for me. I needed that promotion. I needed to somehow feel like I had done enough to earn my parents' praise. Maybe I could work on training my thoughts to be positive, so I'd never get myself in trouble. Think good things about my parents and brother. Think neutral, friendly thoughts about Lucas.

With his shirt on.

Okay. I could do this.

I REMEMBERED to set my alarm that night, so I got to work the next morning at 7:45. I sat in my car in the parking lot, pulled down the visor, and looked myself straight in the eye. It was time for a pep talk.

"Amethyst King. You are smart, confident, and accomplished. You can handle this assignment, and you will get that promotion. You won't totally ruin your life in the next thirty days. You got this."

With a quick nod, I tossed my long hair over my shoulder, gathered my purse, and stepped out of my car. I tried to dress in my most confident outfit: black slacks, a fitted pink blouse, and some shiny black pumps. My shoes clicked on the tile floor of the lobby, and I hopped into the elevator.

As the elevator doors began to close, someone jumped in with me. "Sorry!" she exclaimed breathlessly. "I'm on my way to an interview."

"Oh, congrats! Which company are you interviewing with?" I asked.

"AGD Engineers. I'm an architect." She looked a little

disheveled. Her skirt was wrinkled and turned sideways, and she had stray hairs sticking out all over her attempted updo.

"I hope it goes well! They're really nice up there," I said. *Please don't ask if you look okay. Please don't ask if you look okay.*

"Do I look okay?"

Ugh. The first test of my new assignment. Oh, how I wished it was yesterday and I could have just said, *Yep! You look great!*

"Um," I hesitated, trying to figure out the words. But the elevator kept moving, and I was running out of time. "Your hair is a little messy."

"What?" she exclaimed. "I spent an hour on this!"

I cringed. It was a disaster. "Okay, let me see what I can do." I walked over and started taking out her pins. Years of looking perfectly presentable taught me how to do a five-second sleek bun. I finished it up and pulled out my phone to show her.

"Oh, my goodness. You are a lifesaver! Thank you!" she exclaimed.

The elevator dinged with my floor. "No problem!" Feeling encouraged for doing a good deed, I called into the closing doors, "And your skirt is a little wrinkled and twisted!"

Her eyes widened as she looked down at her clothes. Whoops. Maybe that was a little too far. Not sure she'd have time to fix that one before the interview.

I walked into work and got to my cubicle. Pulling out my phone, I saw it was 8:03. Time to find Gia and give her the good news.

I wandered over to her office. She looked up from her

work through the glass doors, then waved me inside. I opened the door with a smile on my face.

"Is that a yes?" Gia asked excitedly, her eyes wide with anticipation.

"Yes!" I exclaimed, giving a little shake of my fists. I was so weird. Thankfully, Gia didn't seem to mind and got up out of her chair to give me another awkward hug. It's a little weird when your boss only comes up to your shoulder.

"So…tell me how you feel," she said with a wink. "And you know you have to tell me honestly!"

"Very nervous, but also excited. Hopefully everything ends up smoothly and I can write a killer article afterwards."

Gia smiled knowingly. "We'll see, Amy. This is just day one."

A shiver ran up my spine. Tiny villain Gia struck again. "Well, I do have a date with someone I hate on Saturday, so that's going to be interesting."

Gia laughed. "Now I can't wait to hear about that. Make sure you keep me updated."

"I will. I did want to talk to you about one thing, though. I know I have to speak my truth, but I don't think I should be openly telling everyone about the assignment."

She paused, tapping her chin for a minute. "I think you're right. It might affect the way people respond to what you say. We want to just see what happens when you start speaking your mind and let people naturally react."

"Okay, great." I relaxed. I was so worried about having to tell Lucas that I was speaking my truth, and if something suspicious came out of my mouth, he'd know that I wasn't hiding anything. That could be dangerous, to say the least.

"Thanks so much, Gia!" I waved over my shoulder as I headed back to my cubicle. So far, so good. I got a new assignment, made Gia happy, and had an article that was still doing really well. This promotion was mine. What could go wrong?

Eight

I fought a yawn as I checked the clock in the conference room above Maria's head. 4:45 pm. It was a terrible time of day for her presentation about the new website design, and the ten other pairs of droopy eyelids slowly blinked around the table. We were almost done with another Wednesday at work, and concentration evaded me. For the last two days, I hadn't needed to do anything unusual to speak my truth, which was nice, but still made me nervous.

Maria clicked on the projector. "As you can see, the website has a more user-friendly design and a fun, engaging color scheme."

The bright colors jolted me in my seat. Neon green and purple splashed across the screen. It looked like a website for an energy drink, not a professional resource for women navigating the business world.

Maria continued explaining the website, and my heart picked up its rhythm. I realized I would need to speak my truth. It was my first test.

One by one, the other girls around the table praised

Maria for her forward-thinking design. Each person came closer and closer to me, and still no one expressed any concerns. My hands started to shake.

"Amy? What about you? Do you like it?" Maria asked.

I hated saying anything contrary. I looked at Gia with wide eyes, hoping she'd understand and help me get out of it. Instead, she smiled widely and made a "go ahead" gesture.

Taking a deep breath, I prepared myself for Maria's reaction. "Honestly, no. I don't like it. I think the website looks really confusing, and the colors are too bright. They don't match our aesthetic."

Maria's cheeks turned bright red, and she looked back at the projector. I wished I could disappear, or that this meeting had happened two days ago. Was that too harsh? I had no idea. I had never had to speak my truth before.

"Farah? What about you?" Gia asked.

"I agree with Amy," she said. I turned my head to her, and she winked at me. "We want to appear polished and professional. While the colors are fun, they're too flashy and juvenile."

Feeling braver, I looked around at my coworkers gathered at the table. Some looked like they agreed and wanted to applaud. They must have been too afraid to speak up themselves. Others stared daggers at me, so angry at my decision to speak up.

Maria turned off the projector suddenly. "Well, then. I'll work on it some more." She stomped out the door, shaking the floor as she walked past me.

Farah rubbed my shoulder. "That wasn't so bad, was it?" she whispered.

"I feel terrible." I glanced over at Gia, who looked like she was watching her favorite new reality TV show. Was this what she wanted?

"You're fine. Maria needed to hear it." Farah stood up and gathered her things. "It's about time to leave. See you tomorrow?"

"Sounds good. Thanks for having my back."

"Any time." She gave me a wide smile and waved as she walked out the door.

My phone buzzed. *Hey Ames. You have plans for lunch tomorrow? I'd love to catch up.*

Lucas.

Speaking my truth? I didn't have plans for lunch tomorrow. But I guess I did now.

LUCAS SAT at one of the outdoor tables waiting for me. He was dressed in a fitted shirt and nice jeans that showed off his physique. I wished I could appreciate it more without looking like a creeper. He waved me over as soon as he saw me and stood to give me a hug. I tried to make it a sideways hug so I wouldn't be tempted to squeeze him tight, but he had other plans. Full frontal assault. This was torture.

"Thanks for coming," he said. "I already ordered your favorite from high school."

I looked down at the table to see that he had gotten my usual custom pizza order. The fact that he remembered made my heart flutter, but I was also embarrassed that my tastes hadn't changed in eight years. Maybe that was a metaphor for Lucas, too.

"What? Did I do something wrong?" he asked.

"No, no." Shoot. How could I frame this without giving too much away? "It's really sweet of you. I'm surprised that you remembered exactly what I wanted. And a little embarrassed that my taste buds haven't matured."

He smiled widely. "I'm glad you haven't changed." *What did that mean?* He gestured for me to sit down, and we both started eating our pizzas.

"How have you been the last few days?" he asked.

"Good, good." I kept eating.

"What did you do last night?"

I flashed back to last night, where Ivy and I invited Hannah over for a karaoke championship finale. That was normally our little guilty pleasure, but...

"Karaokechampionshipwithivyandhannah," I said under my breath.

"What?" he laughed. "Hang on, say that again."

I set my food down. "Karaoke championship with Ivy and Hannah."

"Is this a regular thing?"

Oh, boy. I folded my hands together and met his eye. "It's been an ongoing tournament. We spent a few weeks competing. Last night was the championship."

He put his pizza down and met my gaze. "And who won?"

I raised my hand meekly.

"And what exactly did you sing?"

I cleared my throat. "Britney Spears. 'Toxic.'"

He ran his hand through his hair and laughed out loud. "Oh, I wish I could've been there. Please, please tell me there's a video."

I glared at him. "There is, but don't you dare ask to see

it." I was in no way prepared for him to see me decked out in my bikini top and short shorts, strutting around like Britney Spears in her glory days.

His laughter faded to a quiet smile. "I would never make you show me if you didn't want to." He chuckled. "But man, do I wish I were a fly on the wall."

I tried not to think too hard about what that meant. "So, what were you up to today?" I asked, quickly changing the subject.

Lucas took it in stride and picked up his pizza again. "I met with Ivy's dance studio owner again, and I played a couple of pieces for her. She was excited to have me play for the ballet classes."

"Have you done that before?" I asked.

"Yeah, it's a fun side gig. I did that for a studio in New York while I was at Eastman. Along with private piano and guitar lessons, I was able to make a decent living out of it." Furrowing his brow, he gestured at his mouth. "Uh, you have a little something..."

I felt my teeth and found a big piece of spinach on my front tooth. "Biscuits," I muttered. He must have thought I was such a clumsy idiot after eight years apart. First, I fell at the beach, now I had food in my teeth?

As if reading my mind, Lucas laughed. "You don't have to be perfect all the time, Amy. I've seen you much worse than this."

"Oh, really?" I asked, teasing. "Like when?"

"Like when you got your wisdom teeth out during spring break of senior year."

"Oh, my goodness!" I exclaimed, laughing. "I wish you didn't remember that."

"How could I forget? You were the cutest little chipmunk."

My cheeks flamed. What a terrible combination of descriptions—a cute chipmunk. Just what every girl wants to hear from her crush.

"What, not a good description?" he asked.

I took a moment to decide how to speak my truth. "That's definitely not flattering. I don't think any girl wants to be described as a chipmunk."

He tilted his head and smiled. "Maybe it wasn't your finest look, but you were adorable. And we had a great time watching movies together while you rested, remember?"

Boy, did I remember. He came over and made me watch the original Superman trilogy with Christopher Reeve. While they weren't my favorite movies, I pretended I liked them for him. "Yeah, I remember. That was fun."

"And that was your first time watching Superman! Remember how much you liked them?"

This was going to be interesting. Too bad I couldn't keep up my fake love for the movies. I pulled a piece of my hair over my shoulder, unable to meet his eyes. "Yeah, about that. I didn't...love them."

His eyes widened. "Oh, really? Then why did you say you liked them?"

Feeling a little bold and curious to see his reaction, I looked straight at him. "I was trying to impress you. And it was fun to watch something you enjoyed." He was so excited, rewinding parts over and over, that I didn't have the heart to tell him how I really felt. Now I had no choice.

He swallowed, then nodded. "I'm sorry?" He said it as a question, unsure how to proceed.

I giggled to lighten the mood. "Don't be. It was one of my favorite days of recovery. You made everything fun, even if I didn't like the movie."

He nodded slightly, then changed the subject. "So, any plans this weekend?"

Ugh. "Yeah...I have a date with Ethan."

His eyes widened. "Ethan Taylor?" He had heard plenty about him from my tales of galas and banquets in high school.

I could only nod my head.

He took a bite of his pizza, chewed, and nodded. "That's...interesting."

"Yep." I wasn't sure how much I wanted to tell him about the situation. Should I explain I was only going because my mother had given him my number? I thought that would sound pretty pathetic. If I didn't say anything, though, he'd think that I was genuinely interested in him. At this point, I wasn't sure which was worse, so I left it alone.

"So!" I tried to change the subject as he took a bite of his pizza. "Any concerts coming up?" If there was one thing I remembered about Lucas, he was always checking out the latest concerts for inspiration.

He looked confused by the sudden change in conversation, but took it in stride. His eyes gleamed with excitement. "I'm going to Stella Knight's concert next weekend."

"No way! That's awesome!" She was the biggest country star in the nation. With big, beautiful, curly blond hair, killer legs, and a voice that sounded like an angel, she had breached the gap between country and pop. Everyone loved her music. A slightly jealous side of me wasn't thrilled about the idea of Lucas ogling her legs all night, but I pushed that thought aside right away before it popped out.

"Yeah, it's at the LA Pavilion. I was only able to get a single ticket way up in the nosebleeds."

I zoned out for a moment, my imagination roaming with the vision of being outside, under the stars, enjoying a Stella Knight concert with Lucas.

"Amy? Where'd you go?" Lucas waved his hand in front of my face.

Well, this was about to be embarrassing. "I was thinking about being at the concert with you. It would be really nice."

Poor Lucas didn't know what to do with that piece of information. "I, uh, can see if there's extra tickets," he stammered.

"No, no, don't do that," I said. "Maybe next time."

Lucas was definitely looking at me funny now. He leaned forward in his seat, putting his pizza down and looking me in the eye. "Okay, Amy, you're acting strange. What's going on?"

"I can't tell you," I said. At least I had covered that with Gia.

"Okay," he said, drawing out the word. "Is something going on with your parents?"

I shook my head. "Nothing out of the ordinary."

"Then it's something at work."

I nodded my head slowly, hoping I didn't give anything away.

"A new assignment?"

I grimaced. "Yes, but stop asking questions."

He laughed and leaned back in his chair. "Oh, Amy. You sign up for the craziest things, just to make your boss and your parents happy. I know you don't love your job, even though it seems like you're good at it." He sighed. "Well, I can't wait to read the article about this one."

Oh, biscuits. I forgot my articles were public. Whether or not I told him about the assignment now, he'd find out in about a month. I put my head in my hands, my head spinning with the possibilities.

"Hey, hey." Lucas gently put his hands on my wrists. "I'm sorry, I was just teasing. I didn't mean to hurt your feelings."

"My feelings aren't hurt," I said. "I just...don't really want you to read this article."

Surprised, he pulled away. "Well, now I just want to read it more," he said, trying to lighten the mood.

I smiled at him. "We'll see how the next thirty days go."

Nine

Ivy's face appeared from the doorway of my bathroom. "Hey, girl! Getting ready for your date with the devil?"

I swiped blush on my cheeks. "Ugh, yes. This is going to be a disaster."

Ivy bounced on the tips of her toes. "It's so fun watching you say crazy things."

"You should come watch the show tonight," I suggested.

"Hah! Like I could afford Magistra's. But I expect a full report when you get home."

"You know it." I picked up the flat iron to work on some loose curls in my long brown hair. At least I could make myself look presentable while I suffered through this evening. I had a cute dark-blue dress in my closet that I saved for these date setups from my family. It was sleeveless, slightly above my knee, and fitted—flattering but not revealing.

Ivy fluffed my hair with her fingers. "You look beautiful. You're sure you're not trying to get with Ethan?"

"Heck no!" I exclaimed. "I just have to make sure my

looks aren't the reason why he doesn't want to see me again. My winning personality will take that award." I smiled a big, toothy grin and crossed my eyes.

Ivy laughed at me. "You're ridiculous. I can't wait to hear what happens."

At 7:30 sharp, there was a knock on the apartment door. Ivy gave me an evil grin from the kitchen. I shook my head at her and opened the door.

There stood Ethan Taylor. Classically handsome, Ethan was a Ken doll. Brown hair that was gelled and combed to perfection. Deep blue eyes. Chiseled jaw line. Tall and fit, not in a way that made him look like a bodybuilder, just that he cared about his body. He wore a crisp navy-blue suit, expensive from the look of it (and if I knew anything about the Taylor family, it had to be).

I raised my eyebrows. He ignored my expression, nodded curtly, and said, "Let's head out. I don't want to be late." He walked out the door, expecting me to follow. I gave Ivy wide eyes, and she returned the look, then shooed me out the door.

I quickly followed Ethan to his car. It was a silver Porsche, and I have to admit, I can appreciate a nice car. As he opened my door, he asked, "Ah, so do you like the Porsha?" Of course he would pronounce it properly. And unfortunately, I had to answer honestly.

I cleared my throat. "Yeah, it's a beautiful car."

His eyes gleamed. "Just you wait. It's a great ride." He waggled his eyebrows suggestively. Barf. I got in and buckled myself in for what was sure to be a bumpy ride.

Ethan and I grew up in the same circles, but thankfully never went to the same school. His parents made sure to send him to the most expensive private school on the coast. For reasons I'll never understand, my parents chose to send me to public school, where I thankfully met Ivy, Hannah, and Lucas. The students who attended Ethan's school went to the most prestigious universities in the country. Ethan attended Harvard and got his degree in finance, while I went to San Diego University and got my degree in creative writing. We didn't cross paths often these days, except for the occasional galas that my parents forced me to attend. I hadn't seen Ethan in at least a year before this night.

We drove to the coast for dinner. It was a beautiful drive, again one of the reasons why I loved living here, even though it was ridiculously expensive. Ethan droned on and on about his work and how well he was advancing through his father's company. I zoned out for a few minutes and enjoyed the view of the ocean. If I had to go on this date, at least I'd try to enjoy some scenery.

At one point, he mentioned my brother. "Scott just got a promotion. I'm sure you heard about that. He's really making inroads with my father," he said with a clenched jaw. That was one time he didn't look completely pleased with himself. I had to wonder why he asked me out, if he felt so threatened by my brother. But he didn't ask one question or even leave a chance for me to say anything.

Magistra's was, by far, the most pretentious restaurant in the area. Dim lighting, waiters who filled your water after you took a single sip, steaks that were incredible but cost an arm and a leg (and you still had to buy the sides separately). The clientele was ninety percent men over the age of sixty with their twenty-year-old third wives.

It was a great place to eat and celebrate, for some people.

I was not one of those people.

Because of who my family was, and who Ethan thought I must be, he brought me here. I'd had my fill of Magistra's, coming here nearly every month growing up. But Ethan said he was going to take care of the bill, so I decided to enjoy myself.

We were seated in the outdoor patio section, and the sun was setting in gorgeous pinks and oranges. The view here was incredible, since the restaurant was on a cliff over-looking the ocean. With twinkly lights above our table and soft piano music from a live musician, I wished Lucas were here with me instead. As much as I hated the ostentatious show, at least I would have enjoyed being with him. I tried to distract myself by grabbing my menu and picking a drink when I was startled by Ethan's voice.

"So, celery juice, eh?" he asked.

I sighed and put down my menu. "Yes, celery juice."

"I'm sure you're glad one of your articles went viral, but that has to be a little embarrassing, right? Chronicling your bowel movements over the course of thirty days?"

My face turned into fire. "Well, I hadn't thought about someone like you reading about my bowel movements. And now I'm embarrassed. But otherwise, I am really proud of myself."

He laughed. "But going viral doesn't mean anything in terms of your salary, right?"

I gritted my teeth. "No, I didn't get a pay raise. But there are a few things in the works."

"That's disappointing," he said, taking a sip of his water. The waiter magically appeared to refill it. "Although I doubt it's really driving the right kind of traffic to the Women in the

Workplace blog. Health nuts aren't the type of people you're trying to attract."

"We're trying to attract all women," I said defensively. "Anyone who might be interested in rectifying the gap between men and women in the world of business."

He waved me off. "I was just joking. You knew that, right?"

"No. I didn't."

He looked surprised. "Oh. Well, I was." He cleared his throat. "I'm sorry."

My eyes widened. I'd never heard Ethan apologize. "That's okay, I guess," I mumbled, and looked back at my menu.

The waiter arrived at our table and asked for our drink order. I was about to order a martini for myself when Ethan said, "We'll take a bottle of your finest red. Right, Amy?"

Hah! "Actually, I hate red wine. I'll take a lemon drop."

Ethan cocked his head at me. "Oh. Then a glass of red for me, and a lemon drop for the lady." The waiter nodded and made his notes.

"Since when are you so forward, Amy?" Ethan leaned toward me with a glint in his eye.

Oh, biscuits.

Maybe this was backfiring.

Ten

I carefully weighed my options. I had to tell him the truth, but I wasn't sure how much I wanted to divulge. Did I tell him all about the article and my assignment? Or just say I was trying something out? I decided to go with the former.

"Normally, no. I'm not usually this forward," I said. "But I'm on an assignment from my boss to speak my truth for thirty days."

Ethan laughed and sat back in his chair. "Well, that sounds fun. How's that going?"

I was surprised by his interest in the topic. "Uh...it's a mixed bag. I made a lot of people upset at a meeting this week."

Ethan nodded thoughtfully. "I could see that." I watched him process this new piece of information. "So...if I ask you anything, you have to answer honestly?"

I leaned my head into my hand that was propped on the table. "Unfortunately, yes."

He drummed his fingers on the table. "Well, this just got interesting."

"Please, Ethan, I'm begging you. Don't ask anything that could get me in trouble."

He shook his head. "No, no, don't worry. I just have a few questions I want to ask you."

Chalk this one up to another failure by Amy. "Let's get it over with."

"Why did you agree to go on a date with me?" he asked.

"Because my mother wanted me to."

"Do you do everything your parents ask?"

"Aside from going to the right college, yes. And that wasn't my fault; I didn't get into USC."

"What does your family think of me?"

I sighed. "My parents love you. My mom was beaming when she told me that you were going to contact me."

"And your brother?"

I thought for a moment. "Honestly? I don't think I've heard him mention you at all. He seems indifferent."

Ethan pressed his lips together and nodded. I wondered what intense rivalry he'd conjured up in his mind. "And you? What do you think of me?"

Oh, boy.

I took a deep breath in and out to calm my nerves and slow my racing heart. "I think you're pretentious and self-absorbed. You care more about appearances than what actually matters."

He laughed out loud, startling me and the other customers nearby. "You should speak your truth all the time, Amethyst King. This is highly entertaining."

Confused, I stared at him for a moment before speaking again. "I'm glad you're so entertained," I muttered, smoothing out the napkin in my lap.

"I'm going to return the favor, Amy," he said. "I'll be honest with you, as well."

I looked back up at him in surprise, and he began to share.

"I only asked you out because my father wanted me to. I think he wants some kind of partnership with your family, and if I didn't make it happen with you, then he would take Scott under his wings instead. I care about appearances because I have to. That's the world I work and live in. And I'm okay with that. I enjoy the things that make me look good, and I enjoy looking good to others."

I nodded. While I didn't feel the same way, I appreciated his honesty. "Well, thank you for telling me the truth. So...is that it? Are we done here?"

"What, for the evening?" he asked. "No way. We're going to enjoy a dinner together and you get to tell me more truths."

I laughed. "I guess I've gotten the worst out of the way."

We spent most of the evening genuinely enjoying each other's company. Not needing to pretend that we were impressing each other, we were honest and forthright. We compared stories growing up with our pretentious families, the people in our parents' circles, and laughed about the ridiculousness of it all.

"And remember—remember," I said, laughing and taking another sip of my second martini, "when your mom threw her cocktail in Susan Carson's face?"

Ethan sat back and roared with laughter. "Who could forget it? It was on TV for everyone to see." He shook his head. "Our families are ridiculous."

"No kidding. I have no idea why you want to have any part in it."

He pursed his lips and looked away. "I do wonder sometimes, too." He looked me square in the eye. "So, who is he?"

"Who is who?" I asked with a laugh.

"The guy you're clearly in love with. You haven't flirted with me all night. There must be someone else."

"Aren't you modest?" I smirked, taking another sip of my drink. I set it down, sat forward, and put my elbows on the table. Very ladylike. "Lucas Carter."

"Tell me about him."

I sighed dreamily. Who was I? "He's perfect. He's got such a good heart. He cares about other people and puts them first. But not at the expense of pursuing his own path and what makes him happy. He's an amazing songwriter, and he's going for it."

"So, basically the opposite of your family."

"Yep, basically."

"And that's why you haven't gone for it."

I gave him a cheesy finger gun. "Bingo."

He nodded thoughtfully. "I might know something about that."

"Oh, really?" I asked excitedly. "Well, now it's your turn."

"No, no, no," he laughed, waving a hand at me. "I'm not the one obligated to speak my truth. But let's just say that I can sympathize with you more than you might think."

"Hmm," I mused. "As unfair as this feels, I can respect that. But I do ask that you keep my feelings for Lucas to yourself, thank you very much."

He returned my finger guns. "No problem."

We enjoyed the rest of the evening together and he drove

me home. He walked me to my door and gave me a simple, friendly kiss on the cheek. "This was a much better evening than I expected," he said.

"I have to agree," I admitted. "Although I was really looking forward to telling you off and seeing you freak out."

He half smiled. "Sadly, I already know my reputation very well. It was nice to be real with someone for the evening." He put his hands in his pockets, looking more like the little boy I remembered running into at family functions. "I wish you the best with Lucas."

"And you with your mystery lady," I said, waggling my eyebrows. He laughed.

"Well, I'll see you around, Amy. Have a good night." He waved and headed back to his car.

I walked in the door to see Ivy watching reality TV and adding even more rhinestones to her students' costumes while sitting in a straddle stretch. "Oh, my gosh. Tell me everything. Why aren't you angrier?" she exclaimed.

"That was definitely not how I thought it would go," I said, as I sat down on the couch. "I was honest with him, and instead of being angry, he almost appreciated it. We spent the evening reminiscing about old times and kind of letting down our pretentious facade. It was weirdly nice."

Ivy stared at me blankly, blinking twice. "Okay," she said, drawing out the word. "I did not expect that at all. You don't...like him, do you?"

"No way." I shook my head emphatically. "He still cares too much about appearances and flashy things. But it was nice to have someone to relate to. I even told him about Lucas, and he said he was in some kind of similar situation."

"Well, that's interesting." Ivy looked at me thoughtfully. "So, I guess you're not seeing each other again?"

"Not romantically. I'm sure we'll run into each other some more. He works with Scott and he runs the same circles as my parents. But I won't mind seeing him now."

"That's so weird."

"Yep."

Ivy patted my leg in solidarity, but didn't say more. Exhausted from the emotional exercise in speaking my truth, I didn't say much else that evening. Instead, we let the True Trophy Wives, including Ethan's mother, who lived ten minutes away, fill our apartment with their voices. They had no problem speaking their truth. But I didn't exactly want to follow their example. I was determined to find a way to fulfill this assignment without ruining any relationships worth keeping.

$$Eleven$$

On Monday morning, I headed to the local coffee shop on my way to work. There was a huge line inside, and my phone buzzed with a call from my mother. Normally I wouldn't pick up my phone in line, but with so much time to kill, I figured I'd get the conversation over with. But that's what she'd always been to me. And I thought it described our relationship pretty well. I clicked the "Answer" button on my phone and put it up to my ear.

"Good morning, Mother," I said cheerily. I had been expecting her, and I was genuinely having a pretty good morning.

"Good morning, Amethyst. How was your date with Ethan?" Cutting right to the chase. No need for small talk with her. My life wasn't interesting enough. To be fair, I had spent Sunday snuggled with Waffles watching more of Lucas's videos, which would not have interested her in any way.

Thinking carefully to make sure I spoke honestly, I chose

my words. "It went surprisingly well. Ethan and I had a great time."

"Oh!" my mother exclaimed. She seemed genuinely shocked. She thought I was such an epic failure that I wouldn't be able to enjoy a date with Ethan Taylor. Although, if I were being honest, I thought the same thing myself. "That's wonderful. Do you have plans to see each other again?"

"No, we don't," I answered. Realizing that part of my assignment probably meant not misleading others, I decided to clarify. "He's not interested in me romantically. We just had a nice time together as friends."

"Nonsense!" she interjected. "I'm sure that's not true."

"No, Mother. It was pretty clear."

But she kept insisting. "You say that now, but we'll work on this. This will be so wonderful for our families. Just you see." And she hung up.

I tried, right? I spoke my truth loud and clear. If my mother chose to misunderstand, that wasn't my fault or responsibility. I didn't think I had to call her back and make sure we were on exactly the same page. That would never work with my mother, anyway. She lived in her own dreamland and believed what she wanted. Wasn't that the point of the assignment? Just to speak my own truth?

Unfortunately, the man behind me decided to strike up a conversation. "Having some trouble with your momma?" he drawled in a Southern accent.

Ugh. I hated when men tried to hit on me in line. In any other circumstance, I would have turned halfway to glance at him, given him a polite nod, then started fake texting to give a clear "don't talk to me anymore" vibe. But now I had to respond.

"A little," I admitted. "But not more than I'm used to from her."

He smiled. He looked like he was in his mid-thirties, and surprisingly handsome, with dark hair and dark eyes. "I didn't mean to eavesdrop, I'm sorry for that. But I just wanted to let you know that you're very pretty, and I'm sure you'll have a better date soon."

Next thing I knew, he'd be saying that date would be with him. I smirked at him and turned back to the line, trying to tune him out. If he didn't stop talking, there'd be some violence soon.

He didn't get the hint and continued. "Mommas always want the best for their kids, but sometimes they just need to get out of the way. My wife is the same way with our little ones, but I worry that she won't mind her own business as they grow up."

My face filled with heat. Married, and just trying to be friendly. I guess I totally misread this situation. "I'm sure she just cares a lot for them," I murmured. I looked forward and noticed the line had moved, so we both took a step.

"I'm sorry if my conversation startled you. We're visiting from a small town in Georgia. I gotta say, no one here has wanted to talk."

While it wasn't a question, I wanted to answer honestly. I paused, formulating my answer. "For the most part, people here are very interested in their own lives and don't want to be bothered."

"Is that why you didn't want to talk?" he asked.

I closed my eyes, preparing for the consequences of

telling the truth. "Honestly, I thought you were hitting on me."

He let out a loud laugh, and a few other customers looked over. "I guess I can see that. But I'm happily married, and I'm buying some coffee for my wife."

I wanted to melt into a puddle. Thinking about our interaction, he didn't stand too close or look me up and down, the way a usual scumbag would. He was genuinely trying to have a nice chat with someone in line.

There was a brief silence, and I felt compelled to redeem myself by starting the conversation back up. "So, what brings you and your wife out here?"

"Oh..." He hesitated for a second, gesturing to the line that I wasn't paying attention to. We scooted forward again. "Have you heard of Stella Knight?"

"Stella Knight? Who hasn't heard of her?"

He chuckled. "Well, she's my wife. We're here for her concert this weekend at the LA Pavilion."

I gaped at him, feeling like my eyes were going to bug out of my head. After an awkward, long pause, I managed to say, "My friend Lucas will absolutely die when he finds out that I met you." And I felt a little like dying for thinking that he was hitting on me. His wife was the most beautiful creature to ever grace the music scene.

He smiled widely, then pointed at the register. "I think it's your turn."

I turned around again and noticed the huge gap that had formed while I was absorbed in my conversation. The customers behind the man (Stella's *husband*) looked pretty irritated, but that barely registered. "Whoops, thanks!"

I trotted up and placed my order, then scooted to the

side to wait for my tea (I couldn't manage coffee, I was too wound up now as it was). Just to make sure, I kept my phone tucked into my side and searched "Stella Knight husband" in my search engine. Sure enough, there was a picture of the man I had just met next to the incredible Stella Knight. With a hand pressed against my forehead, I typed a message to Lucas. *I just met Stella Knight's husband! Don't you have tickets to the concert this weekend?* Almost immediately, he responded. *What?!?! I am SO jealous. And yes, I can't wait!*

I smiled to myself, and Stella's husband walked up just then. "I'm sorry we didn't exchange names," he said, holding out his hand. "I'm Chip."

"Amethyst. Or Amy," I said, putting my hand in his. Then I held up my phone. "And I was right. My friend totally flipped out."

"Your friend, huh?" Chip looked intrigued. "Tell me about him."

At least he didn't ask how I felt about him. I felt a slow smile spread across my face as I thought about how to describe Lucas. I looked off into the distance as I spoke. "He was one of my best friends since high school, and he just moved back home from New York. He's genuinely a good person. And he's a really talented songwriter. He admires Stella's work so much."

Chip narrowed his eyes at me. "You're in love with him, aren't you?" he asked.

I gaped at him, then pressed my hands to my cheeks. And then I realized I had to tell the truth to a complete stranger. "Ugh, yes. How did you know?!"

He laughed out loud. "Darlin', my wife is in the business

of love. Your whole demeanor changed. Your eyes lit up the way my wife's do every time I walk in the room."

Well, that was adorable.

"Hmmm," Chip mused to himself. He patted a couple pockets, then found a business card and handed it to me. "Here's my card. Send me a text later today. I'm going to help you out with your friend. Maybe Stella and I can help things along...backstage this weekend."

"Oh, my goodness. You don't need to do that!" I exclaimed. Were southern people really this nice?

"You've been so kind this morning, and there's nothing Stella loves more than true love. Trust me, we'd love to."

Just then, the barista called us both up for our drinks. I picked mine up in a daze, then started to add my honey. Chip grabbed the two cups for himself. As in, a coffee for Stella Knight. Stella's mouth was about to touch that cup.

"I hope to hear from you, Amethyst!" he called to me on his way out.

"You will!" I called back. "Thank you!"

This morning, speaking my truth was working out *very* well.

As I drove to work, I thought about how this assignment was going. Some moments were awkward, like the meeting where I criticized Maria's design. But there were some unexpectedly sweet moments. Meeting Chip and getting the tickets and backstage passes was obviously the highlight, but connecting with Ethan was such a surprise and gave me a new friend.

How many opportunities had I missed over the years by holding myself back?

I knew that Gia was really hoping to see the professional side of things, mostly how speaking my truth would affect me at work. I wasn't sure what she was waiting for, though. Did she want some kind of blowup at the office? That didn't seem like her. She was very cautious about putting forward a positive look at our company, an example of what all businesses could be like. A catfight would be a bad image.

I shook my head and kept driving. I'd just have to keep going and see where these thirty days would take me. As soon as I pulled into my parking spot at work, I grabbed Chip's card and sent him a text.

ME

Hi Chip! This is Amethyst. It was nice meeting you at the coffee shop this morning!

Hopefully that was enough to jog his memory. Almost instantly I got a response:

CHIP KNIGHT

It was lovely meeting you too! Send me your email address and I'll get you those tickets. Looking forward to seeing you this weekend.

I couldn't believe it. I was going to spend an evening with Lucas, watching and meeting Stella Knight. This was going to be amazing.

Or humiliating.

Either way, I couldn't wait.

Twelve

I strolled down the wine aisle of the grocery store, pausing to find the perfect bottle for the concert tonight. Stella's voice carried through the speakers, the sign of an incredible evening to come.

"Excuse me," came a voice from behind.

I turned around and looked down at a man who was about my age. Shorter than most, he was otherwise unremarkable. I smiled as I scooted over. "I'm sorry, was I in your way?"

"Uh, no. I mean..." he stammered, then drifted off. I waited patiently, but my eyes darted away as I tried to excuse myself from this awkward conversation. I gave him a tight smile and took a couple steps with my basket in arm.

"No, wait!" he exclaimed, grabbing my arm. I looked down at his hand in alarm, and he pulled back quickly. He shook his head, gathering his courage. "You're very beautiful. I wanted to see if you would be interested in going out sometime."

"Oh." Biscuits. How would get out of this one? I used to

lie that I had a boyfriend when rejecting unwanted advances, but now I had to speak my truth. I bit my bottom lip while I thought.

"Thank you, I'm very flattered." That was true. By now, a couple other shoppers were glancing over, hoping to see a love connection. This was getting worse every second. I had to put an end to it quickly, so I spat out the last part. "But I'm not interested."

He cleared his throat and tugged on his shirt collar. "Why not?" he asked.

That was a little aggressive. I expected him to walk away, but instead he demanded more answers. Flying buttered biscuits. "Um, you're not my type."

"How would you even know that? We haven't gone out."

Would he ever give up? This was a nightmare. "I don't date men who are shorter than me." Oh, my lord. How shallow did I sound? I had to end this on a better note. "But I'm really flattered. Thank you."

He huffed. "I guess you're not as beautiful on the inside as you seem on the outside." He walked backwards, then stumbled into a display case of wine. He frantically tried to catch the bottles before they fell, but one slipped from his grasp and broke on the floor, red wine spilling all on the aisle. I ran up to help clean, but an older woman grabbed my shoulder.

"Haven't you done enough?" she scolded.

"I just wanted to help," I protested.

"Go find someone to clean it up. Leave the poor man alone." She whispered in my ear, "Next time, just say you have a boyfriend."

Thanks, lady. Sighing, I left the scene of the crime to find an employee.

~

IVY WAS THOROUGHLY AMUSED by my grocery store encounter, but I was still pretty upset. I busied myself with doing my makeup and getting into a better mental space before Lucas arrived.

A knock on our apartment door interrupted my last swipe of mascara. "Come in!" I shouted.

"We could've been serial killers," Lucas called as he came through the door. "You really should lock your door."

"Lucas. We live in Park City," Ivy said as she gave him a hug. "Besides, we only left it open because we knew you were coming." Nate followed Lucas through the door. With it being their first meeting in eight years, Ivy had confessed that she was nervous about seeing him again. She gave Nate a hug, but made sure not to linger. "Hey, Nate. Good to see you."

"You too, Ivy," he said, pushing up his glasses. His eyes were wide, just like they were in high school. Poor Nate. Ivy was hard to forget. I related to him more than he would probably understand. Just like in high school, Nate was tall and lanky, with dark curly hair. A kind and generous soul, he and Lucas were great friends, but Nate was shy.

The boys were dressed in flannel shirts and jeans. Lucas must have helped Nate get dressed so he wouldn't stick out like a sore thumb. He looked over at Ivy and me, taking in our attempts at looking "country"—button-down shirts, jeans, and braids. "You look adorable," he said. I snorted. "What?" Lucas asked. "Did I say something wrong?"

Ah, biscuits. The honesty already had to begin. "I think 'adorable' is one of the worst words you can use to describe how a girl looks," I said.

He just laughed. "Well, you do. At least we're all making an effort to fit in."

I smiled and gave the boys hugs, a friendly one for Nate and something I hoped was friendly for Lucas.

"Amy, I seriously cannot thank you enough for this," Lucas said. "I am so excited. I can't believe you managed to get these tickets. Just because you met Chip?"

"Yep!" I said, giving Ivy wide eyes. I wasn't about to disclose the part where Chip read my feelings like a book. "He said people here haven't been very friendly. I told Chip that you loved Stella and that we were good friends, and he wanted to help me out." Ivy rolled her eyes at me but didn't say anything else.

"That's pretty incredible. Well, should we get going?" he said.

"Yeah, we're running a little tight," said Nate. "The concert starts at 7:30, and you never know traffic in LA. If we want to enjoy our picnic, we'd better get going."

Ivy and I grabbed our picnic basket, blanket, and bottle of wine. The LA Pavilion was an incredible and historic venue. They encouraged everyone to bring a picnic and enjoy the venue before the concert began. Munching on biscuits, cheese, and salami with some wine before and during the concert was going to make for a fantastic evening.

We hopped into Lucas's car. It wasn't a Porsche but a Mitsubishi Ralliart, a lower end sports car that fit his personality. We girls climbed in the back so Nate could navigate. The car rumbled to life, and we headed down the road.

"Should we listen to Stella's songs to get ready?" I asked.

"No!" Lucas and Ivy both shouted.

"Biscuits! What's with the animosity?" I asked.

Lucas drew in a breath. "You can't listen to the music that you're about to hear at a concert. You can listen to it on the way home, so you can remember how amazing it was to hear it live, but if you listen to it on the way there, you'll get sick of it."

"Fair enough. That kind of makes sense." I turned to Ivy. "Did you get a sub for your rehearsal tonight?"

"Yes! I told my students I got tickets to Stella Knight's concert and meeting her after and they just about lost their minds. I am definitely the coolest dance teacher ever."

"I think you already have that title," Lucas said. "At least that's the word around the studio."

"Yeah, isn't that what you won at the last competition?" I teased.

"Hah!" Ivy barked a laugh. "No, but 'Best Choreographer' was pretty awesome, too."

"So, who's subbing?" I asked.

"Her name is Blake. She's new. She's been in a bunch of commercials and music videos, so the moms are all excited to have her teach their daughters."

Lucas nodded. "I heard a few of the girls talking about her. Everyone is really excited to have her there."

"It's cool, but being an amazing performer doesn't automatically mean she's a great teacher. We'll see how things go."

"Traffic looks pretty bad," Nate interjected, ever the pessimist.

"No worries, man." Lucas slapped his shoulder. "Good thing we have beautiful girls and good company." He winked at me in the rearview mirror. "Amy, how's your new assignment going?" he asked with a teasing glint in his eye.

I narrowed my eyes at him. "Fine." It *was* going fine, but he didn't need to know more than that.

"Anything you would like to share about it?" he continued. What a brat.

"Nope!" I *didn't* want to share anything.

He laughed, then cleared his throat. "And, uh…how was your date with Ethan?"

I glanced at Ivy, who raised her eyebrows at me. I knew what she was thinking: he wouldn't have asked if he wasn't interested himself.

"It went better than expected. We actually had a good time together."

"Oh." Lucas nodded and kept his eyes on the road. "So, are you guys dating now?"

"No, not like that," I answered. "We had a really good time but agreed we're not interested in each other that way."

"He's not…" Lucas trailed off, his eyes flicking at me, then back at the road. "Uh, I'm sorry?"

"Don't be. It was a really nice night. He's a better guy than I expected him to be."

Lucas looked at me again through the rearview mirror, searching for an answer in my face. I'm not sure if he found what he was looking for, but he kept driving and changed the topic back to Ivy and the dance studio.

The traffic was as Nate expected, and we pulled into the

parking lot around six. The venue was a short walk from the parking lot through an underground tunnel beneath Los Angeles Boulevard. We scanned our tickets and found a nice patch of grass for our picnic. We laughed at all the concert-goers, most of whom looked like me and Ivy—southern Californians trying to look country. There were definitely some legitimate dressers, though. Ivy and I pointed them out and wished we had some of those amazing sparkly boots.

At 7:15, we decided to head to our seats. Lucas originally had a seat in the far back, but Chip got us tickets in the VIP section. It was basically in the middle of the venue, but instead of a concrete bench, we had cushioned theater-style seats. Nate sat down on one end and immediately pulled out his phone to start checking on any work issues. Lucas sat next to him, then me and Ivy.

Lucas sat in his seat, looked at the stage, and smiled widely. "This is incredible. We're going to have such amazing acoustics." He turned his eyes to me. "Seriously, thank you, Amy." He was so genuine, my heart melted again.

"You're welcome, Lucas. I can't imagine sharing this with anyone else." I held his gaze for a couple seconds longer (probably too long) and looked away before he asked why I was staring at him. I didn't want to answer that question honestly.

"And we even get to meet her afterwards!" Ivy bounced up and down in her seat. "My girls are going to flip when I post this on Instagram."

"Do your students have Instagram accounts?!" I asked incredulously.

Ivy laughed. "Yep. They want to be famous dancers, so

they need their own accounts. Their parents monitor them, for the most part, though."

I shuddered. "I don't think I'll let my kids have social media until they're at least sixteen. It's too scary."

"Agreed," Lucas said. "But we're not preteens, so let's post a picture." He pulled his phone out to take a selfie.

"Oh, no, no," Ivy protested, hopping out of her seat. "Let me get a decent picture of the two of you." She winked at me. I was going to kill my best friend. She jumped back a couple rows so she could get a picture of me, Lucas, and the stage. Lucas and I turned towards each other in our seats to face her.

"You guys. You're like a mile apart. Get a little closer." Ivy smiled innocently. I glared at her, but Lucas scooted closer and put his arm around me. I froze for a second, then melted into him. That felt heavenly. I looked into his eyes and gave him a shy smile. He put his forehead on mine for a moment, then looked over at Ivy.

"Say, 'Stella'!" she called. We obliged, and she snapped the pic.

She came back to her seat and handed me the phone. "I took a couple," she said. I put the phone between Lucas and me and we looked at the first smiley pic, then scrolled to the left to see the others.

Oh, my biscuits.

She got the perfect picture of the moment when I smiled at him, and then the next of our foreheads together. It looked like an intimate moment between a true couple. I looked over at Lucas in alarm to see his reaction. To my surprise, he was smiling at the picture and didn't seem as shocked as I did.

"That's a great picture," he said, and sent them all to his number. He busily typed on his phone for the next few minutes. The next thing I knew, he posted the picture on his Instagram with the caption, "Looking forward to an incredible night with this one #stellaknight."

Who was "this one"? Me? Or Stella?

More evidence that social media sucks and shouldn't be used by anyone under the age of sixteen. Or maybe anyone at all, for that matter.

"Is that okay?" he asked.

"Yep!" I squeaked. It *was* okay. I just didn't know what he meant. But he didn't press any further, just slid his phone into his pocket and sat back in his seat. I looked over at Ivy in alarm, and she winked. Just then, the lights dimmed and the stage lit up. It was time for the concert.

Thirteen

The LA Pavilion was one of the coolest venues I've ever been to. Built into the California hills, the stage was backed up to green hills, and behind the stage were the infamous "Hollywood" letters. The stage itself had a huge, white domed arch, and inside the arch was another fully lit archway that changed colors depending on the artist's preference.

The concert began with the lights all deep blue, and everyone around me stood up and cheered. The band started playing, and Lucas grabbed my hand. I looked over at him and his huge smile warmed my heart. He squeezed my hand once, sending a jolt of electricity through me, and then he let out a loud cheer. I, on the other hand, clapped politely. My parents raised me to never cheer or whistle too loudly. That would be obnoxious. I watched Lucas with envy, wishing I felt free enough to cheer when I felt the desire.

Stella strutted out on the stage with the utmost confidence, the glittering microphone in her hand, her voice filling the entire bowl and rising to the heavens. I already knew she was an incredible singer, but hearing her voice in person, surrounding us all, gave me chills. Ivy grabbed my arm and jumped up and down in excitement.

"How are y'all doin' tonight?" Stella asked to the loudest screaming I'd ever heard. "I can't wait to enjoy this night together! Thank y'all for being here!" Already I loved her. Just like Lucas, she seemed so genuinely kind and thankful for everyone in the audience.

Song after song, Stella entranced us. Her dancers were incredible, as Ivy kept pointing out. Once upon a time, Ivy wanted to be a backup dancer. But once Katy was born, she put her own dreams on hold to help her parents out. And thankfully, she really loved teaching and coaching at the dance studio. Stella herself was an incredible goddess, her long legs stretching out under her cobalt-blue fitted shorts with flowing fabric creating the illusion of a dress. I glanced over at Lucas, and he looked back at me right away with a big grin. At least he wasn't completely hypnotized by her legs.

Near the middle of the concert, Stella slowed things down and sat down at a gorgeous blue grand piano. "I think that one is nicer than your family's piano," Lucas shouted with a laugh.

"I would hope so!" I answered. "At least someone plays this one."

He smiled at me, and I hoped he remembered the time he played "Clair de Lune" for me. I did.

Stella played the first few notes of her ballad, "Nights Beneath the Stars." The crowd went wild. She gestured to everyone to quiet down, and we all obliged like eager little children. Her voice had magical properties that made even grown men obey.

"I want to enjoy the magic of the California skies," she said, her fingers continuing to move through the introductory notes of the song. "Y'all have been so lovely. Thank you for sharing this evening with me. I want you to grab your loved ones and hold them tight, because that's what this song is all about."

She began singing, and I closed my eyes to enjoy the magic of the moment. I felt Ivy hold my hand on my left, and I opened my eyes to turn and smile at her. At just that moment, I felt Lucas put his arm around my waist. I turned to him in surprise, but he just kept watching Stella with a big smile.

What did this mean? Did he love me? I glanced over at Nate on his other side and figured he wouldn't want to hold him tight, so maybe I was just the next best option. And of course we were friends. But...could it mean more? I tried not to overthink it and hoped he couldn't feel my pounding heart. Ivy still held my hand and squeezed it tight with encouragement.

And for that moment, I felt the true enchantment of the moment and relaxed into it. I listened to Stella's voice, felt my best friend's warmth in my hand and the man I loved holding my waist.

Loved?

I startled myself. Was I in love with Lucas? Eight years ago, I thought I was. At least, as much as an eighteen-year-old can be in love. And now?

I watched Lucas as he watched Stella. It was the same man I knew eight years ago. We were older, possibly wiser, but his heart was still the same: pure and full of joy.

I didn't have any answers, but settled into the moment

and felt at peace. I didn't worry about what my parents would think, or who was watching, or what anyone else thought. I enjoyed myself *for me*. It was so freeing, like a weight on my chest was lifted to the stars with Stella's voice.

All too soon, the song was over, and the band started back up with one of her upbeat songs. Lucas let go of me and put his hands over his mouth to cheer again. We all danced to the rest of the concert (including Nate, believe it or not). She performed an encore, then bid us all good night and exited the stage.

The lights went back on, and we all looked at each other with wide eyes.

"She's incredible," Nate breathed.

We all looked over at Nate, thinking he was talking about Stella, until we saw him looking down at a girl a few rows ahead of us. Her dark hair was cut in a bob, and she wore glasses. She looked just like the Nate of her group, a little awkward and shy, but happy to be with friends. She glanced back up at him and looked away shyly.

"Nate," I hissed. "Go talk to her!"

"Oh...no. I can't do that." He dipped his head in resignation.

"Fine. I'll do it," Ivy said. Before Nate could tell her to stop, she had climbed over the chairs and headed down to the girl.

"I think she wants him to move on," Lucas whispered to me. I couldn't control my laughter, the giddiness from the concert catching up with me. We all watched as Ivy grabbed the girl's arm, talked to her briefly, and pointed up at Nate.

"Oh no, oh no," Nate repeated over and over. I had never seen him so worked up. Both girls pulled out their phones, and then Ivy hopped back over to us. "Her name is Jess. She's a software designer. She gave me her number, and I gave her yours. You're welcome," she said, slapping Nate on the shoulder. He looked dumbfounded.

"Don't screw it up, man," Lucas said. Nate shook his head and grabbed Ivy's phone to copy down Jess's number. He started texting her right away, and none of us stopped him.

"Well, now that's handled, can we go meet Stella?" Lucas asked, clapping his hands. He looked like a kid going to Disneyland.

"Sure," I said. "Let's head down."

We headed out of our seats and down the steep hill with the other concertgoers. There was a huge crowd lined up at the stage door, hoping to get a glimpse of Stella as she left. Feeling like celebrities ourselves, I gave the security guard our names, and he opened the door for us. I looked back at my friends excitedly, and we all walked in.

We wandered down the hallway until we got to a huge open area, and there she was. Stella was sitting on a couch, still in her full costume from the evening, sipping on a bottle of water. Chip sat next to her, with his arm around her shoulders. They looked so sweet I hated to interrupt, but Ivy couldn't hold back.

"Oh, my goodness, hi!" she shrieked.

Stella looked at us and then at Chip, who nodded when he recognized me. "Amethyst, it's good to see you again!" he said. They both got up off the couch and shook our hands.

Stella looked me in the eye and shook my hand. "I heard so much about you! Chip was so happy someone finally talked to him," she laughed.

I thought I wasn't the type of person to get starstruck.

Growing up in southern California, we ran into celebrities on a semi-regular basis, especially with my parents being fairly influential. For goodness' sake, Ethan's mom was a Real Housewife. We'd been around the taping of the show for plenty of our banquets and galas. But meeting Stella up close was something different, especially when she had heard about me. I shook her hand but couldn't say much.

Lucas laughed next to me. "Amy is a kind soul."

I smiled gratefully at him, then found my voice. "Well, I'm glad I decided to talk to Chip. This has been an incredible evening. Thank you both so much."

"The pleasure is all mine! This must be Lucas. Amethyst told Chip you were a songwriter, so I decided to look you up," Stella said, turning to Lucas.

Now it was his turn to look starstruck. "Oh...wow. Thank you?"

Stella laughed. "I was very impressed. Your songs have a lot of heart and soul."

He nodded slowly. "Thank you so much. That...thank you."

"So, what did y'all think of the concert?" Chip asked.

"It was incredible," I said, excited that speaking my truth wouldn't get me into any trouble tonight. "Stella, hearing your voice live is unlike anything I've experienced. And I know Ivy loved the dancing. She's a dance teacher."

"Oh, that's wonderful," Stella said. "I can't dance much myself, but my dancers are incredible."

"They really were!" Ivy exclaimed. "I recognized a few of them from Dance Star."

"Yep, I snatched them up right after the show was over," Stella said. "They were too good. I couldn't let anyone else use them." She looked back at me. "So, what was your favorite part of the show?"

"Definitely when you sang 'Nights Beneath the Stars'. I don't think I'll ever forget that moment."

She smiled, like I had said exactly what she had hoped. "I do love singing that song. Especially for people who appreciate the sentiments." She glanced between me and Lucas, as if she knew exactly what had happened. "You know what? I'd love to hear you play, Lucas."

"Oh, no, that's okay," he said. His eyes widened, and he seemed nervous for the first time in forever.

"No, really," she insisted. "I play for other people all the time, and I never get to hear other people play for me. Please. I've already watched your YouTube videos, so I know I won't be disappointed." She winked, then reached next to the couch for her blue acoustic guitar.

Lucas wiped his hands on his jeans and took the guitar from her. He wouldn't meet my eyes as he sat down on the couch. His knee bounced a bit with nerves, then he started strumming the strings. I glanced at Ivy to confirm that this was a new song; the opening chords didn't sound like any of his other songs. She shook her head and shrugged, agreeing that she didn't know this one either. I turned back to Lucas with renewed curiosity, and he began to sing.

> I remember a time
> When the sun shined
> Brighter than these city lights
> Saw the embers fly
> From our bonfires
> Disappear into the sky

When my eyes close at night
There's still one face that burns bright

Will these words I've scribbled so hastily
Ever be read
Or written so beautifully again?
Can I find that melody
To make me smile
Smile like I did back then?

He stopped with a nervous laugh. "That's all I've got so far. Still working on it." He handed the guitar back to Stella, then finally looked my way. Lightning sparked between our eyes. I couldn't deny the tension that was suddenly in the room.

Oh, my biscuits.

Was it about me?

No, of course not.

But maybe?

"That was absolutely beautiful, Lucas," Stella said. "You have quite a way with words. I'm going to keep you in mind. I might have something for you to help out with in the near future."

He snapped his eyes from mine to look over at Stella. "Oh, wow. I don't think you understand what this means to me."

She looked at both of us and winked. "Oh, I think I do."

～

"THAT HAD to be one of the highlights of my life so far," Lucas announced on the drive home. As we had planned, Stella's latest album was playing on the stereo and we were excitedly pointing out our favorite parts of the concert.

Well, Lucas and I were. Nate said he was going to text Jess in the backseat and figured Lucas didn't need his help to navigate. He hadn't said a word for the entire drive. Ivy "wanted to sleep," so she pushed me into the front passenger seat and curled up in the back. I reluctantly climbed into the front seat with Lucas. We weren't technically alone, but it was just a conversation between the two of us, and it felt oddly intimate.

"That makes me so happy," I said with a big smile. "I can't believe she asked you to play for her."

He shook his head in amazement. "I have no idea what she wants from me, but I can't wait."

"Here, I'll put Chip's number in your phone," I said. Stella had instructed me to give him Chip's number, and that he should text Chip in the morning. Lucas looked like a kid in a candy store. I tapped Lucas's phone and saw that he had made his lock screen the picture of the two of us that Ivy had taken. "Oh, I didn't realize you liked the picture this much." My heart started fluttering in my chest.

He glanced over and smiled. "It's a great picture. And it's been a great night. I don't want to forget it." He paused for a moment, then glanced back at me. "Did you...was it okay? During 'Nights Beneath the Stars'?"

Oh, my biscuits.

What did he mean?

I took in a deep breath and held it in. "Yes. It was definitely okay. I really enjoyed it." I said it as quickly as I could. So awkward, but at least it was the truth.

He nodded. "Cool. That's good."

I nodded back. "Yep."

We sat in silence for a couple more seconds, awkwardness hanging heavy like humidity. I wanted to curl up into a ball.

Instead, Lucas quickly reached over and grabbed my hand. I felt a zap of electricity through the top of my hand and all my fingers. He glanced over at me as if to ask if that was okay. I finally let out that breath and smiled at him with encouragement. He relaxed back into his seat and drove us home.

We sat quietly for the rest of the drive, listening to Stella's voice singing about "that one person," and I felt like we were at the start of something new.

Fourteen

"So, Amy, how's work going?" Scott asked casually at dinner. I had to look up from my halibut (which was delicious) and concentrate on the conversation at hand.

We were at Saturday night dinner, forced yet again by my demanding parents and joined by my angelic brother. But I felt a little more prepared to manage it after the amazing night I'd just had.

When Lucas walked me up to the front door, he gave me a hug and thanked me again for a wonderful night. I felt all sparkly as I went to sleep and spent Saturday getting ready for family dinner.

And now I was here, in the ostentatious dining room, sipping on wine (at least tonight was white wine) and eating delicious food that I could never afford, thinking about Lucas. But time to snap back into reality.

"Work is going really well," I said. "I did get that new assignment and it's been really exciting. I even got backstage passes to Stella Knight's concert last night."

"Who?" asked my father. Remember when I asked Chip who didn't know Stella Knight? I guess I spoke too soon.

"Stella Knight," my mother repeated to him, a conniving glint in her eye. "She's a very famous singer...do you think you could get her to come to our gala?"

That was the last thing I wanted to do, push my mother's "charity" events on a genuinely kind celebrity couple. But things were about to get awkward.

Regular Amy would not have made waves. Regular Amy would have made some noncommittal response along the lines of, "I'll see what I can do." But truth-speaking Amy couldn't say that.

Truth-speaking Amy said, "No, I can't."

My mother dropped her fork in shock. (I told you this was a big deal.) "Well," she said, smoothing the napkin in her lap. "I'm disappointed in you, Amy."

I took it in stride. I expected no less from her.

Scott tried to steer the conversation in a different direction, clearly uncomfortable with my mother's outrage. "Who did you go with?"

"Ivy, of course."

"Who's Ivy?" my father asked. He was really going for the father of the year award here.

"My roommate, Dad. My best friend, Ivy? We've been friends since we were little girls."

"I thought her name was Fern. I don't like her very much."

I took a deep breath in and out, holding myself back from an explosion. Out of the corner of my eye, I saw Scott clench his jaw. Maybe he was tired of the awkward conversations that my parents always directed towards me. "No, Dad. Her name is Ivy. It's always been Ivy."

"And her parents own that farm, right?" my dad continued. "What a mess they've made of their yard."

Why did I need to keep defending her, all these years into our friendship? "They do grow vegetables on their property. It's pretty amazing; they only eat eggs from their own chickens and the vegetables that they grow. It's a lot healthier."

"Messy work. Too time consuming. They should get jobs and pay someone else to do that for them." He barked a laugh. "Maybe that's why they had so many kids, to help with the work. Too many kids..."

"Who else came to the concert?" Scott interrupted. Apparently he was tired of my father's tirades.

"Lucas and his roommate, Nate." I said.

"Why didn't you invite Ethan?" my mother whined.

"I told you, Mother. He's not interested in me like that."

Scott tried again. "How's Lucas?" he asked.

"He's doing well! He asked about you last week. He actually played one of his songs for Stella backstage and she was very impressed." I dazed back into my memories, but was abruptly awoken.

My father, who had tuned us out and started messaging on his phone, perked up. "I never liked Lucas."

"Me neither." My mother wanted to contribute to the fiery arrows aimed at me again.

"He's not so bad—" Scott tried to defend him, but my father interrupted.

"He's just floundering around, doing whatever he wants. That's no way to live in this world. You need to work hard, make money, and settle down with a family." He nodded his head and took a sip of his whiskey. "Don't you go getting any ideas about that boy, Amy. We raised you better than that."

Fighting tears, I nodded meekly. My mother looked admiringly at my father and patted his shoulder. She called Marta over to ask her a question about the food and the plans for the upcoming week.

Scott looked visibly uncomfortable and sipped his whiskey as well. I looked at him sharply. "Do you think so, too?" I asked him quietly.

"Hmm?" He feigned ignorance. "Think what?"

I gave him a "don't mess with me" glare. He sighed. "Lucas is a nice guy, Amy. But he isn't right for you. You need someone who will bring you up in this world, not drag you down." He rubbed my shoulder in consolation, and I shimmied away from him.

"How do you know what's right for me?" I whispered to him. I put my napkin on the table and excused myself to the restroom.

I gave myself a couple minutes to have a pity party as the tears trickled down my cheeks. I was supposed to speak my truth, but what was my truth? Was it the feelings I had inside my heart for Lucas, suppressed for eight years and now bubbling at the surface? Or was it my desire to please my parents? It was hard to know which would win when both were pulling at me so hard.

What was I thinking, getting so close to Lucas last night? I was thinking with my heart, not my head. And my heart always got me in trouble. The music and the moonlight could make anyone do crazy things, but I wasn't just anyone. I was Amethyst King. I needed to pull myself together and be the person I knew I was. I had worked so hard over the last few years to get this promotion, and I was right on the cusp of something amazing. That was my truth. As much as I didn't love my parents' attitude and opinions, they were still my parents, and I needed their approval and support. I would be strong. I wouldn't give in to my heart again.

As if knowing I needed a test to confirm my resolve, my phone buzzed in my purse. I pulled it out to see a text from Lucas.

LUCAS

Thinking of you. Hope you're having a nice dinner with your family.

Of course he would remember that I had family dinner tonight. I wanted to write back, "Thank you, you're so sweet." But it was better to cut off communication. I deleted his text. It was time to speak my truth, to realize that my place was Amy King, successful writer and businesswoman. There was no room for Lucas in that picture.

Fifteen

"How is the assignment going?" Gia asked.

It was Wednesday morning. The last few days were a blur. I spent the entire day Sunday binging The Office and snuggling with Waffles. Ivy popped in here and there, but she could sense I'd rather be alone. Lucas texted again, but I deleted his messages and focused on the TV.

On Monday and Tuesday, I threw myself into my work. I was enthusiastic in meetings, offering genuine feedback to my coworkers, but doing my best to not hurt their feelings. Everyone seemed pleased with my input, and I felt my relationships building stronger with the girls in the office. But my heart still ached for Lucas.

So how could I honestly answer Gia? How *was* the assignment going?

"It's a mixed bag," I eventually answered. "The concert on Friday was great, but I let things go too far with the guy I like. Or liked. I don't know anymore."

Gia tapped her fingers on her desk, thinking for a moment. "Did you tell him how you feel?" she pressed.

"Tell him? No. He didn't ask."

"Amy." Gia sighed. "The point of the assignment isn't just answering when someone asks you a question. I want you to speak your truth, in all parts of your life."

"That doesn't seem very work-related," I pointed out, laughing nervously. This was not going as I had hoped.

"Well, I want you to really commit," Gia said. "You won't get anything compelling from your article if you don't go for it, in every part of your life. Right now, you're playing it safe, just answering questions and giving your opinion. But you need to take it further. Seriously think about your whole life. Don't just sit back and let it go by. You need to speak up, and tell people how you feel and what you think."

If Gia wanted to know what I was thinking right now, it was a list of things I'd rather do than speak my truth *all* the time. Run a marathon. Take one of Ivy's dance classes for kids. Watch scary movies for thirty days. Never mind, not that. I was a chicken and got nightmares. But I did not want to tell people what I thought all the time, that was for sure.

I sat back in my chair. "I don't know if I can really do that."

Gia shrugged. "Then I'm not sure if this assignment was for you. I'll give you a couple more days to think it through and really try to implement it in your life. If you can't fully complete the assignment, then we'll have to pass it to someone who will."

Heck no. That was not happening. I had already gone through two awkward weeks; I wasn't going to give up now. Not when I was potentially getting a promotion. "No, no. I can do it." I said. "I'm all in."

"Great." Gia smiled. "I'm glad we talked."

How was I going to do even more than I already had? I was trying to still keep my life basically the same, just being more honest in conversations. I was headed for trouble. There was no doubt about it.

I HID in my cubicle for the rest of the afternoon. I didn't want to see or talk to anyone, for fear of what I might say if I had to truly speak my mind. Farah took one look at me on her way out and beelined for the door.

Getting home was a relief. I threw my purse on the couch and threw myself down like a starfish, thankful that no one was here to look up my skirt. My mother would have said I looked like a "lady of the night" laid out like this. But who cared? She wasn't here.

The door banged open, and I started, covering up my legs. Ivy stomped in and threw her dance bag on the floor with a groan.

"I just had the worst day." She flopped down on the couch next to me.

Normally, I would commiserate with her and let her complain, no matter how tired I was. But my assignment had changed, and now I had to truly tell her how I felt.

"I don't want to talk about it," I said.

Ivy flopped her head to look at me. "Well, that's new. Did someone else have a bad day?"

"Yep."

She nodded and flopped her head back. "Do *you* want to talk about your bad day?"

"Not really. I don't want to talk. I'm going to get myself in trouble."

Ivy nodded. "TV?"

"No. I'll just go to my room so I don't bother you." I stood up, and Ivy stood up, too. She gave me a quick hug.

"I'm sorry you had a bad day." She was unusually somber, and I felt awful.

"I'm sorry I'm being a bad friend. I need a little decompression time, and then we can talk later."

She put her hands on my shoulders. "That would be good. Go rest."

I retreated to my room, laid on my bed and stared at the ceiling. No sooner had I finally rested than my phone buzzed. I picked it up and held it in front of my face, reading a group message from Hannah to me and Ivy.

HANNAH

Here's my dress! Final fitting tonight with my mom!

She attached a picture of herself in her wedding dress at the bridal shop. Her dress choice was perfection. It had thin spaghetti straps with a ruched satin bodice that came down to a low V. Sparkling gems created a faux belt right under her bust. The dress flowed out from there, a slightly billowing satin skirt to create a beautiful silhouette, but not too much to look like a princess. Because Hannah wasn't a princess; she was a queen.

IVY

You are so beautiful!! Evan is going to go crazy!

ME

Gorgeous, Hannah!

At least I could be a little more enthusiastic over text than I was in person. I laid back down and closed my eyes. My phone buzzed again.

HANNAH

And here it is with the veil!

I blinked a few times, trying to figure out what was wrong. The veil was beautiful on its own. But with this dress, it didn't fit. The veil was long and made of lace. It had gorgeous flowers all over it, but it was the wrong style.

IVY

So beautiful!

I dropped my phone flat on my face. Perfect, now my nose would be sore too. Grouchy with pain and frustration, I hesitated for a moment before typing my response.

ME

I don't know. The veil is beautiful, but it doesn't match your dress.

I pinched my eyes shut and threw my phone against the wall.

"Amy, what is wrong with you?" Ivy yelled through the apartment. She burst through my door, holding up her phone. "Are you serious?"

I turned my head to her. "You know I'm serious. That's all I can be now. Serious."

"Quit the melodrama. You're not on a teenage soap opera. You can speak your truth without being rude."

I shrugged. Ivy's phone buzzed with a phone call.

"It's Hannah," she informed me. "Now I need to do damage control." She answered the call and left my room, slamming the door.

Was that too far? Was I watching too many reruns of One Tree Hill? The answers were yes and yes. But what now? I couldn't take back what I said.

I sat up in bed, a head rush pounding through my ears. Ivy's soft murmurs came through the walls, her attempts at comforting Hannah making their way into my room. I took in a deep breath, then went to the living room to join the call.

Ivy put her phone on speaker when she saw me, and with wide eyes signaled that I needed to be nice. Hannah's sniffles came through the phone.

"I know she has to speak her truth, but that was a little harsh," Hannah said.

"Hey Hannah, I'm here. I'm sorry for hurting your feelings." Ivy's expression told me that I was still not hitting the mark.

"It's my mother's veil," Hannah said softly. "Her feelings are really hurt."

Oh, biscuits. I wanted to sink down and disappear through a hole in the floor.

"I'm so sorry. I had no idea," I said. Ivy nodded at me in approval. "It's just my opinion."

"Well, once you said it, the people at the bridal shop agreed. So now my mom is really upset and I don't have a veil. And my wedding is in three days."

"We're coming right now," Ivy said. "Both of us." She

used her dance-teacher stare on me, and I got a shiver down my spine. No wonder she was such a good coach. No one could hide from the wrath of Ivy. She hung up the phone and fixed me with a steely glare. "You need to fix this."

"I know, I know," I said. "Let's get in the car and I'll think."

Ivy drove us to the bridal shop, while I sat in the passenger seat scouring Pinterest for something that would work.

"Stop getting distracted with cute lunch ideas. You hardly ever cook."

"I'm not! I'm trying to find ways to repurpose a wedding veil."

Ivy glanced over at my phone and pointed at one idea. "I think that could work."

We pulled into the parking lot and found Hannah in the bridal store, sitting in her wedding dress on a chair. She was a vision, even slumped over and distraught. I sat next to her and reached a hug around her shoulders. "I'm so, so sorry," I said. "Will it make you feel any better if I tell you that you belong in a magazine right now?"

She shimmied away from my hold, and despair settled in my belly. Ivy sat on her other side and hugged her, and Hannah settled into her.

Ouch.

"It's not totally Amy's fault that she's being a witch," Ivy reassured Hannah.

"Hey!" I exclaimed.

Hannah looked over at me. "Well, it still sucks. Because normally she would have thought it, but not said anything."

"True," Ivy said. "But at least we may have found a solution."

Hannah perked up as I pulled out my phone and showed her the pin of a beach wedding. "You said you had a pergola, right? Sometimes people use decorative fabric draped over the top. Maybe you could use your mom's veil like that."

"Then you'd get married *under* it. It would still be part of the ceremony and all the pictures. But it wouldn't clash with this gorgeousness." Ivy gestured at her incredible gown.

Hannah pursed her lips, thinking for a moment. "I'll have to see what my mom thinks. It's not the same, but maybe that would help her feel better." She reached over and rubbed my arm. "Thank you for at least trying to fix it."

"I really am sorry for hurting your feelings. And your mom's. I'm supposed to take speaking my truth to another level, but I'm figuring out how to do it without hurting the people I love."

"Ah, that explains it," Ivy said.

Hannah straightened up and wiped her eyes. "I should go get changed. I'll talk to my mom tonight when I get home." She hugged Ivy, then reached for me again. "Thank you for coming. I know your assignment is difficult for you, too. I'm sorry."

Tears pricked my eyes. "I don't deserve you, Hannah."

She smiled at me. "Sure you do. We're all here for each other." She turned and walked into the dressing room.

Ivy and I slumped back into the chairs. "Crisis sort of averted," she said.

"Well, since I'm apologizing, do you want to tell me about your day today?" I asked.

She sighed. "Remember that new teacher, Blake? She's taking over my teams."

"What?" I exclaimed.

"The moms are so excited that she has industry experience. It doesn't matter that her choreography stinks and she doesn't know how to teach technique. Lisa's thinking about taking away my best teams and handing them to her."

"I'm so sorry," I said. "What are you going to do?"

"Quit." She laughed. "Just kidding. The idea crossed my mind. But the studio is like a family to me, and families make mistakes." She nudged my shoulder. "Like you just did with Hannah. We can forgive mistakes."

I nodded, grateful for friends who were more like family than my own flesh and blood. This assignment was getting harder by the minute, but at least I had their support.

<h1 style="text-align:center">Sixteen</h1>

The night before Hannah's wedding, Ivy and I spent the night at Hannah's house for one last night of celebration. After a karaoke tournament with her parents (where I performed a toned-down encore of my award-winning rendition of Toxic), we had a girls' spa night: painting nails, watching old movies, and face masks. The things we assumed she wouldn't have time for when she was an old married woman (although we hoped we were wrong). Even though we were a little sad to be losing our trio of single ladies, we were so excited to celebrate with Hannah. It was the start of a new era, but she deserved all the love and happiness in the world. Her eyes glowed every time she talked about Evan, and she got a faraway smile. We were so happy for her.

We spent Saturday morning having a big breakfast and getting our hair and makeup done. And of course, for me, it didn't come without awkward moments.

The makeup artist worked on my face while the hair stylist created Ivy's updo. We were chatting and enjoying ourselves. The makeup artist, Grace, was gorgeous and tall, with bright red hair and impeccable skin. The hair stylist, Carrie, was short and curvy, with gorgeous curls. Ivy's hair looked incredible, swept back into a low bun with beautiful curls framing her face.

"Okay, all done!" Grace said to me, pulling out a mirror to show me my makeup. Biscuits. I groaned internally, not only because I didn't love it, but because I'd have to openly speak my truth about it.

"Thank you, Grace," I began.

"Okay, Ivy, your turn!" she continued.

"I'm sorry, Grace, but I'm not really happy with it." I cringed internally. *I hate this, I hate this, I hate this.*

"Oh!" she exclaimed. "What exactly don't you like about it?"

"Um...I'm not sure. I don't love my cheeks, I think there's too much blush. And something about my eyes looks funny. I think it's too much eyeliner."

She sighed. "I basically have to start over again."

I slunk in my seat. "I'm sorry. I just really don't like it. But I guess if you don't have time, I can live with it."

She shook her head. "No, no. This is your friend's wedding, and you'll see these pictures forever. Let's see what we can do."

Ivy smiled at me encouragingly. I was so embarrassed. Was this really the way things were supposed to go? I felt awful. I was delaying the timeline, and I probably hurt Grace's feelings. She came with the makeup remover and started cleaning my face off again.

"I'm really sorry, Grace," I said. "I'm on a work assignment to speak my truth, and sometimes it comes out at the most terrible times."

Grace stepped back and looked me square in the eye. "Hon, it's your face. It's a little disappointing, sure, but I do want you to be happy. We'll find a fix that will work." She smiled at me and went back to work.

I sighed with relief. Ivy smiled at me and pulled out her phone to pass the time. Sure enough, Grace fixed my makeup, and I was thrilled. I thanked her profusely and gave her a big tip to thank her for her kindness. She gave me a hug and said she was glad I spoke up after all.

Should I have been speaking up like this my whole life? It was uncomfortable and awkward, to be sure, but at least on these more minor occasions, it worked out for the best. As long as I was kind and understanding, others seemed to reciprocate. I hoped I could implement speaking my truth in a considerate manner once my assignment was over.

We headed to Hannah's room to get dressed. Hannah's dress hung in the window, and the photographer was catching some still shots of the dress and shoes. Sitting in the chair of her vanity, wearing a silky white robe, Hannah looked like an angel. Her hair was pulled back in a sleek low bun, and her makeup was a classic, beach-kissed look. It was simple, but perfect and classy.

"Oh, you girls look incredible!" she exclaimed. "I love your hair and makeup!"

We gushed over each other, started to cry, then remembered it was *not* the time for that. Her mother came into the room to help get Hannah dressed, and the photographer snapped pictures of her mother zipping up the back of her dress. It was such a beautiful moment, and I couldn't help thinking about my relationship with my mother. If I got married, would she let me even choose a dress that she didn't like? At least Hannah's mother gave her the right to make that choice. My mother would probably send me a couple pictures of options that I'd have to choose from.

Would I even want pictures like this of my mother zipping my dress? Hannah turned around and gave her mother a hug, and they both had tears in their eyes. My mother could fake our relationship for photographers and the public, but would I even want pictures of a charade?

What was I doing with my life? Why didn't it feel like my own?

I shook my head to escape my thoughts. It was time for the veil, and Hannah gave us a small smile as she pulled out a new veil that we had never seen that matched her dress perfectly. With a mischievous grin, she asked for Ivy and me to put it on. We took the thin single layer of chiffon with a satin edge from her hands silently, and the photographer took pictures of us sliding it into her bun. Hopefully the pictures wouldn't show the bewilderment on our faces. I looked at Hannah's mom to see if she was upset, but she beamed and wiped tears away. We gathered for a couple more pictures, then the photographer went downstairs to take pictures of the bouquets. Hannah's mom followed them out.

"What. Is. This?" Ivy asked before I could.

"Oh, you mean my new veil?" Hannah asked with a sly grin. "Yes, I think it matches my dress much better. What do you think, Amy?"

I gaped at her, then started to laugh. "It's perfect, Hannah. Truly. So how did this happen?"

She turned to look back at herself in the mirror. Satisfied with her appearance, she explained. "When I came home from the bridal store, I decided to have an open conversation with my mom. I explained to her that I loved her veil, and it was a beautiful memory, but that it didn't match my dress. And while I thought it was a beautiful gesture, it wasn't the right fit for me and my wedding. At first, she was disappointed. But after I showed her the picture you found, she agreed to use it as decoration for the pergola."

A smile spread across my face. "I'm so happy for you, Hannah. And your mom was willing to compromise." I doubted my own mother would ever compromise.

As if reading my thoughts, Hannah gave me a hug. "I never knew how she would react until I gave it a try. I'm glad you said something...although I wish you'd been a little gentler."

"I'm still figuring out how to speak my truth," I said. "But I'm glad it all worked out so well."

Ivy and I then grabbed our teal dresses from Hannah's closet and started to get dressed. Ivy's dress was sleeveless with a crossover bodice. It was fitted to the waist, and gently flared out. My dress was off the shoulder, the sleeves angling down to the V in the bodice, and had a similar skirt to Ivy's. I felt elegant and classy. For a moment, I wondered what Lucas would think when he saw me, but tried to push that away. He had stopped texting me after Wednesday, and I hoped he got the hint to put some distance between us.

Once we had our dresses on, we stood with our arms around each other's waists and looked in the mirrors. No one said anything; we just stayed there for a minute and enjoyed the moment together.

It was the end of an era, but the beginning of something beautiful and new. We three would be close forever, and this was just another momentous occasion that we could celebrate together. We had been through many in the past, and there would be so many more in the future. I was incredibly blessed and thankful to have these two beautiful and caring women by my side.

All too soon, the photographer called up the stairs, reminding us that we needed to take pictures of the three of us before we made our way to the ceremony. We smiled at each other, then made our way down for more pictures.

Ivy and I were waiting with our respective groomsmen, Evan's brothers, at the beginning of the path to the beach. They were very nice but married, so it was kind of a relief that they didn't try to flirt with us. Hannah stood behind us, calm and composed, holding on to her father's arm. He was beaming. We heard the music begin for Pachelbel's Canon, and the wedding coordinator signaled to Ivy that it was time to walk. I watched her go, squeezed Hannah's hand one more time, then headed down for my turn.

I walked down the aisle, trying to enjoy the beautiful decorations. The simple white seats had a teal sash tied around the back, and the end of each aisle was decorated with peach-colored roses. My bouquet had some of those roses in it, along with teal succulents and some coral peonies.

I was too nervous to look at anyone seated while I walked down the aisle, but once I took my place at the front for the ceremony, I got my first glimpse of the attendees. My brother Scott was there. He and Evan had known each other in school and kept in contact. Thankfully, my parents were not invited. I could enjoy myself without their presence and judgment. Ivy's whole family was there, though. Hannah had spent many afternoons and weekends with Ivy's family, too, and they were family to her, as well.

And, of course, there was Lucas, sitting with our friends and family.

At first, I didn't recognize him. He had cut his hair short on the sides but kept some of the length on top. He wore a dark-gray suit, which I had never seen him wear before. When we locked eyes, I inhaled sharply. His eyes were wide and his mouth was slightly open. I thought he was looking in my direction, but I wasn't sure, so I turned to check and make sure there wasn't anything behind me. When I looked back at him, he gave a wide smile and mouthed, "You look beautiful."

Oh, my.

So much for putting distance between us.

I was sure my cheeks turned bright red, but I was holding the bouquet and couldn't cover them up, so I just smiled back and mouthed, "Thank you."

Then Hannah came down the aisle. I snuck a glance at Evan, and I watched the moment he first saw her. His breath caught, he smiled from ear to ear, and his eyes misted over. I looked over to see my friend and understood immediately. The lowering sun made her dress glimmer in the light, and her peach bouquet matched the colors of the sunset. Holding onto her father's arm, she was a vision. She came up to the archway, watched as her father and Evan shook hands, and looked lovingly up at Evan as she joined his hand.

As thrilled as I was for my friend, I felt a pang of jealousy. Her family was ecstatic with her match. Evan may not have been part of her culture, but he was a respectable, honorable man, and they embraced him with open arms. Her parents were able to see beyond his race to understand who he was inside, and that was enough for them.

My parents couldn't see past anything. They knew Lucas, they remembered him from high school as my "musician friend who couldn't find a respectable job." But they didn't look any further to see the man he was inside: the one who cared deeply for others, who put the ones he loved before himself, but who also knew the value of pursuing his dreams and never settling for others' expectations.

But where did that put me? I didn't know if I was ready to push aside my parents' expectations for my own happiness. After everything they had given me, how could I ignore their assistance in my life? But did I deserve to be unhappy just for the sake of their lofty expectations? I didn't know. I looked over at Lucas again, who beamed with happiness for our friend.

I refocused on Hannah and her ceremony. The minister gave a beautiful speech about love, respect, and the marriage arrangement. As Evan and Hannah exchanged their vows, their faces shone with joy and love. It was perfection. After a quick prayer, they shared a sweet kiss to the cheers of everyone attending. We danced back down the aisle, and as a bridal party, we mobbed Evan and Hannah to celebrate. Evan and Hannah shared another kiss, and I felt hope in my heart that one day I'd be able to share the same feelings as them.

Seventeen

Hannah and Evan swayed under the sparkling lights. It was their first dance, and everyone could see how genuinely happy and in love they were. The tables were set with coral-colored roses and peonies in tall teal glass vases, and we sat under the stars with twinkling lights strung overhead. Ed Sheeran's "Perfect" played over the sound of the ocean waves in the background, and I smiled with joy for my friend.

"They look so happy." I heard Lucas's voice from my side, and my heart started pattering. He pulled out the chair next to me and took a seat. My seat was assigned to the bridal party, and Lucas sat with a few other friends from school. But once the first dance began, people milled around and chatted quietly. I looked around to find Ivy, since Lucas was now sitting in her seat, and saw her with her parents and sisters. I tried to give her a "help me!" expression, and she pretended to wipe her hands clean, gave me a wave and a wink, and turned away.

"They really do," I answered Lucas, turning to face him.

Those were the first words I had spoken to him in a week. "I'm so, so happy for them."

He casually draped his arm around my chair, his fingertips brushing my bare shoulder. Despite the fire in his touch, I shivered in my seat. Apparently he hadn't gotten the memo that I was trying to keep him at a distance now.

Lucas flashed me a flirtatious grin. "You look beautiful," he said, repeating his sentiments from the wedding.

"Thank you," I replied. He was impossible. I looked back at the happy couple.

"I cut my hair." He would not be deterred.

I looked back at him. "I noticed."

He looked me directly in the eyes. "I figured it was time to grow up a little."

"You're definitely pulling some Chris Hemsworth vibes."

He laughed. "I remember how much you loved that Thor movie." He winked at me, letting me know that there was more to his haircut than just a change to the style.

What was wrong with him? Didn't he notice that I ignored him for this entire week?

"You ignored me all week."

Ah. I guess he did notice.

I nodded. I didn't want to have to tell him the real reason why, and if he asked, I wouldn't have a choice.

He turned his attention back to the happy couple and sang the lyrics to Hannah and Evan's song quietly under his breath. Startled, I took in a sharp inhale.

How did I not pay attention to the lyrics when he sang this song at the beach? The song was about being kids when they fell in love, and not giving up this time. I couldn't believe the irony.

Just then, the DJ saved me and dropped a beat, inviting everyone to the dance floor. Lucas stood and gave me a huge smile while holding his hand out to me. "Shall we?" he asked, with a mock bow. He was joking, but it still made me swoon. Like almost every girl my age, I'd spent my fair share of time rewatching Pride and Prejudice (the 2005 version).

What harm could dancing in a group do? I realized I had waited too long, finally gave him my hand, and we headed to the dance floor. We spent the next hour dancing together, letting out all of our jitters from the day, all the while stealing glances at each other.

We danced with Ivy and her family, little Katy stealing the spotlight with all the moves her big sister had taught her. She loved being in the center of the dance circle and gave the best facials. Ivy grabbed her by the shoulders and had her tone down the booty shaking, even though she deserved to be a backup dancer for Taylor Swift. Her parents finally had to drag her out of the circle to take her home, to her protestations. Then it was Ivy's turn to be the center of attention. When the DJ played "Single Ladies," Ivy danced in the center of the circle, doing every move from the music video. She spent countless hours watching Beyonce's video on YouTube when we were teenagers, determined to learn the entire dance.

"It's time to slow things down a bit," the DJ announced from the booth. We heard the first few notes of "Nights Beneath the Stars," and Lucas and I immediately locked eyes. I hesitated, knowing that once I danced with him, I wouldn't be able to stay away anymore. But it was like a magnet attracted us to each other, and I couldn't resist the pull. He put one arm around my waist and held my hand in his. I put my other hand on his shoulder and felt like a proper lady. We swayed wordlessly for a couple minutes. Out of the corner of my eye, I saw Scott dancing with Ivy. They looked like they were having a surprisingly nice time together.

But Lucas drew my attention away from them. He put his lips to my ears and whispered, "This is perfect."

A chill went down my spine. I closed my eyes and silently told my heart to slow its pounding. "What is?" I asked breathlessly.

I heard him chuckle. "This song, this lighting, this occasion...this girl." He paused, sucked in a breath, then pressed his lips to my cheekbone.

This was torture. I felt my resolve slipping, bit by bit.

I slowly turned my head to him. "Lucas, I don't know—"

Suddenly, Michael Jackson's voice blared in the speakers, and everyone around us hollered and crowded onto the dance floor. Lucas met my eyes and tilted his head toward the beach. I nodded in agreement, and, hand in hand, he led me away.

We reached the archway where Evan and Hannah had stood just a few hours before. Lucas reached for my other hand and held them gently, keeping space between us. There was a slight breeze from the ocean, the sound of the crashing waves matching the thoughts that kept rushing through my mind. Doubts, insecurities, love for the man in front of me... but it was time.

Before I could say anything, Lucas began. "Amy, I can't take it anymore. Being near you, being your friend—it's torture. I'm still in love with you."

I stood still, in shock. It had been eight years since I'd first heard him say those words, and as much as I daydreamed about hearing them again, nothing matched their sound in my ears. I must have stood silently for too long, because Lucas pulled one hand away to scratch the back of his neck. "Are you...are you going to say anything?"

I shook my head, incredulous. "Why?" I asked.

"Why?" he repeated, bringing his hand up to my cheek.

"Why me? After all this time?" I whispered. I closed my eyes and tried to keep my wits, but it was so hard when his finger was gently caressing my face.

He stopped and put his hand around the back of my head. I opened my eyes and looked back at him. "The day after graduation, I told myself that I'd forget about you. With the whole country between us, I figured I'd move on. But no one compares to you. You are incredible. Intelligent, kind, loyal. You care about your friends and family so much. You see the best intentions of everyone you meet." He paused. "And you're devastatingly beautiful."

No one had ever said anything like this to me. No one listed my good qualities and told me *why* they loved me. Tears pricked my eyes as I felt the weight of his love for me. He brought his hand to cup my cheek, his thumb slowly caressing my cheek. He leaned forward and brought his lips to meet mine.

Like our first kiss eight years ago, this kiss was light and sweet but full of intense heat that passed between our lips. We pressed together for a moment, and all too soon, Lucas pulled back. I opened my eyes in confusion to see him looking back at me, his eyes asking for my permission to proceed.

I decided that speaking my truth didn't just mean words. I leaned into him and kissed him again, with determination to show him how I truly felt. I poured eight years of feelings and pent-up frustration into that kiss.

He groaned and wrapped one arm around my waist, bringing the other hand around the back of my neck. I put my hands on his chest, appreciating how much his physique had changed over the years, but the person inside had never changed. Emotion overflowed in my heart, as I realized that this man I still loved, loved me in return. It was a bliss I had never experienced and had only hoped to feel. Tears began to run down my cheeks. Lucas deepened the kiss, trying to convey his admiration for me.

I felt it.

Slowly, Lucas decreased the pressure and gently kissed my lips once more before trailing kisses down my neck and across my bare shoulder.

"Lucas..." I murmured, and felt his lips smile through his kisses. He slowly made his way back to my lips, then leaned his forehead gently against mine and shook his head slightly.

"Amy," he breathed. "I—"

"Amy? Are you out here?" Scott's voice rang across the beach. A cold wave of reality came crashing over me.

What was I doing?

What would my family think of this?

I pushed Lucas away from me, putting a few feet of distance between us. His eyes filled with confusion and disappointment. But I couldn't let Scott see us like this.

"I'm here, Scott," I called back, my voice trembling, praying he hadn't seen us a minute earlier.

He came to where Lucas and I stood a few feet apart, a question hanging thick in the air. But he chose to ignore the situation and simply said, "Hannah is looking for you."

"Okay. I'm coming," I said, starting to follow him.

But Lucas grabbed my arm. "Hang on," he said. "Amy and I still need another minute."

Scott stepped forward to defend me.

"It's okay, Scott," I said. "We just need to finish our conversation and then I'll be there."

Scott paused, then gave a curt nod. "Fine." He leaned closer to me and whispered, "But remember who you are, Amy. Who *we* are." I nodded meekly at him, and he turned and headed back to the reception.

I turned back to Lucas. The hurt in his eyes stabbed through my heart. "Amy," he said. "I thought...what is going on?"

"I can't, Lucas," I started. "I wasn't thinking. I just—"

He held up his hand to stop me. "Answer me one thing. How do *you* feel about me?"

And there it was. The culmination of my assignment. The time to actually and truly speak my truth. And yet, it felt like the floor was slipping out from under my feet. Finally, *finally* I knew that Lucas still felt something for me, but it didn't mean anything. Nothing mattered, so long as I was my parents' daughter.

I closed my eyes, as if not looking at him would make it easier. "I love you, Lucas. I always have."

I felt his hands run down my arms. "Then what is it? Your family? You can't tell me that they still matter that much."

I opened my eyes. "Of course they do. You know that. Their opinion means everything to me."

"*Everything?*" he asked. "Amy, you're a grown woman. You can make your own choices. And who you love should be your choice, not theirs."

"Maybe it should be my choice, but it isn't. You know them. I can't do this to them." I shook my head, pulling myself free from his grasp.

"You're not doing *anything* to them! This is not their business!" Lucas started pacing and running his hand through his hair. I wished there was something, anything, I could say to explain it to him. But nothing came to mind. I knew he didn't understand. His family had supported his pursuit of his dreams; they never held expectations for him. Whatever he did was golden to them. "Then...what was this?" He gestured frantically between us. "What just happened between us, that wasn't nothing."

"It was a moment of weakness," I said. "I wasn't thinking."

"It wasn't just a moment. This has been simmering for the last eight years, and you know it. But this last week at the concert, I thought...I thought you were ready."

"I don't know what I was thinking," I cried through my tears. "But my parents—I'm never enough for them." He stopped walking and turned to face me. "I can never do the right thing by them. I went to the wrong school, got the wrong degree, have a mediocre job, while Scott does everything they've ever dreamed of and more. I can't keep disappointing them."

"Amy." He stepped forward and took my hands again. "You are enough to me. More than enough. Please let me show you that. You don't need your parents' approval."

I shook my head. "I can't." I closed my eyes. I couldn't face him anymore.

He leaned his forehead against mine again and held my face in his hands. "I wish you could see yourself the way I see you." He kissed my lips lightly one last time. "Tell Hannah and Evan I said congratulations." He turned and began walking away.

"Wait!" I cried out, my voice cracking through my tears. "That's it?"

He turned back to face me again. "I don't know what you think can happen if you're not willing to really do this. I can't hang around waiting for you forever." He pinched his eyes, then shook his head. "I love you, Amy." He shrugged. "I don't know what else I can offer you. But if that's not enough, then at least I know now."

I turned back to the ocean, too afraid to watch him walk away. I couldn't trust myself to let him go. The sound of the waves crashing masked the sound of my sobs, as I tried to get a hold of myself and go back to the wedding.

What had I done? I had spoken my truth, that was for sure. Not only by kissing Lucas and truly telling him how I felt, but by explaining to him we could never happen. I felt a strange relief in getting the truth out there, but the crushing weight of despair in the things that could never be.

Lucas loved me. And now what? What would even happen to our friendship? How could we both expect to move on if we hung out together as usual? We'd already spent years together, and that was before we reopened our feelings and kissed.

Oh, that kiss. It rocked my world, body and soul. The passion between us was just as intense as the first time. No one else had ever kissed me like that. I didn't know how I would ever be able to move on, knowing that Lucas was out there somewhere kissing someone else.

I sat on the sand. I didn't care about my dress getting ruined. It was too much. This was all too much to handle.

A minute later, another teal dress sat next to me. Ivy. She wrapped her arms around me and held me while I cried. I couldn't speak, but she was always there for me. Together, we sat and watched the waves until I felt strong enough to get up and face the wedding again.

I passed the rest of the night in a daze, faking a smile for Hannah's sake. When I walked back into the reception, Scott looked at me with a question in his eyes. I shook my head. He gave a curt nod, and we avoided each other for the rest of the night.

Finally, Ivy and I arrived home, and I asked if I could sleep in her bed with her tonight. I still hadn't explained exactly what happened, but she hugged me and nodded. We climbed into her bed, and I fell asleep almost immediately, too exhausted from all my tears and the emotions of the day.

Eighteen

B*uzz, buzz, buzz.*

"What is wrong with your phone?" I grumbled. It had been buzzing for the last few minutes. I opened my eyes and blinked until I could clearly see the time on Ivy's clock: 2:30 a.m. She rolled over and grabbed her phone off the nightstand. Furrowing her brows, she picked it up.

"Hello?" she asked groggily. A frantic voice spoke on the other side. It sounded like Hazel, Ivy's second younger sister. "Wait, what?" She was more alert this time. "No, no, no," she cried, pulling the blankets off the bed. I sat up in alarm. "Is Katy okay?" she asked. She breathed a sigh of relief. "I'll be right there."

She hung up the phone, staring into the darkness.

"What happened?" I asked.

Dazed, she focused on me. "That was Hazel." She paused for a moment. "My parents took Katy home early from the wedding, and they were in a car accident. They're in the hospital." Her eyes started to fill with tears.

"And Katy's okay?" I asked.

She nodded. "She's a little banged up, but nothing serious. But I don't know about my parents…"

I jumped out of bed with her. "Let's go. Right now."

We gathered what we could as quickly as possible, then rushed out the door to my car. The hospital was about fifteen minutes away, but at this time of night, we were able to zoom there quickly. The cold air and fear about Ivy's family jolted me awake, even though I only slept for about two hours. We pulled into the parking lot and ran inside the hospital.

We were shown to the area where Ivy's family was. Katy was asleep in her room with Hazel watching over her, some scratches and bruises over her body but no internal injuries. Her mother had a broken arm, but otherwise seemed to have minor injuries as well.

But her dad was currently in surgery. The car that collided with them, driven by a teenager who was texting his friends, had smashed into the driver's side. Katy was sitting behind her mom in the passenger seat, so the two of them had fewer injuries. But Ivy's dad had been hit straight on, causing injury to his spine and legs. The doctors were worried.

We were worried.

We talked with doctors in the hallway, and I tried to support Ivy as best as I could. She put on a brave face, trying to hold it together as the oldest daughter of the family. Therefore she needed to make some of the most critical decisions. For now, all she could do was wait.

Waiting was torture.

After two hours of sitting in silence and praying, a doctor came to tell us that Ivy's mom was ready to see her. I squeezed her hand and sent her to follow the doctor to her room. Ivy gave me a quick hug before walking away, and then I was left alone in the hospital.

Despite the bustle of nurses and doctors, I felt completely alone. Worry consumed me. In many ways, Ivy's parents were dearer to my heart than my own parents were. An accident like this would completely wreck their world. Not only did they love their home garden and the projects they did there, but they still had to take care of Katy full time. Thank God she was okay. I couldn't imagine how we would feel if something had happened to her. But even so, I couldn't help worrying the worst for their father.

Fifteen minutes later, Ivy came back down the hallway. She walked slowly but looked slightly brighter than before. "She's doing pretty well," she told me. "She's in pain, and she keeps asking about my dad. But she's doing okay."

"Who's with her now?" I asked.

"Luna's with her. Hazel is still with Katy in the pediatric ward, and they'll switch soon. I should go see Katy, too."

"I'll stay with you, don't worry," I said.

She squeezed me again. "I'm so sorry you're here. You know you don't have to be."

Tears pricked my eyes. "I love your parents, and I love you. I'm not going anywhere."

She smiled and kissed my cheek. "You're the best. Let's go see Katy."

We wandered through the hospital together to find Katy's room. She was still asleep, and Hazel was awake, just watching her.

"Hey," Ivy whispered. "How's she doing?"

"She's good," Hazel said. "She whimpers and tosses around every now and then, but she's going to be okay."

Ivy nodded, then looked at her little sister lying in the hospital bed. Tears filled her eyes again, and she walked over to pick up her little hand. Katy stirred, but didn't wake up. "She's just so little. She shouldn't have to deal with this."

I rubbed her arm, trying my best to be supportive. But what could you say to someone in this situation? All I could do was be there for her, so she knew she always had me through whatever happened.

"Hazel, you can go see Mom if you want," Ivy said to her. "I'll stay with Katy for a little bit."

Hazel nodded, exhausted. She must not have slept at all tonight. She gave Katy a kiss on the forehead, hugged Ivy and me, then left to go see her mom. Ivy and I settled into the chairs next to Katy, all while Ivy held onto her sister's hand like a lifeline. We sat quietly for a few minutes, and then Katy began to stir.

"Mom?" she asked, her eyes blinking open.

"Hey, Katy girl," Ivy said softly. "It's Ivy and Amy."

Katy smiled. "Hey. Is Mom here?"

Ivy shook her head. "She's in her own room. She's okay though."

"And Dad?" Katy asked.

Ivy bit her lips and shook her head again. "He's in surgery right now."

"Is he going to be okay?" Katy asked.

Ivy looked at me for help. I didn't know what to say.

Katy looked at me. "Amy? You have to tell me the truth. What's happening with my dad?"

My stomach dropped. She was right. I did have to answer

her truthfully. This little spitfire wasn't letting an accident get in the way of her finding out what was really happening.

"Um…your dad is in surgery."

"That's what Ivy said. Is he going to be okay?"

I tried to not let the tears fall. "We don't know, Katy. He has a big injury to his back and legs. I know the doctors are trying their absolute best."

She nodded, her big blue eyes filling with tears. "Thank you for telling me, Amy," she said. She looked up at the ceiling, then looked back at Ivy. "I'm scared," she said.

Ivy let the tears fall from her face. "Me too, Katy girl. Me too."

Nineteen

Exhausted and spent from crying, Ivy and I fell asleep in our chairs while Katy watched TV. Her parents always tried to limit her screen time, so she was happy to watch as much as she could.

When the sun finally rose around seven, Hazel came into the room and gave Katy a quick kiss on the head. "Hey, the doctor said they're done with Dad's surgery, and he wants to talk to us."

Ivy jumped up from her chair. "I'll stay with Katy," I offered. Ivy nodded gratefully and left the room with Hazel.

Katy pouted as they left. "I want to go, too."

I reached over to her and squeezed her hand. "I know, sweet girl. We'll get the info from them as soon as they come back."

We watched them leave, and Katy heaved a big sigh for such a little girl. "This is hard," she told me, her eyes up at the ceiling.

I nodded at her. "Which part is the hardest?" I asked her.

"I hate that they think I'm too little for them to talk to

me. And I hate that I'm stuck here in this bed." She looked at me. "At least you don't think I'm too little."

"I do think you're too little. But I have to be honest with you," I said with a smile.

She laughed, then sobered. "And I'm scared about my dad."

"Me too, Katy," I said.

"What if he doesn't wake up?" she asked me, her eyes filling with tears.

"I don't know. I don't want to think too hard about that," I said. This was such a big conversation to have with her, and I didn't want to mess it up. "I'm keeping hope."

She nodded, blinking away her tears. "Then I will too." She took in another deep breath. "At least we had fun together last night. If he doesn't wake up, at least we had fun. He knows that I love him and that he's the best dad." She turned back to the TV, satisfied with her conclusion.

Oh, wow.

I blinked away my tears, processing what this little speaker of truth had just said. She at least resolved that she had been open about her feelings towards her dad, and she never left any strings untied. On the other hand, I couldn't even tell my parents that I hated my job, or that I loved Lucas.

How would I feel if my parents died? Sad, of course. They raised me, sort of. And in a terrible way, I would feel...relief? That I didn't have to live up to their expectations anymore. This was too heavy to process right now. I needed to focus on the Jones family instead. I shook my head to clear my thoughts, then focused on Katy and her show.

After a couple more episodes of Bluey, Ivy came back into

the room. "Hey, let's talk in the hallway," she said to me. Before I could get out of my chair, Katy grabbed my hand. "You know you have to tell me everything when you come back," she whispered.

"That's not how it works," I whispered back with a smile.

She rolled her eyes and slumped back in the bed. "I'll get it out of you," she said, shaking her finger at me. I had to admire her feistiness.

Stepping out into the hallway, I put a hand on Ivy's arm. "What did the doctor say?" I asked.

She took in a deep breath and looked around, trying to gather her words. "He had damage to his brain and spinal cord. He still hasn't woken up yet, but they won't know the full extent of the damage for a little while. He's stable, though, which is good."

I nodded slowly, not sure I understood completely. "So... what's the worst-case scenario?"

"Paralysis."

My eyes widened. I couldn't imagine Brent Jones being paralyzed. His life was in his garden. He loved to be active. He was the dad who would skateboard with the kids in the neighborhood. I swallowed, then nodded again. "Okay. And how long until he wakes up?"

"Hopefully in the next couple of hours." She looked down at her hands. "You don't have to stay, though. You should go home and rest."

"I'm tired, but I don't want to leave you."

"I'm okay right now. I have my sisters, and my mom is awake. I'll call you as soon as I hear anything."

I gave her one more hug and headed out to my car. The sun was finally up, but it felt like the middle of the night to my body. I was so exhausted, even though I had slept in Katy's room.

I thought again about how I would feel if my parents were the ones in this accident. I'd be worried and upset, but the despair I felt for Ivy and her sisters was on a completely different level.

And then there was the relationship that Ivy and her sisters had. I would never have that with Scott, and my relationship with my parents would never be anywhere near the relationship the girls had with their parents. Ivy was comfortable with me leaving because she had her sisters. If my parents were in the hospital, I would beg her to stay with me. I would need her support.

What did that say about my parents?

What did that say about me?

My phone buzzed in my purse. I hadn't checked it since we left the wedding last night, afraid I'd see something from Lucas. But now he had sent a text. My heart raced as I unlocked my phone and read his words.

LUCAS

I heard Ivy's parents are in the hospital.
What happened?

I started to text him back, but realized a phone call would make more sense in this situation. He picked up right away. "Hey." He sounded distant.

"Hey. I'm leaving the hospital to go home right now."

"What happened? Are they okay?"

"They were in a car accident. Katy's okay. Rachel broke her arm but is awake and fine. We're not sure about Brent yet. He hasn't woken up and had some damage to his spine."

I took in a shaky breath. "Ivy and her sisters are here, though, and they promised to keep me updated. I'm going home so I can get some rest."

Lucas was silent for a minute. I could imagine him nodding or running his fingers through his newly cut hair. "Are you okay?" he asked.

I bit my lip, trying to formulate an honest answer to that question. Finally, I said, "I don't know."

"Do you need anything?" he asked.

I laughed sarcastically. "How could you ask that after last night?"

"Amy," he said firmly. "I haven't turned off my feelings in one night. I still love you. And I know how much Ivy's family means to you. Regardless of what happened last night, you're still my friend and I want you to be okay."

Friend. We're still friends. No matter how much I wanted to be more than that. "Thank you," I whispered. "I still love you, too. And I'm so thankful for you."

He laughed quietly. "We probably shouldn't keep saying that we love each other, though."

"Probably not," I agreed. Although, I was speaking my truth. Maybe after the assignment was over, we could go back to normal and not worry about our feelings getting in the way of our friendship.

"Okay. Let me know if you hear anything about Brent. And send my love to the family."

"I will. Thank you for texting. I'll...talk to you later, I guess," I said.

"Bye, Amy."

I hung up and put my head on the steering wheel and started to sob. The last twenty-four hours were the biggest roller coaster of emotions I'd ever experienced. Joy and elation for Hannah and Evan, thrill and love for Lucas, heartbreak over the realization that we couldn't be together, and despair for Ivy's parents. I didn't know how I'd come back from this.

I GOT HOME and threw my purse on the couch. Exhausted emotionally, I still wasn't ready to sleep. Instead, I grabbed my calligraphy notebook and markers and settled in. I turned on The Office for distraction and flipped through my notebook.

I was so proud of my progress. The hobby I started for fun in high school (and to impress Lucas, if I'm being honest) had turned into something that satiated my soul. I turned the pages slowly, assessing how much I'd improved since I'd started this notebook a year ago. Then the last page appeared, with the quotation I had doodled before I received my assignment.

"Not enough for me? You are everything."

Tears filled my eyes as I remembered the words Lucas had spoken to me last night. *"You are enough for me. More than enough. Please let me show you that."* The words I had longed to hear my whole life—that I was enough for someone. I always reached for more with my parents, yet I was never enough for their expectations. But here was someone willing to accept me exactly as I was. Was I such an idiot, that I would turn down a love like this?

What was I even turning him down for? My parents' unrealistic goals and indifference towards my desires? But I still couldn't think of any way to get out from under their watch, unless I completely severed the relationship with them. I wasn't ready for anything like that.

I flipped to a new blank page and just stared at it. I figured I'd doodle Ivy's family names, almost like a prayer for their health. I started with Brent and Rachel at the top, then each of the four girls' names: Ivy, Hazel, Luna, and Katy. As I drew each name, I said a prayer for their health and healing. I didn't know if it would really help, but it at least gave me the calm I needed to come down from the emotional roller coaster of the last day.

I looked at the page with a sense of satisfaction. Just then, my phone rang, Ivy's name appearing across the screen.

"Hey, is he awake?" I asked.

"No, not yet. But I figured I should call and see if you're okay. Did I wake you up?"

"No, I'm too wired to sleep. I was just doing some calligraphy."

"Well, you're always welcome to come wait here with us, if you want," she said. "Or if you want to be alone, that's fine, too."

"No, I want to come back. My brain is going crazy here. Does anyone need anything?" I asked.

"Actually, if you can bring me a book and some drawing things for Katy, that would be awesome," she said.

"Perfect. I'm on it. I'll be there soon." I hung up and packed everything up for them, along with my iPad for Katy to draw on, too. Thankful for a distraction, I headed back to the hospital.

~

WHEN I GOT THERE, Ivy, her mom, and her sisters were all in Katy's room. Rachel had been discharged, and Katy was going to be soon. They wanted to keep her a little longer, since she was so small, to make completely sure that she was fine before she left.

I hugged Rachel as soon as I got in, trying to be careful of her arm that was in the sling. "I'm so happy to see you up and moving around," I told her.

"Me too," she said with a smile. Her hair was tossed up on top of her head, likely the work of one of the older girls. She was exhausted, but still looked like she was whole. She looked at her girls with a smile. "At least we're all here together."

"How's Brent?" I asked.

"Still the same. We're just waiting for him to wake up so we know what to expect from here." She sat down in a chair by the window, a little bit away from the girls, and gestured for me to sit down next to her.

"How's Katy taking everything?" I asked.

"She feels fine, which is a relief. And she's excited to have so much attention from her sisters. But she's worried about her dad."

"Of course," I said. "And you?"

She looked at nothing, her eyes far away. "I'm worried for his sake. His life will never be the same, even if he's not fully paralyzed. It's going to be difficult, to say the least." She sucked in a breath. "But at least we've spent the last thirty years doing what we've loved. No regrets. We've been together, raised this beautiful family, and made our home into exactly what we wanted." She smiled at me, her eyes shining with tears. "Even if everything changes from here on out, we'll know that we did everything we could to be happy. We'll figure it out together."

I bit my lip to hold in my tears. "You are both so blessed to have each other," I finally said with a wavering voice.

"And we're blessed to have you, as well," she said, giving me a hug. "You're family, too, Amy. Thank you for being here for my girls. We love you."

The tears fell freely then. Rachel had been more of a mother to me over the last fifteen years than my own, and her words cut into my soul. How would I feel in thirty years if I had a life-altering accident? Would I feel like I had lived my life the way I wanted until that point? What regrets would hang over me?

As if reading my thoughts, Rachel pulled back and looked me in the eye. "Amy, are you happy?"

"Right now?" I asked with a laugh. "Not really."

"I don't mean about the accident. In general, are you happy with your life?"

I thought for a moment, making sure I answered honestly. Was I happy?

I had incredible friends. Most people didn't have that support system. Ivy and Hannah were more than I deserved. Ivy's family had given me the love and encouragement I desperately craved from my parents. But other than that, was I truly happy? I spent every day at a job I didn't enjoy, and to what end? All I wanted now was to be with Lucas, to feel his embrace, to know that he would be there for me at the end of each day. Instead, I pushed him away (twice), making myself miserable in the process.

I looked down at my hands before answering. "I'm beyond thankful for Ivy. And your family is amazing to me. But overall...no, I'm not happy."

Rachel rubbed my back. "Why do you think that is?"

I narrowed my eyes at her. "Why are you comforting me? This is backwards."

She laughed. "Helping you is taking my mind off things. Humor me."

The weeks of speaking my truth led up to this moment. I didn't want to choose my words carefully anymore. I wanted to speak my truth, and I knew Rachel wouldn't judge anything I said.

I sighed. "I don't do the things that will make me happy, because I'm worried about what my parents will think."

Rachel nodded. "I can see that. You've always wanted to do what would make them happy. Except for your college."

"Well, I didn't really have a choice there. I didn't get into USC."

"And I feel like you've been beating yourself up for years over that." She shifted in her chair, her knees touching mine. "If you could start over from scratch, what would you do?"

"Calligraphy." The answer came out without thinking. Guess I was really speaking my truth. "I love it, and I already have a decent following on Instagram. I could address invitations, teach courses, make instructional YouTube videos. There are a lot of ways I could make it into a career."

"Seems like you've thought a lot about this," she said, cocking her head with a grin.

"I guess so," I replied. "I didn't realize it until I said it."

She paused, considering how to proceed. "What would happen if you did it?" she asked.

"Oh, my parents would be livid. It's like being the artisan in medieval times. No one respects them."

She nodded. "I could see that. I've only met your parents a few times, but they don't seem like the types who would be happy with a daughter who's an artist." She paused. "Would that really be so bad?"

"Well...they're my parents," I said. "They paid for my college tuition. I owe them. And my mother holds grudges like you wouldn't believe. She would never speak to me again." I glanced at the other girls to make sure I wasn't disturbing Katy, but they were all busy painting Katy's nails.

"I know, Amy." Rachel smiled sadly. "But remember, your tuition is a drop in the bucket to them. And more than that, you are a person whose thoughts and feelings matter. You are important. Your feelings are important. If you're unhappy, you need to change that. And I don't mean by bending over backwards to please them. You need to do what will make you happy." She smoothed my hair, ran her hand down my cheek, and cupped my chin. "I will always be here for you." She stood and went back to her daughters.

My head was fuzzy like cotton candy. I watched a beautiful, loving mother with her four girls. Her heart was breaking for her husband, but she had created a life she loved that was filled with love. She didn't have regrets.

Would I have regrets at her age?

Did I have regrets now?

A doctor came into the room then. "Mrs. Jones? Your husband is awake."

Twenty

Brent Jones was awake and conscious. He was in a lot of pain, but his mind worked well. While he could move his hands and arms, he was currently unable to move the bottom half of his body. We wouldn't know for a little while if it was permanent. He was upset and in pain, yet the joy he had at knowing that his wife and daughter were fine was overwhelming. I only saw him through the window, and I was moved to tears (again).

I found Ivy in the hallway on my way out.

"You're leaving?" she asked.

"Yeah, I think it's time for me to go home."

"I was actually going to go home, too. My mom told me to go take a shower and come back later. Now that we know Dad's awake and stable, I can breathe a little easier."

"Good timing. Let's head home." I put my arm around Ivy and we walked out to the car. We didn't say anything, each of us processing the last twenty-four hours. We climbed in my car and I turned it on. But before I could shift into reverse, Ivy grabbed my arm.

"Hold up," she said abruptly.

"What's wrong?" I asked, alarmed. I thought something might have happened in the hospital.

"Why were you crying on the beach last night? Oh my goodness, Lucas! What happened with Lucas?" She was so shrill, I had to plug my ears.

"Girl, lower your volume!" I laughed. "It's been a long day. I can't deal with your banshee noises."

"Stop redirecting. Tell me what happened."

I rested my head on the steering wheel. Slowly, I recounted the whole evening to her. Talking with him during the first dance, dancing together. Our kiss on the beach, Scott's interruption. Our declarations of feelings, and my realization that we could never work. Ivy sat silently until that point.

"Never?" Ivy finally interrupted. "Amy, come on. The man told you he loved you. What more could you ask for?"

"I know, I know," I said. "After today…I'm not so sure anymore."

She nodded. "I know that you want to make your parents happy. I don't understand it, but I know you do."

"Ivy, you *should* understand. Don't you want to do the things that will make your parents happy?"

"That's different, Amy, and you know it!" Ivy's face flamed with passion. The events of the day had caught up to her, and she was letting it loose. "My parents may not be perfect, but they want *me* to be happy. They're not selfish, they don't care about appearances, they don't care how much money I make, as long as I'm happy. Your parents care only about themselves and how you make them look. And you only care about them, too. That's a twisted relationship.

I've sat by and watched you lose all your joy for their sake, and you need to take a stand." She huffed and sat back in her chair, her speech completed.

"Maybe you're right," I murmured. "I just wouldn't even know where to start."

She turned her head to face me. "If you're really ready to do this, let's go get some sleep and then we'll plan later." Her eyelids were drooping. She must have been so exhausted, not just physically, but emotionally. I nodded and backed the car out of the parking spot, then headed home so we could crash into our beds and sleep the day away.

I called in sick to work the next day. I wasn't ready to go in and face everyone. It was partly because I was exhausted from a lack of sleep and emotionally worn out, but also because I wasn't sure if I was going to keep working there anymore. I loved Gia and admired her passion, but it wasn't my passion. I wanted to do calligraphy full time. I knew I was good enough at it to make it a full-time job, but I needed the courage to take that leap and go for it.

Ivy and I rolled out of our beds the next morning around ten. Her dad was still in pain, still paralyzed from the waist down. Katy and Rachel were both discharged now and headed back home, but Rachel was going to need help watching her for the next few weeks. Potentially even longer, depending on how much help Brent needed once he got out of the hospital.

Ivy hung up her phone and sighed. "I think I might need to move back home."

"What? Why?" I asked.

"My mom will need my help with Katy. Hazel and Luna are both in college. It's not really the right time for them. If I can help watch her, then she can help with my dad."

My eyes widened. I didn't want to lose my roommate, but I understood where she was coming from. I pursed my lips, trying to think of a solution to my rent problem without being selfish.

Knowing what I was thinking, Ivy smiled at me. "You know, you could probably move in there, too. There were a few years where all four of us girls were living at home. There's enough room for all of us, since Hazel and Luna are out."

I nodded slowly, processing that I could now actually move away from my apartment if I wasn't worried about what my parents were thinking. Did I really want to move back into a house with...parents? I wasn't sure about that, but at least I had the option.

Ivy grinned wickedly. "Or maybe you'll just get married to Lucas and move in with him."

I barked a laugh. "You're moving a little fast there, don't you think?"

"Uh, no. Let's get down to business, girl. Are you doing this or not? Are you going to go for what *you* want now?"

I nodded slowly. "Crazy enough, I feel like this is really the culmination of my assignment. I'm not speaking my truth in my life right now, and that's really what I'm supposed to do. Speak my truth."

Ivy smiled from ear to ear. "I'm so proud of you. I knew this day would come. You've finally grown up." She laughed and gave me a hug. "So...what's first?" she asked.

I took a deep breath. "I've been thinking about that. I think the first thing needs to be quitting my job. I don't feel like I can really move forward with anything else until I start there."

Ivy nodded. "And then Lucas?"

"And then Lucas," I said with a big smile.

I PEERED into Gia's office the next morning. My heart pounded thunderously in my chest. I couldn't breathe. But I needed to do this.

"Hey Gia. Can I talk to you?"

"Sure, Amy. Come on in." I entered her room and sat down. It was eight on Tuesday morning, and I needed to get this done as soon as possible.

"I was going to ask you to come in, anyway," she said. "We didn't get to catch up on your assignment yesterday."

"I'm just going to say this so I don't chicken out," I said quickly. "I'm quitting."

Gia's eyes widened, and then she smiled. "That was faster than I expected."

"I'm sorry, I should've given you more of an intro, but—"

"No, no. That was faster in the course of your assignment."

I cocked my head, confused. "Wait, what?"

She leaned forward in her chair. "You're doing a great job here, and I'm really grateful that your celery juice article went viral. Our views have gone through the roof, and our email subscription list has tripled in size. We have plans for expansion, new sponsors, everything is going great. And a lot of it is because of the article you wrote."

"So, what exactly is the problem?"

"The problem is you. You don't love this job. You're not happy here," she said. "As much as I would love to keep you, I know that this isn't where you belong."

I blinked quickly, trying to understand. "Am I being fired?"

She laughed. "No! You just said that you quit. I'm not going to fire you. I'll gladly write you a glowing letter of recommendation for any employer you need. But I did give you this assignment with the goal of you finding your purpose. Speaking your truth, not just in conversation, but in life."

I nodded, slowly grasping what she was saying. "So, you gave me the assignment, hoping that I'd quit."

She shrugged. "Either you'd quit, or you'd decide you loved it here and embrace the lifestyle. Whichever one was most true to yourself."

"But what about the article?" I asked.

"I would still love for you to write it. I think this is a powerful point for anyone to hear, not just women. Let me ask you: are you happy you took this assignment?"

I thought over the last three weeks. I'd met Chip and Stella Knight, gotten in a fight with Hannah but patched things up, finally told Lucas how I felt, and now had the courage to do what I wanted. "Yes," I answered. "I think that speaking my truth has changed everything, but in the best way."

"Then I want people to know that. We need to be honest with ourselves, and others, about what we really want and feel. This isn't just about work, it's a way of life. And as much as I have a business to run here, I also understand that people need to be happy and fulfilled. I want you to have that, and I want you to share that with others."

"I'd be happy to," I answered. "Do you want me to stay on until I finish it?"

She shrugged. "You don't have to come in anymore, if you don't want to. Just finish your article by the end of the month and we'll consider it your farewell letter to our readers." She stood then, and I got up as well.

I gave her a hug. "Thank you," I said above her head. She was so tiny, but apparently, she was more like a benevolent fairy godmother than a formidable dictator. "You gave me a gift. I don't know how long it would have taken me to get the courage to live my life as I choose."

She pulled back and put her hands on my arms. "You will do amazing things, Amethyst King. I just know it. And I'm glad I got to be part of your journey."

My eyes teared up. I was finally getting the recognition and approval that I craved from my parents, but again from another source. Maybe stepping out of their shadow didn't mean I wouldn't have anyone to look up to; I'd just have to change my perspective.

I gathered my things and went to see Farah. She was my one true friend at the office, and I didn't want her to hear about it from anyone else.

"What am I going to do here without you?" she asked.

"Well, I hear there's a promotion up for grabs," I told her with a shrug. "But you didn't hear it from me..."

"Ooh," she said with a smile. "Expect some texts from

me. I'll let you know if Maria goes off the rails again with her new website."

"Sounds good." I gave her one more hug. "I'll miss seeing you every day."

"Same," she said. "But I'm really proud of you. You deserve to do what will make you happy."

Waving goodbye, I headed out to my car. I had a whole day ahead of me, and a plan of what to do to win Lucas over. It just had to work.

Twenty-One

That night I sat on the beach waiting for Lucas, pizza boxes and a brown wrapped package in hand. I watched the few people who wandered along the beach. It was crowded for a Thursday evening, but school had gotten out for the summer and there were more people enjoying the evenings now. A few clouds streaked across the sky, their pink and orange hues preceding an incredible sunset. I checked over my shoulder and saw Lucas heading my way, a towel in hand for his seat. "Ah, you're feeding me," he called with a smile.

"Nope, these are both for me," I teased with a grin.

He laughed. "I should go…" He gestured over his shoulder with his thumb.

I patted the sand next to me. "Sit," I commanded. He obeyed with a smile. He spread his towel out on the sand, then pulled his knees up and put his arms around them.

"So, are we trying to hang out as friends again?" he asked. "I'm not exactly sure why you asked me here."

"I quit my job," I blurted out.

His eyes widened. "Oh. Congratulations?"

I nodded. "It's the first decision I've made for myself in a long time." I paused. "Probably ever."

"What do your parents think?" he asked.

"They don't know yet," I said.

He laughed in disbelief. "That's going to be an interesting conversation."

I nodded. "But...it's not just about my job. I'm done living for them. I want to do things for myself now. And if they don't want anything to do with me anymore, then I'm willing to accept that."

He looked deep into my eyes, as if searching for the answer that I didn't vocalize. But, because this was Lucas, and he cared more for others than for himself, he had to ask another question. "What brought this all on?"

I took in a shaky breath. "When I was in the hospital, Rachel told me she didn't have any regrets about the life she and Brent had built. They had followed their dreams, and no matter what happened from here, she was happy they had lived their truth together." I swiped quickly at the tears gathering in my eyes. "I can't say the same about myself. If something terrible happened tomorrow, I would be full of regrets over the things I never did or said."

Lucas finally reached for me, gently brushing the tears off my cheeks with his thumb. "And what would you wish you had done?"

I gathered my courage and looked deep into his sea-blue eyes. "More than anything, to be with you."

Those magic words moved him to action. He leaned in and kissed my lips. This kiss felt like a sigh of relief. Finally, we knew we would work this out together. He turned his body towards me, and I angled to meet him as my hands found his firm chest again. He kissed me softly, knowing we had all the time in the world, that there would be an infinite number of kisses in our future.

He pulled back, then gently kissed me on the forehead. He pulled me into his lap and rested his head on mine. "So, what now?" he asked.

I wiggled as close to him as I could. "Well, right now, we enjoy this sunset while eating our delicious pizza that is probably really cold."

He laughed. "You know what I mean."

I turned my head to face him. "I'm serious about being done with my parents. But my mom's big gala is this weekend, and I promised I'd be there. I want you to come with me. As my date."

He shook his head. "I don't know if that's such a good idea."

"I need you by my side. Please. They won't make a huge scene with all their friends around, so it shouldn't be too awful."

He shifted uncomfortably. "Fine. But I don't want to make a habit of going to these events."

"Trust me, I don't think we'll be invited to any more of them after I tell them about my job."

He nodded, still clearly uncomfortable. "Okay. One event." He looked over at the pizza and then noticed the other package. "What's that?" he asked, pointing at it.

Feeling a little shy, I removed myself from his hold and reached to get it. "It's a gift for you."

He untied the twine, then unwrapped the brown craft

paper to reveal my collection of his lyrics that I had written in calligraphy.

I explained, "These are just the copies I made for myself, but I wanted you to have them. I've been keeping them since we first met. Even for the last eight years, I've watched your YouTube videos and written down all the lyrics." I tried to read his expression, but couldn't understand what he was thinking. "I've loved you this whole time, Lucas. I just wasn't brave enough to be true to myself."

He slowly rifled through the pages, a small smile growing on his face. "You know, I still have the originals of these at home." He held up a small stack, the ones from high school.

"Really?" I asked. "I thought you burned them after graduation."

"The gorgeous girl I love writing my lyrics in beautiful letters? Of course I kept them." He rifled through the pages. "Although I do cringe when I read the first ones I wrote. 'Your eyes are brown, your dress is green, you're the coolest girl I've ever seen.'" He chuckled to himself.

"My calligraphy was pretty awful back then, too."

"It looks like we've both grown together." He put the pages down and gathered me back in his arms, pressing a kiss to the top of my head.

"Like that song you played for Stella?" I twisted to look back at him. "Where did that come from?"

"Let's just say I have my muse sitting right here," he said. "I've been working on that one for a very long time."

My cheeks burned red hot, my hopes confirmed. The song really was about me. I figured as much after our kiss at Hannah's wedding, but to hear it from him made me feel like I could float across the waves. We sat peacefully for a few minutes, watching the orange and pink sky reflected on the water, the sound of the waves crashing the perfect backdrop for our beating hearts.

And Lucas's growling stomach.

I laughed and sat up. "Sorry, I've kept you waiting long enough. The pizza's probably awful now."

"It's been worth it," he replied. "Oh, pizza—from our lunch date! I knew something was up. Are you ever going to tell me what your assignment was?"

I nodded. "I think I'll just let you read the article. It's going to explain a lot."

Twenty~Two

"I do not understand why Ethan owns five of these," Lucas said, looking at himself in my mirror. "I mean, I look awesome. But can't you just rent a tux when you need it?"

I stepped in front of him and put on my earrings. We made quite a pair, all dressed up. His black tux and bow tie matched perfectly with my gown. I rented a high-neck sleeveless black gown with a black floral overlay. The back had a teardrop shaped opening that exposed just the upper part of my back. It was the perfect combination of classy and sexy. "When you go to galas and special events as often as Ethan, it's easier to own them."

"Like Dwight and his hazmat suit," Lucas said.

I turned around and pulled his jacket close to me. "I love when you quote 'The Office' to me." I punctuated the statement with a quick kiss. "Ethan's got all the colors he needs to match his dates. And he made sure to get them tailored just for him. You should be glad you fit in the same size as he does."

When Lucas told me he didn't have a tux, I figured I'd give Ethan a call. We were friends now, after all, and he had encouraged me to go after Lucas. He was kind enough to allow Lucas to borrow the tux for the evening, especially when I promised we'd get it dry cleaned.

"Oh, really?" he asked me teasingly, wrapping an arm around my waist. "Be honest, were you tempted by his good looks and charm?"

I laughed. "Nope. Not like that. But he did turn out to be a nice guy, after all. He's just hiding it from everyone." I sighed. "I hope he can get the bravery to step out and be himself. I know I'm already happier for it."

"Well, I'm enjoying you in this dress." He pressed a kiss to my neck, sending a shiver down my spine. "I haven't seen this one on you before."

"And that's because I'm too poor to own anything this amazing," I breathed, trying to compose myself. "I rent all my dresses, even for family dinners. But don't tell my mother."

"I have no intention of telling your mother anything." He squeezed my waist.

"Hopefully we can just make a quick appearance. Then we can go have fun somewhere else."

"I like the sound of that." Lucas leaned in for a slow kiss.

Ivy interrupted our moment by loudly opening the front door. "Warning! Warning! I'm walking in!" She hung her purse by the front door, visibly exhausted from another visit to the hospital.

Lucas winked at me. "I'm coming back later for more."

This boy was trouble. "How's your dad?" I asked Ivy, composing myself.

"He's okay. Coming to terms with his new abilities, I guess."

"That makes him sound like a superhero," Lucas said, trying to lighten things up.

Ivy laughed. "I'm going to text him that. It'll make him happy." She shrugged. "It's going to be a big transition, so I'm trying to help as much as I can."

"You're a good daughter," I told her and gave her a hug. Over her shoulder, I saw the clock on the oven. "I'm so sorry. We have to run."

"I expect a full report when you get home," she said. She grabbed my shoulders and gave me a serious expression. "I'm really proud of you."

My eyes misted over, and I quickly fanned them so I wouldn't ruin my makeup. I couldn't go into the gala looking like a mess. I looked back at Lucas, who held his hand out to me, and we left.

As we got into his car, I pulled down the visor and applied my lipstick. "No more kissing," I said sternly. "Can't afford to mess this up."

He laughed. "Bummer," he said. "We'll just have to wait until afterwards." He gave me a sexy little wink. I refocused on the mirror so I wouldn't get distracted and kiss him right then.

The drive was quiet until we got onto the freeway. I could tell Lucas was nervous. He kept tapping the steering wheel and jiggling his legs. I put my hand on his to calm his nerves, and he gave me a smile.

"I'm pretty sure this will be the fanciest event I've ever attended," he confessed.

"Just remember: you've met Stella Knight. And you have her phone number." I tried to make him smile, and it worked.

"Either way, I want to get in and out quick."

"Mmm, In-N-Out. Let's get some after."

He turned to me seriously. "Come on, Amy. You're not nervous?"

"Oh, I'm terrified," I said truthfully. I had to think less and less about speaking my truth these days, especially now that I was open about my feelings with Lucas. "But at a public event, my mother is less likely to make a scene. And besides, it's part of my assignment."

"Your assignment for your job that you quit..." Suspicion filled his face.

"Well, the assignment was good for me. I promised Gia I'd still write the article, because it really has changed my life. After all, it brought us together."

"I guess I can't complain about that." He picked up our joined hands and kissed mine.

Just then, we pulled into the valet area of the Royal Cove Hotel. "My car is the cheapest one here," he whispered as we waited for the valet to come.

"Yep!" I said. "Good thing we brought your car and not mine, though. Mine would have been even worse."

We stepped out of the car and into the hotel, and I led him into the ballroom for the gala. My shoes were invisible under my dress, but my heels clicked on the floor and matched my pattering heart. I tried to exude confidence and calm, but inside I was shaking.

The ballroom glittered with crystal and roses. Beautiful piano music played in the background while everyone mingled and drank. Dripping in opulence, I wondered once again why all the money was spent on hosting a gala instead of given to the charities they claimed to support. Surely there would be a more cost-efficient way to get these people together to support a good cause.

On the other hand, I looked around at the attendees and should have known better. All the important families from Orange County were here, including some of the True Trophy Wives. Like Ethan's mom. I hated that they got featured as "real" housewives, while Ivy's mother Rachel was the most real person I knew. If anyone should have had a TV show, it was her.

"Do you see anyone you want to talk to?" Lucas asked.

"Not really. But we should mingle anyway." I spied Ethan by the bar with a beautiful, tall blond woman. "At least I know Ethan won't bite." I pulled Lucas over to them.

"Looking sharp, Lucas," Ethan called, waving us over with his free hand, then taking a sip of his drink.

"Thanks, man," Lucas said, shaking Ethan's hand. "I really appreciate it. Hopefully we won't be here too long, so I won't ruin it."

Ethan waved his comment away. "It's fine. I have a few."

"Ethan, aren't you going to introduce us?" I asked, gesturing to the lovely lady beside him.

"Oh, yes. This is Bethany Stone. She's a lawyer in the area."

Dang. Gorgeous and brilliant. My parents would have loved her as a daughter. Lucas and I took turns shaking her hand as she said she was "charmed" to meet us. I couldn't quite tell if her accent was real or fake. I raised one eyebrow and cocked my head at Bethany as if to ask Ethan if this was the woman he referred to on our date. He shook his head slightly.

"Have we missed anything?" I asked.

"Not much," Ethan answered. "My mom already had a few drinks and yelled at Samantha. The usual." His gaze wandered over to a red-headed waitress who was walking around with champagne glasses. His eyes glossed over a bit as he got lost in thought. Was this the mystery girl? No wonder he hadn't done anything about it yet. A waitress would possibly be worse than a musician, and I already had enough trouble coming my way.

"Have you seen my parents?" I asked, pulling him from his trance.

He blinked a few times, then refocused. "Last I saw, your mother was fussing at someone about the floral arrangements. But I think they should have fixed that by now." He looked around the room, then pointed over towards the dance floor. "There she is. Your dad, too."

As if summoned, they turned around and looked directly at us. I couldn't see who they were talking to, but my mother clearly saw me with Lucas and frowned with fury. I hoped her dermatologist wasn't here, since he'd be thrilled about the new Botox injections she'd need. She turned back to her conversation, but knowing I'd been seen, I decided that it was time to head over there.

"Who is she talking to?" Lucas asked Ethan.

Ethan, the tallest of us four, tried to look over and see. "I don't recognize her. She looks like a petite Asian woman."

Startled, I looked over at Lucas. Gia wasn't the only petite

Asian woman in the area, but of course, that's where my mind went. And if Gia were here, she might have accidentally told my parents that I quit before I was ready.

"It's probably not Gia," he reassured me. "She hasn't been to these things before, right?"

I shook my head, but part of me had a sinking suspicion that it was her. "Come on, let's go." I grabbed his hand, waved goodbye to Ethan and Bethany, and headed to my parents. Lucas squeezed my hand in support.

I was stopped by a hand on my shoulder and turned to see Scott's alarmed face. "What in the world are you doing?" he asked.

"Saying hello to Mother and Dad," I replied.

"Amy," he said gently, pulling me away from Lucas. Lucas looked like he wanted to punch Scott, but I shook my head at him. This relationship was going to be difficult to mend; they kept meeting up with each other in the worst situations. "Don't do something you're going to regret later."

"I regret letting them rule my life for as long as I have," I said. "Maybe you're happy, taking the job they set out for you and living the life they expect, but I'm miserable."

He put both hands on my shoulders. "I don't want to lose you, Amy."

I pulled back in surprise. "Lose me? I'm right here, Scott. You don't have to make the same decisions as they do. You can still see me. I'm your sister, and you're my brother. No matter what happens with them, you can still choose to be there for me."

Uncertainty clouded his eyes. He pulled me in for a hug. "I love you, Amy. I don't think this is a good idea. But I don't think I can convince you otherwise." He pulled back, gave me a quick kiss on the head, then sent me back to Lucas. Scott kept his eyes on me, watching to see what happened next. Lucas reached for my hand, and together we headed to my parents.

Twenty Three

"Hi, Dad. Hi, Mother." I swept around them to get in their eyeline. My dad gave me a quick side hug, and my mother gave me air kisses, the kind she always did when we were in public.

"Hello, Amethyst. Lovely to see you. And who is this?" my mother asked, as if she didn't know.

"You remember Lucas, I'm sure," I said.

"Ah, yes, of course," my mother said through her teeth. "Good to see you again."

My father narrowed his eyes at Lucas and reluctantly reached out his hand. If we didn't have company, he probably would have walked away.

Speaking of company...

"Gia, what are you doing here?" I asked her. It was Gia, after all. But she had never attended one of my parents' swanky events, so I was really shocked. I tried to play it off, since everyone here had to always act like they were smooth and in control. Except the True Trophy Wives. They could do whatever they wanted.

"Your mother invited me," she explained. "I'm happy to see you!" She gave me a warm hug.

I looked over at my mother in confusion.

"After you mentioned your successful article, I figured I'd invite your boss to our event," my mother explained. "It would be good for her to network and mingle with our circles."

My mind whirled. Apparently, my mother had processed more about my article and business than I had anticipated. Now I had gained her approval, to the point that she thought my company was worth having at her gala. Now the people I chose to associate with were enough to be part of her social circle.

I was finally enough.

The irony was not lost on me. Finally, I had done enough to gain my mother's approval, but it had come too late. I didn't need her approval anymore.

Besides, I already quit.

I wasn't sure if she knew that already, though, so I proceeded cautiously. "I'm really glad to hear that. I know there are so many people here who would love to be a part of Women in the Workplace. Gia has an incredible vision."

"One that she says you are no longer a part of?" my father asked.

I glanced at Gia for confirmation, and she mouthed "sorry" at me. It wasn't her fault that I hadn't told my parents yet, so I smiled at her and looked back at my father. "Yes. I was hoping to discuss that later, but I guess you already know now."

"Would you look at that? There's...someone I need to talk to." Gia pointed off in the middle of nowhere and scurried away from the brewing storm in front of her. I decided to demote her from fairy godmother to just regular godmother. This was a tornado about to destroy everything in its path.

Without Gia's eyes and ears, my mother's facade fell. "What is going on? First Gia says you quit your job, and now you're here with *him*?" She waved her hand up and down at Lucas in disgust.

"Yes, I didn't mean to—"

"Amethyst, you know our expectations of you, as one of the Kings," my father said. "We have a reputation to uphold."

I looked between my parents and realized I had no choice but to have this conversation right here, right now. "I didn't intend to discuss this tonight, but it seems that we need to now." I took in a deep breath. "I understand your expectations, but I will no longer live under them."

My parents' eyes shifted between me and Lucas.

"Are you *pregnant*?" my mother hissed at me.

"No!" I exclaimed. "We haven't even...not that it's your business...No, I'm not!"

"Then why else would you disrespect us in this way?"

"Because I'm not happy," I said with gritted teeth. "I'm so tired of trying to live up to whatever image you conjured up in your mind. That's not me. I deserve to forge my own path."

"But don't you see? You were finally there! You were doing so well, and to throw it all away, for him?" My mother gestured at Lucas.

"Quitting my job has nothing to do with him. Well... maybe a little. But more in the sense that I'm not letting anyone get in the way of what I want anymore. I *want* to be with Lucas. And I *wanted* to quit my job. This is my life, my choice. I won't let you dictate that for me anymore."

"Well," my mother huffed. "If that's how it's going to be, then I'm going to ask you to leave so you don't embarrass us in front of our colleagues."

"No problem," I said. "I think we had other dinner plans anyway." I shifted my eyes to Lucas, who beamed with pride. My mother turned and stormed off to find some other friends of hers to fuss at.

My father looked at me, as if examining me for the first time. "I'm not happy with your choices, but I didn't think you had it in you." He patted my shoulder and walked away.

I stood for a moment more, processing what had just happened. Although the conversation was short, the impact was monumental. A life without my parents' expectations hanging over it seemed freeing, but also frightening.

Looking around, I noticed that many people were watching and whispering. They pointed in our direction, and some even had their phones out. I felt a little sorry for making such a scene at my parents' gala, but at the same time, I needed to be clear about our relationship from this point on.

"I think it's time for a cheeseburger," Lucas said to me, shaking me out of my daze.

I turned to face him, wrapped my arms around his neck and kissed him firmly. "Make it a Double-Double. And a chocolate shake."

"...TWO ORDERS OF FRIES, and a large pink lemonade."

"Don't forget my chocolate shake!"

"Oh, and a chocolate shake."

We were ordering our food at In-N-Out, and I was beyond thrilled. We decided to go inside and enjoy a few more moments in our fancy clothes. We were like those teenagers who went out after prom for burgers, except we were much older and a little wiser. Lucas was paranoid that he would get some ketchup on Ethan's tux, but we decided it was worth the chance.

"Actually, maybe we should order something for Ivy, too. Let me call her."

I pulled out my phone and saw that I had twenty-five text messages and ten missed calls, mostly from Ivy. "She must be desperate for an update," I laughed. "Just go ahead and order an extra Double-Double."

The cashier took Lucas's card and gave us our order number. As we picked up our ketchup and drinks, we noticed some whispers and people pointing behind us. We both turned around to see who they were pointing at, but couldn't see anyone of importance.

"Do you think they're pointing at us because we're all dressed up?" Lucas asked.

"I wouldn't think so. This isn't the craziest thing you'd see at an In-N-Out," I replied.

Finally, one teenage girl broke free from her pack to come talk to us. "Are you Lucas Carter?" she asked.

"Um, yes," he said, looking at me with confusion. "Do I know you?"

"I wish!" she exclaimed. "I love your songs."

His eyes widened in alarm. "How do you know about my songs?" he asked.

She held her phone out to him. His YouTube channel was pulled up, and his videos now had hundreds of thousands of views each. "What...how?" he asked, dumbfounded.

"You don't know?" she asked. She glanced at our outfits. "I guess you must have been busy. Stella Knight posted one of your videos on her Facebook page."

I pulled up the Facebook app on my phone, and sure enough, Stella had linked one of his videos on her account. "Check out this guy, y'all! I think I might need to add him to my team." She ended the caption with a winking face.

"Did Chip or Stella reach out to you?" I whispered to Lucas.

"No, I thought they had moved on," he replied.

"I guess not." I gave him a kiss on the cheek. The girl glared at me, and I smiled sweetly back at her. "Thanks for letting us know!" I said with a wave.

With a pout, she went back to her friends, but not before snapping a candid picture of us.

"Better check Instagram later for that one," I said, laughing. "Is your account private?"

"I have a public account just for my music, but my personal stuff is a separate private account."

"That's a relief. I bet you have a ton of new followers."

He shook his head. "This is too much. I'm not sure I want to check it right now."

I wrapped my arms around his waist to give him a hug, and he put his arm around my shoulders. "We can deal with it tomorrow. But maybe you should check if Chip or Stella has reached out."

He pulled out his phone. He had even more notifications

than I did, but he went straight to his texts and saw a message from Chip.

CHIP KNIGHT

> Hey, Lucas. Sorry we didn't give you a heads-up before Stella posted. We'll call you tomorrow with a proposition, if you're interested. Hope you're having a good night!

He showed me his phone, a smile growing on his face. The shock must have worn off, and now he was getting excited. I grabbed his face and gave him a quick kiss, unsure who was filming or photographing us now. "I am so, so proud of you," I whispered.

He leaned his forehead on mine and grinned from ear to ear. "Thank you. And I am so, so proud of you. Sorry for turning the night into something about me."

I laughed and pulled away. "Are you kidding? The universe is telling us we're heading in the right direction. I'm thrilled!"

He looped his arm around my waist and gave me one more quick kiss. Our number was called, and we grabbed our food and headed home to see Ivy.

Twenty-Four

Knock, knock, knock.

Buzz, buzz, buzz.

Bleary-eyed, I picked up my phone. "It is seven on a Sunday morning," I muttered to myself. "What is wrong with some people..." My mother's number blared across the screen of my phone, followed by more knocks on our front door.

I jumped out of bed, my alarm bells ringing. Worried that something had happened to my family, I picked up my phone. "Mother? Is everything okay?"

"Come to your front door, Amethyst."

I ran to the front door and opened it. My mother had never visited me at my apartment before, but here she was. She stepped inside without so much as a greeting and surveyed her surroundings. She wrinkled her nose at the bright colors in the living room and the dishes left in the sink. Not that she ever did any housework herself, but anything left untidy would surely offend her.

"Is everything okay?" I asked again.

"I've just been thinking about our conversation last night," she began, still looking around the rooms. "I think that maybe we were too quick to judge your decisions last night."

I couldn't hide my shock. "Really?" I asked. My heart raced with excitement. Maybe my parents would be willing to accept me as I was, after all. Maybe I would be enough for them, just as I was.

"Yes, well, some things have come to my attention, and I think that it was impulsive of us to cut you off so quickly," she said, still not meeting my eyes.

Hang on a hot second. "What things?" I asked, my excitement fading to suspicion. This didn't seem like a mother trying to reconcile with her daughter. Once again, there was some hidden motive I couldn't find right away.

Just then, another knock sounded on the door. I looked through the peephole to see Lucas with a box of donuts.

I opened the door for him.

"Hey! I didn't know if you'd be awake already, but—" Seeing my mother in the kitchen, he stopped short. His eyes widened as he looked at me in confusion.

"Oh, Lucas!" my mother exclaimed, floating over to him. "Lovely to see you again."

He returned her air kisses, looking at me for help. "Good to see you, too?"

"Why didn't you tell me that you played such wonderful music?" she asked.

"You knew about his music, Mother," I said. "I told you about the time he played our piano."

"Oh!" she laughed airily. "How could I have forgotten? Yes, of course, Lucas and his music. Such an accomplished musician. It's wonderful for you to be part of the family now."

Finally, the pieces all clicked together. The people staring at the gala last night—it wasn't because of our disagreement. It was the same reason why people were staring at In-N-Out. And my mother, as much as she wanted to be in everyone's business, couldn't stand social media. Which meant she didn't know anything about Lucas's newfound fame until...

"When did you find out?" I asked her.

"Find out what?" She played the innocent angle.

"Find out about Lucas and Stella Knight?"

"Stella who?" She yelped as Waffles brushed against her legs. She gathered herself and began again. "I'm sorry. You'll have to explain what you're talking about." My mother blinked her eyes like an innocent doe. I didn't buy it for one second. When we were at the family dinner two weeks ago, she practically begged me to invite Stella to the gala.

"Stella Knight. The biggest country star right now. The woman whose concert we attended two weeks ago. The woman who promoted Lucas and his music yesterday, which I'm sure all your friends were talking about last night." I stepped next to Lucas and put my arm around his waist. "How many of them asked you if we were dating?"

She waved her hand dismissively. "Don't make it sound like a bigger deal than it was. They just asked if he was now part of the family."

I laughed. "I'm sure they did. They probably asked if they could book him to perform at their parties, and you pretended that you could get us in contact with them."

She narrowed her eyes at me. "It would be a great opportunity for him."

"And a great opportunity for you to gain some points with your 'friends.'" I looked up at him. "Lucas, you're right here. What do you think?"

He looked down at me with a big smile. "I think that anyone who wants to get in contact with me can do it themselves." He faced my mother. "Thank you for your interest in my career, but I can handle it myself."

She looked at us with fire in her eyes. I watched the moment she chose to intentionally soften her face and appeal to me one more time. "Amethyst, my dear daughter. We shouldn't let things be so strained between us. I'm sure we can all come to some kind of happy arrangement."

My heart broke hearing her attempt at making amends, but it was too late now. All the things I wished she would have said to me, growing up as a child and throughout my early adult life, were never going to be enough now. It was too little, too late. I was going to speak my truth to her one last time.

"Mother, I love you. You will always be my mother, the woman who birthed me and raised me. Thank you for making me into a strong woman. And as a strong woman, I know that I need to change our relationship. I am not happy living under your expectations, and you cannot expect me to live that way. I am a grown woman, and I can make my own choices. Please see yourself out."

She lifted her nose into the air. "Well. You know where to find me." She swept past us toward the entrance.

"Feel free to take a donut!" Lucas called to her. She purposely ignored him and slammed the door.

I stared at the door, a weight lifted off my shoulders. I felt like I could fly.

"Have I told you lately how proud I am of you?" Lucas said.

I sighed and relaxed into his arms. "This has been the wildest twenty-four hours of my life," I said to him.

"More wild than meeting Stella after her concert?" he asked, turning to hold me in his arms.

"Hmm," I mused. "Okay, let's say this has been the wildest two weeks of my life." Lucas started to lean down for a kiss, but we were interrupted by a bleary-eyed Ivy.

"What in tarnation is going on around here?" she asked, wiping the sleep from her eyes. "It is 7:15 on a Sunday morning. This is totally unaccep—ooh, are those donuts?" She rushed over to the kitchen counter and perused through the assortment Lucas brought with him.

"I brought you coffee, too," he gestured toward the cupholder. "And tea for you," he said, giving me a kiss on the forehead.

"Was that your mom?" Ivy asked, her mouth full of a chocolate glazed donut. "I would've loved to hear what she thought of our place."

"Yep. She didn't really comment on it, but her face said it all."

Ivy laughed. "Oh, man. So why was she here?"

"She heard about Lucas's newfound fame and wanted to reconcile. You know, now that her friends want Lucas to perform at their parties, she didn't want to have a strained relationship with his girlfriend."

"That's just sad," Ivy said. "She only wants a relationship with you when it will benefit herself."

I nodded. "Yeah. Doesn't feel great."

Lucas gripped my chin gently and turned my face to meet his. "Hey. You have people who want to be with you just because of who you are. Not because of the benefits we get from that."

Ivy cut in. "Speak for yourself. I'm only friends with her because her boyfriend brings us donuts and coffee in the morning."

I shook my head at her and turned back to Lucas. I pulled his hand, leading him into the living room for a little bit of privacy. "Thank you," I said, pulling him to me and giving him a quick kiss.

"For what? Tea and donuts?" he teased.

I stuck my tongue out at him. "That, and for wanting to be with me for *me*. For helping me feel like I'm enough."

He pressed a slow, sweet kiss to my lips, lingering for a moment before quoting my favorite line ever from The Office.

"Not enough for me?" he asked with a smile. "Amy, you are everything."

We spent the rest of the day lounging around in our pajamas, watching TV, and snacking. I worked on some calligraphy posts for my Instagram. Not only had Lucas's account gained thousands of new followers, but the posts of us at In-N-Out had also blown up and I had thousands of new followers, as well. Things were working out very well for both of us. With a following, I could start to actually monetize my platform.

"You should post some of my lyrics that you've worked on," he suggested, looking over my shoulder at my phone.

"Is that okay?" I asked. "I know you're not thrilled with the lyrics you wrote when we were younger."

"I didn't say you should post what I wrote when we were seventeen," he laughed. "But one of the songs I wrote a few years ago would be fine. Actually, I'll post it on mine too."

"Can one of you guys post one of my videos of choreography, too? I wouldn't mind getting Insta-famous for my dance routines," Ivy teased.

I smiled at her, and Lucas and I busied ourselves with posting. Lucas jumped when his phone began to ring. His eyes widened and he showed it to me: *Chip Knight.*

"Answer it!" I exclaimed.

"Hello, this is Lucas," he said into the phone.

"Hi, darlin'! So sorry for not calling sooner." Stella's loud voice blared through the phone. Lucas put it on speaker-phone for us all to hear.

"No worries, I know you're busy," he said.

"Well, that's kind of you. Especially since I just rocked your world yesterday!" She laughed. "How's the newfound fame?"

"Uh, a little overwhelming, to be honest. But I've just been hanging out with Amy and hiding out for now."

"Oh, yes, I saw the pictures of you two at the In-N-Out last night. You two are just the cutest! I'm so glad you finally made that happen."

He raised his eyebrows at me and I just shrugged. I still hadn't explained my conversation with Chip and how he and Stella knew I was in love with Lucas.

"Well, I'll get right to it," Stella continued. "I'm writing a new album and I'd like to have you on my team. I write all my own songs, but I do like to have people for creative collaboration. There may even be opportunities for you to help write songs for some of our newer stars; I've been putting your name out there."

"Oh, wow, Stella, thank you," he replied.

I gestured at him, mouthing "Where?"

He understood what I meant. "Would I need to relocate for this?"

"Well," she said, drawing out the word. "For a few weeks, no. We could do our sessions with video conferencing. But I do want to get together in person at some point."

"And where is 'in person'?" he asked.

"I write my music in Georgia, and I record in Los Angeles. So, I'd need you out here in Georgia for a few months, and then in LA when it's time to record."

Lucas looked at me for confirmation, and I gave him an enthusiastic thumbs up. As much as I'd miss him while he was in Georgia, I couldn't be the reason why he'd hold himself back from his dreams.

"That sounds amazing!" he exclaimed. "Thank you so much, Stella."

"You're welcome, darlin'. I may want to talk to you about that song you sang for me backstage. I noticed that one wasn't on your YouTube channel."

He glanced at me with a mischievous smile. "I wasn't done with it yet, but I'm finishing it up now." He winked at me, and I just about melted.

"Ah," she said with a laugh. "I can understand that. Well, you say hello to my lovely Amethyst and I'll be getting in contact with you soon with all the details."

"Sounds great, thank you, Stella!" he said, hanging up the phone. He ran his hands through his hair and put his head back on the couch. "This is crazy!" He suddenly reached for my face with both hands and gave me a huge kiss. "We're going to Georgia!"

"Wait...we?" I asked.

"Well, yeah! You can work from anywhere, right? Come with me!"

I looked at him, dazed. I hadn't even thought about going with him. But now that Ivy was moving back home and I couldn't afford rent on my own, I hadn't made official decisions for my living arrangements. I looked over at Ivy to see her smiling at me encouragingly.

"Girl, this will be an amazing adventure. You have to go!"

I nodded, then beamed back at Lucas. "We're going to Georgia! But first...I need to finish that article for Gia."

Twenty-Five

Thirty Days of Speaking My Truth

Hello, my beautiful women in the workplace! I'm sad to say that this will be my last installment of the "Thirty Days" series. While I have enjoyed experimenting with different trends and lifestyle changes, I have made the decision to leave my position at Women in the Workplace and move on to other pursuits. And it's all because I spent the last thirty days speaking my truth.

Before you worry that speaking my truth drove me to misery and led me to quit, let me reassure you it is the exact opposite. Speaking my truth has taught me many things about standing up for myself and believing in myself, and for that, I will forever be grateful to Gia and this company. They have my full support and endorsement.

What exactly did "speaking my truth" entail? At first, I took it to mean giving an honest opinion when called upon. For example, I met a woman in the elevator who was on her way to an interview and she asked me how she looked. I honestly told her that her hair looked awful. I told a coworker that I hated her new design for the website. I went on a date with someone I despised, and I told him exactly what I thought of him. I told my friend that her veil looked awful with her wedding dress three days before her wedding. It was awkward, uncomfortable, and terrifying.

But each of those situations turned into a positive experience. I fixed the woman's hair in the elevator, and she got the job (and looked way better)! The man I went on a date with actually loved that I told him what I thought of him, and we're now friends. I never got a chance to apologize to my coworker, but the website looks fabulous now, don't you think? And my friend was able to change her veil in time, while mending the relationship with her mother.

Unexpected benefits came to me, as well: backstage passes to Stella Knight's concert, all because I allowed a conversation with Chip Knight. He was kind enough to strike up a conversation with me, and if I hadn't spoken my truth, I would have ignored him. Instead, three friends and I had our lives changed by meeting Stella after her concert two weeks ago.

By speaking my truth in everyday conversations, though, I realized that I needed to speak my truth, not just in word, but in action. My life was being ruled by choices others made for me and expectations that had been set by others. I decided I was done living that way. I wanted to embody the assignment and live my truth, not just speak it.

I told the man I love how I feel about him.

I quit my job to pursue my lifelong dream.

I severed ties with the people who were holding me back from happiness.

And now, I feel free. And I feel like myself.

While I will miss Women at the Workplace and the assign-

ments that pushed me outside of my comfort zone, I feel that leaving has been the right choice for me.

So, what does this mean for you, dear reader? Don't be afraid to speak your truth. If someone asks for your opinion, give it. Especially if you can do something to help fix it. It may allow for collaboration that you never knew could exist.

Don't shy away from conversations with strangers. You never know when you might run into Chip Knight at a coffee shop and get backstage passes to his wife's concert (sorry Chip, hope I'm not blowing your cover).

Be true to yourself. If you're unhappy with any facet of your life, change it. *Your life is your own. Take control, make the change, and speak your truth.*

Lucas cleared his throat. I put a couple more books into a moving box, then walked over to his seat at the kitchen table. He kept his eyes on the computer screen, processing. "That explains a lot," he mused. "When exactly did it start?"

I tapped my fingers on the table, remembering the first time I spoke my truth with him. "Our pizza lunch date was the first time I had seen you since I started the assignment."

He sat back in his chair at my kitchen table, replaying the events of that day. "That's why you told me that you didn't like the Superman movies."

"Yep."

He tapped his foot. "And that's why you told me about the karaoke championship."

"Yep."

He pointed a finger at me. "I think I deserve to see the video now that we're dating."

I laughed. "Maybe when we're married." I slapped my hand across my open mouth. "Oh, my biscuits. I did not just say that. I think I need to retrain my thoughts to stay in my brain." I rushed back to my bookshelf, taking a few more books and tossing them into the moving box. I was so mortified, I couldn't face him. His steps sounded behind me, then I felt his arms wrap around my waist.

"What's wrong with talking about getting married?" he asked.

"Lucas, come on. I have to keep packing. We're leaving for Georgia in two days."

He rested his chin on my shoulder. "What's wrong with talking about getting married?" he repeated.

"I cannot believe you're so casual about this." I buried my face in my hands, leaning my back into his chest.

Gently, he spun me around to face him and pried my hands off my face. "Amy, I love you. I've loved you for years. I'm not afraid of getting married."

"You're not?"

He pulled me a little tighter. "If you wanted to get married today, I would be one hundred percent in."

I widened my eyes at him as a big smile spread across my face. "Don't make empty promises."

He laughed again. "I'm not! You want to? Let's go!"

I thought for a moment about what he was suggesting. He knew I didn't want to share a room in Georgia unless we were married. Was this completely crazy? We'd only been officially dating for two weeks. But he was the one I wanted to be with for the rest of my life. There was no doubt about that. Why would I delay the inevitable? Why not speak my truth?

He saw the moment I made up my mind and gave me a firm kiss, making my head spin. "Wait, I haven't officially asked you yet." He pulled away and slowly got down on one knee, keeping eye contact with me the entire time. Slowly, he pulled a gorgeous princess cut solitaire diamond ring out of his pocket.

"Where on earth did that come from?" I exclaimed.

"I've been holding on to it, waiting for the right moment. I bought it the day after we started dating. I'm sorry there's no extravagant gesture with trumpets blaring and a dove swooping in with the ring, but this is all I have to offer you." He cleared his throat, some moisture gathering in his eyes. "Amethyst King. You are the love of my life. There is nothing I want more than to spend every day with you. Will you marry me?"

I thought my cheeks would burst from the smile on my face. "Yes, yes, yes!" I exclaimed, and Lucas slipped the ring on my finger. He stood up, picked me up, and spun me around.

"We're getting married!" he exclaimed.

AND THAT'S HOW, three hours later, we gathered in the small Canyon Cove courthouse with our closest friends: Ivy, Nate, Hannah, and Evan. Hannah and Evan came back from their honeymoon that morning. I wore a knee-length white dress, and Lucas wore a white button-down shirt with gray slacks. I held a small bouquet of red roses in one hand and Lucas's hand in my other.

"How do I know you're still speaking your truth?" Lucas whispered to me with a smirk.

I let go of his hand and playfully slapped his arm. "I'm

still speaking my truth, whether I want to or not. That's how we ended up here today."

He grabbed my hand again and brought it to his lips. "I'm so thankful."

The officiant cleared his throat. "It's time for your vows. Lucas Carter, will you have this woman to be your wife to live together in the covenant of marriage? Do you promise to love her, comfort her, honor and keep her, in sickness and in health; forsaking all others, be faithful to her as long as you both shall live? If so, say, 'I do.'"

Lucas looked me straight in the eye. "I do."

"And now for Amethyst. Amethyst King, will you have this man to be your husband to live together in the covenant of marriage? Do you promise to love him, comfort him, honor and keep him, in sickness and in health; forsaking all others, be faithful to him as long as you both shall live? If so, say, 'I do.'"

Speaking my truth?

"I do."

After exchanging the rings, the officiant said, "I now pronounce you husband and wife. You may now kiss the bride."

Lucas gathered me into his arms and put his forehead on mine. "I'm never letting you go."

"You better not," I replied.

He pressed his lips to mine, a romantic but quick kiss for the sake of our friends. They cheered and hollered, then gathered around us for a big hug. We piled into Ivy's family's van and drove to Mike's for a celebratory dinner.

"Ah, the van," Lucas laughed, sitting next to me on the middle bench. Hannah and Evan sat in the far back row together. "Ivy, I can't believe they haven't gotten rid of this thing yet." He turned to me. "I have a lot of memories of flirting with you in the back row."

I giggled, but Ivy interrupted our walk down memory lane. "Whatever their reasoning, I'm glad they still have it for moments like this," she said, looking at us in the rearview mirror. Nate sat up front with her, but things were going well with Jess and he was happy to maintain a friendly relationship with Ivy. "They were happy to let me borrow it for this event."

"How has it been, living back at home?" Hannah asked.

"Not too bad. They're pretty respectful of my boundaries and understanding that I'm an adult. My dad has a hard time asking for help, but I'm glad I'm there. It's only been a few days, though." She shrugged. "It's just temporary."

"I'm glad you'll have company while we're in Georgia," I said. "I hope you won't miss me too much." She looked back at me in the rearview mirror, and I winked at her.

She huffed a laugh. "Don't worry, I have other friends."

"Oh, yeah? Like who?"

She shrugged her shoulders. "Other people."

I furrowed my brow and looked at Lucas. He raised one shoulder and shook his head. It wasn't like Ivy to keep secrets, but maybe she was just uncomfortable in front of Nate, so I let it go.

"Well, I'm going to miss you," I said.

"I think you'll be too busy to miss me," Ivy retorted, wagging her eyebrows. I blushed furiously, and Lucas pinched my side. "Busy with calligraphy! What did you think I meant?" Ivy said with a laugh.

I shook my head at her. "I have a lot of work to do there, that's for sure. And Lucas will be busy with Stella, anyway."

"We'll have to take a proper honeymoon once we get back," Lucas said, giving me a quick kiss on the forehead.

"So, Amy, when does the article come out?" Hannah asked. "I feel like I'm so out of the loop. At least you texted me that you and Lucas were together and that you quit your job."

"I finished writing it this morning, so probably another week or two. That's actually why Lucas and I ended up here today."

"I think it's her best work yet," he said.

"And are you happy, Amy?" Hannah asked.

Even though I wasn't on my assignment anymore, I knew I had to speak my truth. I looked at my friends in the van, my husband by my side, and my heart was about to burst. Lucas looked intently into my eyes, and a slow smile spread across my face.

"Yes. I am so, so happy."

THE END

Embers

I remember a time
    When the sun shined
    Brighter than these city lights
    Saw the embers fly
    From our bonfires
    Disappear into the sky

When my eyes close at night
    There's still one face that burns bright
    Will these words I've scribbled so hastily
    Ever be read
    Or written so beautifully again
    Can I find that melody
    To make me smile
    Smile like I did back then
    I remember my heart
    Beat louder than the echo
    Off these subway tiles
    Undeniable sparks

That sent these cars apart
For miles and miles

When my eyes close at night
There's still one face that burns bright
Will these words I've scribbled so hastily
Ever be read
Or written so beautifully again
Can I find that melody
To make me smile
Smile like I did back then

Is there another story to write?
Or is this one worth the fight?

Acknowledgments

Writing acknowledgments for my first book feels so surreal. I have many people to thank, because I never could have done this alone.

My beta readers: Whitney, Christina, Linda, and Mandi. You helped me shape the book so much, and your enthusiasm meant everything. Sending the book to you was the most vulnerable experience, and you gave me the encouragement to keep going! And Lola: thank you, thank you, thank you. You read random chapters whenever I needed it, you brainstormed ideas with me, and you were so excited for me every step of the way. Malarie, thank you for reading close to the end and giving me the last boost of encouragement I needed, as well. Cindy and Jennifer, thank you so much for your editing and proofreading. You did an incredible job, and I was so thankful to have you on my team!

Ben, thank you so, so much for writing Embers. For months, the manuscript said, "THE SONG GOES HERE." I was terrified to write any kind of lyrics or poetry. The song is perfection and is exactly what I hoped for. It adds so much to the story. Thank you!

To my parents: thank you for all your support growing up. Dad, I remember writing an essay freshman year that you tore to shreds, but it made me a better writer. And Mom, thank you for being nothing like Ruby King and encouraging me to go for my dream of being an author. I'll never forget when you told me that I could be a mother AND an author. To Dee, I never would have wanted to be an author without our unrelenting obsession with the Baby-Sitters Club. You were my first and most important reading buddy. I love you.

Most importantly, thank you to my husband and my kids. Caleb, you are the only reason why I was able to finally make my dream come true. Your support means the world to me. You never said a negative word about my writing, and always told me you were proud of me for doing this. From the bottom of my heart, thank you so much. I hope I can be the same support to you for the rest of our lives. And my kiddos, thank you for enduring Mommy's writing time and giving me the love and support I needed. You're the best kids ever, and I love you so much.

And finally, thank YOU for reading! I cannot believe someone is actually reading the words I've written. Thank you, dear reader, for taking the time to sit and go on the journey I've written. I hope you'll come along with me again in the future.

About the Author

Marie has had two goals since she was seven years old: to be a mother, and to be an author. She has been a storyteller her whole life and can't wait to share these stories with the world. When she's not writing, she can be found watching The Office, playing the piano, sewing a dress, or reading a book (while consuming copious amounts of chocolate). She lives in sunny Southern California with her husband of 16 years, four children, and their chickens.